School of Freedom

Michigan Monograph Series in Japanese Studies
Number 58

Center for Japanese Studies
The University of Michigan

School of Freedom

Shishi Bunroku

Translated and with an Afterword by
Lynne E. Riggs

Center for Japanese Studies
The University of Michigan
Ann Arbor   2006

Original title: *Jiyū Gakkō*, by Bunroku Shishi
Copyright © Atsuo Iwata, 1951
Originally published in Japan by Asahi Shinbunsha
English translation © Lynne E. Riggs 2006
All rights reserved.

Published by the Center for Japanese Studies,
The University of Michigan
1007 E. Huron St.
Ann Arbor, MI 48104-1690

This book has been selected by the Japanese Literature Publishing Project (JLPP),
which is run by the Japanese Literature Publishing and Promotion Center
(J-Lit Center) on behalf of the Agency for Cultural Affairs of Japan.

Library of Congress Cataloging in Publication Data

Shishi, Bunroku, 1893–1969.
    [Jiyu gakko. English]
    School of freedom / Shishi Bunroku ; translated and with an afterword
by Lynne E. Riggs.
        p. cm. — (Michigan monograph series in Japanese studies ; 58)
    ISBN 1-929280-40-8 (cloth : alk. paper)
    I. Riggs, Lynne E. II. Title. III. Series

    PL830.W33J5913   2006
    895.6'35—dc22

                                                            2006051846

This book was set in Palatino Macron.

This publication meets the ANSI/NISO Standards for Permanence of Paper
for Publications and Documents in Libraries and Archives (Z39.48—1992).

Printed in the United States of America

Contents

School of Freedom

Chapter 1
"Get Out!"

That whirring and clanking, clanking and whirring! To a man's ears, the noise of a sewing machine is intensely disagreeable. Beyond that, it conveys the mood of the user all too eloquently.

A treadle worked by an angry spouse can be quite a performance. They say that women only began to assert themselves after the end of the war, but there is good reason to believe it goes back much further, to when sewing machines began appearing in Japanese homes. At any rate, households were infinitely quieter in the days when women did their needlework by hand, seated on the tatami beside their sewing boxes.

"It's time you were going!" Komako's voice, shrill and piercing, rose above the clatter of the machine.

Komako was just past, or just approaching, the age of thirty. She was wearing a short-sleeved housedress with black and white stripes, and her feet were bare as they pedaled furiously at the machine. Some women might look sloppy, even sluttish, going around barefoot, but a degree of informality in a wife can be a relief for a husband, and it was, after all, quite warm. Despite her bare feet, there were few women as organized and as efficient as Komako. There was nothing about her that was casual or superfluous. Her compact figure had no excess weight or height, and her proportions were well balanced, with a head that was not too large nor a bosom too ample. Her hair, neatly curled under, was abundant but not to excess. Her features, too, were not overly conspicuous, and the boldness of her eyes was softened by an appealing dip in her nose. The somewhat masculine set to her lips and her slightly tanned complexion prevented her from having a beauty that might have aroused envy among her own sex. There was nothing unnecessary in her neat features, except perhaps the sprinkling of freckles on her cheeks.

Economical in her movements, Komako continued to work the treadle without turning her head or giving so much as a sideways glance.

"It's seven minutes past eleven!"

She was aware of the exact time displayed on the clock on the bookshelf behind her.

The bookcase was filled with works of literature, from nineteenth-century English authors to American writers introduced to Japan after the war—both in the original and in Japanese translations. They were all books that she herself had acquired and had nothing to do with her husband. However, when her husband was at home, Komako was not one to be found reading. By busying herself each day at the sewing machine making children's clothes, she could bring in some money as well as drive her spouse out to work, if only to escape the noise.

The house they were living in was small—in fact, not much more than a storage shed. It had two rooms and stood a little distance from the landlord's large, thatched farmhouse. At that moment, Komako's husband, Minamimura Iosuke, was sunning himself on the veranda, his large frame stretched full-length on the warped, weathered planks.

The sunshine of late May was already quite strong, and Iosuke was sweating as he lay there. His threadbare flannel pajamas must have made him feel even hotter, but he showed no sign of discomfort. Though the weather had turned warm, he was the type of man who lacked either the energy or the good sense to stop this habit he had begun during the chilly days of midwinter. That same lethargy might explain why he failed to respond to his wife's repeated calls.

The whirring suddenly stopped.

"Are you asleep?"

"No." His voice seemed to resonate from the bottom of a deep well.

"If you're not asleep, why aren't you answering?"

"I am answering."

"And I'm telling you it's after eleven."

"I know."

"If you know, you should be getting ready to go to the office!"

Iosuke grunted but did not move. He seemed totally inert. The undulations of his huge body lying prone on the veranda brought to mind the famous sand dunes on the shores of Tottori Prefecture—neck muscles, bulging like the thick trunk of a pine tree, and wide shoulders, back, and buttocks covered in the worn gray pajamas. And, just as immovable as any landscape, Iosuke was not about to be roused.

"Up to your old tricks again!"

The sewing machine started once more, and Komako's voice grew shriller.

"Do you think there's anything admirable about acting so indifferent? It's ridiculous! You're behaving like a complete fool!"

4

"You think so?" was Iosuke's drowsy reply.

If he didn't give some kind of answer, he knew she would become even more insistent. His response was mild, but his thoughts were far less so.

She speaks to me so rudely these days, he mused. She wasn't like that before the war. Must be the hard times we've been through.

"Yes, I do. You're infuriating! Lying around all the time. You're completely useless! Like one of those balloons used for carrying bombs, just drifting about aimlessly! A typical East Asian, you are! And what do you . . ."

Iosuke ceased listening. Instead, he decided to be lulled by the humming of the sewing machine and enjoy the growing warmth of the sun.

Komako and Iosuke had been married in November 1941, only twenty days before the Pacific War began. Life was already getting difficult then, but all the same they had held their reception in the Imperial Hotel with champagne and even a wedding cake. Indeed, Iosuke's family could readily afford such luxuries then. Although his father, who had been vice-president of the Manchurian Transport Company, had passed away, the family fortunes had not yet declined. The Minamimuras still owned stock in the company, and they had the wise guidance of Iosuke's mother and the support of those who succeeded his father in the business. Behind his back, Iosuke was called as useful as a neon sign in daylight, or a clock that has stopped, but no one had any worries about the family's wealth.

What happened after that is testimony to the fickleness of fate. The reason Iosuke and Komako were living in this tiny outbuilding of a farmhouse way out in the country—a twenty-five-minute walk from Musashi-Hazama Station on the Chuo Line—was due in part to the war. But more of that later . . .

"Now listen to me! Stop lazing around and go to work."

This time Komako's voice was right next to Iosuke's ear. She had abandoned her post at the sewing machine and was looming over him. That meant trouble.

Before he knew it, a hand came down—it was uncanny how it reached out, attached itself to his pajama collar, and half-lifted his hefty bulk into a sitting position. It was like a kitten picked up by the scruff of its neck. Scenes like this—where a woman's will can defy the laws of physics—were not uncommon in this household.

"Now get going!" Komako's tone remained even.

Blinking, Iosuke crossed his legs. As he did so, the bright light hit him full in the face, revealing an extraordinary set of features.

One rarely encounters a face like this except on heroic figures from history, such as the thirteenth-century Buddhist priest Nichiren or the nineteenth-century rebel leader Saigo Takamori. Eyebrows bristling like hairy caterpillars, a nose as rounded as a bun, a pair of flashlights for eyes, lips thick as hamburgers, and the whole enclosed within broad lines as generous as the outfield of a baseball diamond. But even with these features his head did not look disproportionately large because he was a man of above-average height and considerable weight. His head actually looked small, reminding one of the knob on the lid of an iron kettle.

Most people were awed by Iosuke's bulk and imagined that something impressive lay behind the imposing features. But those closest to him, Komako and his late mother, Akino, knew why his head looked small; they knew, sad to say, that he was by no means great or noble. He was not petty or mean, but when it came right down to it there was nothing of great import behind that huge countenance.

Iosuke had gone to good schools—Gakushuin, the choice of aristocrats, followed by the elite Kyoto University—but after that he had remained unemployed for quite a while. The year he married Komako, a former employee of his father's had found him a job at the Tokyo News Agency. As the agency had no idea what to do with this massive person, he was first put in the Sports Department, partly because it was the least busy but mainly through the misguided assumption that anyone that big must have an affinity for sports.

However, ever since he was a boy, Iosuke had disliked all forms of physical exertion, had never taken up a sport, and had no aptitude for athletic pursuits. He was an anomaly among men of his age in not even knowing the rules of baseball. The sports he detested most of all were kendo and rugby, the reason being that competitiveness was essential and winning was paramount.

Contention of any kind went against his grain. With a physique like his, Iosuke no doubt possessed considerable strength, but not once in his life had that been put to the test. He had never been involved in a fight, possibly because his size was enough to frighten off anyone before matters came to blows, but also because he took pains to give that kind of confrontation a wide berth.

He knew he was ill suited to sports journalism, but he was not the type to come out and say so. Indeed, his employment was marred from the start by an embarrassing incident. He had gone along with a senior reporter to cover the 7th Japan Athletics Meet, but watching the 5,000-meter races was tedious and he decided to go to the stadium toilet. He took his time there—after all, there was no hurry—and he may even have dozed off, he couldn't be sure. When he realized that the races must nearly be over, he decided to go back, but for some reason the toilet door was stuck. To someone as strong as Iosuke, it would have been no problem simply to break down the door, but he was not the sort to break things. So he patiently waited for someone to enter an adjacent stall. When someone finally did, he called out.

"Sorry to trouble you, but could you please phone the Tokyo News Agency in Marunouchi and tell them that their employee is locked in the toilet and can't get out."

It was a strange plea indeed, but the middle school student or other well-meaning fellow faithfully carried out Iosuke's request. The person at the agency who took the call was puzzled by this message when there was another reporter in the stadium. Fearing there might be some kind of trouble, a tough-looking staff member was dispatched in a company car flying the agency flag. When this man found that his sole purpose was to let Iosuke out of the toilet, he was speechless.

From that time on, Iosuke's name was familiar to everyone in the company. He was soon transferred to the peripheral and virtually defunct News Research Office, and there he had remained ever since. He would surely have been fired if the person who had introduced him to the agency had been less influential.

It was not only that Iosuke was unsuited to the Sports Department; he also lacked all trace of journalistic shrewdness. In fact, were one to ask what occupation would have fitted him better—office worker, businessman, soldier, lawyer, artist, or anything else—it would immediately become clear that none of them was right for him. Perhaps he might have managed a job in a temple, but not as an officiating priest or an acolyte, for such positions involved duties; it would have to be as the head priest or some such post that did not involve any work and in which one could sit and sip tea all day. Yet such a job does not exist. In short, he was not a man cut out for any ordinary work.

Iosuke had been born to a good family and reared under the protective wing of an unusually wise mother. After marriage, his life had been completely controlled by a wife of unrivaled capabilities. Komako had graduated from the English literature department of a well-known women's college. Since the end of the war she had been teaching English to girls on neighboring farms and doing translations for the Allied Forces controlling the country. She also knitted, and made clothes and accessories. Thanks to the sewing machine that she had been working so furiously until a moment before, she was the mistress of all sorts of skills to supplement the household income. When it came to preparing meals with meager ingredients and managing on a shoestring, she was far more resourceful than the average housewife.

Komako had not always been this type of woman. Before the war she had enjoyed the comfortable and sophisticated lifestyle of what was considered the upper class. But her fortunes had taken two sudden downturns: first, in her childhood, when her father had been implicated in a case of graft; and then, after marrying Iosuke, when the Minamimura family had lost its fortune. These experiences had turned her into a woman who survived by her wits.

> Whatever hardships may come
> I pray for more,
> The better to test my limitations.

That memorable verse by a well-known seventeenth-century scholar may be hoary with age, but as a description of pushing the limits of endurance, it aptly conveys her psyche. Komako was the type whose abilities shone more brightly the greater the adversity she faced. No doubt pride played a part in this, but it was also the result of her own temperament. Standing next to her was like standing next to a stove that burns all year round, generating a heat—fueled by blood, spirit, or whatever—that is almost palpable. "Strong-willed" was too inadequate a word to describe her intensity.

It was this intensity that Iosuke's sagacious mother, Akino, had spotted and placed her confidence in.

"You can see what type of man Iosuke is, so think of him more as you would a son," she once advised Komako after the engagement.

Akino's words clearly carried an important message. She meant that even if the couple should have children, Komako should continue to look upon Iosuke not so much as a husband but as a grown-up child. In other words, Akino did not expect any woman to love Iosuke as a man or as a husband. Of the two kinds of affection of which a woman is capable, it was to the maternal instincts of her future daughter-in-law that Akino appealed. Recently, Komako found herself recalling the words, thinking how well the mother had known her son.

At the time, Komako had been young and inexperienced, and had taken Akino's words for a mother's modesty. Komako had been thoroughly infatuated with Iosuke. For some reason difficult to fathom, this monolith of

8

a man had held inexplicable allure. When they had become engaged, she remembered smiling as she declared, full of confidence and authority, to a classmate, "He's totally different from anybody I've ever known. I've never come across anyone like him in real life—not even in a novel. In a way he reminds me of a bull, but that doesn't explain him either. Maybe you could liken him to . . . to the ocean. You feel he has the breadth and the depth of the ocean—you know, a kind of vastness, an unknown quantity. It's an incredible adventure to marry someone like that."

Komako had been a spirited girl, quick to turn up her nose at this and that fellow, spurning the smart and the handsome in quick succession without the least sign of regret. It defied all logic, therefore, that she should fall so completely for someone like Iosuke. Perhaps it was more a case of a calamity brought about by too much logic.

As long as his mother, the wise Akino, was alive, Iosuke's appeal never weakened, since right up to her death she took great care to prevent his worst side from showing. Once she was gone, however, and all through the war years, Komako suffered one disillusion after another. Far from the "vastness" of the ocean or even a good "bull," Iosuke turned out to be truly useless. Until the final months of the war, when he was drafted into the military for a stint in the construction corps, Komako had her hands full dealing with a husband who was incapable of lifting a finger to help cope with the hard times.

Komako was one of those women who, like many men, adamantly refused to admit defeat, and she bore everything without a word of complaint. What can one do, she would think, when this is what fate has meted out? Persuading herself of the inevitability of her destiny, she adopted a heroic fatalism. Since she had married Iosuke, he was her responsibility and she would not shift the blame onto anyone else. Even though she knew she had married someone so utterly good for nothing, she had no wish to seek a divorce. She would stick by him, no matter how condescending that might appear. It was not an attitude that recent champions of women's rights would have been likely to condone.

The decision to accept the path one has chosen is, after all, the result of conscious resolve, as witness the great swordsman Miyamoto Musashi. Yet how vast are the unplumbed depths of the human heart—the female heart in particular—that even the self is not aware of. What writhes and squirms within us we know not.

Although Komako never spoke of it, deep in her subconscious she knew she had been duped. As much as she might be determined to carry the responsibility she had accepted on a conscious level, her inner voice could not be silenced.

Many a woman resents the forces that play havoc with her life. All married women harbor such feelings to a greater or lesser degree—they are universal, lodged in odd corners of the psyche of even the most fortunate of wives—so Komako could hardly be faulted for having them. However, the intensity of the anger and resentment that lurks in such women is enough to make one's hair stand on end.

All is well if these sentiments remain buried or forever dormant, yet from time to time they will surface, appearing like corrected words that, though papered over, emerge faint but still legible. Komako had recently begun to grind her teeth in her sleep, an eerie sound that disturbed the silence of the night. During the day, too, she had begun to let out long sighs, and her eyes sometimes took on a disturbing glint, while the taut skin of her cheeks betrayed an occasional tic.

Komako was finding Iosuke's behavior so irritating that she had taken to speaking to him quite brusquely. Yet he seemed completely impervious to whatever she said, which only made her redouble her assaults. The woman of good breeding who had so beautifully mastered the lilting honorifics of those who considered themselves members of the gentility now spoke with the vulgar meanspiritedness of an undertipped barmaid.

One could hardly blame Komako—she was barely conscious of how she had changed. Of course, she admitted there was plenty in her life that was unfair and disagreeable. Nobody who shoulders a heavy burden can be entirely free of such thoughts. Iosuke's basic salary was 12,000 yen a month, and with various benefits came close to 20,000 yen. After deducting taxes, union dues, expenses for entertaining colleagues, and other payments, his take-home pay was usually less than 10,000 yen. It would have helped if he had handed over his entire pay packet to Komako, but Iosuke had not lost the spendthrift habits of a son of the wealthy Minamimura family. For him, a month's salary was meant to be squandered on a night out in Ginza. Indeed, there were few men as oblivious to the value of money as Iosuke. Since he had always taken money for granted, he assumed his wife did the same. There were months when he did not bring home a penny, and no matter how Komako might rant or rail at him, he had nothing to say. In such circumstances, all a wife could do was to come up with a long-term plan of her own.

Komako herself had faced worse adversities. After Iosuke's mother passed away, she had single-handedly borne all the misfortunes that came their way—hardships due to the war, evacuation to the countryside because of the air raids, payment of the inheritance taxes, and tidying up the family's affairs after the business went bankrupt. All this had made her wise and tough beyond her years.

The long-term strategy devised by such a woman is not to be underestimated. She does not indulge in anything so straightforward as taking out insurance or hoarding cash in secret places. She strikes a bargain with Heaven and Destiny and is fiercely determined to survive by her own resources. Such a resolve can border on the terrifying.

It was not long before Komako was earning more than 10,000 yen a month by giving English lessons and making clothes, but that was only the initial step. Since she could not rely on a steady salary from Iosuke, she would get as much as she could by making strident demands like any grasping landlord. And this was merely the prelude to more serious tactics. Her true colors began to show when she started to study the text of the new constitution that went into effect in May 1947. Once she began developing a philosophy of her own, she was obviously not the girl she had been. She decided that maternal love notwithstanding, there was a limit to how far a husband could be indulged.

From the outset it was inauspicious to have been married in the year the Pacific War began. Her life was rocked, tormented, and totally transformed by the event. The world may know a lot about war widows, but it should know more about wartime wives, for they are widows, too, in a way. The only difference is that the war widow has lost her husband, while a wartime wife loses sight of hers. As a result of the war, Japanese women became bitterly disillusioned with their menfolk and ceased to rely on them or take them seriously. Essentially, one could say they ignored them. The women learned to survive by their own devices, to think on their own, to feed themselves through their own efforts, and to pursue any cravings they might have by themselves. They decided everything, and their ideal was never to become dependent on a husband.

"Freedom!" was their battle cry. And freedom was their booty of war. Yet you would not find any of them standing around being grateful for it. When the war took a turn for the worse, these were the women who traded kimonos for baggy work trousers, who stood in line for rations, who rushed over with buckets of water when fires broke out, who stood in crowded trains stooped under loads of food bought in the countryside to feed their families in the cities, and who even ladled out the latrines. They assumed that amount of freedom was only natural, but it was still far from sufficient.

The reason was that now, in the year 1950, they were supporting themselves solely through their own efforts, and they were very conscious of this. The realization itself was momentous. The fact that Japanese women had started to fend for themselves was revolutionary.

All right, I'll do you the favor of letting you eat half! That was Komako's message to Iosuke. Things had come to such a pass in the house. Deep down, Komako felt pride and not a little superiority at being in the role of breadwinner, the one dispensing sustenance. Girls of the working classes do not think this way, but when one has been born into wealth and has only recently discovered the brave new ability to earn one's own living, that awareness is fresh and vibrant.

What Komako found most irritating was Iosuke's laziness, which was daily becoming worse. His job at the news agency might be easy, but not leaving for work until noon was disgraceful, especially because it infringed upon her own time, when she was free of her wifely duties. If she did not badger him, he would not get moving until mid-afternoon. It smacked of more than plain indolence—it made her suspect something was afoot.

"Here you are! Your socks. Your shirt." Komako began tossing his clothes at him, one item at a time. This treatment might appear harsh, but Iosuke was not your ordinary husband. If she did not resort to such extraordinary measures, he wasn't likely to get the message at all.

Inured to his wife's behavior, Iosuke hardly batted an eyelash. Without a word he began to get dressed, putting his socks on one at a time and buttoning his shirt, but his movements were as languorous as a movie running in slow motion. Today it was taking him especially long to dress.

"I can't find shirts your size in the stores, so don't get any stains on it!" Recently Komako had noticed yellow stains down the front of one of his shirts, perhaps from spilling something when he was out drinking. She never missed things like that.

Iosuke was too large to fit into the ready-made clothing most people wore, not even undershirts and underpants. Before the war there had been one department store that stocked extra-large sizes, but it no longer carried them. So, Komako looked for any suitable material she could lay her hands on and made all his clothes herself. That alone required special care. A feeling that could be described as either pity or pride—imagining Iosuke's miserable appearance had he married any other woman—was perhaps one thread that bound her to him.

"Here's your wallet with your train pass. I've put in 300 yen."

This, at least, she did not throw at him. Iosuke took it and put it in his inside pocket, as was his custom, but he still did not stand up.

Komako knew that after he had been poked and prodded to that extent he would leave in five minutes or so, and she turned back to her sewing machine.

Once more a noisy whir and clatter filled the small house.

"What? You're still here?"

In all the time it had taken her to finish sewing the back of a girl's dress, Iosuke had been sitting there calmly with his legs crossed. Komako was appalled at his immobility.

"What's the matter with you?"

She went over to him and stood there, towering above him like a telephone pole.

"I was thinking it wouldn't be much good to go out."

It was the first thing he had said without being prompted. Like his movements, his speech was slow.

"What do you mean, 'not much good'?" she snapped.

What an odd thing for a husband useless to begin with to say! She couldn't help growing slightly hysterical. But Iosuke continued, his voice a model of composure.

"I don't think it makes sense to go out every day and just stroll around killing time."

What on earth could he be saying?

"Who are you talking about?" Komako practically screeched.

"Me, of course."

"You? Strolling around? Killing time?"

"Yes. Recently, anyway."

"What do you mean? I don't understand!" Komako felt as though she was enveloped in a thick fog, which made her mind go temporarily blank. Then she realized what he meant.

"You mean you haven't been going to the office?"

"Yup." He didn't sound the least perturbed.

"So all this time you've been pretending to go to work but you were going out and having a good time?"

"Well, not exactly. It just happened that way."

Komako was accustomed to Iosuke's replies being as ungraspable as clouds, so his words hardly surprised her. But she never dreamed that his laziness had reached the point where he had stopped going to work.

"I don't . . . believe this!" she said, stumbling over her words in her dis-

13

may. "You're acting like a child cutting school, for heaven's sake!"

All she could do was to glare, like an angry mother, at this truant husband who was acting no better than a grade school boy who did not want to study.

Komako had believed she had her husband completely under her control. She was convinced she knew his every move, and the thought that he had lied to her made her livid.

"Oh, now I understand," she said caustically. "You've been fired, haven't you?"

Everyone at the agency knew that Iosuke was good for nothing. The man who had introduced him had lost his position during the purge of business executives accused of complicity in the war, and he now worked elsewhere. Without him there to protect Iosuke, it would have been no surprise had Iosuke been fired.

"No," came Iosuke's calm reply.

"You weren't fired? Then what? You mean you just stopped going to the office and just dawdled around?"

That, too, was unforgivable, but it was easier to tolerate than if he had been fired. She could force him to make up for it by getting him to report for work regularly from now on. Even though there was not much left of his salary by the time he got home, it was better than nothing. Besides, a wife has some peace of mind if her husband has a job.

"No, it wasn't like that. I told you." Iosuke was still unruffled.

"Then what happened?" Komako could barely hide her exasperation. "Will you please come to the point?"

"I quit. Of my own free will," he said simply. That was all he had to say.

"You quit? You mean you handed in your resignation?"

"Yes."

Komako was astounded.

"How could you do that without telling me?"

"If I told you, you weren't likely to have agreed to the idea."

"Of course! And when did you do this?"

"About a month ago."

"A month ago? You mean you've been deceiving me all this time! But why did you quit? What made you quit?"

Iosuke began to inch away from Komako, but she followed, her eyes fixed on him, demanding answers.

"I wanted freedom."

How dare he say that, she seethed. *He* wants freedom! Who does he think he is talking to? *He's* not the one saddled with a spouse more trouble-some than a big baby! *He* doesn't have to take in work at home as well as go out to a job, and on top of that do all the household chores! He's not the one who's always pressed for time and money! He's not burdened by maternal instincts or inconvenienced by the Minamimura name and the feudal conventions still followed in Japanese society. It should have been she, Komako, to say that first. Indeed, were they not the very words she had been murmuring to herself, not only in the dark recesses of her heart but also in broad daylight?

What is he talking about—this worthless husband who was living off her earnings? It was outrageous! How dare he utter those words first?

"I quit because I wanted freedom," he repeated.

Such was Komako's shock that at first she thought she had misheard. Then she burst out laughing.

"You! It's farcical. It's so funny!"

"Why?"

"How can you ask why? Oh, it's too ludicrous!"

She felt giddy. Her arms flailed about as she tried to control her laughter, and her eyes took on a strange glint. She glared at him with such intensity that she seemed to drill holes in his face. Mirth mixed with anger borders on the fiendish. But Iosuke was so gentle by nature that her rage went unnoticed.

"I've had a lot of questions on my mind lately," Iosuke started. "Questions about our society and about the company. And what they all boil down to is the freedom of the individual, of human beings." As he spoke, he seemed to warm to his theme.

"Will you shut up!" Komako's composure had snapped. There was no holding her back.

"Here I am, having to teach English to the spoiled neighborhood brats, sewing and knitting for a pittance, taking charge of rites and rituals for your relatives, paying for the upkeep of your ancestral graves. I've been working myself to the bone to keep our heads above water, and you've been loafing around for a whole month? You quit your job without so much as a word to me, and you still walk out of the house with the 300 yen I give you. Isn't that right?"

"Well, you gave it to me, so I took it. I had my severance pay, so I didn't need more."

"Severance pay? You've even kept that hidden from me?"

"I didn't hide it. But it wasn't easy to tell you I'd quit, so . . ."

An uneasy silence descended. Komako was trembling from head to foot, and she bit her lip so hard it almost bled.

"Get out!" she blurted.

Komako's voice rose like a clarion cry. Both the vehemence and the significance of her words surprised even herself. It was a voice that welled up from deep inside her. But by the time she realized what she had said, she knew she had no wish to retract her words. She merely said more calmly, "I'm sorry, but I don't think I can live with you any more. It would be best if you left."

Iosuke turned to cast a sharp glance at Komako, then with a heavy voice replied, "I see."

Slowly he rose to his feet, took his hat from the nail by the door, and added, "I'll be going then. Goodbye. By the way, the rest of my severance pay is in the desk drawer."

Chapter 2
The Goshokai Society

A week had passed since Iosuke had left. The third day had come and gone, then the fifth, and by the time Wednesday came around again Komako began to feel a little worried. Still, she could not take the situation all that seriously. How could a man as spineless as Iosuke survive without someone like her to look after him? Most probably he was staying with a succession of friends, so there would be a limit to how long he could sponge off them. Although he was not the sort to notice when he had outstayed his welcome, if they suggested it might be time to leave, he would take the hint.

Furthermore, he would run out of money.

After Iosuke left, Komako had looked inside the desk drawer and found a little more than 17,000 yen in it. Tokyo News Agency was not known for its generosity, but that amount could only be a fraction of the severance pay Iosuke would have received for over nine years of employment. She seethed at the thought of how much he must have squandered on food and drink around town while pretending to be going to work. What made her especially angry was the 300 yen she had given him every three days in her ignorance.

The day he had left home, his wallet had not contained much money, so he could not have had more than the three 100-yen bills she had inserted. After two or three days, she guessed, he would not even be able to buy cigarettes. None of Iosuke's friends would have any cash to lend him, so lack of funds, if nothing else, would soon put a stop to his wanderings. Of all Iosuke's weaknesses, his dependence upon money was the greatest.

Komako envisioned Iosuke appearing in the garden, his huge hand scratching his head in embarrassment, and saying, "Well, I thought I'd better come back." She was prepared to give him a piece of her mind and a good tongue-lashing that would leave such an impression on body and soul that he would never be tempted to try the same thing again. But when an entire week went by with no sign of his return, it rather took the wind out of her sails.

It's very odd, she mused, that he should be able to stay away so long. On the lookout for his reappearance day after day, she was reminded of abalone divers. You never knew when they would bob to the surface again; you were just confident that they eventually would. In the interim, you wondered how they managed to stay underwater so long.

It suddenly came to Komako that he might have gone to his uncle's house to borrow money. Iosuke's uncle, his mother's younger brother, was a retired law scholar and something of an eccentric. He lived in the resort area of Oiso on the Pacific coast, an hour from Tokyo by train. Although he held the title of professor emeritus at the prestigious T University, he had long ago withdrawn from the city to lead a hermit's life in pursuit of his own pleasures. He was by no means rich, however. Some royalties no doubt trickled in from his books, and lately, to the despair of his former students, he had taken to writing articles for low-brow magazines, but any income from that source had to be minimal. Komako knew he had a perverse streak, too, and although he could be more than generous if he opened his wallet of his own accord, he would refuse anyone who came asking for a loan. So Oiso was out: there was no way he would lend money to Iosuke. Moreover, this uncle was not one to be partial only to his own kin, and he had always treated Komako as warmly as Iosuke. For this reason Komako felt comfortable paying him a visit to discuss the situation.

Knowing Iosuke, there was no way to be sure he had not sashayed down there to borrow money, been refused, and ended up taking advantage of his uncle's hospitality nevertheless. If she went to Oiso, Komako thought, she might gain some news of her errant husband. The uncle was one of the older members of the family, and even if she learned nothing, at least she would be doing her duty as Iosuke's wife by reporting that he had left home a week ago and not returned. It might not be appropriate to reveal the exact nature of their marital spat, but it would be easier to talk to this eccentric relation than to other members of the family.

I might as well go and see what I can discover, thought Komako.

After tidying up early, she shuttered the house and left. She stopped by the main house to tell the landlady she was going out and to ask her to keep an eye on things. It was convenient not having Iosuke around; she could leave the house anytime simply by letting the landlady know.

In Shinjuku she purchased the requisite gift for the Oiso relatives and reached Tokyo Station in time to catch the ten past eleven train bound for Atami. Being a weekday, the train was not crowded and there were several vacant seats. The last time she had taken this train just after the end of the war, the windows had been boarded up with planks, but now the glass had been replaced. Beautiful scenery of blue sky and lush greenery rushed by as the train made its way along the coast.

Komako was surprised how light-hearted she felt. She had not been so carefree since an excursion to Kyoto as a schoolgirl. She would have liked to hum a tune or take out a bar of chocolate from her handbag. Was this the way a woman whose husband had left home more than a week ago should feel?

Come to think of it, before leaving that morning she had spent longer than usual on her makeup. She had been surprised to see how youthful she looked in the mirror. She had chosen a blue-gray suit with a double-checked pattern she had recently made, and she carried a dark blue leather handbag that complemented it. She wondered why she had gone to such lengths to make herself attractive. It wasn't like her, unless she was hoping to win over that withered stick of an uncle in Oiso, which would have been a waste of effort to begin with.

As the train pulled into Yokohama Station, a well-dressed man—a businessman or an officer in civilian clothes—who was walking arm in arm with his wife stared openly at Komako as he passed her window. His expression clearly conveyed his appreciation at having discovered a pretty flower where he had least expected it. Komako quickly looked away, but her face reddened. It had been a long time since she had blushed like that.

Do other wives feel lonely when their husbands disappear? she wondered.

What was strange was that from the first night after Iosuke had left she had not felt a single pang of loneliness. Indeed, it was a relief not to have that mountain of flesh stretched out beside her. The small tatami room where they laid out their bedding each night now seemed wonderfully spacious. Instead of constantly worrying about Iosuke, she found herself sleeping straight through until morning. It surprised her that her actions implied she had no affection for her husband. She quickly dismissed the notion, however, reasoning that it was because she was convinced he would be back soon.

As the hills of Oiso came into view and she prepared to alight, Komako began to regret that she could not stay on the train. She wanted to travel on and on, to some faraway destination—ideally as far as the United States.

Distracted by the excitement of the journey, she had forgotten all about the sandwich she had made for lunch, but that was not important. From the station she walked briskly along the tracks heading in the direction from which the train had come. When she was a child, her father had had a summer cottage in Oiso, and she knew the area well. The cottage had been in the affluent section, but the neighborhood where Iosuke's uncle lived had fewer houses and the land was low-lying and untidy. As she descended the gentle slope, her daydreams, too, came quickly down to earth.

The smell of the ocean was carried on the breeze, and the path through the pine trees took many twists and turns before bringing her to a simple wooden gate set in a hedge of Chinese pine. The crabbed calligraphy on the wooden name board was so weatherworn that the name, "Haneda Chikara," was barely legible. The house looked similarly shabby, hardly the sort one would expect a respectable scholar to inhabit. It had been hastily constructed some fifteen years before, when her uncle had been no better off than he was now.

As Komako slide aside the cheaply made door of the house and called out a greeting, she was surprised to find several pairs of shoes lined up inside the earthen-floored entryway. From within the house came the sound of chatter and laughter. How unusual, she thought, for a couple she had considered not fond of socializing. She had never heard of them having large gatherings before. So absorbed were they that nobody seemed to hear her.

This may not be a good time, Komako thought. It won't be easy to talk in private.

Still, she did not want to turn around and leave, so she went to the back entrance. The kitchen door was open and she could see Iosuke's aunt, Haneda Ginko. She had a white apron on over her kimono and was wearing spectacles as she sliced some pickles on a cutting board. Ginko looked up, startled.

"Komako! My goodness! It's so unsightly back here."

"Well, I called out at the front door several times, but . . ."

"Oh, yes. We've got an unusually full house today. But it's only the Goshokai Society, and they're no trouble. Now, go to the front door and come in the proper way."

"If it's all right with you, I'll come in this way. I can see you're busy, so I won't stay long."

"Oh, don't mind them. They've all brought their own lunches, so I'm just serving some homemade pickles. I'm not busy at all. I suppose they'll stay for drinks in the evening, but we'll see about that when the time comes."

Iosuke's aunt was warm and openhearted, as always. She had none of the haughtiness assumed by many scholars' wives and refused to have a housekeeper, taking care of all the housework herself. There were only the two of them, so the chores were not demanding, but the way she managed the many little domestic tasks without any sign of being burdened—indeed, even with a certain grace—was surely the result of her family background in the upper-class Yamanote area of Tokyo.

"Do come in, then."

With a "There, that's ready," she finished arranging the dish of pickles.

"Now please come into the sitting room."

As Komako followed Ginko down the corridor to the small tatami-matted room, she peered into the rooms along the way but saw no hint of Iosuke's presence. Casually she asked whether Iosuke had been to visit, but the answer was a brisk no. In that case, thought Komako, I'll tell Aunt first about Iosuke leaving. But Ginko was brimming with such cheerful chatter that Komako could not get a word in edgeways.

"Komako, you must have a bowl of *ochazuke* rice with me. I've got some nice salted saurel and pickled plums to go with it."

"Please don't bother. I've brought a sandwich and that will do fine."

"Come on, don't act like a stranger! We can talk while we eat."

Soon they were absorbed in a stream of chitchat. As Komako found herself talking and laughing, she had no opportunity to bring up Iosuke's disappearance.

Occasional bursts of laughter reached them from the parlor where her uncle and his guests were gathered.

"They certainly are a jolly bunch," commented Komako. "Are they Uncle's students?"

"No. It's the Goshokai Society. This is the first time they've got together since the war, so they're having a really good time!"

"The Goshokai Society? What's that?"

"Haven't you heard of it? Iosuke knows all about it—at least, I think he does. It's difficult to explain. It's a crazy group of friends and your uncle's the leader!"

"Are they studying something very odd?"

Ginko let out a giggle.

"Well, I suppose you could call it 'studying,' but it's not the usual sort."

"What kind of a group is it?" asked Komako, curious.

"Just listen and you'll understand. After all, when you get five folks together who are funny up here"—her aunt pointed to her head, which had a neat coif set in traditional style—"and their leader is that husband of mine . . ." She gestured in the direction of the *zashiki*.

"I can hear a woman's voice, too," said Komako.

21

"Oh yes, that's Horan. She's the widow of Mr. Hori, the businessman. She's very clever—does noh drama, tea ceremony, Chinese-style painting, and she's quite accomplished. Her husband was one of the group's founding members, and she joined after he passed away. She said it was her late husband's wish. But she's the only woman."

"You mean Mr. Hori of the Japan Hydroelectric Company? I met him once with Iosuke. He was walking in Ginza with his son, about sixteen or seventeen years old."

"That would be Takabumi. Mind you, Takabumi's grown up since then. Hori was a good friend of your father-in-law, so Iosuke must know him, too. All the Goshokai members know Iosuke, not just Hori. After all, the group's been around a long time. In 1936, when those young army officers staged the coup d'état on February twenty-sixth, Haneda was so indignant about it that he started the Goshokai."

Just then, staccato thwacks on a hand drum came from the direction of the parlor, signaling the start of a festival tune.

"There they go!" said Ginko, giggling again.

The thumps of hand drums and the high-pitched sound of a flute announced a gay festival melody, but the music soon tripped and faltered. The large and small drums were not in time, the gong had started too briskly, while the flute languished with agonizing solemnity. The performance finally collapsed in comical disarray amid a burst of laughter.

"This is awful," pronounced Haneda in a concerned voice.

"That's what we get for not doing it for so long!" came a middle-aged man's voice.

"I've been practicing for a couple of weeks. I didn't think I'd be so bad once we got together." This was the voice of an older man.

"Oh, it's all my fault. My teacher showed me the basics, but I've gone back to my old habits and played it like a noh song." The woman's voice was husky but sensuous.

"No, it's my gong. I was trying to copy Father and thought I'd mastered it, but when it comes to actually performing, I'm far from . . ." A younger man was speaking.

"Your father was quite good on the gong," the older man said. "It made you wonder what his real profession was—medicine or the gong. Anyway, we miss him terribly."

"The gong is an instrument that's easy to play but difficult to master," observed Haneda with unusual gravity. "It has four tones, but even if you learn to produce all of them properly, it's still hard to achieve the touch

22

that pulls the whole performance together. To learn that, you have to be able to play all the other instruments as well. In that way dear old Henmi was first-rate."

"You're full of praise for Henmi, but do say something nice about Hori's flute. Otherwise the poor man will reproach you from his grave," pleaded the woman.

"Sorry, but I can't say anything good about Hori's flute, even if I should. Not many men are as untalented as he was. Not only that, but he was tone deaf! Yet he did so love the flute! Far more than most people! And he was such a gentleman, in the truest sense of the word."

"Well, praise in one breath, blame in the next."

"There has never been a bad apple in the Goshokai, and old Henmi and Hori were the best of fellows. To think we have lost both of them!" The older man's voice conveyed deep emotion. "Our gatherings in the old days were wonderful. They were so invigorating and gave us all a new lease on life."

As she listened to the voices drifting down the corridor, Komako began to grasp the nature of the Goshokai.

"All right," came Haneda's voice. "Let's leave the nostalgia and try again. This time let's chant the rhythm aloud. Ready? *Ten-ten-tenya, ten-tenya, suke-ten-ten, iya, do-don . . .*"

"Is that *kagura*?" Komako was thinking of the ensemble music played during ceremonies at shrines.

"Oh no. They'd be upset if they heard you say that," her aunt admonished. "Even the instruments are different. This is the popular festival music called *waka-bayashi*."

"You mean what's called *baka-bayashi*—'fool's music'?"

"Yes, it's better known by that name. It's not the sort of thing you often find respectable old men doing."

"I never knew it was a hobby of Uncle's."

"The group started before you and Iosuke were married, but what with the war and everything they couldn't practice. They've started up again today, the first time in years. This crazy racket will go on for a while now. Actually, at first it was just a group for telling funny stories. All sorts of disturbing events were happening back then—like Dr. Minobe Tatsukichi being forced to resign from the House of Peers for saying the emperor was merely an organ of state. We began to wonder what the world was coming to. These old fellows—they weren't old then, of course—started the group in order to cheer themselves up with funny stories.

23

"There were always the same five members. I'm not really sure how they came up with the name Goshokai. It means "Five Laughs Group" and has something to do with human beings only having five ways of laughing. The members got along famously. There was Hishikari, who used to be a viscount, Dr. Henmi, who had his own hospital, Mr. Fujimura, the chief engineer at Mitsuboshi Heavy Industries, Mr. Hori, whom I mentioned earlier, and my husband. They all had different professions, but they enjoyed each other's company immensely and got to be closer than family. When Henmi passed away and then Hori, your poor uncle was so depressed! Men can become really attached to one another, Komako. You should never underestimate male friendship."

"And where did this *baka-bayashi*—or should I say *waka-bayashi*—idea come from?" inquired Komako.

"It was dreamed up by your uncle. Only he could have thought of something so absurd. A festival ensemble has five members, two players on small hand drums, one on the big bass drum, one on the flute, and one on the gong. Since there were five of them, it was a nice coincidence, so he suggested they form a band. Your uncle used to be a bit of a connoisseur of country *kagura* music, and he had a big collection of records of it."

"I'm surprised they learned to play it so quickly," remarked Komako.

"Not at all! They couldn't play for anything, but, my goodness, were they enthusiastic! They got a man by the name of Hasegawa, who knew all about this type of music, to come and give them lessons. At first, he wouldn't let them even touch the drums. He'd make them practice drumming on a thick piece of bamboo wrapped in straw rope. There they'd be, fully-grown men, solemnly singing *ten-tenya, ten-tenya, iya, suke-ten-ten* at the tops of their voices! I swear you couldn't watch and keep a straight face!"

"It sounds as though Uncle's become quite good. Isn't he playing one of the drums?"

"He plays both the drum and the gong, but I'd say that his tendency to lecture has advanced more than his playing."

"I think it's wonderful they can enjoy themselves like that in times like these," Komako began. Then she suddenly remembered the problem that had brought her to Oiso.

"Oh dear! So Iosuke has left home." Her aunt's expression of bemusement gave way to concern as she listened to Komako's account. "You should have told me right away! That's what you came here to talk about, right?"

"Well, yes."

It was not just because her aunt was so relaxed that Komako had been chatting on without mentioning the purpose of her visit. In fact, she was not that worried about Iosuke's disappearance, though she could not say so outright and just sat there with her eyes lowered. Misinterpreting her silence, Ginko chided Komako.

"Now don't be shy. If it was as important as that, why didn't you tell me straight away? If you'd said something, I'd have fetched Haneda immediately."

"But Uncle and his friends are having such a good time."

"All they're doing is fooling around with those instruments. Wait here and I'll get him."

"Please don't trouble him now. There's no need."

"There is a need," said Ginko firmly. "All right, come with me, if you like. I'll take them some tea and we'll see what the situation is. I'll find a way for Haneda to get away."

She quickly prepared a tray with tea and cups, and arranged some Saigyo *manju* sweets, a specialty of the district, in a blue-and-white porcelain dish. Komako picked up the dish and followed her aunt down the corridor.

The L-shaped corridor led to the parlor used for entertaining. From the garden, which was a neglected lawn with five or six pine trees, came the rasping of early cicadas.

"Well," exclaimed Komako's uncle from the back of the room, acknowledging her with a slight bow of his cranelike frame. "When did you get here?"

With his small, lozenge-shaped spectacles, graying mustache, and bushy shock of hair, he resembled Hiranuma Kiichiro, who'd been prime minister before the Pacific War.

"She's been here for a while," his wife answered for Komako.

"Well, I hope you've put her to good use in the kitchen. Everyone, allow me to introduce Komako, my nephew's wife. She's a talented woman, if I may say so. Not only is she a connoisseur of English literature, but she's accomplished in the handling of *nukamiso* pickles. And when it comes to handling her husband . . ."

"Uncle, please!" protested Komako.

"So you're young Minamimura's wife."

"Iosuke's your husband?"

Turning to Komako, the group greeted her with welcoming smiles.

"I hope you'll get to know all these people well," urged Haneda. "You'll

25

find no better or more wonderful friends on earth. The elegant gentleman with the hand drum is Hishikari, who used to be a viscount."

Obviously in high spirits, Haneda began to introduce each member of the group in turn, making Komako feel extremely awkward.

Hishikari Otomaru, aged fifty-eight, had held the title of viscount until the peerage was abolished in 1949. He had been a member of the Kenkyukai Party in the House of Peers and was also chairman of the Japan Dog Association. Both positions, however, had been purely honorary, for Hishikari was a man dedicated to the pursuit of pleasure. He was adept at the games of Japanese chess and *go*, was skilled at hunting, fishing, and golf, and was a habitué of the teahouses. He had been a neighbor of the Hanedas in the days when they lived in the upscale Aoyama area in central Tokyo, and had been a member of the group from the beginning. Endowed with natural dexterity, he could play all the instruments in the ensemble and was its most accomplished member. Today he was playing the first hand drum. He was short and rather wizened, but one could detect traces of an aristocratic mien in his broad forehead. The faded thin coat he wore over his Oshima-*kasuri* kimono suggested that his circumstances were recently much reduced.

Fujimura Koichi was a little older, at sixty-one years of age. He had a degree in engineering and had been the chief engineer at Mitsuboshi Heavy Industries. He was a man of great integrity, but he had no hobbies other than this group. When the Occupation forces purged business executives thought to have cooperated in the war effort, he avoided that fate but had retired of his own accord, keenly feeling his responsibility for the war. He was currently serving as advisor to an electrical engineering company. No one had been more delighted than Fujimura at the resurrection of the Goshokai after the war. He had been a good friend of Haneda's since they both attended the same high school, and he, too, was a founding member. Today, as always, he was on the second hand drum. When it came to practicing, he was enthusiastic, but his talent was no match for his enthusiasm. He was wearing a navy blue suit.

Henmi Takashi, aged thirty-five, was the youngest member of the group, but his demeanor was as grave as if he were the oldest. He had been taught to play the gong by his father, Henmi Hirota, a physician. On his father's death, he had asked to join the group, saying his father had wanted him to succeed on the gong. Sent off to serve in the war, he returned a vulnerable, timid man. In fact, his true motivation was not the music but the atmosphere of the group, which provided an escape from the unpleasantness of the real

26

world. He was employed at a pharmaceutical company, but from time to time, like today, he would call in sick and take the day off. He could probably get away with this because he was a major stockholder, as his father had been. He was wearing an elegant suit and a dark necktie.

Hori Horan, the only woman, was probably around forty-four or forty-five years of age. She had apparently been a geisha before becoming the second wife of Hori Daisuke, then managing director of Japan Hydroelectric Company. Her husband had also been a founding member and had adored playing the flute even though he was hopeless at it. Horan had sometimes accompanied him to the gatherings, so she was well acquainted with the other members. By nature she was anything but polished but had cultivated hobbies such as the tea ceremony and ink painting, most probably to conceal her humble origins. At first, she had scoffed at this type of music, but after her husband died she had developed an interest in it. She displayed the candor and practiced coquetry of a middle-aged woman who had weathered many storms. When she heard that the group was to be revived, she asked to be allowed to take over the flute, saying she played the noh flute. Horan, which literally means "Fragrant Orchid," was the artist name given by her ink-painting teacher, and she invariably used it in her correspondence rather than her real name. She loved vivid colors and was wearing a russet-colored kimono decorated with cherry-blossom crests. Her makeup was thick, and her hair was done up in a rather unchic swirl. She cast flirtatious looks at all the men and made clever chitchat in a raspy voice. She had a habit of boasting about her son.

"It is a great pleasure to meet you," Komako said, bowing deeply to them all, but finding the carefree atmosphere of the group somewhat irritating.

What a bunch of old fogies, she thought. Not a single face there reflected a contemporary intellect. Her unsentimental gaze swept over the members, each seated primly behind an instrument—the drums bound with their worn red cords, the gong looking like the lid of an old tea kettle. Yet they obviously loved these primitive instruments.

"Komako, you should come and join us sometimes. It's great fun. We wouldn't want you jumping to the conclusion that true music only resides in the likes of Beethoven and Mozart. Music is at its purest and most creative in this festival music."

Today Komako felt nothing but disdain for her uncle's garrulity. She was even reluctant to tell him about Iosuke.

Having poured the tea for everyone, Ginko murmured in her husband's ear, "There's something we have to discuss," and asked him to excuse himself. With that, she and Komako withdrew and returned to the family sitting room. Soon they heard Haneda's footsteps in the corridor.

"What's going on? Surely it's nothing so urgent, is it?" he asked, beginning to lower himself by the low table but stopping halfway, poised to return immediately to his guests.

"There's a little problem, dear," said Ginko, keeping her voice low. "Komako tells me Iosuke has left home."

Haneda let out a guffaw.

"Left home? Most husbands nowadays would like to do that, I'd say. They're just putting a brave face on things."

"Do be serious! It's no joking matter! Iosuke left a whole week ago."

"Since he's decided to leave, he'll be gone for some time. But don't worry. He's bound to come back to our Komako in the end."

Judging from her uncle's reply, he seemed to think there was no problem at all, and this was not just because he wanted to get back to his drum. He appeared fully confident that he was right.

"I also believe he'll be back," murmured Komako, "but I thought I should let you know." Actually, she was rather relieved at her uncle's lack of concern.

"No need for you to report all your private affairs to us. It's just some husband-wife tiff, isn't it?"

Komako had too much pride to let her uncle think that both sides had been equally responsible, and making excuses would have hurt her vanity, so she gave an honest account of what had happened.

"So, Komako, it was you who told him to get out?" said her aunt, looking shocked.

"But more importantly," pressed her uncle, "tell me again exactly what Iosuke said."

Haneda cocked his head to one side as though trying to remember something.

Komako didn't understand what he meant.

"You mean how he confessed he had quit his job without telling me?"

"No, no. You told us he said something—some smart remark—about his reason for quitting."

Uncle Haneda frowned as he tried to recall what he had just heard.

"Iosuke isn't the sort to make smart remarks," declared Komako. "I'm sure I didn't mention anything like that."

"No, he did say something. Let me think. It was unusually intelligent for

28

Iosuke. Gracious, my memory's terrible these days."

"I wonder what it was. He said something like he had 'questions' about his company and society in general, but . . ."

"No. It wasn't as obvious as that."

"He said his questions were about the freedom of the individual and human beings, whatever that means. It's not the type of comment you'd expect from Iosuke."

"Not true. Phrases like 'individual freedom' and 'human freedom' are everywhere now—you see them in all the newspaper editorials. No, I think it was something more straightforward."

"Apart from what I've told you, he didn't say much. Well, he talked about wanting freedom or some such . . ."

"That's it!" exclaimed her uncle. "That's the sort of thing you can't afford to ignore."

"But, Uncle," protested Komako, "even elementary school children are talking about freedom."

"That's right," said her uncle. "This freedom and liberation business is on everybody's lips these days. Back in the 1880s—the freedom and people's rights era—it was the intelligentsia who were always going on about freedom this and freedom that. Today it's the talk of the town. The way people go on about it, you'd think freedom was something given automatically. It was exactly the same back then."

"Iosuke must have been talking about it that way, too—superficially. I don't think it could have had any deeper meaning. He must have been repeating what he'd heard other people say," asserted Komako.

"I disagree. I have great respect for your intelligence, Komako, but this time I think you're wrong."

"But Uncle," Komako persisted, "Iosuke is not the type to care about the latest trends. As a matter of fact, until 1945 he wouldn't deign to wear the khaki that all men in Japan felt they had to, to show support for the war effort. When it comes to copying others, he's awfully slow."

"I'm sure he wore khaki because he wanted to. You can bet his decisions have nothing to do with trends or fashion. When he said he wanted freedom, I'm positive he meant it. He wasn't just mouthing what other people are saying. It's a definite message."

"Are you sure, Uncle?"

"Komako, how long have you two been married?"

"Nine years."

"Well, I've been watching that young man for thirty-five years. Iosuke won't come back for one month, maybe two. So you'd better be prepared to wait it out."

Komako slipped away from the Hanedas a little before four o'clock in the afternoon.

"I shouldn't leave the house empty too long," she said by way of an excuse. She had no need to worry about the house, however long she might be gone, but listening to that eternal *ten-ten-ya, ten-ten-ya* was starting to grate on her nerves. Besides, it was obvious from what her uncle had said that he did not take her situation seriously, and Komako was not one to put up with that attitude for long.

He'd be quite nice if he didn't talk so pompously, she thought.

It seemed preposterous that Iosuke's lethargic remark about "wanting freedom" might have some special meaning. It was her uncle's usual bad habit of hatching a theory and basking in its cleverness. One might even say it was his trademark. When you have seen the same game played a few times, it starts to irritate you. Yet something in what her uncle said showed he may not have just been showing off today.

Well, birds of a feather! A bemused grimace passed over Komako's face as she thought of the blood bond between Iosuke and Haneda.

Despite having traveled so far, Komako had little to lift her spirits. Reluctant to head straight for the station, she had a sudden urge to go to the beach. It had been a long time since she had smelled the sea breeze, and she was fond of this western part of Oiso where her father used to have his summer cottage.

She strolled out onto Terugasaki Beach. The southerly wind that was blowing buffeted her face, and the outlines of the lush green landscape were distinct all the way from Enoshima and the Miura Peninsula to the mountains of Hakone. She remembered how the old caretaker at the cottage used to say that when you could see everything so clearly it was bound to rain the next day.

Despite the strong wind the waves were not particularly high and there was no wind-blown spray. She began to walk westward along the sand, just beyond the reach of the waves. By midsummer, this stretch of beach would be full of temporary beach shelters. They had reed screens to give shade from the sun's glare and offered drinks and snacks for sale as well as a place to change clothes. Each summer cottage had an arrangement with one of them, and Komako's family always used the one called Izumatsu. Even now she could recall how delicious the sweet barley tea there had tasted.

So silly, dreaming of old memories!

Some women who were born into wealth and married well became stubborn and proud people after they lost their fortunes as a result of the war. They resisted any temptation to show sentimentality, for they knew full well the pitfalls that awaited them if they let themselves sniffle and sigh over the past.

Komako was one such woman. She refused to indulge in nostalgia by wondering what her father's cottage among the pines might look like now, or who was living there and how it might have changed. None of that had any connection with her present reality.

When she had walked as far as Sorokaku, the imposing residence of the Meiji statesman Ito Hirobumi, she decided to turn around and go back. As she did so, she caught sight of a young man and woman, both city-bred by the look of their clothes, running down the dunes toward her. She thought that she had been completely alone, except for a few children playing baseball, so the sudden appearance of a couple like that startled her.

"I wish you'd just decide. I hate people who dither!" said the young woman, obviously upset. She was a picture of fashion—red sweater, light blue gabardine skirt, white shoulder bag. With that hairdo and makeup, thought Komako, she could be a streetwalker from the Yurakucho district of central Tokyo. But if you looked at her more carefully, her face revealed the glowing health of a girl of good family. Young women today are like mushrooms, Komako mused; it's difficult to tell the healthy from the noxious.

"I told you—if you're going, I'll come, too. All I was saying is that if we're going to stop in Yokohama on the way home, we should deliver the gift quickly instead of strolling along the beach."

The young man was slim and looked as though he was still a student. He was also fashionably dressed, wearing a wide-brimmed fedora, a colorful tie made from what looked like the lining of a woman's kimono, a jacket with a rough texture, pale gabardine trousers, and red Cordovan shoes. They were all brand-new, and he looked no different from other young dandies often seen in Tokyo. Still, the features of his slender face were as finely chiseled as carved ivory and had a vulnerability and refinement that clearly showed him unsuited for fisticuffs or any shady activity. His voice was soft and his manner quiet. The girl was walking quickly, and as he trailed behind carrying what looked like a heavy parcel, he brought to mind the women of feudal times, who always walked a few paces behind their husbands. It was an almost comical sight.

"Oh! Come on! You're such a nitwit! I bet you haven't the least intention of going to 'Hama for some fun. You're just making excuses. I bet I know why. You're in *a pinch*, huh? If you haven't got the money, why don't you just say so. Go ahead, just admit it! I've got money—plenty of money—to go to 'Hama for Chinese food. It's a cinch!"

"*Never happen*—no way! No, I won't have it. How could I let you pay?"

"That's what I can't stand! Can't you forget such weird customs? *Never suki*—I'll never like that kind of thing!"

Shouting, the girl in the red sweater stormed across the sand with great, hip-dislocating strides. The young man scrambled after her with a worried expression on his face but could barely keep up.

What was all that about? Komako murmured to herself. She had no idea why they were quarreling, and even had trouble understanding the new slang they were using, which incorporated English phrases. If it was proper English—even more difficult expressions—she would have understood, but their speech did not resemble the language she had read in books. Was this the new Japanese for the new era? Whatever it was, Komako realized with a shock how little of it she understood.

The two stopped again and continued their argument. As their language was so littered with the slang used by the young, Komako gave up trying to follow. She was about to pass them when she noticed the young man staring at her.

"Excuse me, but aren't you Mrs. Minamimura?" he said, raising his hand to the brim of his soft hat. The friendly manner of this rather effeminate young man took Komako by surprise.

"Yes, I am."

"I thought so! Sorry, but I nearly didn't recognize you!"

With a charming smile that revealed gleaming white teeth, the young man addressed her politely. The awkwardness he had betrayed when arguing with the girl had vanished, and his words came out easily.

"Excuse me, but you are . . . ?" Komako could not recall who the young man might be.

"Have you forgotten me? How disappointing! We met once in Ginza. I am Hori Takabumi."

With that, the young man raised his hat and made a formal bow.

"Oh, that time in Ginza." Instead of recalling the actual occasion, all Komako could think of was that this young man was the son of the strange woman she had just met at her uncle's house. The encounter in Ginza had taken place five or six years ago, and she had little reason to remember a young boy in his school uniform. Nevertheless, she responded politely, noting wryly how quickly an adolescent boy can acquire such a grown-up air.

"You must have been visiting the Hanedas," the young man continued. "We're about to drop by there, too. Mother and Uncle Fujimura asked me to bring down this present for them. It's a delicacy that's made in the morning and only sold after midday, so Miss Fujimura and I bought it and caught the five past one train. Oh, let me introduce you. Yuri, come over here." Chattering on as though to himself, the young man beckoned to the girl, who was standing a little apart.

Komako watched as the girl, who until a moment ago had displayed such a temper in her argument with the young man, came toward them looking perfectly composed. Her movements were exaggerated, like an actress making a stage entrance. She introduced herself formally.

"My name is Fujimura Yuriko. It is a great pleasure to meet you."

Her gesture—a brief curtsy, without bending her head—was an odd one, though.

Could this really be the daughter of that grave-looking person? Komako wondered. She recalled the face of the courteous gentleman seated primly in front of the second hand drum.

"What a coincidence meeting you here," said the girl, in a manner as familiar as if she had known Komako all her life. "We're going to drop this off at the Haneda house and then we're going to Yokohama to have some fun. Would you like to come with us?"

Chapter 3
First Blooms of Summer

A month had passed since Iosuke had left. Komako visited every single place he might have gone, even his erstwhile employer, Tokyo News Agency. All she learned—just as he had told her—was that he had resigned about a month before the day he disappeared. She also approached colleagues and his former classmates at Kyoto University, but he had not been in touch with any of them.

Komako took great care never to say outright that Iosuke had left home or to ask expressly if he had dropped by. It was only to the Hanedas that she had confided the whole story. For the rest, she contrived to confirm what she needed to know without giving any reason for her inquiries. She had no wish to publicize what had befallen her or to let people realize she was asking where her husband was. She knew perfectly well what effect that might have on his future.

In fact, Komako's attempts to locate Iosuke had less to do with wanting him back than with wanting to know what had happened to him. If she could learn that, she could just sit and wait until he ran out of money and came meekly back home. She did not want to lose track of his whereabouts, but she was not going to make it easy for him, either.

When she thought of how he must feel, it was not as easy to be so dispassionate. He had left home wearing a woolen suit, and now, with the summer heat and humidity, she could imagine how hot he must be. She could not bear to think of the state he must be in if he were still wearing the same shirt and underwear. In those days, only standard-sized shirts and underwear were available in stores. She even toyed with the idea of finding a way to slip him the clothes he needed if she knew where he was. In the end, however, she did not pursue that plan, wanting him to suffer for having left her.

So where had he gone? He should have come back by now. Whatever situation she imagined him in, she thought he would have long since given up and set off for home. She had never thought Iosuke had much staying power. If proved wrong, it was an aspect of her husband she had known nothing about. The very thought vexed her. That was what she found most infuriating. Who in the whole world could possibly know Minamimura Iosuke better than she?

That was why she had been so irritated when her uncle in Oiso had said, "Iosuke won't come back for one month, maybe two." At the time she had scoffed at the idea. How could he make such a confident prediction, like some sort of street fortuneteller? It was preposterous! But as the days passed it became more probable that his pompous assumption might turn out to be true.

Are you thinking of never coming back? Komako put the question to her absent husband, but there was no reply.

All right then!

If you're going to be like that, just wait and see! This was her response to Iosuke's imagined resistance. The fact that he was still away only proved that he was not in any big trouble. Convinced that he was not the sort to put up with discomfort for the sake of pride or appearances, she took it for granted that he would be quick to return as soon as his circumstances became unbearable.

This time, she had to admit, she had been outwitted. Another possibility that occurred to her was that Iosuke was living under the protection of someone she did not know. That could be the only explanation for his long absence. If that were the case, she was furious that she had been unaware of the existence of such a person, whether male or female.

It was an act of rebellion, a clear case of betrayal. For the first time in nine years of married life Iosuke had dared to stage a revolt. It wouldn't be surprising if he'd been planning it all along, she thought. There was something suspicious about the way he had gone without a word of protest, when all she had said was, "Get out!"

The fact that he had merely answered, "I see," put on his hat, and left might mean he had been biding his time. He must have been prepared to make his move. He had quit his job a month before. He had made free use of his wages and severance pay (even though he had left a small amount in the desk), proving that he had planned his departure.

And you actually did it! You just walked out and left me looking like a fool!

What was it that Iosuke found lacking in his life to turn him into a rebel? He had enjoyed all the comforts of home. His action was as unthinkable as that of an employee who has a secure job, only works a thirty-hour week, and has his room and board paid for but decides to go on strike. It was as outrageous as if the current Yoshida Cabinet were to seek the support of the Soviet Union as well as the United States. Maybe it was the very ease and comfort of Iosuke's life that had brought this about.

I think I've put up with enough, Komako decided.

The idea of women's rights and more freedom for housewives was not exactly new to Komako. She had read *Lady Chatterley's Lover* even before the war, and although she was indifferent to recent movements calling on women to "awake," the postwar reforms giving equal rights and suffrage to women and the new constitution of 1947 were certainly welcome to every Japanese woman. She was often moved by reports of the courageous actions of women and girls carried by newspapers and magazines. She sometimes found it absurd that she had to be sitting at the sewing machine, pedaling steadily away. What kept her there, tolerating it all, were her overriding maternal feelings toward Iosuke. And if he had betrayed those sentiments . . .

If that's what you've done, just you wait! She had an idea how she might get even.

"I hope I'm not intruding."

Hori Horan's son was mopping his forehead as he came through the garden. It was his second visit.

"Hello, Takabumi. How are you? Do come in."

Komako rose from her desk, where she had been translating a piece by Eleanor Roosevelt, transforming the horizontal lines of the original into vertical Japanese script.

"Today I've come to invite you out," said Takabumi.

"Where to? A movie?"

"No, to an exhibition of French fashion," he said. He was still addressing her respectfully, as a younger man would a contemporary of his parents. "I thought you might find it useful for your work."

"Thank you. Which department store is it in?"

"It's not open to the public. It's at the Franco-Japanese Gallery in Ginza, and it's by invitation only. I managed to get some tickets."

"I suppose we can go in the afternoon. Anyway, come in."

"Thank you."

Apparently young men these days were not unduly concerned if they were disturbing someone. The house had no formal entryway, and as he sat on the veranda to remove his shoes, Komako noticed his socks had scarlet and navy blue stripes.

"Oh, you were working," he said, seeing her papers. "How I envy you, being able to do that. If only I knew enough English."

"It's nothing to envy. I just like doing it. So how's Yuri?"

"The same as usual. I'll never understand why she has to be so wild. She's such a handful. And your husband—is he still away on business?"

"Yes. It looks as if he'll be gone for a while this time, perhaps six months. Would you like some tea? Or if you don't mind just having some of these chocolates, that would be easier."

It should not alarm the reader how Komako came to be on such familiar terms with young Takabumi. That day in Oiso, after visiting the Hanedas, Komako's thoughts had been in turmoil and she had accepted the sudden invitation from Takabumi and Yuri to join them for dinner. They had taken the train to Yokohama, boarded a bus, and ended up eating *wonton* noodles in a dirty shack in Chinatown. The two had led the way, insisting that they knew the best place in Yokohama for the dish. Komako had paid the bill. After all, she could not have imposed on someone so young as Takabumi. In return, the two had done their best to fuss over Komako and treat her with the respect due to an elder.

Komako discovered a great deal about them as they took her into their confidence. Apparently, with the consent and blessing of both sets of parents, an engagement had been arranged for Yuri and Takabumi. However, they despised this custom, which they considered feudalistic, and declared that they would respect each other's freedom. Komako learned from Yuri that her father was an inflexible character, while Takabumi's mother, Horan, was a classic example of prewar vanity and retrogressive thinking. Yuri even disliked the sentimentality implicit in her name—*yuri*, meaning "lily," a symbol of purity and innocence—and insisted on using the American style of given name first, surname last, pronouncing "Yuri" like an English name.

Komako had responded to their frankness with the good grace befitting their senior, and had come to know them quite well during the course of the evening. However, their deferential attention, which included the frequent use of honorifics in their speech, far from raising her spirits, had left her feeling somewhat lonely.

Komako never once doubted her own youthfulness. She had never experienced childbirth but did not think she wanted children anyway, which in itself was proof she still took her youth for granted. She had complete trust in her youthful body, but, more than that, her confidence derived from her up-to-dateness and awareness of modern values, which was so much greater than that of her husband or her friends, or anyone else for that matter.

Her knowledge of English exposed her to the latest intellectual trends from abroad, and although she might not follow them as closely as an influential literary critic might, as a woman she felt engaged and interested. She also took satisfaction from the fact that, anonymous though she was, there were women among the well-known novelists and leaders of the women's movement who held values far more old-fashioned than hers. She had intended to keep up with the vanguard at all times and seemed to have succeeded.

Komako's self-assurance resulted from her mental and physical youthfulness and doubtless lay behind her domineering attitude toward her husband. Iosuke, as one might guess from his physique, was innately indifferent to trends, while Komako was a woman who kept pace with everything in this era of transition.

Despite that, trekking around Yokohama for three hours with Takabumi and Yuri had thrown Komako off balance. It was as if the two of them were forcing her out of a rut. They were overwhelming, but she had no inclination to admit defeat.

These postwar people are vulgar, she decided.

The way Yuri slurped down her noodles was simply horrendous. Indeed, there was nothing in the behavior of the two young people that merited praise. Yet there was no denying the existence of this new generation, sitting there eating in front of her.

The way they talked, the rapport between them, their relations as man and woman went against all convention. Komako had thought that she and Iosuke were a fairly modern married couple, but they were nothing like the two youngsters. Takabumi and Yuri must be still at the stage when they were simply good friends, but neither displayed any affection or deference for the other. Even Komako, misguided though she may have been, had been in love with Iosuke at first, but Yuri betrayed no sign of being emotionally involved. Neither did Takabumi give the impression he was courting Yuri. Yet you could tell that the two got along famously and enjoyed each other's company. It was all quite baffling.

In the curious relationship between Yuri and Takabumi, Komako was perceptive enough to detect evidence of the new era. At the same time, she could not suppress an aching loneliness in herself, like the sense of approaching autumn on seeing the large leaves falling from a paulownia tree.

Being fascinated by someone she had little respect for may have been inevitable for a woman like Komako, but she had been caught by surprise when this example of postwar youth had first appeared at her house a week earlier.

"I've been to visit my father's grave in Tama Cemetery," Takabumi had explained as he walked up to the veranda. "On *Mommy's* orders." He used the fashionable American term for his mother.

Before leaving Yokohama, Komako had given him her address without thinking much about it, never dreaming he would bother to come to this remote place. On his first visit, moreover, he'd been wearing his college student's uniform, which made him look more like the young innocent she remembered meeting in Ginza years earlier. At the time there was nothing to put her on her guard.

On that occasion Takabumi had sat on the veranda's edge and talked for an hour or so before going home. It may have been a mere hour, but for Komako, who had been growing bored with her life, it was rewarding. It allowed her to fill out the impressions of the younger generation she had gained during the three hours in Yokohama.

Her instincts about Takabumi had not been wide of the mark. He was definitely the latest specimen of youth, a product of the new age. You could find plenty of faults in him—he was unreliable, careless, superficial, off-hand, brazen, effeminate. But these qualities, like those of the new mass-produced materials such as plastic and nylon, were striking for their novelty and texture. Komako may have been accustomed to handling more traditional goods, but she possessed an above-average capacity for appreciating the newer qualities.

Her association with Takabumi and Yuri brought Komako into contact with the new era, and it was a stimulation she consciously sought. Perhaps there was an ulterior motive, too. Sensing that she had fallen behind the times, she thought that befriending the two young people might allow her to keep abreast of current attitudes.

Takabumi's visit today, less than days after his first, surprised her, but it was not unwelcome.

"Since you've gone to all the trouble to invite me to an exhibition, perhaps I could treat you to a meal," suggested Komako lightheartedly.

She had been wondering what to do about lunch. Cooking for one person was such a bother that Komako kept little food in the house apart from some bread, and could not have prepared a meal anyway. By offering to take Takabumi out to lunch, she could have something substantial to eat as well.

"Oh, Madam, that would be wonderful!" Takabumi sounded genuinely delighted. Komako's research into the modern age had not reached the stage when she knew that being taken for a meal by an older woman could make a young man extremely happy; she merely thought his response charming and typical of a hungry adolescent. However, his use of "Madam"—a title more usual for a bar manageress—in place of his customary respectful address was unpleasant.

"Since we're going to Ginza, let's have lunch there. I'm going to change, so please wait here," Komako said, standing up. The house had only two rooms, divided by sliding panels, and there was a sharp smack as she slid the panels closed.

The outing did not merit her best dress, which she had worn to Oiso, but she had what she called her "second batter," a pleasing top and matching skirt that would do fine. With a final glance at the mirror, she was about to open the door panels when she saw that they were not completely shut. Through the gap she caught sight of Takabumi, looking suspiciously nonchalant.

So you were peeping, were you? she thought.

The determined innocence of Takabumi's expression was proof that he had done something he should not have. Komako showed no embarrassment, not so much because of her confidence as a woman married for nine years as because she did not consider Takabumi an adult yet.

"Shall we go?"

After locking the glass doors to the veranda, Komako let herself out through the back, slipping into her white summer shoes for the first time that year.

It was quite a walk to the station, but a pleasant early summer breeze was blowing through the new leaves of the trees along the path. As they walked, it was apparent from Takabumi's height, a couple of inches more than Komako's, that he was a fully grown man. He was wearing chestnut-colored slacks of a thickish material, and the fabric of his off-white shirt—neither linen nor flannel—caught her attention.

"That shirt you're wearing—it's quite unusual, isn't it?" she commented.

Her interest in the material was not so great that she felt compelled to ask about it, but since leaving the house Takabumi had fallen strangely silent, so she used the question to restart their conversation.

"Yes," he said simply.

According to Yuri, Takabumi would pester his mother for money and spend it all on clothes; he never wasted money on anything else. He took meticulous care of his hats, shirts, shoes, and so forth, brushing them when necessary and using cleaning fluid to remove stains. It was strange that someone so concerned about his clothes would not respond to her remark.

"Is that what they call sharkskin?"

"Yes."

"It's all the rage this year, isn't it? You're certainly up with the latest fashions, Takabumi. Are all university students like you?"

"No."

He was saying only a fraction of what she was expecting.

Why would this boy, who had been so full of cheerful chatter until a moment before, suddenly clam up like that? Clearly there was some reason for his silence.

Maybe he's embarrassed to be seen walking with me. Komako had started to enjoy herself and had not expected Takabumi, who must have been used to walking with Yuri, to be shy.

No, it must be that!

When she was changing, unaware that she was being watched through the crack in the sliding doors, she had struck various poses in front of the mirror, dressed only in her petticoat. Perhaps Takabumi was regretting he had spied on her.

Silly boy, he shouldn't take it so seriously.

As they came in sight of the street leading to the station, Komako was still overestimating the naiveté of the younger generation.

On the train there were plenty of empty seats, so they were able to sit side by side. However, as it was not crowded, people were staring at them.

I wonder what they think we are. Komako was curious. Takabumi was about ten years younger than she, and a woman going out with her youngest brother would not raise any eyebrows. So perhaps they think we are . . .

As they approached the city center, the carriage began to fill. More people were standing, and she ceased feeling they were being watched. When they got off at Yurakucho Station and left by the east exit, they were soon swallowed up in the crowd. No one was paying any attention to anyone else, but this left Komako feeling vaguely dissatisfied.

I wish somebody would notice us.

He may only be an awkward boy, but she wanted people to notice that here she was, walking with a man in this fashionable district called Ginza.

"Anywhere is fine with me," she said to Takabumi, moving closer to him. "Why don't you take me somewhere you know."

In fact, Komako knew hardly anything about restaurants and suchlike

41

in postwar Ginza. Occasionally she went there to buy fabric or buttons for the clothes she made, but when she had to eat in the area she always chose Shiseido, which she was familiar with from long before. She had heard that a number of good restaurants had opened recently, but it had never occurred to that useless husband of hers to take her out for a meal. And you wouldn't feel right going into a nice place without a man beside you.

"Would you like somewhere that has good food or somewhere quiet enough to talk?"

Now Takabumi was acting like an adult. Coming to Ginza had clearly restored his spirits.

"How about good food as well as quiet surroundings?"

Komako knew that such a restaurant was bound to be expensive, but today she had an irresistible urge to spend recklessly. Iosuke's severance pay—or what was left of it—was still untouched.

As they started across the road at Sukiyabashi, Takabumi was quick to offer Komako his arm. Apparently, it was the latest form of etiquette, although it may have meant something more. But Komako was feeling rash, so she took his arm and immediately realized this was the current way for a couple to walk.

Even after they had crossed the street Takabumi did not lower his arm, and Komako continued walking with her arm in his. No one gave them a second glance, since one in every ten couples was walking in the same fashion.

This must be how an actress feels when no one in the audience notices her, thought Komako. And what was it that made her so want to perform? For whom was the play intended?

Well, my worthless husband, are you here somewhere?

Komako was thinking about Iosuke as they crossed the tram tracks and stepped inside a restaurant with "Petrushka" written vertically in *kataka-na* lettering beside the entrance. Her spine tingled with the possibility that Iosuke might see her there.

The walls of the restaurant were painted rose pink, with floral motifs in pale blue and gray—a sort of Marie Laurencin pastel effect—and in conjunction with the strategically placed potted plants they created a contrived romantic atmosphere. The Ginza district had been struggling to regain, superficially at least, its prewar elegance and mood and had succeeded to a large extent.

"This is nice, don't you think?" Takabumi asked, manipulating his hors d'oeuvre knife with some skill. He had again reverted to the form of address suitable for a respected aunt.

42

"Yes, I suppose so."

Komako was thinking she would have preferred somewhere more opulent and more of an adventure. If this was all postwar Ginza had to offer, it was disappointing. There was nothing in the ambiance or the decor to rival the intimate booths of restaurants she had read about in Western novels. Why did the thrill of walking arm in arm with a younger man recede as soon as they stepped inside the restaurant? Was it simply frustration that no one noticed?

After serving them, the waiter had quickly withdrawn, perhaps to leave them alone. Takabumi put down his knife and fork and placed his hands on the tablecloth.

"You know, I was really glad to meet you in Oiso."

He looked into Komako's eyes and smiled winningly, like a child trying to appeal to an adult—or a woman to a man.

"Oh, and why's that?"

Komako was watching Takabumi's fingers. Slender and white, like some attractive confection, they were never still. His nails had obviously been manicured. In her mind, Komako could see Iosuke's fingers: as large and fat as well-fed caterpillars, making the cigarette lodged between his first and second finger look tiny in comparison. The image was so comical that it brought a smile to her face. Takabumi was still talking with great earnestness.

"I was sixteen when I first met you. Was it in front of the Daitoku hat shop or Senbikiya, the fruit parlor?"

"You have a good memory."

"How could I forget? You were wearing a very attractive suit—I think it was blue-gray."

"Really?"

"Yes. You were so beautiful. To be honest, I was jealous of your husband."

"Well, Takabumi, you were a bit advanced for your years, weren't you?"

"When you're sixteen you think of all kinds of things. It's just that adults don't know."

"That's an unsettling thought. But if I made such an impression on you, I should feel honored."

"At that age I liked older women."

"At sixteen, most women would be older than you."

"Not only then, but now, too. I'm twenty-one and I feel it even more. Maybe it's a kind of Virgin Mary fixation. Not that just any older woman will do. What I always imagine is . . ."

Their fish course arrived.

Takabumi went on to describe his ideal woman with all the detail of a "Wanted" poster. It was an exact match for Komako's features and figure.

"She has a soft complexion—I think they call it lightly tanned—which shows truly fine sensibilities. And there's a sprinkling of faint brown dots. . . ."

"Don't you mean 'freckles'?" Komako's hand went involuntarily to her face.

"Yes, without freckles my image of the ideal woman would just shatter. All really intelligent women, I think, have freckles."

If this is Takabumi's way of seducing me, thought Komako, he must take me for a fool, and if he's serious, it's too ridiculous for words. Nevertheless, there was no denying the passion of his appeal.

Komako had never heard such praise of freckles. She suppressed an urge to laugh out loud; yet it flustered her to feel a wave of happiness at being complimented on a feature she had always considered a defect.

Indeed, Takabumi's approach was a new experience for Komako. No man had ever said anything like this to her. Before she had married Iosuke, one man had declared his love for her, but both she and he had been around the same age and belonged to the same social stratum. And here was Takabumi, looking up at her, so to speak, and murmuring compliments at her feet in an almost feminine voice. In eighteenth-century Europe, did the young pages of court ladies whisper sweet nothings to them like this?

"That's the kind of woman I'm waiting for," Takabumi went on. "I could devote my whole life to a woman like that. Don't you think that's where happiness lies?"

"I don't know about that. I thought Yuriko was more your type."

"Yuri? Couldn't ever happen! 'Tornado Yuri' is what I call her! She's not interested in anything but acting wild. Just imagine how uncouth I'd end up if I put myself in her hands!"

"You shouldn't say that. You're the same generation. People are happiest when they fall in love with someone who's their own age and from the same background."

Having said that, Komako's thoughts turned to her own situation. She and Iosuke did not seem to belong to any era and were a classic example of a mismatched couple. By the same logic, theoretically she should be dismally unhappy.

"I disagree." Takabumi was defending himself. "I couldn't care less for anyone my own age. Besides, there's nobody around worth bothering about. All this talk about equality between the sexes—only country bumpkins talk

44

like that. Me, I want a woman to worship, a woman to lead the way in every part of my life. Ah, what joy that would be for me! That is what I want."

The waiter brought their entrées.

It was already after two by the time they finished lunch and left. They had taken a long time over the meal, but Komako felt the food had fallen short of the excellence promised by the tableware. The bill of 4,125 yen, indisputable though it was, was a blow.

Takabumi, meanwhile, was almost ecstatic and grinning from ear to ear. Being treated by the woman he worshipped was a supreme form of pleasure. For Komako, paying for him was a display of her womanly prowess. Takabumi had not rated Komako's financial resources too highly, but, witnessing her generosity, he naturally wanted to express his appreciation.

"I enjoyed that immensely! Thank you so much!"

Being thanked so ardently and with such enthusiasm made it easier for Komako to forget the expense.

Afterwards, the two went to the exhibition at the Franco-Japanese Gallery. Included in the display were many items that had been in fashion the previous year, but Komako was nonetheless fascinated by the imagination and creativity of the famous French designers. What surprised her was that the styles were closer to the chic of Japanese *iki* taste than the "new look" then in vogue.

However, not much use for my sewing work, she thought. She was quick to observe the gap between European fashions and the realities of the Japan of her own time.

Once they had finished at the gallery, there was nothing left to do.

"Oh, you're going home already?" asked Takabumi, looking downcast.

"Well, as you saw, I didn't shut the house up properly, so I need to get back."

"At least let me see you home."

It needed considerable persuasion before he would agree to walk her only as far as Tokyo Station.

"So when can we see each other again? And do I have your permission to write to you?" Takabumi asked anxiously as they approached the Yaesu entrance of the station. His nervousness was almost pitiable and, as the time to part drew near, seemed tinged with sadness.

This could be dangerous, Komako thought. I'd better tread carefully.

But she did not want to pass up the opportunity to prolong this risky relationship a little more. After all, she was free to do as she wished with the young man. If their relations reached a point beyond which she had no wish to venture, she could make him obey her and do whatever she wanted. She felt capable of that because she was sure he had not touched her emotionally. She had never experienced this kind of freedom before, and would never have the chance again. It was a fascinating diversion. Depending on how you looked at it, she had the "new age" literally at her feet, and it offered proof that she was still young.

Komako felt a warmth spreading throughout her body.

"You may visit anytime you like. And, of course, your letters . . ."

She was about to continue when she noticed the back of a very large man who was turning in the direction of Ginza. Startled, Komako stopped, but before she could get a better look, he had vanished. It might have been an illusion, for Iosuke had never been one to move as quickly as that.

Chapter 4
Feelers Out

It had grown quite hot and still there was no sign of Iosuke. Komako was convinced he would come back eventually, if not for a while. She had resigned herself to that.

Fortunately, she was busy with her translation of Eleanor Roosevelt's memoirs. Working on the book helped to distract her from her disgruntlement with Iosuke and supplemented her income. Now that her husband was no longer in the house, she could devote almost the whole day to the translation.

In truth, a husband's absence can be a liberating experience for a wife. Even though Iosuke had been firmly at her beck and call, now that he was gone Komako felt a tremendous sense of freedom. A Japanese wife carries a heavy burden indeed.

The profession of housewife in Japan does not pay. A subservient spouse, of course, is invariably the loser, but even a domineering one such as Komako finds it difficult to come out ahead. In the insect world, whoever heard of a queen bee doubling as a drone? A wife may act high and mighty, but to what avail? If Iosuke returned, she could seize him by the collar and give him a good shaking, but the little satisfaction that might bring would soon pass. And then what?

If I were smart I might take this opportunity to change my profession, Komako thought.

Until now, Komako had taken her job as a housewife seriously and had always regarded divorce with disdain. The realities of the past two months without Iosuke, however, had forced her to reconsider. It was not that she had stopped caring for her husband; it was just that her regard for herself had been awakened. This can happen to housewives anywhere and is not particularly unusual in itself.

Takabumi's infatuation had little to do with her interest in changing occupations. He had become a regular presence in her life, sending letters that arrived morning and evening and visiting her at least once a week. He made no attempt to hide his feelings for her, but, despite his efforts to act older than his years, he was basically an adolescent with the smell of his mother's

47

milk still on him. His fawning, devoted attentions were entertaining, but they did not stir Komako's passions.

Komako treated Takabumi's overtures with motherly tolerance since they provided diversion that helped her to while away the time. He did merit some respect, after all, as the first of what might become a succession of men entering her life. If she did decide to change professions and become free again, the path before her would be open and the field would be wide. Nothing seems as vast and limitless as the future.

To freedom! That was the call that sounded frequently in Komako's ears. One moment she would be fretting about how Iosuke would manage in the heat without a summer shirt, the next moment she would be pondering the recently revised Civil Code. She knew one clause stipulated that if it was impossible to establish whether a spouse was still alive after an absence of three years, divorce would be granted automatically. But that was still two years and ten months away. There was also a clause granting divorce if the wife has been "willfully abandoned," but that might raise the question of whether or not Iosuke had left home with willful intent. Indeed, he may not have intended to abandon her at all. It might even be argued that Iosuke had been the one abandoned.

Humph! The new Civil Code isn't so new after all!

A brief note arrived from Haneda, Iosuke's uncle in Oiso: "Would like to hear how things have been since your last visit. Please come to the address below at 1:00 P.M. on the 28th. Cordially."

Enclosed was a map with directions to Fujimura Koichi's house in Kasumi-cho, an upscale residential neighborhood in the Azabu area of central Tokyo. Komako recognized "Fujimura Koichi" as one of the Goshokai members and Yuri's father. This must mean that the group was meeting there this month. Perhaps stirred by a touch of familial concern, Iosuke's uncle had the idea that since he would be making the trip to Tokyo, he could arrange to see Komako and check up on her situation. In typical Haneda fashion, the note implied that asking her to come was an afterthought.

Komako ate an early lunch and left the house. A gathering of the Goshokai was not much incentive to dress up, so she opted for a simple dress she had made from one of Iosuke's Echigo linen kimonos and put on a pair of white socks. She seemed unaware that a woman like herself looked more attractive in casual clothes than in anything more elaborate.

At Shinanomachi she got off the train and boarded a tram. A man who was sitting in one corner doffed his hat to her. It was a Panama hat of good

48

quality, and the man was wearing a light-colored suit of fine linen. Komako recalled the gathering in Oiso. He had been the one behind the gong.

"Mr. Henmi, I believe. I'm sorry I interrupted your practice the other day."

"It's become very hot, hasn't it? May I ask where you are going today?"

Henmi spoke with an affected gentility. It crossed her mind that he must be one of those people who copied English manners. He was the only man in the crowded tram wearing a necktie, and he had on white gloves and was carrying a walking stick.

"To Mr. Fujimura's house. I received a note from my uncle asking me to come."

"Really? I'm on my way there as well. So let's go together. This is the third time the group has met since Oiso."

"You must be looking forward to it," Komako remarked in an attempt to be friendly. Then, thinking she might risk a little candor with a man who was relatively young, she couldn't refrain from adding, "But don't you find it somehow absurd?"

"Not at all," he responded lightly, and then said, "Well, it's not the music that attracts me so much as the atmosphere. There's no other place in Japan today where you can truly feel we're at peace."

"Well, it may represent peace, but doesn't it strike you as somewhat antisocial? Isn't it a rather exclusive pastime of people concerned solely with enjoying themselves?"

"Well, as I said, I just go for the atmosphere. By the way, I understand that you are well-versed in English literature."

Apparently, the gentleman did not like to argue and preferred to change the subject.

"Can you tell me whether you think the novelist George Meredith is important or not? I don't know anything about literature, but I did enjoy reading one of his novels called *The Egoist*."

In the course of their conversation it became apparent that Henmi Takashi was a person of considerable culture.

Prefacing his remarks with "while I myself don't know," he proceeded to offer perceptive comments on music, art, and current affairs.

As they talked, however, Komako concluded that his views were conservative and a trifle outdated. When it came to the arts, his criteria were those current before the war, and if Komako mentioned a contemporary American novelist, he had nothing but critical comments.

49

Nevertheless, their conversation did not lag even after they got off at their stop by the cemetery and made their way from there on foot. Komako noted that Henmi was careful not to walk ahead of her. Ever since they got off the tram, he was displaying all the courtesies of a gentleman solicitous of a lady. Moreover, he managed this without any of the exaggeration that characterized Takabumi's attempts at gallantry. Henmi seemed a person of some depth, which made it hard for Komako to believe that he was a participant in the Goshokai foolishness.

He's unusually refined, she concluded.

Of late, upon meeting a man for the first time, it had become her habit to compare him with Iosuke. Just as she had contrasted Takabumi's slender white hands with Iosuke's thick-fingered ones, she now set Iosuke against Henmi's obvious store of learning and culture, his thoughtfulness, and the air of elegance that was manifest in everything he did.

How different they are! she mused.

Although the two were about the same age, Komako detected in Henmi almost everything that Iosuke lacked, not only as regards knowledge and culture but also in breeding and good manners. One other difference was that Henmi seemed to have plenty of money.

She had learned from chatting with Iosuke's aunt that Henmi's income was considerable. He and Hori Horan were called "the Goshokai *zaibatsu*," the wealthy members of the group. Komako had been brought up to appreciate the importance of money, so she naturally wanted to keep on good terms with it and was annoyed that money seemed to be giving her a wide berth lately. One of the factors that had persuaded her to marry into the Minamimura family had been her assumption that she would have no financial worries. She had thought that if she were allowed to indulge her interest in English literature she would have few complaints, no matter what else she might not like about her marriage. She never imagined that she would end up toiling to support the household with dressmaking and other odd jobs.

"If you are ever in the area, please come and visit." Henmi was inviting her to his house. "I am a little out of the way, though."

It would have been more conventional to allude to his home as "a miserable place," and the fact that he mentioned the inconvenience of its location instead may have indicated the pride he took in his house.

"Thank you very much. I would love to come, especially if I could meet your wife as well."

Komako had decided that befriending as sophisticated a person as

50

Henmi would be pleasant. However, in a voice that betrayed some emotion, Henmi replied, "I'm afraid my wife is presently at Fujimi."

"Do you mean she's ill?" asked Komako, recognizing the name as a place in the foothills of Mt. Fuji known for its spas and sanitariums.

"Yes. She's been there for more than a year now."

"Here we are," said Henmi, pointing to a large house surrounded by a tasteless concrete wall. Komako was disappointed that their conversation had to end. Henmi seemed to feel the same way, but it could not be helped.

"Greetings, greetings," Fujimura called out from the entryway. "Haneda has been waiting for you." Mrs. Fujimura was standing there, too. She looked like a serious-minded woman and could well have been a schoolteacher.

"I hope you had no trouble finding us," she said. "Sorry it's so inconvenient."

"Not at all. I was fortunate to run into Mr. Henmi. He showed me the way."

Komako was led to a sitting room on the second floor. There was nothing unusual about the house except that it was twice the size of her uncle's. It was neat and well kept.

"It's presumptuous to keep a man waiting," said Haneda in place of a greeting. He was seated by the *tokonoma*, wearing an old-fashioned black alpaca jacket unbuttoned at the front, and was fanning himself vigorously. "When it comes to rendezvous like these, they say it's the latecomer who has the advantage," he said with almost comical pomposity. "In other words, the one who keeps the others waiting is the winner. As a woman of experience, what do you think?" He was addressing Horan, Takabumi's mother, who was sitting next to him. Apparently they had been the first to arrive.

"Oh, how would *I* know? I wouldn't *dream* of using such tactics!" she protested. She was dressed in a kimono of fine linen with a hatched pattern. The coquetry of her look belied her words.

"Come, you are far too modest," countered Haneda. "Your late husband, my dear friend Hori, told me the whole story—about a snowy evening at a certain place where he was waiting patiently for you . . ."

"Professor, you mustn't tease me!" Horan interrupted. In an attempt to distract him from his offensive, she turned to Komako.

"Dear Mrs. Minamimura! I've been so remiss! I must thank you for treating Takabumi to a meal in Yokohama the other day. How very kind of you!"

Finding herself the target of such a polite greeting, Komako's face reddened. Since Horan only mentioned Yokohama, it seemed that Takabumi had not told his mother about their lunch in Ginza.

"That boy is so shy, Mrs. Minamimura. He still can't enter a restaurant by himself!" she bubbled. "Now he tells me he wants you to teach him English, and he's thrilled about it. So we look forward to your wise guidance."

Komako felt extremely awkward on hearing this, but her uncle intervened and saved her from having to respond.

"Komako, you mustn't stop at English. It's not too early to give him lessons on how to be a good husband, which will be a great help to young Yuri one of these days."

Encouraged by the general laughter, Haneda turned to Henmi and continued.

"I must tell you that our Komako is a mistress of the art of being a good wife as well as a bad one, both of which she employs with great skill and discrimination. She's something of a rarity in Japan these days. I would suggest," he said, now looking expectantly at Henmi, "that the young gentleman here could benefit from such guidance as well."

"Oh indeed, I myself would love to benefit from her wisdom," Henmi replied, attempting to pass it off as a joke but speaking with more intensity than he intended. He had clearly developed an interest in Komako.

"Our friend Hishikari is very late. These aristocrats do like to take their time!"

Constantly hopping from one topic to another seemed to be a trait of Haneda's, and Komako guessed that he was rarely serious, even with his wife.

"It's not that late," said Fujimura in the latecomer's defense. "Besides, we don't have the right drum in the house and Hishikari promised to bring his own. That must be a lot of trouble."

"What about playing a tune like 'Tama of Shichome' to warm up. I'm dying to start." Haneda seemed as impatient as a child.

"Excuse me, Uncle," Komako broke in, unable to wait any longer. "You sent me a note."

"Oh yes, that's why you've come, of course. Perhaps we could ask our host to let us use another room so we can talk."

"I'd be grateful."

"On the other hand, it's not as if we're plotting to overthrow the cabinet or anything. Everyone here is like family, so there's no need to go elsewhere, is there?"

"But . . ."

"The fact is," Haneda continued, addressing the gathering, "that Minamimura Iosuke has left home. Well, it might be more accurate to say that he was driven out of his home . . ."

Komako could not prevent Haneda from blurting out everything he knew. Not one to keep even his own secrets, he seemed totally oblivious to the loss of face he would cause Komako by broadcasting her story.

The others made sympathetic noises.

"The way I understand it is that Iosuke has taken a leave of absence, let's say. Even we older folks understand the necessity of such a thing from time to time," declared Haneda with a chortle. "But in this case, my friends, what do you think the good wife should do? If you ask me, I might suggest that if a leave of absence taken by a husband seems unfair, the wife should consider taking one, too."

"Please, Uncle!" Komako was deeply embarrassed, and her face was flushed as she tried to stop her uncle from continuing. She felt she was being made a laughingstock.

"Komako, you should ask these good folks what they think you should do. Hishikari is not here yet, but you won't find a group of people with better judgment anywhere in the country. They are sure to give you calm, considered opinions about anything you may ask. Don't you think you should keep an open mind and listen to what they have to say?"

It hardly mattered what she thought, Komako reflected. Glancing to one side, her eyes met Henmi's sympathetic gaze.

"Reason! Reason is the key," Fujimura began earnestly. "When it comes to solving all sorts of domestic problems, nothing can take its place. It may not resolve everything, but at least it won't lead to unhappiness. Reason can guide us to an agreeable solution much more effectively than emotion, I believe."

Komako was surprised that Fujimura should be the first to speak. She had believed him to be one of those stern men of the old school who rarely volunteered an opinion. There was nothing he said that Komako found particularly helpful—it was as conventional as it was abstract—but his attitude was pleasantly candid and, indeed, reasonable.

These Goshokai members are certainly a curious bunch, she thought.

"That's easy to say," said Horan, pushing back the collar of her kimono with the assertiveness of a woman accustomed to arguing with men. "But in relationships between men and women most things cannot be measured rationally, with a ruler or some such yardstick."

"That may be so, if you use such primitive devices. But if one uses a precise enough gauge, I believe that all things can be measured. Naturally, I am speaking of scientific accuracy, not absolute truth, because we do not live by philosophical truths in our daily life." Fujimura was speaking with great solemnity.

"I'm not sure what you mean, but such fancy theories are just stopgap measures," Horan continued. "Men like to emphasize 'accuracy,' whatever that means. But since time immemorial, women's hearts have been deep and difficult to fathom. The old saying that 'A man may father eight children, but he still needs to be on his guard when it comes to his wife' is precisely because of that complexity. And that's not saying anything derogatory about women."

Horan appeared to be speaking from personal conviction and was reluctant to yield to Fujimura. She was calmer than he and spoke with a brisk assurance.

"I think I understand perfectly the mores and complexities of a woman's feelings," Fujimura replied, "but that is not something that cannot be clarified by medical science or psychology. All the intricacies of the female psyche can be explained in psychoanalytical terms. In fact, as a subject of scientific inquiry, the female psyche is not overly difficult."

"How can you say that? How can anyone believe a person like yourself, who has such a moral and impeccable lifestyle. In real life, it is experience and actual exposure that's important. Your study of this topic is limited to your wife, is it not?"

"I don't see anything wrong with that. The worst sin that can be committed in research is overdiversification. I have examined a single case with great thoroughness."

"Fascinating!" Haneda exclaimed. "Both arguments are well founded, and seeing them matched like this is most enlightening. Komako, don't you find this helpful? It should give you much food for thought." Eager to see the discussion proceed, Haneda urged them on.

Even after Hishikari arrived, the Goshokai members continued to debate the inherent natures of men and women, their music practice all but forgotten. The sparring between Fujimura and Horan—with Haneda offering gratuitous comments without taking sides—showed no sign of abating.

Komako began to gain a clearer idea of what the Goshokai was all about. The members enjoyed lively arguments just as much as practicing their music. What made them unusual was the degree of enthusiasm with which they pursued these two pastimes. Nevertheless, having her domestic situation made the subject of their leisurely diversion was unpleasant, and she was grateful that Henmi had ventured no opinions.

Earlier, her uncle had tried to draw him into the discussion by saying, "How about you, young man? You ought to have something to contribute."

"Oh, a young person like me should just listen," he had said, tactfully declining and directing a kind smile at Komako.

It was rather hot in the second-floor room, and both Haneda and Hishikari had removed the jackets of their woolen suits. Only Henmi kept his on. Now and then he would take a white handkerchief from his pocket and dab at his face, and each time he did so the fragrance of his eau de cologne would drift in Komako's direction.

When Komako had met Henmi at Oiso, she had dismissed him as simply another member of this odd group, but observing him more closely she realized that he was different from the others. She noticed, too, that after he heard about Iosuke leaving home, his smile had grown gentler and more sympathetic.

He may be conservative, but in view of his background that's inevitable, she concluded.

While studying Henmi, Komako had the curious sense of returning to the social class of her birth. According to the upper-class code, feminine modesty does not allow a woman to display excessive warmth toward someone she has met just once or twice. Komako adhered firmly to this rule and only allowed herself to return Henmi's smile most discreetly. His expression showed her that he understood her intent within the framework of that etiquette. Without this wordless exchange with Henmi, there was no reason for her to linger in the hot second-story room.

"Well, Komako, having heard all these sound ideas and opinions, you have probably made up your mind. There's nothing to be done but prepare yourself for the long haul and wait until Iosuke comes home."

Komako had fallen into a reverie and ceased listening to what was being said, so Haneda's words startled her. She mumbled a noncommittal reply.

"So if that's settled, we have business to attend to."

With this, Haneda began to tap his drum impatiently. He made it seem as if he were testing the sound, but the action could be interpreted as a hint for her to leave.

"Is that all you wanted to say to me, Uncle?" Komako blurted out, greatly annoyed. Not only had she come all this way and had her private affairs bandied about, but she had been forced to listen to their irrelevant homilies. Now she was being summarily dismissed. Who would not be upset at such treatment?

Is this the only reason he called me here?

Bristling, Komako left the room. She came close to walking out the door without even saying farewell to Henmi, but fortunately he came to the top of the stairs to bid her goodbye. He had been sitting nearest the door, so it was easy for him to slip out.

"So sorry to see you go. Until another time, then."

His voice was low, but the "sorry" sounded heartfelt. The innuendo of the brief "another time" echoed down the dim stairwell after her.

"Thank you very much." Komako's reply had an undertone that complemented his and confirmed the rapport between them. Superficially, however, their exchange was so formal that anyone overhearing it could not have detected the slightest impropriety. Human beings, especially those who are highly sophisticated, have all sorts of subtle ways of conveying meaning.

In any case, the brief exchange with Henmi completely dissipated Komako's anger. She quickly went downstairs and was moving toward the front door when she decided that it would be too ill-mannered simply to put on her shoes and leave. Women could not afford to omit the proper courtesies to one another.

"Mrs. Fujimura, thank you very much. I'll be going now," she called out in the direction of what appeared to be the downstairs sitting room.

"You're leaving already?" came Fujimura's wife's voice, and Komako heard the soft padding of her footsteps. Simultaneously, there was a loud clatter from the opposite direction. Another voice called out and into the entryway burst Yuri. She was wearing a casual sleeveless dress with a wide collar.

"Yuri, what has got into you?" Mrs. Fujimura appeared at the same moment and scolded her daughter. "For heaven's sake, try not to make so much noise!"

Yuri paid no attention to her mother.

"I only just heard you were here," Yuri said to Komako. "I need to see you. There's something I want to talk to you about."

The way she had her arms folded across her floral-print dress was far from ladylike.

"Your parents are very busy with guests, so I shouldn't stay," Komako replied.

"Don't worry about them! All they're doing is jangling on their gongs and such. It gets on our nerves. You're no trouble. Besides, my room's like another world."

"Yes, by all means please stay as long as you like," urged Mrs. Fujimura.

Komako was finding it hard to leave.

"Come, there's something I have to talk to you about!" Yuri practically ordered Komako to follow her.

"This used to be my brother's room," said Yuri, showing Komako into a small square room that projected into the garden like a separate wing. The room was as cluttered as it could possibly be. The ill-fitting curtains hanging in the bay window were dirty, and the desk standing on the tatami mats had a thick layer of dust. The walls were covered with photographs from *Time* and *Life* magazines and three-color prints. On one wall hung the white shoulder bag that Komako remembered from Oiso. It was a room devoid of taste—at least, of an ordinary young girl's taste. No French dolls or photographs of stars in the Takarazuka theatrical troupe.

"You have an older brother?" asked Komako.

"He's married and has moved out. It's maddening how men can go off and be independent just like that!"

Yuri threw herself onto a shabby rattan chair in front of the desk. There was no other chair in sight, so Komako pushed aside some magazines and sat on the ledge of the bay window.

"Would you like one?" Yuri was holding out a packet of Lucky Strikes.

"Not for me, thank you."

Komako had been teaching herself to smoke from a packet of cigarettes Iosuke had left in the house, but she had no desire to smoke at that moment. Yuri did not insist but took a cigarette for herself and lit it with a lighter. She blew out two streams of smoke from her nostrils.

"You don't get scolded for smoking?"

Komako could not help comparing her own girlhood with Yuri's behavior.

"Of course I do. But *I don't care*," Yuri replied, using the English phrase.

Calmly she tapped the ash into an ashtray on the desk. Komako concluded that her smoking must be an open secret.

"You were born in a good age, weren't you?"

Komako's remark was half irony and half conviction.

"Not especially. From now on we have to fight for what we want—all kinds of things. Anyway, there's just one thing now. I want to ask a favor."

Yuri's style of speech had grown even blunter than when they had gone to Yokohama. She sat in front of Komako, her bare legs crossed, swinging one foot back and forth. It was an attitude that could have been taken as friendly, but it also carried a hint of challenge.

"What can I do for you?"

Komako masked her wariness with a smile.

"It has to do with Candy Boy."

"What boy?"

"Don't you know what that means? It's a young dandy like Takabumi— you know, where the packaging is everything."

"I understand."

"It also means someone who's sweet-talking and sticky."

"I see," said Komako with a chuckle. "You young people are certainly inventive."

"It's not an invention. Just a new word."

"Never mind. So what about this Candy Boy?"

Yuri turned to stub out her lipstick-stained cigarette and continued.

"Would you please take him in?"

"What do you mean by 'take him in'?"

Komako was not sure how to react to these words.

Yuri knitted her brows and sighed. "If you won't do something about him, I don't know what to do."

"Why am I responsible for doing something about Takabumi?" said Komako with a light laugh.

"How can you say that! That's why adults make me so mad! Aren't you carrying on with him? Taking him to lunch at Petruschka and going for walks."

Komako suddenly realized that the young woman was jealous and feeling petulant. Not that she had any reason to be, since Yuri could have him back anytime. Komako hadn't the slightest need for young Takabumi or anyone like him. But, that aside, how did Yuri know about the afternoon in Ginza?

"Well, you certainly know a lot about what I am doing," she said.

"Of course! I know everything! What he writes in his letters to you, what he talks to you about—everything!"

"I wonder. Are you clairvoyant or something, Yuri?"

"I don't need to be to know what's going on! He tells me everything!"

Yuri's reply was offhand, but Komako was completely floored.

She did not understand them at all. Just as she had not understood the new slang they had used in Oiso that first time, she felt exactly the same way now. Takabumi had nothing good to say about Yuri, yet it turned out that he had been pouring out all his feelings about himself and Komako to her!

"Some parts of his letters were actually thought up by me," added Yuri without batting an eye. "He used quite a lot of my ideas."

Thrown off stride by this revelation, Komako could only conclude that the youngsters had deliberately planned to insult her.

"What on earth are the two of you up to?" Komako erupted, words almost failing her as she voiced her utter perplexity about the relationship between Takabumi and Yuri.

"Please calm down," Yuri said. "The situation is simple. Him and me, we're just friends. But you're more than that—you're like his lover. He and I are close, but we can never become lovers. Any way you look at it, we're not suited to each other. Besides, we mustn't be lovers. We have to fight the feudal system that made us get engaged. We really need someone like you so that we can always remain good friends. You're our savior!"

"Well, if so, that's all for the good. But what did you mean by 'take him in'?'

"I wanted to make sure you understood. I want you to marry Takabumi."

Chapter 5
A Lunch of Sweetfish

Ten days had passed, but the shock of that conversation with Yuri still lingered.

Are girls like that typical of the new generation? Komako wondered.

Komako had known right away that Yuri was a bit wayward—from how she spoke, her opinions, and the clothes she wore. Yet Komako had never imagined that the postwar model of woman could be so different—head, heart, and all.

"All you have to do is marry him!" Yuri had declared. "If you just made up your mind!"

It was all the more astounding that Yuri could come up with the idea so calmly, even though she was supposedly unaware of Iosuke's disappearance. She appeared to think that marriage was as casual as visiting next door.

Komako had laughed out loud. "What an absurd idea! Do you realize the difference in our ages?"

That had not deterred Yuri in the least. "Well, I guess about ten years. It would be exactly right. There are lots of couples like that now. These days all young guys want to marry older women. Even me—I'm not interested in marrying a man who's not twenty years or so older. Don't you think that someone who hasn't developed his abilities to the fullest can't be considered a real man, can he?"

That made Komako wonder whether young people had found they could not trust a partner their own age. Had the winds of war been so devastating that they had blighted the buds of youth in this unnatural way? If so, the new generation, which had seemed enviable for having everything that could be desired—peace, material abundance, democracy—might deserve to be pitied as victims. Komako was beginning to feel this when Yuri spoke again.

"I'm happy just being friends with Takabumi. Even if he marries someone else, we'll always be close. We'll go dancing sometimes, or camping."

Although it sounded as if Yuri's idea of friendship with a man went no further than an enjoyable platonic relationship, more than that was implied, but it was not clear where she drew the line. The stark truth might be that Yuri wanted to line men up as a convenience to cater to her whims—one to rely on for practical support, one for romance, one for fun and games.

Komako wondered what Yuri really wished for in a man, and whether she had any such wishes at all.

And then there was Takabumi. Perhaps he was the same. Komako felt able to deal with an unwanted suitor who professed total devotion, but how sincere were the intentions of a young man who not only recounted every detail of his relationship with her to Yuri but also went so far as to seek the girl's advice about the wording of his love letters? Could both of them belong to a breed that had no particular wishes vis-à-vis the opposite sex?

They're just a couple of outrageous adolescents!

Komako tried to convince herself of that conclusion. Otherwise she would end up in a slippery place indeed, the victim of their scheming. In any case, a man of a more conservative character would suit her better.

A letter arrived from just such a man, written on crisp imported notepaper that was white on one side and light tan on the reverse. The sheet was folded in two and enclosed in a large envelope of a matching color. It was the kind of stationery favored by English gentlemen, so Komako deduced that it must be stock purchased overseas before the war.

The message was brief and to the point—less than a tenth the length of Takabumi's missives.

> Hoping to continue our conversation about English literature, I would like to invite you to join me on a visit to my friend Mogi's country house in Inada-Noborito on Sunday. Mogi is an old friend of mine. I understand that he and his wife were also friends of your parents, and he hopes you will be able to accompany me. His wife is eager to display her skills in Western-style cuisine with local river fish. Mogi says he will send a car to meet us at Shibuya Station at 11:00, and if that is convenient for you, I will be waiting there at the appointed hour.

That was all. Talk of English literature, joining his friend and wife, enjoying home-cooked freshwater fish—not a single inappropriate innuendo on the page. The letter did not contain a word that was improper, and she could have shown it to anyone. It was an invitation she could not be faulted for accepting.

Yet Komako detected a whiff of danger in the elegant note. It was the fragrance of the eau de cologne she had noticed when Henmi had flourished his handkerchief in the gathering at the Fujimuras. Komako recognized it as the mark of a Western-style gentleman, and it was a scent to which she was susceptible. Nevertheless, she believed that whatever danger there was lay within herself, and she did not regard the invitation as a trap.

One aspect that made her hesitate was Mogi and his wife. The Mogis were indeed old family acquaintances, but the friendship had been between the previous generation, so Komako had never met the current head of the family, who was Henmi's friend. This Mogi had a reputation as a playboy. He had studied in the United States for several years but had returned to Japan during the war. After the war he started a business that had flourished, and was now doing extremely well through his contacts with overseas buyers. Since Komako's own fortunes had turned in the opposite direction, she was not overly enthusiastic about meeting someone so prosperous.

If it had been just the two men, there may have been no problem, but the presence of Mrs. Mogi was an extra concern. Never having met her, Komako worried that she might be the haughty type who looked down her nose at everyone. That would be enough to put someone with as much pride as Komako out of sorts for a week.

Nevertheless, the presence of the Mogis was the factor that made it possible for Komako to accept Henmi's invitation. Otherwise it would not have been proper to have a rendezvous with a man she had met only twice. Clearly, the invitation provided a valuable opportunity to further the acquaintance.

There was the added allure of a nostalgic day spent in the social milieu of her youth—country cottages, luncheon parties, chauffeured automobile rides. It had been a long while since she had been invited to a gathering of which all that was a part.

To help make up her mind, she tried counting off on her fingers—"to go," "not to go," "to go," "not to go"—and ended with "to go."

That fine Sunday morning the crowd at the bronze statue of Hachiko in front of Shibuya Station was dense enough to make even that faithful dog howl. White hats, white shirts, and white blouses sparkled in the sun, and the smell of sweat was everywhere.

"Ah, Mrs. Minamimura!"

Henmi was surprisingly quick at locating Komako in the crowd despite the fact that she was not particularly tall.

He had arrived first. Komako herself had come ten minutes before the appointed hour and had been a little fearful that this might betray some eagerness on her part, so she was relieved that Henmi was there even earlier.

"Thank you for your kind invitation," she said with a bow. She was wearing a simple white cotton dress chosen especially for the excursion. It may have been a little informal for a first visit to someone's house, but if she did not want to wear the same outfit twice in her encounters with Henmi, it was her only alternative. She had also counted on it being easier for the wealthy Mrs. Mogi to accept someone who looked sporty rather than elegant.

"Not at all," said Henmi. "I was afraid my invitation might be awkward, but the Mogis' cottage is quiet and relaxing. It's cool there, too, so it's a good place to talk."

Henmi was speaking less formally than at their previous meeting. While talking, he replaced a white safari hat on his head.

He, too, was dressed in white, and had elected to come without a tie, leaving the top button of his shirt undone. He was wearing shorts, his knees showing above long white socks. Only his shoes were of pale yellow leather. Whether he had adopted the dress code of an English gentleman for the heat of summer or for a visit to the country, she was not sure, but he stood out from the crowd inasmuch as he was wearing a jacket despite the warm weather. The fact that his shorts and jacket were of plain white cotton made it look as if he and Komako had coordinated their attire ahead of time. To all appearances, they could pass as a harmonious couple who preferred cotton to linen and dressed in the style of European colonists in the tropics. As they became aware of the impression they created, they both began to feel light-headed, as if they had been drinking champagne on an empty stomach.

"The car is waiting at the corner over there."

Henmi led the way through the throng. Many people who could not afford a trip to the seaside were milling about the station entrance, waiting to catch a train to go swimming in the Tama River. The two slipped through the crowds like a pair of minnows darting upstream.

Two or three cars were parked at the curb. Komako was about to pass a pale green one that looked too big to be used by anyone except a foreigner, when she heard Henmi call out to the driver, "Here we are. Sorry to keep you waiting."

The driver jumped out and doffed his cap.

"After you," said Henmi, turning to Komako and taking off his hat as the driver opened the door.

The car was marvelously comfortable, like riding on a cloud, and so quiet that she had no trouble hearing what Henmi was saying.

"There's no need to worry. The Mogis are very casual people," he explained as they set off.

"But this is not exactly casual, is it?" remarked Komako, with a hint of a smile. She knew it was not considered good manners in this setting to say anything too formal.

"Oh, it's all right. Let's get them to treat us extravagantly today," said Henmi. "Mogi has made quite a bit of what they call 'easy money,' so we'll be virtuous and help him share his wealth."

"I suppose I don't mind helping with that sort of socialism," said Komako, finding herself in a matching jocular mood.

"*Money*," said Henmi, flaunting the English word, "does have a curious power. It can make a person quite vile or it can be the source of great good."

Laughing, Komako allowed the genteel inflections of her upbringing to return to her speech. "I am the sort who would not dismiss a little 'vile money' if I could be its manager." Being in the habit of speaking brusquely to Iosuke, she had almost forgotten she could still talk with the refinement of the upper classes.

"Naturally, you fully qualify as someone who would use money well, and so in my opinion your present circumstances are quite regrettable."

Henmi spoke as though he were familiar with her financial situation, perhaps having heard about it from Iosuke's uncle. Komako was embarrassed, but she did not have to take it in a negative way. Although she was aware that Henmi was trying to flatter her, she was pleased nonetheless.

"Gracious, how can they in this heat?"

As the car passed over the concrete bridge spanning the Tama River, they saw crowds of boats on the shallow water as well as countless bare bodies, like so many black beans, on the riverbank below. Looking down, Komako did not believe the river could provide much relief in this weather, and it struck her as a pastime of the poor and wretched. She had allowed herself to forget that she, too, was one of them.

After crossing the bridge, the car turned right. They were moving slowly, but all at once a child jumped out into the road in front and the car had to swerve a little. The two passengers had been sitting some distance apart in the back seat, but the sudden movement threw them closer. As the vehicle continued, Henmi's bare knees brushed against Komako's skirt at times. The two fell silent. Then Komako, pretending that her legs had tired of being in the same position, managed to move away without it seeming to be unnatural. It was not that the closeness had been unpleasant, but the thought of being sucked into a situation against her will was disagreeable.

However, the two seemed to have developed a certain rapport since leaving Shibuya Station, and as the car turned off the paved road to jolt over dirt roads leading through fields and orchards, they drew closer in a physical way as well.

Eventually, they came in sight of another river, and Henmi leaned over to point out a hill on the left, saying, "The Mogis' house is up there."

Although it was said to have been built by a German, the house looked more like an English cottage, with an unpretentious front door.

The driver had sounded his horn to announce their arrival, but Henmi rang the doorbell on the porch several times just for the fun of it. He was clearly in high spirits.

"Welcome! You certainly made good time!" Their hosts came into the hall just as the maid opened the door. Mr. Mogi was in his shirt sleeves and was sporting a bow tie, which made him look like the popular comic storyteller Matsui Suisei. His wife was dressed in an aloha shirt and white shorts.

"*Missus Minamimura!*" she exclaimed in English, thrusting out a hand with American-style gusto. "My goodness, it has been a long time!"

The remark caught Komako off guard. Nonplussed, because she could not remember ever having met the woman before, she simply touched Mrs. Mogi's hand.

"Well, well, do come in!" urged Mogi. "It's cooler inside." Though he was not tall, he led the way with long strides, his footsteps echoing in the dim hall. Unlike most houses, no indoor slippers were provided, so they kept their shoes on. This saved Komako from leaving the only pair of white shoes she owned in the entryway and exposing the shabby lining for all to see.

They were ushered into the living room, which seemed to be two large rooms combined into one, serving as both parlor and dining room. On the far side was a wide terrace swept by a cool breeze, with a fine view over the river and the railway bridge.

"Oh, how splendid!" exclaimed Komako. Her father's summer cottage at Oiso had been in the traditional Japanese style, and this was the first time she had been inside a Western-style cottage. She was especially impressed by the row of attractive bamboo chairs on the terrace.

"If you'll excuse me," said Mrs. Mogi, "I have to check on things in the kitchen."

Mogi, too, disappeared inside the house, leaving Henmi and Komako alone. There had been no introductions and none of the customary greetings—it had been simplicity itself. But Mogi's wife's remark when they arrived still bothered Komako.

"You know, Mr. Henmi," said Komako softly, "I really have no recollection of meeting Mrs. Mogi before. Do you think she was in another class at the same high school or something?"

"Oh, don't worry about that!" said Henmi, laughing. "It's the way she greets everybody. It's the sort of person she is. As I told you, they're both eccentrics, so please bear that in mind." He seemed rather amused.

"What would you like to drink, Mrs. Minamimura?" asked Mogi, appearing at the door by the terrace, cocktail shaker in hand. Just like a professional bartender, he began to take down various bottles from a cabinet in the dining room.

Small sweetfish deep-fried in olive oil were served. Mogi sprinkled salt on the golden-colored crescents and ate them with his fingers.

"These little ones are from around here—they're what we call 'willow-leaf sweetfish,'" he explained casually. "The ones we'll have later come from the Nagara," referring to the river in Gifu Prefecture famous for sweetfish.

"Mmm, delicious!" said Henmi.

"Indeed! Mrs. Mogi, they're exquisite!" added Komako.

Henmi and Komako stuck to eating with knife and fork.

"Really? The maid deep-fried them. I don't care much for freshwater fish, but I've been trying not to eat meat."

Mogi's wife, too, was eating the fish with her fingers and taking long drafts from a can of juice.

"You mean you don't like meat?" inquired Komako politely.

"No, it's because meat is fattening," said Mogi. "Our Blondie is worried about her weight."

"*Hey, you!*" she retorted in English, glaring at him.

Everything about them seemed to be in the American style. Mrs. Mogi had also spent her college days in the United States and had shed all concern with the usual conventions and manners. Generous and forthright, it did not seem to bother her that she was a couple of inches taller than her husband, or that, with her mannishly square face and big mouth, Komako was the more attractive woman at the table. She ignored the Western table manners Komako had learned at school, smoked a cigarette during the meal, sat with her chin cupped in her hand, and drank a good deal of juice and ice water.

Mogi was similarly unconventional. He made a brief allusion to the connection with Komako's family, but that did not seem to be the reason for his hospitality. He gave the impression of someone interested only in the immediate present, who considered it a waste not to have an enjoyable time with guests come especially to visit. He was also unlike many of the nouveau riche in his disinclination to boast or hang on to the fortune that had come his way. He seemed a somewhat spoiled fellow who loved spending money.

When the larger sweetfish prepared in the *meunière* style arrived, Mogi began to tease Henmi. "Are you still carrying on with that festival music group?" He was referring to the Goshokai.

"And what's wrong with it?" retorted Henmi. "You've been blowing away on that saxophone of yours, haven't you?"

"That's different. For one thing I was never so caught up in it. Mrs. Minamimura, don't you agree it's odd he should be so serious about that old music?"

Komako gave a noncommittal chuckle, but inwardly she had to agree. She wished Henmi would leave the ensemble.

"Our children would love those dances!" This irrelevant interjection by Mrs. Mogi, said with great earnestness, made the others burst into laughter. It emerged that the couple had sent their two children to the beach at Zushi with the housekeeper. The Mogis had bought the cottage purely for their own pleasure, they said, and they intended to enjoy all sorts of pursuits that were not possible in their more traditional-style residence in Tokyo's exclusive Yoyogi district. Komako found herself musing that theirs was a household that revolved around the husband and wife rather than the children.

Following a huge salad of fresh vegetables, some kind of gingerbread was served, and lunch was over. Having imagined that there would be a succession of lavish dishes, Komako felt slightly disappointed by the meal's simplicity. On second thought, perhaps not going to extremes was the American way of entertaining. However, they were then offered large slices of melon and a pile of well-chilled Alexandria grapes.

After coffee, Mogi stood up.

"Now I hope you two will make yourselves at home."

Henmi, sounding surprised, asked, "Does that mean both of you are going somewhere?"

"At two o'clock we've got a game on with some friends," said Mrs. Mogi. "And today it's my turn to win. I've been raring to go since morning." Indeed, she did look the picture of anticipation as she gazed down at her baggy shorts.

It obviously had not occurred to either of them that it might be impolite to invite guests to their house and promptly go out for a game of golf in the afternoon.

"Do you mean you're leaving us on our own?" asked Henmi, pursing his lips exaggeratedly.

"It's still quite hot. The two of you should relax, take a nap, whatever. You're welcome to use our bedroom."

Mogi seemed to think little of this, but it was enough to make Komako blush.

"All right, then!" Henmi responded. "We'll collect our house-sitting fees by emptying your refrigerator." He sounded pleased, almost grateful to be abandoned by his hosts.

"I mean it," said Mogi. "Help yourself to whatever you want. Ask the maid if you need anything."

With that, Mogi disappeared into the rear of the house.

"Don't you think we ought to leave?" Komako suggested quietly to Henmi.

"It's all right. As I told you, it's their style of doing things," said Henmi. "Of course, if you are in a hurry or something . . ."

"I'm in no particular hurry."

If Henmi were going to act the perfect gentleman, Komako was reluctant to say anything that would make her sound prudish.

"Look at me!" Mogi called, reappearing at the door. "A regular caddy on a busy day."

He was loaded with golf bags, his own and his wife's, one hanging from each shoulder. Mrs. Mogi was wearing blue-tinted sunglasses and a white baseball cap. Her long legs were bare, and she presented a strikingly Amazon-like figure.

"We're off now. Enjoy yourselves."

In this way Henmi and Komako found themselves seeing their hosts off at the front door as if they were the owners of the house. The car that had brought them from Tokyo was waiting outside. Shortly before, the Mogis had mentioned that one of the reasons they had bought the house was that it was an easy drive to the Sagami golf course.

"Bye."

68

One couple left and the other stayed.

"Please bring us whiskey and some water," Henmi told the maid as if it were his own home. "And some Coca-Cola, if you have any."

It had grown too hot on the terrace, so the two retreated indoors to the northerly side of the sitting room. A breeze cooled by the foliage along the river blew over their shoulders as they sat side by side on the sofa under the window.

"Do you drink often?" Komako asked.

Komako recalled the time when Iosuke finished two bottles of whiskey in a single day. He had not been out of control, but when she complained, he had fixed her with a terrifying stare. His look had such an unaccustomed fierceness that he must have been drunk. For the past year he had been drinking mostly cheap liquor, and she disliked the smell more than she probably should have.

"Yes, I normally take a little after meals," said Henmi. "It's good for the digestion, you know. Why don't you have some, too?" Pouring a small amount of whiskey into a tumbler, he mixed it with chilled Coca-Cola.

"It might make me drunk," said Komako, hesitating.

"You'll be all right," Henmi reassured her.

Komako liked the smell of Western spirits, despite having come to curse alcohol because of Iosuke. Today, however, she felt like having a drink. The brown-colored cola Henmi had added to the whiskey was something she had only heard about, and she was curious to try it.

"It's rather good!" she said, finding the drink pleasant.

"Wasn't I right? They say this is the best way to drink American whiskey."

After sipping from his own glass, Henmi pulled out his handkerchief and dabbed his lips. The fragrance of his cologne drifted across.

"Incidentally, what's the latest about your husband?"

Henmi was one of those who did reconnaissance before making a foray, like a *shogi* player who starts out by moving his pawns.

"Well, I wonder myself. For all I know he may have become a meth addict."

Komako had wanted to say something cruel, like throwing a stone, to drive away the image of her husband that had floated into her mind a few moments before.

"More important than that," she continued, "is your wife any better?"

"Well . . ." Henmi started with the same word as Komako, but he would naturally avoid introducing anything as vulgar as meth. "She hasn't had a fever for more than six months, and there doesn't seem to be any need for her to stay. Something else must be keeping her there, I suppose." Henmi was laughing, but his eyes betrayed no amusement. A sympathetic listener could have detected the loneliness in his voice.

"You mean she's over her illness?"

"Yes. So she must be there not so much to convalesce as just to be away." Again, Henmi's tone was wistful.

As Henmi Takashi described it, his marriage had not been a happy one from the start.

His mother's belief in the old adage, "Get your daughter-in-law from across the street," was where all the trouble began. His wife was the daughter of the owner of a fish store that supplied the Henmi hospital. She had been educated at a regular girls' high school, but her tastes veered toward the lowbrow, and she was not what one would call cultured. She could sing traditional ballads well enough, but if he took her to a piano recital she would nod off. Similarly, she would watch a Japanese movie spellbound, but a Western movie bored her. She disliked Western clothes, too, claiming that Western-style undergarments gave her a headache.

Henmi's mother had not been mistaken as far as the girl's wifely skills were concerned. She was an early riser and liked to clean house, working with an antlike fervor. She turned out to be a dutiful girl more attentive to her mother-in-law than to her husband. In the end, Henmi felt that he had simply married a housekeeper and developed little affection for her. As his feelings cooled, she began to fancy herself wronged. She would tell him that someone uneducated like herself could not be expected to please him, so perhaps he should find himself a sophisticated mistress.

Taking a mistress went against his gentleman's code, but there were times when he could not help regretting his misfortune. When his wife contracted pleurisy and was ordered to live outside the city, Henmi was honestly relieved. Apparently his wife, too, felt as if freed from captivity, and once at the sanitarium she quickly recovered. She never wrote to him, and he concluded that when she returned she intended to go to her parents' house instead of his.

"I've begun to think it a crime to stay married any longer," he said, looking mournful. "After all, it's illogical as well as immoral to act as if you're a couple when there's no love at all between you."

"You may be right, but what does your wife feel? She may be fond of you but the way to express it is blocked." Komako was thinking less of Henmi's wife, whom she had never met, than of herself.

"Even if there's some affection, when a couple is so far apart in character and education, the affection can be expressed in the wrong way, making the situation worse than when there's no affection. At times I was so irritated that I wanted to weep."

"I can understand that," said Komako, although in her case her irritation would drive her not to tears but to explode like a volcano.

"I'd say compatibility of personality, education, and interests is indispensable for a couple," said Henmi. "Look at the Mogis. They're not particularly cultured, but they fit well together. It makes me envious to see them go out hand in hand for a game of golf. I also want a partner with whom I can enjoy my type of golf. As a man, I think I have a right to declare that I need that. Up until now the idea has been nothing but a fantasy. It was to forget my loneliness that I joined the Goshokai, but . . ."

With her conservative friend warming to his subject to the point of forgetting his usual reserve, and the whiskey and Coca-Cola going to her head, Komako found herself falling into a sort of trance.

It was premature to assume she harbored any special feelings for Henmi. For a woman such as Komako to fall in love, the menu would have to be as elaborate as a French king's banquet. Neither her tastes nor her instincts would have been satisfied by spartan servings of character and cultivation. How could Henmi be so naive as to talk solemnly of compatibility of character and education in a husband and wife? These are superfluous elements when a woman falls for a man. A man's potential horizons are far wider. The fact that the woman in that novel felt so much more attracted to the gamekeeper than to the baronet is surely proof of this.

The heady feeling Komako was enjoying that day was due not only to Henmi's charms but to the allure of his social class. This house was not Henmi's, but it belonged to someone of a similar level. It exuded Western taste, which Komako liked since it represented prosperity in the Japan of the time. Any poor woman hungers for wealth, but no one feels its attraction more strongly than someone like Komako, who had once known wealth but had been forced to live without it.

Luxury is certainly nice, she reflected.

An atmosphere of comfort and ease emanated from the furnishings and fittings—even from the tableware—and she loved it. Oh, how miserable to scrimp and count every penny she spent!

"Would you like a cigarette?"

Henmi was holding out a box of imported cigarettes, a brand she had never seen before and obviously far superior to the Lucky Strikes Yuri had offered her the other day. Komako could not resist, and Henmi quickly produced a lighter.

Komako had smoked enough by then to know how to enjoy a cigarette. The whole day was so pleasant that she inhaled with abandon, drawing the delicious smoke deep into her lungs. The smoke immediately went to her head and the world began to swim. She could feel the effects of the whiskey as well. The feeling was not unpleasant, but Henmi's voice sounded far away, as if in a dream.

"Are you not feeling well?"

She remembered Henmi's surprise, and how he had helped her lie down on the sofa, but then . . .

When she regained consciousness, her forehead felt cool. A damp cloth had been laid on it: Henmi must have soaked his handkerchief in the ice bucket, for it smelled strongly of eau de cologne. The handkerchief was covering her eyes, so Henmi had not noticed that she was awake.

Henmi's hand was warm—he was holding her hand tight on the pretext of checking her pulse. Komako decided to pretend to be asleep a little longer.

"Oh, Komako, Komako!"

The grip on her hand tightened, and through the handkerchief she could see Henmi's face loom closer as he bent forward. He came within an inch of kissing her, but immediately withdrew, too timid to follow through. Despite that, he seemed unable to stop, for soon the face loomed near once more, then receded, over and over again.

Komako decided it was time to abandon her pretense and sit up.

Chapter 6
A Bad Day

Komako wished she had not witnessed that. As she lay recovering from her fainting fit, Henmi's movements had been as comical as a circus clown's. He had been bending stiffly from the waist, lips puckered and a bead of sweat forming on the tip of his nose. If his lips had achieved their goal, that might have been one thing, but despite drawing so close they had soon retreated. Did he lack courage, or had something else been on his mind? Whatever the reason, by the time the lips had loomed and receded three times Komako had been dangerously close to bursting into laughter. Not once in her life had she seen a man look so ridiculous.

I never realized men could be such winsome creatures, she thought.

In the old days, when red-light districts were a commonplace feature of life, the entrance to such quarters often had a bridge called "Stop-and-Think Bridge" or a tree called "Stop-and-Think Willow." That was where men would pause and consider whether to proceed or turn back. Such landmarks reveal the nature of male hesitation.

Now Iosuke . . . at least he was not like that.

Come to think of it, Komako had never seen Iosuke vacillate, in either thought or deed. On the other hand, she could not recall him ever deciding to do something and carrying it out with determination.

In any case, it was definitely not to a man's credit to appear silly even once. After Komako opened her eyes, Henmi had pulled himself together and been the perfect gentleman, but that had only increased the caricaturish impression she had formed of him. He now appeared to be not merely a clown but a hypocrite. On their way back to Shinjuku they spoke very little, unlike on the outward journey. Thankfully, conversation was not necessary, for the Odakyu Line train had been crowded the whole way.

Men like Henmi, mused Komako, were not a rarity among the upper classes. To be sure, their manners were impeccable, but they were not what you would call reliable. They were the second-generation beneficiaries of parental wealth. They were impressively schooled and often good-looking, but their first and foremost concern was to protect their inheritance by any means. They knew all about the art of self-preservation but nothing about how to love a woman. To be the wife of such a man must be a disaster. She could think of more than one case in point—the son of the businessman K, and the eldest son of Baron M. And another was Henmi, whose wife who had grown so tired of him that she had escaped to a sanitarium in Fujimi Highlands. No wonder the woman had no wish to come home.

On her visit to the Mogis' country cottage, Komako had felt a momentary relief to be back in the social class of her youth; yet at the same time there was a certain rankness about that circle—detectable only to those who had once belonged to it—that she had almost forgotten.

Where can I find a real human being, a real man? Does such a person even exist?

Seeing a man reduced to a buffoon may give a woman a sense of superiority, but it is not a feeling she enjoys. Although heady at first, the aftertaste is a distressing loneliness.

There was no reason whatsoever for Henmi to comprehend Komako's disenchantment that day. On the contrary, he seemed to become more confident and ardent, and had let her know that he sought another opportunity to pursue his attentions.

He did this through letters. Written on the same crisp imported stationery as before, they began to arrive regularly. Gradually they grew longer until they rivaled Takabumi's epistles. Unlike Takabumi's letters, however, which gushed with admiration and pleaded for her affection, Henmi's correspondence made no explicit mention of his sentiments. It was inevitable that his letters would run to several pages, for he adopted an elaborate style, taking meticulous care with the wording so they could never be produced as evidence of impropriety. It was only natural that such fastidiousness would exacerbate Komako's irritation.

If he's in love, why can't he just come out and say so? It's no longer a crime, is it?

And of course, as she read his letters, she could not avoid the ludicrous image of him bending over her, his bottom thrust out and his pursed lips looming and receding.

The rather conservative Henmi should have been a good match for a woman such as Komako, so it is odd how such men inevitably turn out to be spineless. By postwar standards, "rather conservative" is another way of saying "liberal"; it is a natural extension of good breeding, but one wonders why such men always look depressed. Criticized by leftists before the war and bullied into subservience by militarists during the war, the liberals only came into their own for a brief six months immediately after the nation's defeat. As a result of being constantly pushed around, they tended to sulk, and it was natural that women should find them unappealing.

In this respect, Takabumi lay at the other end of the spectrum. His overtures might be effeminate in tone, but they displayed intensity and courage.

"Please let me hold your hand just for a moment," he would plead.

He now made such requests without the slightest hesitation. When she had held out her hand one time, he had stroked the back of it as carefully as if he were painting a picture, before pressing it to his cheek.

"Stop it!" she scolded as she would a naughty child, but he seemed not at all chastened.

Unfortunately, his mother had told him that Iosuke had disappeared and that Komako was living alone, and it made him even more demanding. Komako guessed that he and Yuri had come to an agreement on some sort of summer campaign. Their strategy was so direct, unlike Henmi's, that she had to be careful not to underestimate Takabumi, child though she considered him.

The shortcomings of both men notwithstanding, Komako found it not disagreeable to be the target of their affections. After all, this was one of the blessings of postwar freedom. Times were different now from the days of "Tekona, the beauty of Mama," who had committed suicide when she found herself surrounded by suitors, as told in the ancient legend.

The days passed, and autumn was in the air. It was cooler in the country where Komako was living, but the summer heat still persisted in the city. Bombarded by invitations and messages arriving by express mail, she had finally agreed to accept Henmi's invitation to visit his house in Omori-Sanno and was now getting dressed.

She took little care with her makeup. Her interest in the encounter was not even one-half what it had been when she set out to meet him in Shibuya. The high season for romance, like the ripeness of a banana, is very short. Alas, if Henmi had not turned out to be such a fool, her heart might indeed have been ready for peeling.

"Hello? Is anyone at home?"

Thinking it must be a local woman come to pick up the children's clothes she had finished, Komako called out warmly, "Be right with you!" before stepping onto the veranda.

"How wonderful that you're home, Mrs. Minamimura! I had a terrible time getting here. I've been all over the place."

It was Horan, Takabumi's mother. She was flushed and panting, her plump figure clearly suffering in a thick cotton kimono that was more suited to autumn. She was laden with a heavy basket of fruit she must have carried all the way from the station.

"Oh, please come in."

"You're on your way out. I promise I won't keep you long. Just ten minutes."

The older woman's practiced eye had taken in Komako's makeup and clothes and sized up the situation, but this did not deter her from stepping into the house.

"I've been most remiss. It's been such a long time." She began with the usual pleasantries before plunging on. "I thought I should pay my respects at least once. I understand Takabumi has been coming here quite often."

As she raced through the predictable litany of greetings, what she intended to say was crystal clear, innuendoes and all.

It was this formality, not to mention this type of personality, that Komako found most trying. Though neither commanded her respect, she could do little to counter Horan's assault. Presented with a gift that was too extravagant for the occasion, she found herself expressing more gratitude than was necessary.

"It's been so hot that I let the stove go out," apologized Komako, getting up to prepare tea.

"Oh, no matter, Mrs. Minamimura," said Horan. "I'd rather have a glass of cold water, if you wouldn't mind."

"Well, if you're sure."

Her guest had usurped the initiative again, but Komako set off obediently to draw a glass of water at the pump. She felt helpless and defensive, partly because she was embarrassed at having come down socially in the eyes of this status-conscious person and partly because, in the world of women, a matron in her fifties tends to exude a sergeant-major aura, demoting anyone under forty to the role of common foot soldier.

"It's a nice quiet place you have," remarked the guest. "But you must feel lonely out here all by yourself."

Komako realized she had been cast in the role of the abandoned widow.

Tempted to protest that she did not feel the least lonely, Komako decided that rather than aggravate the situation by contradicting Horan she might ensure the woman's early departure by humoring her, and so she responded as ambiguously as possible.

"Well, there are times when . . ."

Horan nodded emphatically.

"I understand completely. I'm a widow, as you know. Sometimes, it just gets so lonely. The house seems so indescribably empty," she continued melodramatically, "that there's nothing left but air. You say to yourself, 'Will I only have air to keep me company from now on?' and you end up in tears."

"I wouldn't go so far as to say that," replied Komako.

"Of course, in your case it's not as if you were parted by death," said Horan. "It's different for people like myself. Yet we have our daily rituals—the household altar to tend to, the monthly visits to the grave, all of which keeps us occupied. Without that, you feel at loose ends, with nothing to pass the time."

Horan seemed determined to pigeonhole Komako as a widow. Komako was not sure what Horan had been told by the Goshokai members, but she seemed to think that Komako had been abandoned by Iosuke and was therefore to be pitied.

"When a woman loses her husband, she's like a wilted morning glory—no chance to blossom at all. And for you—still so young—to be without someone to sprinkle you with the watering can every morning . . ." At this, Horan broke into an earthy chortle.

Disgusting! Komako was thinking. This woman was oblivious to the fact that Japan had a new constitution, not to mention a revised Civil Code. Komako could not think of anything to say in the face of such vulgarity.

"The very best way to forget one's loneliness," advised Horan gravely, "is to take up an art. You could try noh chanting or ink painting. But let me warn you that even with lessons it's not easy to make progress. And, of course, if it's not in your blood . . ."

"Is that so?" said Komako, playing along.

"So what I recommend," said Horan authoritatively, "is for you to marry again, and as soon as possible. You know I wouldn't recommend anything not in your best interest."

"I appreciate that," said Komako with a polite smile.

"If you like," offered Horan, warming to her topic, "I'd be happy to help you find someone. You know Mr. Henmi. He didn't have much luck with his marriage, and his present wife . . ."

So that is why she's come all this way, thought Komako. Henmi put her up to it and she agreed to help him persuade me. As Komako put two and two together, Horan struck her as completely ludicrous.

"I must remind you that I'm legally and morally a married woman."

Komako may have overemphasized the fact that she was still a wife, but her sudden comprehension of the reason for Horan's visit had prompted this strong announcement.

"Minamimura Iosuke's not at home now, but he's still my husband."

Immediately Komako began to regret saying this. If Iosuke had been a good husband, she would not have found herself in this situation. Words have a way of slipping out of their own accord.

Horan gave a sly smile as she adjusted her position on the cushion, then launched into what seemed to be a lengthy apology.

"Oh dear, I surely spoke out of turn. You must forgive me," she said with a giggle. "I was jumping to conclusions. I do hope you'll forgive me."

"There's no need to apologize," Komako replied lightly. She was ruing her emphatic words.

"No, I'm sure what I said was out of place. Mrs. Minamimura, you spoke with great pride of your marital status, and there's something I'd like to ask."

Horan sat up straighter. She was facing Komako, but spoke slightly to one side.

"Really? What's that?"

"Now don't pretend you don't know what I'm going to ask. I mentioned I'd be happy if you'd teach my son English, but I don't remember asking you to teach him about amorous matters."

Her language and facial expression finally revealed her true nature. Komako was stunned by this sudden offensive.

"How can you say that?"

"Oh, don't act so surprised! You know exactly what I'm talking about. I couldn't care less that your husband has abandoned you, but if you're lonely, that's no reason to play around with a boy barely out of his teens. Think of the difference in your ages!"

By this time Komako was trembling as if she was suffering a bout of malaria.

"How can you say such a preposterous thing?"

"If you think you can hide what's going on, it's too late. Takabumi told me everything. You've got him wrapped around your little finger and he's asking me to let him marry you! How could you do this to him?"

"But that was Takabumi's idea! I had nothing to do with it."

"Oh no, you can't get away with that! If you hadn't encouraged him, it wouldn't have come to this, that's certain. The boy is engaged to a fine young girl, Fujimura Yuriko, so you should be ashamed of yourself. It's not as though there's any shortage of men around."

Nothing is quite so vulgar as a quarrel between women, and a spat between a mature younger woman and a tough older one exceeds anything one wants to set down in print. Even attempting to record it might be seen as exulting in the reactionary and the belligerent.

Horan finally left. No doubt she was feeling triumphant as she marched out of Komako's house, for Komako had failed utterly to repulse the older woman.

Komako at that instant was different from the person who had stood over her husband and ordered him to leave. That forceful woman had been rendered speechless by Horan's onslaught. Her throat had gone dry, and she had hemmed and hawed ineffectually. She seemed to be admitting her guilt, and that had fanned the flames of Horan's righteous indignation. Finally, Komako found it impossible to respond at all; words failed her.

How someone as strong-willed as Komako could be defeated so miserably is hard to explain, but perhaps it was precisely because of that trait. She was twice as angry as any normal person, and her fury threw her nervous system into chaos, which short-circuited her usual ability to join the fray. To be unjustly accused was bad enough, but against the flood of words unleashed by the older woman it had been impossible to say anything. Faced with this coarse and vulgar barrage, moreover, the educated Komako had quickly sensed it was not a duel to be won without stooping to the level of her adversary.

After Horan left, she cried out loud in humiliation and frustration, her emotions boiling over. But that did not dissipate her fury. Even picking up the basket of fruit Horan had brought and flinging it into the garden had done little to assuage her anger. The bitterness of defeat seemed to seep into her bones.

I won't let Candy Boy hang around here any longer! she decided.

Of course, no matter what she might resolve, it was too late. This was her first bad experience since Iosuke had left. Indeed, up until now everything had been proceeding a little too smoothly. To drive your husband out and expect life to continue as usual is asking a lot.

As she struggled to contain her tears, images of Iosuke flashed through Komako's mind, but they were not as a deliverer who would rescue her from distress. Rather, images of past and present overlapped. The scene of Horan's attack leaving her speechless mirrored her treatment of Iosuke, giving her a sense of déjà-vu.

For heaven's sake, where is he? Enough is enough.

It had been a long time since such a desperate lament had escaped her lips.

After a while, Komako's tears ceased and she remembered her appointment with Henmi. What with Horan's disruptive visit and the time it had taken for her to recover, a considerable period had passed. It was already four o'clock, and Komako had lost any interest in visiting Henmi. However, she could not leave him waiting for her, so she decided to go to the station and call him from the public telephone there.

"Oh, please don't worry about the time." Henmi's voice over the line had a pleading note. "Couldn't you come anyway?"

"That's very kind of you, but I've had an awful headache since noon." This excuse was not invented. Stress had sent the blood to her head, which had been throbbing painfully since Horan left.

"A headache? That's not good. Do you have a fever? What? I can't hear you very well."

Henmi finally gave in, though obviously unhappy about it.

"Well, if that's how it is, it can't be helped. But you sound depressed. Has anything happened?"

What amazing intuition! Was it the sensitivity of a man in love? For a moment Komako regretted disappointing him. Her suspicion that Horan was acting as his agent had been mistaken, she realized. Horan's purpose was to break off the relationship between Komako and her son.

It was all Komako could do to prevent Henmi from rushing over to make sure she was all right. In return, she had no choice but to promise him that if she felt better she would visit him the next day.

"Well then, I bid you good day." She hung up with a rather formal farewell.

She realized how desolate she must have sounded, and it was not hard for Henmi to sense that something was amiss. Their conversation had been a long one, twice the cost of a three-minute call, but the fact that she did not begrudge the money was a measure of how much she had been made to suffer by Horan.

It was the season when everyone suddenly notices the shortness of the days, and summer lingered only in the lightness of people's apparel. The leaves on the cherry trees were already turning yellow and the shadows were growing longer. The evening was filled with the rasping of autumn cicadas, borne on a humid breeze.

How dismal! Komako thought.

There was a new progressive constitution, and you could almost hear the outmoded conventions breaking down. It may have been a period when one could do virtually what one wanted and no one would care, but how much happiness could Komako say she had found? Was it because she carried within her the remnants of old, feeble values? Here I am, Iosuke seemingly gone for good, and me ready to throw my life away on a roll of the dice if the right man comes along. But obviously one can't gamble alone.

Perhaps I'm aiming too high and I should lower my sights. Thoughts like that did little to push back the wave of her loneliness.

Suddenly she heard a clatter of footsteps behind her and a familiar voice.

"Is that you? I'm so glad I found you!" Takabumi was out of breath and perspiring. "I just got off the train to come and see you."

He looked as if something important was on his mind.

Komako made no reply. She was trying to decide whether she should mention anything to him. Had she not vowed she would not let Candy Boy near her? It was not easy to lower the barrier so soon after she had put it up.

"You must be very angry with me. I know, and I'm sorry. I'm so sorry. Really, I don't know how to apologize." He bowed repeatedly, causing his milk-colored jacket to ripple with his movements. "She's so ignorant, that mother of mine. Ignorant, vulgar, selfish, and brazen. She treats good manners like inessential surplus goods. She's just terrible." Had his mother been listening, the string of insults would have been enough to make her faint on the spot.

"I can't tell you how many times I've been embarrassed by Mama's interference, but she's never gone this far before. She's made a real mess of things. This time I'm determined to fight back. I'll even go to the family court if I have to. It must be an infringement of family law or marriage law or something. I turned twenty on the twenty-fifth of last month, so legally I'm an adult, and an adult does not need parental permission to marry, let alone to fall in love. Anyone who tries to stop me is infringing on my human rights."

"Takabumi, how did you know your mother came to my house?"

At last Komako had found her voice.

"If I'd known beforehand, I would have stopped her, but I only learned after she'd left. I heard it from Yuri. Mama told Mr. Fujimura she was going to visit you."

"Never mind, it's all over. People who want to misunderstand can

81

go ahead and do so as much as they want—that's my philosophy. But, Takabumi, I've decided we should discontinue our association." Komako made herself sound cold and distant.

"Please don't say that. If you do, it'll just be giving in to Mama's old-fashioned ideas!"

"I'm not doing what your mother says. I'm saying—how shall I put it?—I'm rejecting you of my own free will."

"That's not fair! I cannot accept that! Are you saying you don't like me?"

"No, it's not that, but your fancies are getting dangerous for me. Do you understand?"

"I don't. You say 'fancies,' but I . . ."

"Let's walk while we talk about it." Standing in the middle of a busy street, Komako was finding the conversation uncomfortable.

Even as they headed for open country, along a road flanked by broad-leafed taro plants waving in the breeze, Takabumi persisted with his pleas. Komako, determined not to let him into her house that day, had taken a road leading in the opposite direction, and the unfamiliar surroundings were making her uneasy.

"You and I belong to different generations—there's a huge gap in our ages and our way of life. It makes me laugh to think of what it would be like to marry you. Besides—and I'm going to be blunt—I don't have that kind of respect for you."

She had thought these words might give him pause, but he continued regardless.

"But I respect you. If love needs respect, isn't it enough if I have respect for you?"

"A woman has to feel it herself."

"That's so old-fashioned. Why is it wrong the other way around? If a man worships a woman and devotes his life to her, I believe he can find happiness."

Indeed, in ancient Japan there was once a matriarchal society, and that may have been one form of conjugal love a long time ago. It might be interesting if the system were revived, Komako thought, but as she gazed at the young man before her, the idea appeared ludicrous.

"When that day comes, women may be happy, but I'm not going to live so long. Takabumi, you ought to stop dreaming and try to appreciate Yuri more. Now let's go back—it's getting dark."

"Please wait! I want this settled today. I came here determined that if I can't win your love I'm not going back home. It will be a good lesson for Mother. She said such nasty things to you."

Komako turned to retrace her steps, but Takabumi blocked the way.

"Takabumi, I didn't think you had it in you," Komako said with a laugh. "Are you brave enough to defy your mother and set out on your own?"

Komako was tempted to indulge in some mischief making. It might be sweet revenge on Horan to fan the fires of Takabumi's affections and see what would happen.

The young man, however, was not to be underestimated.

"Love," he said with surprising composure, "can give you new courage and strength."

With a "Please forgive me," he approached Komako and put his arms around her. It was like being gripped by the tendrils of a clinging vine, and Komako was repelled to discover that Takabumi obviously had some experience with women. She struggled fiercely and was about to free herself when a figure stepped out of the shadows of some nearby trees.

He was a small man wearing a striped shirt and black trousers. A dirty cloth covering the lower part of his face and his blue-tinted sunglasses made it hard to see his features.

"Better not be too lovey-dovey," the man growled. "See this? Understand?"

He showed part of something protruding from the pocket of his trousers. Was it a knife? A gun?

Takabumi raised both hands as he had seen people in American movies do.

"Good. Now you, girl, put your hands up. You've probably read about me in the papers. I like bothering couples. I've come all the way from Tokyo."

His voice was high and by no means menacing, but Komako had never been in this situation before and was trembling, her body rigid.

"You want money? I'll give you some," Takabumi called shrilly.

"It's not just money I want. But give me what you've got."

Takabumi kept one hand in the air and lowered the other to extract two or three 100-yen notes from his pocket. Komako had to admire Takabumi's presence of mind and the fact that he could even speak at such a time. She had no idea that affluent students were frequent targets of shakedowns in the night-life districts of the city.

Before handing the man the notes, Takabumi let go of them and they fluttered to the ground.

"That was stupid! Don't do anything hasty now." While the robber was gathering the money, Takabumi took to his heels, running like the wind. Watching him, Komako thought of taking the opportunity to flee as well.

"Oh no, girl, I'm not letting you go."

The ruffian seized the sleeve of her blouse.

"Please don't hurt me. I'll give you anything you want." Now that she was resigned to her fate, Komako suddenly found her voice. Or maybe the ruffian calling her "girl" had dispelled some of her tenseness. She had promised to give him anything, but she had left home with just enough change for the phone call and was not even wearing a watch.

Naturally, the man was not pleased.

"Tsk, you're real cheap! All you've got is twelve yen?"

He gave her back her handbag, not bothering to take the money.

"I'll have to keep you with me for a while," he said.

He was even rougher than Takabumi. Pulling her by the wrist, he began dragging her into the nearby stand of cedars. Komako's strength had returned, and she was putting up a spirited resistance when suddenly the man was knocked to the ground. He had been punched hard in the face, and not by Komako.

Komako's savior turned out to be Heiji from the ration office, a gruff ex-army man who had once been in prison camp in Siberia. Komako was impressed by his strength. With one blow he had sent the ruffian sprawling on all fours like a squashed frog.

The man Komako had assumed was a hardened criminal was now groveling at Heiji's feet—a boy seventeen or eighteen years of age. His sunglasses had been knocked off and the towel had fallen away to reveal round cheeks and tired eyes. He hardly looked the type to turn to highway robbery.

When Heiji punched him again, the youth began apologizing, pulling out Takabumi's money and meekly returning it. The piece of tree root or branch that had convinced Takabumi and Komako that he had a knife or a gun fell out of his pocket at the same time.

Komako was struck by the absurdity of the situation, and although Heiji wanted to take the boy to the police box by the station, she persuaded him to let him go.

"I've seen you around here before," Heiji told the youth. "You're from Shimosawa, right? If you ever come bothering people again, I won't let you off so easy." Heiji slapped him once more for good measure and sent him on his way.

84

The incident had taken place on the other side of town from Kamisawa, where Komako lived. Evening was approaching, so Heiji accompanied her back to the edge of town.

He was indeed a man of few words. In the twenty minutes the walk took, he made only one comment, and that was murmured as if he was talking to himself.

"Getting youngsters to behave these days isn't easy. The kids in Russia were real sweet by comparison."

He walked quickly, and Komako could barely keep up. On his head was an old army cap, soiled with sweat, worn in the approved military fashion. This headgear, once almost universal, was now a rare sight. He was also wearing an old khaki shirt and army pants held up with string, and he must have dressed the same way during the war. He had the smell of someone used to handling horses and leather harness. Recalling the terrible wartime days made Komako frown, but she felt no repugnance toward him. In contrast to Iosuke, he was thin and wiry, but this physique concealed great strength, as he had shown. Moreover, there was no denying his courage.

"I don't know how to thank you."

As they reached the edge of town, Komako bowed in farewell, but Heiji did not even pause.

"It's nothing," he said and walked on. The sky behind him was a sunset yellow and overhead was a sliver of new moon.

The next morning Komako bought a carton of Peace cigarettes and went to the ration office. The attacker may have been a boy imitating a recent spate of crimes, but she owed her rescuer some token of gratitude.

"I want to thank you again for yesterday."

Heiji was sitting behind a table in the dim warehouselike building, dressed in the same clothes as the day before.

"You don't have to do this, ma'am." He seemed determined to ignore the gift she was holding out.

His indifference did not seem pretended or caused by modesty. He genuinely appeared not to attach any importance to what he had done. His voice had a languid, almost melancholic note. However, Komako pressed the gift on him, saying that she could not take it back.

"If it'd be such a bother," he said, conceding, "I'll take it."

Flushed with embarrassment, he took the package from her and threw it on the table, where it landed with a bang. His awkwardness made Komako want to smile. She could see that Heiji, though well past thirty, was very shy.

Savoring her superiority as a mature woman, Komako was about to leave the building when Heiji called her back.

"Just a moment, ma'am!"

Thinking she had forgotten something, Komako retraced her steps.

"I hear your husband is away. Is he not coming back for a while?"

"Well, no."

Komako was surprised that Heiji knew about Iosuke's absence, although news like that soon got around the community.

"If that's so, you should report it to the authorities. It's wrong to collect your husband's ration when he's not here."

He was looking straight at her, and his face with its ruddy complexion was coldly bureaucratic.

Komako had not reported the matter, but not for the purpose of collecting double rations. Still, it must have looked that way, and Komako admitted that Heiji had bested her on that score.

"Sorry about that," she said mildly. "From now on, the ration can just be for one."

With that, she left the office.

Curious fellow, she thought. A cynic, I suppose!

Most people would have chosen another time to bring that up, rather than immediately after receiving a thank-you present. A man who could distinguish between public and private matters would have waited for a different opportunity to remind her of this administrative detail. Most likely Heiji, feeling he had been forced to accept her gift, had decided to confront her as a way of getting even. Even if that was reading too much into it, Komako found it interesting that Heiji could switch so quickly from private to public, speaking to her in that severe fashion.

When she arrived home, the landlady intercepted her to hand her an express postcard that had come while she was out. It was from Takabumi. Komako lingered a while to chat on the landlady's veranda, and by chance the subject of Heiji came up.

"He's a stubborn fellow, that one. Since he took charge of the rations, there's no give and take. He can be so cantankerous!"

The landlady spoke at some length about Heiji's personality and habits. She said the reason he was bad-tempered was that after he was called up for the army, his wife got involved with another man and disappeared. Heiji was the son of a relatively well-off farmer in the village, and had even gone to agricultural college. When he returned from Siberia and found his wife gone, he gave up farming and took the job in the ration office and was now

86

living there.

"He didn't used to be like that, so people think he's really bitter. In any case, you'd better not do anything to cross him."

Even after she got home, Komako was still thinking of Heiji. She recalled his rugged, farmerlike features and his honest expression with an air of pathos. She was not sure this was how he really looked, but it was how she perceived him. There was something wholesome about him that appealed to her.

Suddenly she remembered the postcard and read Takabumi's message. It was scribbled hastily, perhaps at a post office on his way home the day before, and gave his excuse for abandoning her. He had intended to go to the police box and get help, he wrote, but then he thought of Komako's reputation and decided not to.

Don't worry, my boy, nobody expected you to become a knight in shining armor.

The wind caught the postcard and blew it into the garden.

Only then did Komako remember that she was supposed to go to Henmi's house. There was still plenty of time, but she did not feel like it.

Henmi wouldn't have been any more use in yesterday evening's situation, she concluded. It was amazing how rapidly the appeal of the slightly conservative gentleman was fading.

And what would Iosuke have done?

She wasn't sure. Iosuke had never lifted a finger against anyone, so he might not have been capable of punching the man. However, had she been with Iosuke, his sheer bulk would have been enough to discourage anyone. It was clear, at least, that no respectable lady could be satisfied with a knight in paper armor.

So is Heiji, the ration officer, the only knight left?

The thought made Komako feel silly, and she almost doubled over with laughter. I must be hysterical, she thought.

Komako had been by herself for more than three months. Women are not as impervious to thirst as men suppose, but while seeking fresh water she might become unhinged if she was denied too long.

I can't put up with this forever, she said to an invisible Iosuke. Just show yourself and tell me what's happening.

Chapter 7
In Search of Freedom

What was Iosuke up to, indeed? In the more than three months since he had left home, a great deal had happened to him. He had neither fallen ill nor joined the demonstrators demanding jobs, but had stayed pretty much in one place. Where he ended up, moreover, was not in some faraway camp flying red leftist flags; he was right in the heart of Tokyo.

Why draw out the suspense now that the story shifts to Iosuke? Why make any ado over such a good-for-nothing fellow? Well, if I were to simply report Iosuke's present whereabouts and what he was up to, few would be interested in what he had felt and done before that. To relate Iosuke's story properly, I have to go back to the beginning, to the day Komako had said, "Get out!"—no, to a little before then.

What husband, no matter how meek and mild, could you imagine just getting up and walking out the door?

Would Iosuke just have murmured, "I see," and left, with no more than a searching glance at Komako, if he had not had some scheme in the back of his mind? What scheme? you might ask. To grasp his freedom when the right opportunity presented itself.

A person as indolent and tolerant as Iosuke was not likely to take resolute action or make any purposeful moves of his own accord. Still, given the chance, he was not so slavish as to continue his bondage passively. So, when his domineering spouse loosened her grip and told him, "Go! You're free!" all he had to do was obey her command and make the most of it.

It takes both energy and depravity for a husband to abandon his wife and home willingly, resources that the patently passive Iosuke had never possessed. In fact, he had become resigned to his situation, so it was quite by chance that Komako had provided the needed impetus.

Iosuke had only begun to find his wife a nuisance after the war. Everything had gone wrong because of the war. His family fortune had been lost and Komako had started to take in work at home, which had turned her into a most irksome woman. He did not mind being ordered to sweep the garden or fetch water for the bath from the well, and so on. He was not even averse to such chores as scrubbing his wife's back in the bath or polishing her shoes. What he could not stand was her domineering attitude, constant-ly ordering him about and nagging him for one thing or another, which he found genuinely tedious.

She had become arrogant and overbearing, demanding and oppressive, keeping him constantly in check. If it were a burden suffered for love, he would have happily borne it. He would not have objected at all if their marriage had been like those of hairdressers in olden times, where the husband played a supporting role while the wife brought in the money by dress-ing people's hair in the intricate traditional styles. But since the war ended, Komako's expressions of wifely affection tended to be like the delivery of rations—late or not forthcoming at all.

Equality between men and women, equality in marriage—that was all well and good, and no one would disagree. Iosuke was not arrogant or violent by nature; he preferred an easy give-and-take in all matters, and he never thought about comparing wins and losses. He was not one to criticize the new parity between husband and wife decreed by postwar reforms. What piqued him was how their husband–wife roles had swung from one ex-treme to the other.

In the old feudal tradition, the man of the house had been all-powerful, and that was how it was until the end of the war. Recently, however, Komako had started to resemble an old-style husband in female guise. Sometimes she treated Iosuke like a slave, and occasionally she spoke and behaved in ways that insulted his dignity—that violated his "human rights." True, she was taking in sewing and making handicrafts, and indeed covered half their living expenses. But, just as imperiously—if not more so—as the prewar husbands who made their wives feel obligated because they were the sole breadwinners, Komako made a great fuss about providing her share. To Iosuke, it did not add up—even mathematically.

The democratic ideal of a conjugal relationship was that everything should be split equally between husband and wife, including love and re-spect, and should follow the fifty-fifty or "going Dutch" rule. That was fine with Iosuke, but Komako seemed to expect him to practice democracy while she persisted in despotism. Who would not protest?

Another aspect that troubled Iosuke was whether Komako's behavior reflected her true feelings. If it did, there was little he could do. She was, after all, his wife of nine years. She may have fallen victim to some evil ail-ment, but you could not just bid her farewell. Yet the way Komako treated him was reminiscent of the erstwhile Imperial Rule Assistance Association.

Launched to mobilize resources and raise public morale for the war effort, its members had acted self-righteously, though their fervor was only skin-deep. They had been in the grip of "principles." Principles can be a shelter, providing protection for delicate flesh, but in their case the result had been unsightly, as if they were parading their calluses for all to see. Considering how people had suffered during the war for being obsessed with one set of principles, he mused, you'd think they'd have learned their lesson, but lately they seemed to have traded that set for another to obsess about. And there were signs that Komako was bent on bringing the trend right into their home. It was all very tiresome for Iosuke.

After the war, Iosuke's home life had gradually grown less comfortable. With no children and no mother-in-law, life should have been relatively simple, yet it wasn't. This very simplicity, in fact, was what allowed the waves of the postwar age to slap so intrusively against their doorstep. The atmosphere had rapidly soured after they moved to their present quarters, and Iosuke began to feel like a mere lodger in a house run by Komako. Deep down, any man—even an easygoing, tolerant one such as Iosuke—craves a home where he can relax. The male of the species is not strong enough to do any respectable work without such a refuge.

Perhaps I'd be better off staying in the company dormitory—at least I could sleep in some mornings.

Iosuke had started entertaining such thoughts more than a year ago. But that was not the only reason he had left home.

The new constitution was lauded for its "fundamental freedoms." Freedom from Komako was the important one that impelled Iosuke to leave, though that is not to deny there were other, lesser freedoms to be won as well. For example, he had been unhappy with his employer, Tokyo News Agency, for some time and had indeed quit without telling Komako, but not because he did not like the work. Throughout the war years a dark, oppressive atmosphere had gripped the agency and was still pervading it. He could endure it no longer.

Iosuke had begun to have his doubts about the company from the time Mr. K, the executive who had obtained the job for him, was purged for his war responsibility and forced to resign. K was a liberal, no matter how you looked at it. If those in charge of the purge decided to condemn somebody as "complicit in war crimes" because he was an executive in a company that had cooperated in the war effort, it probably could not be avoided. But what upset Iosuke was the way employees had treated K like a war criminal. It offended Iosuke that the people who had gone out drinking with military officers and government officials during the war took to speaking ill of K after he left. They themselves had escaped his fate simply because they had not been in positions of responsibility. Moreover, they treated colleagues who had been favored by K, such as Iosuke, as if they were tainted by association.

The worst was how nervous the new company executives had become, even more so than during the war. A telegram arriving from abroad would change everyone's attitude 180 degrees, and so the workplace was always tense and edgy. And there were plenty of other unpleasant aspects more difficult to identify that even the stolid Iosuke could not stomach. The company was generally becoming a cramped and stifling burrow from which he urgently sought escape.

He felt hemmed in, and not just at the news agency. Life in Tokyo was becoming unbearable, and he could not remember any other time when things were so bleak, both materially and spiritually. You could say very little without being criticized. If you suggested that the numbers of police should be increased because of instability, you might be accused of advocating national rearmament; if you talked about peace too often, you might be suspected of being a spy for the communists in Yoyogi. You could not talk about anything that mattered. Just walking down the street you would be accosted by fund-raisers demanding subscriptions for welfare projects, or by people collecting signatures for one campaign or another. Even if you managed to extricate yourself, you would be assailed by deafening commercial announcements, or your way would be blocked by sandwich-board men behaving as if the street belonged to them. Iosuke wished people could be left alone to live in peace.

Feeling in need of a drink, you might drop by a cheap drinking place. Saké would be too expensive, so you would have to order the low-grade *shochu* liquor. You wouldn't spot a single prosperous face inside, and the bar owner himself was likely to be burdened by this tax or that. Indeed, the problem of high taxes was on everybody's lips. People had tired of complaining about them; now the talk was of the huge interest charged and the frightful fines levied if you were late paying your taxes. Some told how, even after paying their taxes, they found themselves slapped with fines for not declaring everything. People whispered such tales to one another as if exchanging horror stories. Who could enjoy a drink in such an atmosphere? The government might be short of funds, but making the people suffer was unforgivable.

The state, the society as a whole, and even the household conspired to make life hard for the individual. It was enough to rile even the most docile person and make him yearn for a different life. Just as Iosuke was considering the idea, his wife told him, "Get out!"

Thus, although his motive in leaving home was rather different from that of the brave heroine of Ibsen's *Doll's House*, Iosuke was striding out into the great beyond, as light as a feather borne on a gust of wind.

It must be said, however, that he was still fond of Komako. She could be infuriating at times, but he did not hate her. Indeed, it would have taken something quite dire to make someone like Iosuke hate a woman, no matter who she was. He was not about to sever ties with her just because she had ordered him to leave. In fact, he was concerned whether she would be all right on her own, which was what made him glance at her as he left. What he saw, however, convinced him he need not worry.

"I'll be going then. Goodbye."

He had told her where he had left the rest of his severance pay, so for the time being he had no worries about her. Indeed, his mind was at peace and his stride was easy. Anyone in the neighborhood would have assumed he was heading to work as usual.

"Off to work?"

When their landlady greeted him at the dry goods store on the corner, his thoughts were as easy as ever.

"Well, yes." He smiled congenially.

The sky was clear and the sun was shining brightly. In winter, the open country west of the city could be quite desolate, but early summer was the pleasantest of seasons, and as he walked between fields of rapidly growing barley, a fragrant breeze was blowing, as if to wish him well.

He did not pause even when he reached the station. His rail pass was still valid, and anyway the ticket collector knew him and hardly glanced at it. As always, he took his time walking across the bridge leading to the inbound tracks. Indifferent to the time, he sat on the weathered bench there until the shabby carriages of his train drew into the platform.

It had taken some practice, but now, without the least haste, he could position himself exactly opposite the carriage door when the train stopped. The doors opened automatically, and everything seemed to be progressing smoothly that day. And, sure enough, there was one seat empty, as if waiting for him. "Human rights" could still be maintained with these few passengers, even if the crowds at rush hour constituted a possible violation of the terms of the Potsdam Declaration.

Feeling completely at peace, Iosuke dozed off. He could sleep until the end of the line, or he could get off wherever he happened to wake up. It was different from the days when he had skipped work, or during that whole month when he left home each morning on the pretense of going to the office. He no longer had to feel uneasy, and riding the train could be rather pleasant. You did not have to worry whether it was going too fast, did you? It would have been too much to expect friendly treatment from the railway staff as well.

"Shinjuku!" called the conductor, and Iosuke automatically stood up to get off—a habit acquired when he was pretending to go to work.

Iosuke strolled down the main avenue of Shinjuku, his huge frame towering above the chattering crowds like the colossal warship *Yamato* sailing across the open sea. Not only his stature but his unusual features made people look at him twice. Komako could not be blamed for having been lured into marriage by those bushy eyebrows and those large, round eyes. And today, filled with the joy of liberation, Iosuke was standing especially tall, his face exuding confidence. He had eaten a good breakfast at eleven that morning, so he was not feeling hungry, and none of the tempting restaurants he passed—Western-style eatery, Chinese restaurant, pork-cutlet shop, grilled teriyaki eel stall, cake shop, confectionery, sweets shop—distracted him or slowed his pace. He walked with a detached and almost lordly air.

Hawkers clamored, urging him to buy military surplus cloth, rolls of cotton for summer kimonos not seen on the market in wartime, leather satchels at half price, brown shoes with rubber soles, but he showed not the slightest interest. This was not only because he had little money but also because he never shopped; he relied entirely on Komako to buy his clothes and personal items. The wish to loiter at shop windows gazing wistfully at some much-desired article was completely absent in his character.

He moved down the street with a measured, leisurely gait, swinging his arms, for all the world like an underworld boss making the rounds of his territory. Komako would have thought it strange to see him looking as if he knew these streets well. In fact, when going for a drink after work, he had preferred the more sophisticated Ginza district to other parts of the city. But even a wife cannot always know where her spouse's wanderings may take him. In the month since he had quit the company, he had felt more relaxed in unfamiliar surroundings. He had tried Asakusa and Ueno, but because his train pass was good only for stations between the news agency and his home, more often than not he ended up in Shinjuku. There he would kill time at the movies or drop into the light comedy theaters. In this way he came to know the names and faces of popular actors and learned a good deal about the new fads of postwar speech. Previously, he had little knowledge of the arts, and in Shinjuku he had often passed by the Ao-fusen Theater, famous for light comedy, mistaking it for some sleazy bar.

By now he had visited every theater or cinema in Shinjuku at least once, from the Ao-fusen and the Mukashino on down. He had walked through the new district on the western side of the station, the alleys to the north and south, and even the shady Sakura Shindo quarter. Every day he had been forced to kill time from noon to around six o'clock, and thus he had become something of an expert on the area.

Today, he did not turn into any side street but walked straight up the main avenue to Oiwake. He considered going to another movie and began checking the posters but changed his mind. On an impulse, he decided to go to the Nyoro-Nyoro Show, advertised as being on the fifth floor above the movie theater. He did not know what "*nyoro-nyoro*" meant—it usually meant "wriggling" or "squirming"—but he could hazard a guess at the show's nature. The very idea of such a show had embarrassed him before, and he had never been to one. Liberation can have a startling effect on a person's psychology.

As he took out his wallet to buy a ticket, Iosuke was brought back to earth with a jolt. From its brown leather folds, cold reality stared him in the face: 300 yen. Komako had put the money in only a short while ago, so he knew exactly how much was there; she never gave him more. Until yesterday, whenever he went out he had taken one or two 1,000-yen notes from his severance pay envelope. He had spent all the money he had on him the previous night, so it had been a mistake not to stock up before he left. If he had been planning to leave home, he realized, he should have set aside at least 10,000 yen, but it was too late now.

"You going in or not?" demanded the ticket girl, scornful of this man gazing into his wallet.

"Yes. One ticket."

Now there was no turning back. He put down two 100-yen notes and got back 50 yen in change. He had just spent half the money he possessed.

If Komako had been watching, she would no doubt think it served him right. It was as if a bucket of cold water had been poured over the spark of his infidelity, and his feet were heavy as he climbed the concrete stairs. The four flights were steep and filthy—hardly befitting a staircase leading to the heavenly delights of Eros, and by the time the overweight Iosuke reached the top he was panting.

On the fifth floor was a vestibule like any regular movie theater, and the merry warmth of the crowd within the auditorium wafted into it.

Well, things will work out somehow, Iosuke thought. With that, he felt his momentary depression lift. It was often this way with him. He might become anxious or depressed, but never for more than an hour. He had no capacity for being in low spirits for long, and his gloom would dissipate as quickly as the passing of a summer shower, although he never knew what would bring about this effect. At such times it was his habit to repeat the magic formula, "Well, things will work out somehow." It was not a world in which you could afford to be optimistic, but for Iosuke, who had always depended on his wife's resourcefulness, everything had gone fairly well. From now on, though, things were unlikely to be the same.

"This way, please."

An usher opened a side door. The interior was almost pitch black, but the heads and shoulders of people standing in the aisles were silhouetted like the rugged peaks of Mt. Myogi. The theater was packed and filled with a stifling, sweaty, midsummer heat, yet an incongruous silence reigned—it was as quiet as a mountain temple. Iosuke had never before seen such a hushed, well-mannered audience, even more so than in a noh theater, but you could not call it relaxed. A palpable tension was pulsing through the silence.

Peering through the forest of heads, Iosuke could only see half the stage. There were curtains on both sides, and what looked like a magic lantern in the center. A naked woman with a jar on her shoulder was standing completely motionless on the stage. Like the audience, she, too, was silent.

The scene changed several times, and each one revealed a composition based on a famous painting. After one of "The Source" by Ingres came "The Abalone Diver" by Utamaro. Whatever famous picture was being represented, the actual impression was entirely different. The red kimono draped over the woman's hips was nothing like the vivid crimson of the Utamaro print, and the woman's flesh had the dull yellow gleam of hard-boiled eggs in simmered *oden* stew rather than the luminous whiteness of the original. In the glare of the floodlights, her skin took on a glittery sheen.

That did not bother Iosuke nearly as much as the fact that there was nothing particularly titillating about the show. He had no interest in lewdness, but having spent half of all the money he possessed, he had hoped for an experience enthralling enough to warrant the investment. If what one got from these notorious strip shows was no better than the lithograph on a box of handkerchiefs, he had wasted his money. What surprised him was how all the men around him were completely absorbed in the scene and became excited at each change.

Eventually the "famous paintings" show ended and the lights came on. The silence was broken as the audience began to move, those standing at the back surging forward for seats, especially those nearest the stage. The sight of mature men scrambling like rats to secure a front-row seat was reminiscent of soldiers running for the trenches.

Iosuke barely managed to obtain a seat to one side. The curtain opened again. This time it was a pantomime. The scene was set somewhere under the railroad tracks in the middle of the night. Two streetwalkers got into a fight, and as the skit progressed they tore each other's clothes off until they were nearly naked. It was slightly more titillating than the series of elegant paintings, but he still did not find it erotic.

Could it be that I'm not interested in nudity? he wondered.

Iosuke fell into a reverie. He realized that he could not picture what his own wife looked like naked. For their honeymoon, he remembered, they had gone to the hot spring at Yugawara, and in their previous house in Akasaka the bath had been so large they had often bathed together. Last summer they had both taken to washing in a tub in the kitchen to save the cost of going to a public bath, and thus he had had plenty of opportunities to see Komako undressed, but he could not remember what she looked like. He did have a vague memory that her skin was not particularly white.

The desire to gaze at the unclothed body of a member of the opposite sex was as strong in Iosuke as in other men. However, it would not have been polite to ask Komako to let him stare at her in that state, so he must have avoided looking at her even when she was right beside him. Perhaps that was the reason he could not recollect her body unclothed.

He had certainly seen enough naked women in the theater today, but he did not feel particularly gratified and this bothered him. Was it because nudity in itself had no value? Was it because the bodies could not really be described as naked? Or was it because the nudity was embellished, since the women had spangles over their nipples and wore G-strings?

"Excuse me, are you . . . ?"

Someone came up from behind and tapped him on the shoulder.

"Just as I thought! It's Mr. 'Nami, isn't it? What a surprise seeing you in a place like this . . ." The man trailed off, chuckling.

He was about forty years old and was wearing a suit. Who on earth could he be? Iosuke could not remember where they might have met. Anyone who called him "Mr. 'Nami," however, would have to be a regular at the bar he had frequented in Yurakucho called O-Riki. The woman who ran it had taken to shortening "Minamimura" to "'Nami," and the other customers had followed suit. She liked the idea of calling her large customer by the name of the heroine in a popular melodrama.

"Oh, hello."

Iosuke replied casually, but just then the person next to him left and the man promptly sat down.

"I wanted to thank you for helping me out that time. I went to O-Riki many times to pay you back, but you were never there."

Iosuke still had no recollection of the man or the incident he was referring to. It was true that since he had been coming to Shinjuku, he had not visited Yurakucho.

"So I'd like to settle that later. But, Mr. 'Nami—this show isn't half bad, is it? Me, when I'm not at the baseball stadium, I make a point of coming to see it. I think it's uplifting. Just look at the body of that girl! Isn't she something? It makes me feel so happy. When I'm looking at Teri Teramatsu, I forget all Japanese girls, my wife included—everyone!"

The woman he called Teri was just making her entrance on stage, bare breasts thrust forward, hips swaying seductively. She did have a splendid body, tall at 5 feet 9 and well filled out, with long, elegant legs. She looked neither Japanese nor Western. The dusky tone and texture of her skin recalled the beauties of Bali, and she had the well-chiseled features of South Sea islanders and a slightly feral look—sure to please postwar appetites for the exotic. What a strange country Japan is! If the demand is there, it has a way of importing whatever is required, even a fine body for this kind of appreciation.

"She's got a great figure, hasn't she? I know nothing about music or dance, and I'm no good at following plays, but I never get tired of gazing at a body like that. I end up staying for show after show."

Indeed, it must be agreed that the nude body is a natural work of art that does not easily become boring. So hard were the men concentrating on this art, in fact, that you could hear a pin drop. Iosuke began to see the man's point. It helped him understand why the theater was full of fortyish men like himself.

But I shouldn't have squandered 150 yen on this, he thought. I wish I'd gone to one of those movie reruns instead.

While Iosuke was pondering the state of his wallet, the grand finale began.

When the show was over, Iosuke stood up to leave like most of the others. He had no wish to stay for another performance.

"Well, I'll see you around." Even as he prepared to depart, he still hadn't recalled who the man was.

"Are you in such a rush, Mr. 'Nami? Well, if you're leaving, I will too."

Reluctantly, the man rose and followed Iosuke. They descended the four flights of stairs, but as they came out of the building he showed no sign of going his own way. Iosuke began to feel uneasy.

"We can't talk here. Let's go and sit down for a while." He led Iosuke across the road and into a coffee shop that had been there since before the war.

I'm not going to pay for this! was all Iosuke could think of as he followed the man inside and sat down. Usually he never gave a thought to money, but his altered circumstances had begun to change this.

"Two coffee and cake sets," the man said to the waiter before turning to Iosuke.

"I want to apologize for that other time. I haven't forgotten how rude I was, even if I was drunk. Here's my card. We know each other by sight, but this is the first time we've introduced ourselves properly." Taking a name card out of his wallet, he handed it to Iosuke.

Iosuke glanced at his family name—Takayama—but made no effort to absorb the other information on the card before putting it into his pocket. However, out of politeness he had to give the man his own card.

"So you're Minamimura—that's an old name, isn't it? And you live in Shimozawa? That means your nearest station is Musashi-Hazama, right? My station is Nishi-Ogi—not far away. Maybe I could visit you sometime?"

"Well, at the moment, it's not . . ."

Iosuke was caught off guard, aware he was now homeless. From today he could not receive visitors or mail or anything else. It was a forlorn realization.

"Whatever you say. In any case, you did take care of my bill that night. A bill is a bill, and I want to settle it. It's the way I am, so if you'll let me . . ."

With that, he opened the wallet into which he had put Iosuke's name card and took out a number of 100-yen notes.

"What on earth is this about?"

"You must take it. I'd be mortified if I didn't pay you back."

Takayama began to explain. One night at the O-Riki bar he was about to pay his bill when he found that his wallet had been stolen. Iosuke had noticed his predicament and had paid the bill for him.

Iosuke finally recalled the incident vaguely; it had happened a long time ago.

"I was determined to repay you," Takayama continued, "so I went back to the bar many times—although it's not one I'd usually go to—thinking you'd be there. That was my first time there, but I remembered the name 'Nami, and because of your size I remembered you."

If Takayama had been a regular customer, even Iosuke, who had a terrible memory for faces, would have recognized him. But what about the five or six hundred yen on the table in front of him? If Iosuke took it, not only would it replace what he had squandered on the Nyoro-Nyoro Show, but he would be able to eat a decent meal tonight and tomorrow and still have some change left. To have such a windfall within a few hours of leaving home must mean that the gods were watching over him. Indeed, it was like manna from heaven. He wanted that money so badly he thought his hand might dart out of its own accord and seize it.

Yet for some reason he let the money lie there. He felt numbed, as though he had taken a dose of sleeping pills. Iosuke was not a man of great pride or vanity; if he wanted something, he would not hold back. But, today of all days, he did. He didn't know why, but it wasn't easy to take the money. To begin with, when he had paid for other people, he never wanted to be repaid, although now he had good reason to break this rule. It may be hard to believe, but he had never put much store by money. However, his eyes had been pried open for the first time today, and he understood why ordinary people were so concerned about it.

Still, he could not bring himself to pick up the notes.

"There's no need to pay me back, you know." His voice was low and a little sad.

"There is a need," Takayama insisted. "Think of how I feel! I can't let you pick up my tab and not pay you back." He obviously felt strongly about it.

Iosuke turned to one side so the money was no longer in his line of vision. It was a tense movement filled with regret and took a supreme effort of will.

"Oh, have I upset you? I certainly didn't mean to. No offense or anything. All right, I'll take the money back."

Takayama gathered the notes and put them away. Involuntarily, Iosuke's head drooped.

"Instead, Mr. 'Nami, I'd like to ask a favor. Come with me to Kanda. There's a nice little tempura restaurant I know. Let me treat you to dinner there. If you refuse, it'll be my turn to be upset."

He stood up to leave. The two servings of strawberry shortcake lay untouched.

The taxi passed under the railway at Suidobashi and followed the tram lines in Minowamachi. Takayama directed the driver from the back seat: "Turn at that corner. There it is, on the right."

The restaurant looked like an ordinary residence with its own gate. It did not seem to be one of the many unlicensed establishments that had sprung up. An elegant sign revealed that it was a tempura restaurant. For a postwar building it was surprisingly attractive.

Takayama slid open the door. "The owner used to have a fish store, so the fish is excellent," he said, acting as if he were some sort of gourmet. They were greeted by the aroma of tempura being deep-fried in a vat of hot oil just behind a counter near the entrance.

Iosuke felt his stomach growl. He had been hungry for some time and the memory of the untouched cake in the coffee shop was starting to haunt him. Being overweight, he was liable to sudden pangs of hunger or thirst, but today these were accompanied by misgivings. To satisfy his appetite, he would either have to part with money or accept the hospitality of Takayama, whom he did not even know. Neither option appealed to him since he preferred to be the one treating others.

Rather than taking a seat at the tempura counter, Takayama headed for the tables in the tatami-matted room at the back. A woman, who seemed to be the manager despite her youth, came to take their order.

"I hope you'll give us a feast tonight," Takayama said to her. "I'm sure my guest will happily put away enough for ten people."

"I see what you mean!" she said, appraising Iosuke's size. "Do I remember you from the ring somewhere?" she added.

Seated in the guest-of-honor place in front of the tokonoma, Iosuke did not look pleased at the intended compliment. Now it had been made to appear as if Takayama had brought his favorite boxer for a feed.

Before the main tempura course, some hors d'oeuvres were served— vinegared fish and sashimi. Two servings of each were placed before Iosuke: generosity is one thing, but wasn't this a little insulting? An unfamiliar reaction welled up inside him. He never realized he had such a strong streak of self-respect.

"Is something the matter? You haven't touched anything," said Takayama, looking perplexed as he plied Iosuke with beer, urging him to try this dish and that. Iosuke had no trouble accepting alcohol, but for some reason he found it hard to eat. It was as though he was in the grip of the same pride that makes a starving street urchin refuse charity.

On an empty stomach, the alcohol stimulated his appetite even more, and to stave off the hunger he downed one beer after another. He could feel himself getting drunk.

I won't eat! I refuse to eat! He made this silent declaration, and then his eyes began to glaze over and his breath came in audible rasps through his nose. Finally, the tempura arrived—shrimp, conger eel, delicate white-fleshed fish, and much more—a mountain of it!

They had begun drinking around five in the afternoon (daylight saving time was then in force) and continued until the city grew quiet as the night advanced. They had switched from beer to saké and drank until they could not remember how much they had had. Takayama's speech quickly became slurred, but he kept on chattering about his brokerage business and complaining about his family. Half of what he said was unintelligible, and it was not long before he was stretched out beside the low table fast asleep.

Iosuke had started to feel tipsy at one point, but unluckily for him his capacity for alcohol was considerable, and beyond a certain point he did not become any drunker. He would have preferred to get dead drunk—not in order to forget everything but to give him the courage to reach for the tempting tempura before him. Since Takayama was unconscious, Iosuke thought he might as well eat, but he still could not bring himself to do so. It was cruel how memories of being scolded by his mother for bad table manners came back to haunt him at such a moment.

Glancing at his watch, he realized it was past ten. Whatever the state of his appetite, his stomach was bloated with drink.

"Hey!" He shook Takayama to wake him.

"Umm, let's go to Fujimicho," mumbled Takayama before sinking back into a stupor. Iosuke decided it was time to leave. He pressed the service bell and the woman who had served them appeared.

"I'd like to leave, but…"

"Oh, Mr. Takayama's out of it, is he? Never mind. We'll call a taxi and you can be on your way."

"In that case, please bring me the bill." As soon as Iosuke had said this, he mentally berated himself as a fool. The words had come out by sheer

101

force of habit.

"Oh, that would never do," she said. "Mr. Takayama would be angry with us."

Her words were more welcome than those of an angel of salvation.

Iosuke made a hasty exit, and as he did so his tenseness lifted and a feeling of relief flooded through him. He stopped to gaze up at the sky and noticed that unlike the clear daytime weather, the night was overcast. The city lights glowed reddish against the low-hanging clouds. It would not be long now before the rains of early summer set in.

Without thinking, he hurried toward Suidobashi Station, but at the wicket there he halted.

I can't go back home, he realized.

But neither could he linger in the station. Gazing along the train tracks in the Ochanomizu direction, he could see the dark slope beside the railway line. The darkness seemed to beckon him. The tracks ran along the top of a concrete embankment; on the opposite side was a large building with no lights on. Not a soul was on the street. As he relieved himself against a concrete wall, the lights of a train going west along the embankment passed overhead. Was it heading for Tachikawa, or Iosuke's station at Hazama?

Iosuke slowly climbed the slope. Halfway up he came upon a modest two-story building that had obviously been constructed after the war. A square paper lantern with the word "inn" was hanging outside. The lights in the windows made it look like an oasis. This is exactly right, he thought; I'll stay here.

He turned to walk through the gate under the lantern but stopped again. Cheap as it might be, it would cost at least five or six hundred yen for a night. Even if he did not take any breakfast, it was sure to come to more than he had in his wallet.

Better give it a miss.

Iosuke continued walking. No one passed him, and even after he reached the top of the hill there was nothing in sight but the lonely funnels of light under the street lamps.

Looking around, he realized that the area lay between the burned-out section of the city and an area that had escaped most damage. On one side, large residences and a hospital loomed black in the night, while down the hill toward Kanda was a grassy expanse punctuated by the remains of some walls. Walking beside the burned-out section, Iosuke came to a striking building on the left. It had a red façade and the sign "Women's Library" was strung between two pillars.

So this is women's territory, eh?

The doors were shut and a single light shone at the entrance. No one would complain if a man took shelter there. He climbed the wide stone steps and slumped down exhausted beside a pillar. He had not walked very far, yet he felt he had traveled a great distance.

Phew! This search for freedom is not going to be easy.

His prospects had appeared rosy when he left home that morning, but twelve hours later he was already exhausted. How long could he keep this up? If you set out in search of freedom and ended up with even less than before, it would be an exercise in futility. Even if he was little more than a slave to Komako, it might make more sense to go back to her.

All I have to do is apologize and she'll forgive me, he thought. Judging from her outburst, she wasn't so angry with me.

Iosuke may have pretended indifference, but in reality he knew Komako's moods and temperament very well, though he rarely revealed this.

The first question was whether he should go home today or tomorrow. If he hurried, he could get to Suidobashi Station in time to catch the last train to Hazama. The next question was whether—after he had walked all the way from the station and knocked on his front door—Komako would let him in. It was warm enough for mosquitoes, and if he ended up outdoors in that rural area, he would be eaten alive. If it was up to him to find shelter for the night, he would be safer in the city. And if he did penance for one night and said he had learned his lesson, that would probably be sufficient to assuage Komako's fury.

So he made up his mind to spend the night beside the pillar. However, he soon found the concrete floor too uncomfortable. Moreover, realizing that he had run out of cigarettes, he became all the more desperate for a smoke and doubted if he would get any sleep at all.

As the night wore on, Iosuke leaned back against the stone pillar but was unable to sleep. He had no idea how much time had passed when he heard faint footsteps. Across from the library were some ruins. There was a stone wall, a gate with no door, and a pitch-black void beyond. Two figures emerged from the darkness, a young man in a suit and a woman. The man, hatless and carrying a briefcase, came out of the gate, clearly on the lookout. Once he had checked there was no one about, he beckoned to the woman inside and she came through the gate, taking care her heels made little sound. She looked like an office worker or a shop assistant.

Finding themselves alone, the two shapes merged into one as they embraced. They were as familiar with the latest ways of lovers as any Westerner. Their "timeless moment" lasted a long while before they finally disengaged.

"Till tomorrow then," said the man.

"Yes, tomorrow," answered the woman.

With that, the man turned and walked briskly in the direction of Suidobashi Station, while the woman hurried off toward Surugadai, her small steps echoing in the darkness.

Just a couple of youngsters!

Iosuke recognized lovers like these from the time he worked in the Marunouchi district, where office workers often held their rendezvous in the plaza of the Imperial Palace. Instead of making him think about the "decline in sexual morality," a common topic of discussion since the end of the war, the scene stirred feelings of sympathy, since from his experience that evening he knew what it was like not to be able to use the nearby inn. No doubt the two had jobs in the Kanda district but little cash to spare. Many young people had to conduct their lovemaking in the ruined areas of the city. They were a pitiful sight, like so many alley cats in the spring.

But for Iosuke there was a more pressing matter. To survive the night he needed to find somewhere more comfortable, and the two young people had given him a valuable hint.

Plucking up his courage, Iosuke went through the doorless gate. Inside was a small compound, with a grassy area leading to a steep slope. Somewhere in all that he should be able to find a secluded spot to rest.

Feeling in his pockets, he found that he still had his lighter. He searched by the light of the small flame and, sure enough, in a slight dip in the land was the entrance to an old concrete bomb shelter. He went inside.

It was a real find! The earth was dry, and there was even a mat of woven straw. Extinguishing the flame, Iosuke lay down on the mat. A faint perfume hung in the air, no doubt that of the young woman who was just there. Iosuke's thoughts drifted and he fell into a deep sleep.

"What's the matter with you? It's time to go."

Komako was shaking him awake.

"Oh, let me sleep. I've quit the company."

"What'ya saying? Come on, wake up! Quick!"

She was certainly tough. Iosuke's huge frame was being rocked like a ship in a heavy sea, and to make matters worse his head was being yanked up by the hair.

"You're too rough," he protested, but when he opened his eyes, it was dark and there was a strong earthy smell.

"What do you mean, 'rough,'" boomed a man's voice in the darkness. "Who're you to come in and take over a man's place without his permission?" The voice was right next to him, and was accompanied by an unpleasant odor.

Iosuke had no idea what was happening, but then his mind cleared and he realized that the square of dim light he could see was the entrance to the bomb shelter.

"So it's you who's been messing up my place. Every time I come back there's some rubbish left behind. Don't you have no sense of what's proper, eh?"

"I'm sorry," answered Iosuke meekly. His head was still thick from being roused so suddenly, but apparently the bomb shelter was someone's home, and that someone had come back in the middle of the night to find a stranger in his bed. Who had been "messing up" his place, however, was not something Iosuke could know.

"I been livin' here for three months—just ask around. They all know it's mine. You're one of those homeless, aren't ya? Where'd ya crawl out of, anyway? Are you one of those bums from Nogami?"

"Sorry."

At least he had to apologize, thought Iosuke, and he bowed his head in the dark.

Now look at what he'd got himself into. He let out an involuntary sigh. Property rights! Someone had even staked a claim to a place like this and was ready to defend it. Iosuke felt that most of society's problems stemmed from this "right of possession," which everyone was so sensitive about and protected with such zeal. The very words "right of possession" made him feel sick.

"If you're sorry, you'll be on your way then!"

"Yes."

"So get out!"

Iosuke was shocked. He never thought he would hear the same words spoken twice in one day. Although he could not see the man, judging from his voice he must be an older fellow.

"Please don't say that," he entreated. "I've been thrown out of my house and I need a place to stay."

"Thrown out? Who by?"

"My wife."

The sky began to lighten.

Iosuke had avoided being driven out into the damp and was fortunate enough to spend the rest of the night in the warm and dry shelter. As soon as Iosuke had said he had been thrown out by his wife, the old man's attitude had changed. Not only had he let Iosuke stay, but he had even given him the cigarettes he had been craving. On the debit side, Iosuke had had to listen to the old man's diatribe against women in general and wives in particular. However, it was the price he had to pay and he put up with it.

"Ya can't be too soft on women. All women are thieves, no doubt about it. All they do is take, take, take. They never know how to give." The monologue continued until he suddenly announced, "Dawn's 'ere. How about that? We talked the night away!"

This man, too, had had difficulties with his wife. As the morning light began to filter into the shelter, the two men stared at each other in surprise. Before Iosuke was a tramp about sixty years of age, dressed in tattered old clothes. Iosuke was taken aback by the shabbiness of his host, but the latter seemed more astonished that the owner of the voice that had spoken so gently belonged to this huge person in a good-quality suit.

The man's tone switched from one of disdain to one of respect.

"Please help yourself, sir," said the old man, offering the can of half-smoked cigarettes. Iosuke had accepted quite a few of them during the night, and although surprised, he was not disgusted at having smoked them. He may have had an upper-class upbringing, but he was not squeamish and thanked the old man politely.

Selecting a longish butt, he saw it was a foreign brand.

"So this is what you do?" he asked, holding it up. There was some money to be made in cigarette stubs, using the tobacco in them for hand-rolled cigarettes.

"Sure, I do that, too, but I'm not fussy. I'm a trash-picker and I'll take anything. Hey, it's time to go to work. Haven't slept a wink, but too bad. I got to get out into the streets before people wake up or there won't be nothing left!"

So saying, he ducked out of the shelter, with Iosuke close on his heels. The old man performed his morning ablutions the same as anyone might in his own home. Parting some weeds to one side and removing a stone, he uncovered the broken end of a lead pipe with a trickle of water coming from it. He used this to wash his face carefully and he even gargled. Then, facing east under the overcast skies, he clapped his hands twice in the ritual of morning prayer.

"So what're you going to do?" he asked Iosuke, who, following his example, was washing his face. "If you like, you can go ahead and sleep here."

"Thank you," said Iosuke, "but I thought I'd go home and see if I can make up with my wife."

"Are you sure you wanna do that? Well, it's your business. So sayonara."

As Iosuke watched the old man walk unsteadily down the slope, he felt he had found a friend.

Why should that be? Did he feel indebted for the board and lodging (though he'd received cigarettes instead of food)? Or had Iosuke found a kindred spirit in their shared experience of domineering wives? There was something else that attracted Iosuke to the old man and his unburdened, simple way of life.

What shall I do now? Iosuke wondered.

He asked himself this question only when he reached Suidobashi Station. He was still bloated from too much drink the night before, so he had no wish to eat. If he were to feel hungry, the thought of Komako's *miso* soup and hot rice would surely tempt him homeward. For the moment, though, it seemed too early to head back.

Most of all Iosuke wanted to sleep. Searching for a place to nap, he took the train to Shinanomachi Station, which was covered by his commuter's pass. He would go to Meiji Shrine. In the weeks when he had pretended to go to work, he learned that the Outer Garden there was a good place for passing time.

It was still early, so the only people there were commuters cutting through the park on their way to work. Both their pace and direction were different from Iosuke's. Aware of being unemployed, he felt awkward but at the same time curious, as if he had stepped into another dimension.

He walked to the back of the Picture Gallery building. There was no one about, and the abundance of trees in full leaf beneath an overcast sky made it as quiet as a world apart. Iosuke stretched out on a bench.

I'll just take a nap and then it'll be time to go home. Placing his hat over his face, he fell into a deep sleep in no time.

He wasn't sure how long he slept, but he dreamed about Komako, who was apologizing to him.

"Everything that's happened is my fault," she was saying. "I regretted what I said the moment you left. Marriage is not a matter of balance of power but of harmony, don't you agree? It's not singing together so much as singing in unison, right? From now on I'll change, and I promise to take good care of you!"

107

"You don't have to go that far," he was saying, but then he woke up.

He seemed to have slept quite a while, but since it was cloudy he could not tell what time it was. Looking around, he saw a middle-aged couple, evidently on a sightseeing trip to Tokyo, sitting companionably on the bench next to his and enjoying sweet-bean buns. Two younger people, students perhaps, were deep in conversation beneath a large tree, their legs stretched out in front of them. Was it noon, or past noon?

Should be time to go home now, he decided.

As he looked at his wrist to see the time, he realized that his watch was gone! The hat he had placed over his face was gone, too. Startled, he searched around the bench, but there was no sign of hat or watch. He reached into his inside pocket for his leather wallet, but that was gone, too. He only had his lighter, which was in his trouser pocket.

I've been robbed!

You could never let down your guard. Iosuke had lost all his money, his train pass, his watch, his hat—everything.

The hat was a Borsalino he had bought before the war. It was old and worn and no great loss. What was harder to accept was losing his Vacheron watch, a world-famous brand and a souvenir from Switzerland he had received from an uncle in the diplomatic corps. Komako, too, knew how much he treasured that watch; even after Japan's defeat, when times had been hard and they had sold one valued possession after another, she had not let the watch go.

Now I'm finished. Iosuke felt as if the doors of fate had slammed shut in his face.

The Komako who had been smiling in his dream seemed to have sprouted fangs and, with her hair standing on end, was ready to pounce on him in fury. No excuses would placate her now. No way would she believe that he had lost his precious watch in this innocent way. She would be sure he had got drunk, ended up in some place of ill-repute, and been forced to pay the tab by pawning the watch. Iosuke was aware that her strategy of giving him 300 yen every few days, either in change or notes, was to keep him on a short leash. It was enough money to go drinking but not for fooling around with women. That this had happened the day after he had left her would make it even harder for her to accept his apology!

No way I can go home now.

Gloom at the tongue-lashing he would receive settled over him. The big man with the small heart felt no different from a child who goes shopping for his stepmother but loses the money and has to face her anger. His commuter pass was gone, and he had no money for a ticket, which meant he had no way of getting home even if he wanted to.

Iosuke spent the rest of the day in the Outer Garden. He moved to the area in front of the public swimming pool and the sumo wrestling ring, but he stayed within the park. His reason for moving from place to place was to be near water fountains, for he needed to drink a lot, not only to recover from his hangover but also to fill his stomach.

Once the alcohol had worn off, hunger struck hard. A man with a body that size had an appetite to match, and since his late breakfast the day before he had not eaten as much as a single grain of rice. Hunger was making him giddy. Where he was and what he was doing all seemed as though in a dream.

Before long, the sun had set and he had left the Outer Garden. Trains, trucks, streets, bridges rushed by him like so many apparitions. The next thing he knew he was standing in front of the bomb shelter where he had spent the previous night. The old man was sitting outside.

"I thought you'd be back, so I've waited for you. Now let's eat."

Chapter 8
The Way of the Trash-Picker

Five days had passed since Iosuke became the old man's guest—as far as food was concerned, that is, for he imposed on the man for very little else. It was not a way of life that required tableware, bedding, or other creature comforts. Despite the old man's vigorous claim to the shelter, it could not really be said to belong to him.

The food they ate consisted mostly of hard buns of wheat flour that had been kneaded and roasted until they were covered with scorch marks. Apparently, these were sold somewhere.

"Help yourself," the old man would say, pulling out of his pocket several of these buns wrapped in newspaper. He would say he had already eaten and had brought them for Iosuke.

The buns were rock hard, but if you chewed them slowly, they did not taste all that bad. After two of them, washed down with water from the tap outside, Iosuke would feel he had had a proper meal.

Once the old man surprised him by producing a large wedge of Dutch cheese—a little rancid but edible nonetheless.

"'Course I didn't buy it! I pick up things, remember?"

Some of the houses and hotels in the area had been requisitioned by the Occupation forces, the old man said, and those places had all kinds of stuff that could be sold—from leftover food to empty cans and bottles, and occasionally used clothing and shoes. You could find just about anything in the trash there, the old man added. It gave Iosuke a good idea where the cheese had come from, but he decided not to dwell on that.

On his daily rounds the old man collected an assortment of items, but he would only bring food and cigarettes back to the shelter. Apparently there was a place where he could exchange what he picked up for cash. Others in the same profession lived in dugouts on the hill, he said, and Iosuke had confirmed this when he sought a secluded spot to answer the call of nature early one morning. Every corner of the vacant lot was used for this purpose, and the old man had lectured Iosuke both to cover everything up with earth and to make sure to do his business either early in the morning or late at night. The old man was conscious of the importance of cleanliness, and of the need to avoid complaints from respectable residents living nearby.

On the third day it rained, and the old man spent most of the afternoon in the shelter with Iosuke.

"I've actually got a proper home," he said proudly, "but I moved out here three months ago. One of these days it'll come empty and I'll take you there to live. We're not moles, and we shouldn't have to be in a cave forever."

This revelation about having a home led Iosuke to conclude that the old man had not always been a vagrant. Even though he had turned to scavenging, he retained some integrity. He came out with occasional odd statements, and the world he inhabited was clearly different from that of regular city folk. In the five days Iosuke had been there, the old man had not once asked his name nor mentioned his own. He never asked Iosuke what he intended to do, and he gave no hint that he expected Iosuke to be indebted to him for the food.

As the days passed, the normal world of wife and home began to recede into the distance. It was not that Iosuke ceased thinking about them, for the desire to go back, eat his fill, and get a good night's sleep on a comfortable futon was never far from his mind. However, with each new day it became less realistic to hope that he would ever be permitted to cross his own threshold again. The difficulty of apologizing to Komako seemed to increase daily. It must be hard for people of the postwar generation to understand how a faint-hearted man like Iosuke thinks or feels.

What really stopped him from going home was a feeling of obligation to the old man. He had had no qualms about Komako working to supplement the household income, but he felt ashamed of accepting three (more usually, two) meals a day from the old man.

Finally, on the morning of the fifth day, he could stand it no longer.

"Let me work as well?" he said.

"Work? What work can you do?"

"I can come with you. Help you pick up things."

"It's not easy work for an amateur." The old man seemed reluctant. "But I suppose you could carry stuff. All right, come along then."

But when the time came to set out, a problem arose. Even though Iosuke had no hat, the quality suit he was wearing would have been out of place for a trash-picker. He needed to look the part.

"Somehow I don't think you were cut out for this," the tramp sighed, shaking his head. In the end, he made Iosuke remove his jacket and shirt and hide them under a stone at the back of the shelter. In his dirty undershirt and muddy trousers, Iosuke looked like someone down on his luck, but side by side the two of them gave an impression of a burly bodyguard taking an old thief into custody.

It was early morning and the city was still asleep. From Misakicho to Jinbocho and then Surugadai, the old man followed his accustomed route, like a seasoned angler moving along the banks of a familiar river. And when he reached "a good fishing spot," he would come to a halt. There, outside the closed doors of large and small publishing companies would be piles of wooden crates, straw mats, rope, wrapping paper, and so on. Deftly, he would gather and pack them into the large cloth bag Iosuke was carrying.

"A year and a half ago I was picking up twice as much, sometimes three times," he said. "Business must be terrible for bookstores."

As they climbed up the slope at Surugadai, his attention switched to cigarette butts. People connected with the Occupation forces used this street, he said, so good-quality butts could be found. According to the old man, tramps who specialized in cigarette butts used tongs, but he did not have any. He might pick up the odd butt, but he was first and foremost a trash-picker, and his respect for the "specialists" made him avoid using tongs. Another specialty involved searching the ground for valuables, which the old man also did. Before the war, he told Iosuke, scavenging had been neatly split up so that specialists in one sort of trash avoided infringing on other people's lines. There had been a distinct order observed by everyone.

"Those were the good old days."

So Iosuke went along as the old man's assistant. All he was required to do was carry the large bag, so it was not taxing work. Since the streets were quiet and deserted at that hour, and the only people awake were those on duty in police boxes, he felt no embarrassment.

However, as they were walking down the slope in front of Meiji University and came in sight of a hotel used by Occupation personnel, the old man spoke to him sharply.

"Hey! Can't you see that really good butt—right there at your feet!"

On the corner lay a cigarette with only about a third of it smoked.

"Quick! Pick it up. What're you waiting for?"

But Iosuke couldn't. An inexplicable aversion overcame him, and his hand would not move.

He had seen people picking up cigarette butts everywhere and was not disgusted by it, but when it came to doing so himself he was suddenly paralyzed. Was it a lingering awareness of the social class of his birth? Despite his impoverished lifestyle since the war, picking up that first butt represented a psychological barrier.

All the color drained from Iosuke's face as he struggled with the conflict between his body's resistance and his mind's moral imperative.

I have to do this at all costs, he told himself.

The old man had kept him alive for the last five days, and Iosuke was deeply in his debt. There was the old man picking up anything and everything, and Iosuke could not even pick up one cigarette butt. If he couldn't do that, it would prove he was a coward and would be an insult to this kind and gentle old man.

One, two, three!

Turning his head to one side, he reached for the cigarette and slipped it into his pocket as he had seen the old man do.

Having done it once, it was nothing earth-shattering. Like everything else, the first time was the hardest, and for Iosuke the first time for anything was particularly hard. He may have had few talents, but he had been blessed with an easygoing nature, and as the two men continued down the hill Iosuke gathered his second butt without any prompting.

That first cigarette butt marked a turning-point for Iosuke. The same day the old tramp, assisted by his sturdy packhorse, collected twice as much as usual, and as they neared Okanenomizu Station, he turned to Iosuke.

"I'll go and take care of this stuff. You head on back. Today I'll bring you some delicious white rice."

He was as good as his word. An hour later he appeared at the shelter with a huge ball of steamed white rice wrapped in paper. My, how good that tasted! And it was a meal Iosuke had helped earn.

From then on, Iosuke went out to work with the old man every morning.

Since this was how events had turned out, Iosuke thought he might as well accept the situation and become accustomed to this way of life. At the same time he began to feel a certain attraction to the job of scavenging. He did have some reservations, however. He saw nothing wrong in collecting cigarette butts; after all, one was simply picking up what had been discarded. But he wondered if it was legal to walk off with the wooden crates, boxes, straw mats, and other items placed in front of stores.

"Isn't that what you might call," he began, grinning at the old man as he searched for the right word, "pilfering?"

"Don't be stupid!" the old man retorted. "We're not doing anything wrong! Stuff left on the street doesn't belong to anyone. It's thrown away.

Folk who leave things on the street expect it to be taken."

In short, the old man's argument was that people's private possessions and what they considered valuable were always kept within their doors or gates. This was not his arbitrary conclusion; it was the custom at the time. Leaving something on the street rendered ownership ambiguous, which was the basis of the trash-picker's trade. Was it not proof enough that after the owners noticed the items had gone they did not report it to the police? Even if a trash-picker was caught red-handed, the worst that could happen was that he would be yelled at. There was clearly a tacit rule in society that recognized the trash-picker's role; it was quite different from stealing.

"That makes sense," said Iosuke. "Perhaps the world is not as rigid as I thought."

Iosuke was delighted, for discovering this latitude amid the stifling fussiness of Tokyo life came as a surprise. He had heard of such attitudes in other, large countries. In China, if someone had something stolen it was considered that person's fault for not looking after it properly. In France, if a wife committed adultery it was the husband who took the blame for not being a better lover. It came as a relief to find, even in this confining society with its island mentality, that the winds of freedom blew in some places. It gave him a feeling of ease and space, a kind of pride even.

After mulling this over for a while, Iosuke found himself becoming attracted to the trash-picker's trade, where the heavy chains of ownership were non-existent. He thought of taking up the occupation himself, except that his clothes were not right. He did not look the part and this would affect his performance. For every sort of life one had to dress appropriately. If he was going to be a trash-picker, he had to dress like the old man, but even the shabbiest clothes required money.

"Why don't you sell that suit of yours?" the old man suggested. "Then you can buy work clothes and get some change into the bargain."

The old man was about to set off to visit a buyer friend in order to sell Iosuke's suit when something unexpected occurred.

"First," he said, with the voice of experience, "we should take a good look at the jacket to see how much we can get."

He brought the jacket out into the light and began to inspect it carefully. The fabric was good, he judged, but the large size would be a drawback.

"But it might be better than a small one," the old man muttered to himself. "It should fetch seven or eight hundred yen."

He turned all the pockets inside out and removed the contents. There was the cigarette lighter that had run out of fuel, the name card Takayama had given Iosuke, and a now-filthy handkerchief. That was all. One hardly expected to find anything of value.

"Hey! What's this?" the old man suddenly cried out.

From a small pocket in the jacket lining he pulled out a crumpled bill.

"Look at that! It's a big one!" The old man's voice was quivering at the sight of the 1,000-yen bill in his hand.

Iosuke had no idea how the money got there. He must have taken it from the envelope of his severance pay and tucked it away when he had gone out drinking. He had forgotten all about it. Komako was in the habit of inspecting her husband's clothes, but perhaps it had not occurred to her to look into that small pocket for holding name cards.

"What kind of guy are you, carrying so much money around and not even knowing it," the old man lectured. "No wonder your wife threw you out!"

Smoothing out the wrinkled bill, the old man continued. "Now you won't have to sell your suit. You can use this to buy work clothes. Hang on to the suit. It may come in handy one day." With that, he handed the bill to Iosuke.

"No, no!" said Iosuke immediately, remembering the trash-picker's rule. "You found it, so it belongs to you!" If he could not follow that rule now, it would be meaningless to be part of this new community.

"Don't be silly!" said the old man. "Things is different among pals."

The old man refused to take the money, but after a lengthy exchange he suggested a compromise.

"Here's an idea—why don't I use this to get my home back? We can move in there and you can stay as long as you like. We'll be joint owners. It's got a roof and even a floor—far better than this."

That settled, the old man began to talk about himself. Three months earlier, he had built a hut under the large bridge between Hongo and Kanda and had lived there with his wife. But she wanted to get ahead in the world, and soon she began to nag him for his lack of ambition, finally driving him out. With nowhere to go, he had chanced upon the bomb shelter. People sometimes came to the area under the bridge, which functioned like a barter market, to buy what the scavengers had picked up, and when the old man went there he often saw his wife. She was not going to let him come back, but if he paid her 1,000 yen, she would vacate the house, she said.

What to do with the windfall was settled, but that still left the problem of

115

buying work clothes for Iosuke without selling his suit. No second 1,000-yen note seemed likely to turn up. Wondering if the jacket was a magic money tree, Iosuke went through the pockets once more but found nothing except fluff. However, the old man had been moved by Iosuke's generosity. He made a trip to the "market" under the bridge and a hurried search through a pile of rags produced a jacket that looked like an Occupation army reject and a pair of rayon trousers. These he bought for Iosuke at what he called an "insider's price"—practically nothing.

The blue-gray cotton jacket was a snug fit on Iosuke, who had the build of an American soldier, but the khaki trousers were too short and exposed part of his calves, making him look as if he was wearing long-johns.

Gazing at the results, the old man shook his head. "I picked what I thought were large ones, but they're not big enough. Never mind. All we have to do is adjust them a little," he said. With deft fingers he undid the stitching along the lower trouser legs and rolled them up to the knee like shorts. "After we get back," he promised, "I'll use a needle and thread and stitch them proper."

"You must've been a tailor," said Iosuke admiringly.

"Naw, just made shirts for a big company. Never had my own shop."

"But with your skill you don't need to be a trash-picker."

"Don't make me laugh!" The old man refused to take Iosuke seriously.

At any rate, Iosuke cut a very different figure in his new outfit. It was as if the respectable citizen Minamimura Iosuke had vanished and in his place had appeared a solidly built scavenger. The old man gazed at him with increased camaraderie, and Iosuke himself felt lighter, as if he had become a new person. The change was probably greater than that achieved by Komako putting on her best dress to visit Oiso. Iosuke's transformation was proof of the magic power of clothes.

"So, my friend, welcome to the trade! How about a bottle of saké to celebrate? You look like you can drink, but I couldn't take you to my usual place the way you were. You'd stick out too much and someone'd punch you in no time. But now you're fine. Let's go."

The old man stood up, but when Iosuke looked as though he was going to leave his suit in the shelter, he got a scolding.

"You put valuables like that in a sack and hide it."

Their destination was a market near Kanda Station.

The sight of this shabby Laurel-and-Hardy pair walking down Ogawamachi street at three in the afternoon drew stares and smiles. People

116

stopped to look at them, but the old man was unaffected. Iosuke found it hard enough to feign that indifference; it was even harder to maintain the old man's level of concentration on their journey. Wherever you were and whatever you might be doing, a true professional has to remain alert for business.

After turning off the main street and continuing further, they came to a market beneath the railway tracks. Since he'd been living on his own, the old man said, he'd started coming here for his dinner.

Small stalls lined up like matchboxes were familiar to Iosuke since he had seen similar ones in Shinjuku, but the food and drinks sold there, their prices, and the faces of customers and passersby startled him. Nearer the station were neat little coffee shops and places to eat and drink, but the market was like another world, dark and completely cut off, yet coursing with the energy of a racing muddy current. There was also a distinctive smell, a stench beyond that of animal fat and scorched grain.

It was early for the evening meal, so few customers were at the stalls, and not one could be called well-dressed. They all wore shabby, ill-fitting clothes like Iosuke and the old man. None of the passersby, moreover, could be termed "ordinary citizens." Yet anyone walking down the street was the target of the hard scrutiny of those sitting at the stalls.

Iosuke was scared. He tried to keep to the middle of the narrow street, but the stares not only followed him from the stalls but confronted him head-on as he passed people in the alley. He took care not to bump into anyone accidentally, and he had to dodge several times, but he was often surprised when others moved aside first. There were some, in fact, whose glance seemed to hold a certain respect, and even a few nods in greeting. Why that should be he wasn't sure, but it was unnerving.

"Everybody thinks you must be an important member of some gang," the old man whispered to Iosuke. "You're big, and you've got those bulging eyes."

They peered into one stall after another—selling noodles, steamed buns, rice balls, buns filled with bean-jam, stew, yakitori, fried noodles—but none seemed right.

"I've got my own favorite," said the old man, "but we may as well look at all of them. We have to spend wisely. How's your stomach? If you're very hungry, it's best to have a drink—it makes you feel happy in no time. If you're not that hungry, let's stop by this stew place here. It's real good— better than anything you'll find even in Asakusa. It'll do you a world of good."

117

The stall was hardly two meters wide with a bench and a long table that jutted into the street. They ordered, and two large bowls were set down on the black table, shiny with grease. With them came two slender, lead-colored spoons.

"Strangely enough, if you eat a bowl of this stew in winter, it'll keep you warm all day." The old man's expression softened as he blew on a spoonful.

The stew was hot and thick. Iosuke had a sensitive tongue, and it was too hot for him to eat right away. As he stirred the stew with his spoon, the contents were revealed—chunks of pork and canned corned beef, chicken bones, potatoes, carrots, celery stumps, and a lot more. As far as he could tell, the dish was richer than the cheap Western-style stew he had eaten before the war. Indeed, there was lots of meat, as well as canned corn and green peas, pieces of cheese with the foil still attached, and what might have been button mushrooms, making it quite a fancy dish. It also contained some dubious ingredients that looked like adzuki beans and strands of wheat noodles. Even more puzzling were fragments of Lucky Strike cigarette packs in the broth. How could they possibly improve the taste, he wondered.

"Tastes good, doesn't it?" The old man's question spurred Iosuke to try a spoonful. It was thick, cloyingly sweet, and greasy, like an adzuki bean broth made with meat, with a taste that instantly filled you up. Somehow it reminded him of the "boeuf à la mode Español" that Komako had made with disappointing results some time before.

Whatever it was, it was nutritious, as the old man had said. It was an unpretentious substantial dish that had not existed before the war, made without the least care as to where the ingredients came from or whether they blended well or not. Everything was just thrown into the pot and placed on the stove. This postwar goulash, reflected Iosuke, certainly had the taste of defeat about it.

After one bowl of stew he felt completely full. It cost twenty yen; there could be nothing cheaper than that. When he marveled how they could stay in business charging such prices, the old tramp explained where the ingredients came from. Like the cheese he had brought back the other day, they were leftovers scrounged from garbage cans at dormitories of the Occupation forces and at hotels catering to foreigners. Shouldn't the Japanese consider themselves lucky, the old man asked, to be occupied by a people with such largesse?

"Now let's get something with a little fire in it." With this, the old man led Iosuke into a neighboring shop selling cheap liquor. One glass was thirty yen, but the old man said it was a waste of money because a full stomach stopped it having any effect. Instead he ordered something called a "bomb"; only two glasses, he said, and the world would turn upside down.

Nothing happened to the world, but Iosuke felt himself projected into a realm he had never encountered before. It felt as though the air of the market as well as the tastes of the food and drink were sucking him farther and farther away from the life he had shared with Komako. And he might never be able to find his way back there again.

Chapter 9
Under the Bridge

In early July Iosuke and the old tramp finally moved from the bomb shelter to his shack under the bridge.

Looking back, it had been a long month. During the drenching rains of the monsoon season, their takings from scavenging fell by half. Water seeped into the dugout shelter, making life miserable, and the old man began earnest negotiations with his wife to make her vacate his shack. She had been quick to accept the compensation but slow to keep her end of the bargain. Only after she had found a job as a live-in cook for a medical equipment manufacturer in the Hongo area did word reach him that she had finally left. The old man was so delighted that he danced a jig. And on the day of the move, the weather changed and the endless rain lifted.

They may have been moving house, but they had no need of a truck. The two simply filled large bags with their possessions and slung them on their backs. With all the free time they had during the rain, they had begun cooking their own meals, so they also had pots and pans, but these were easy to string together and carry by hand.

"Make sure we haven't left anything behind," said the old man, taking a last look inside. There was nothing that deserved such scrupulousness.

The two men walked up the main street of Surugadai, crossed Okanenomizu Bridge, and turned right. In the wartime drive to collect iron, the railings had been removed, and access to the river below was easy. A well-beaten path wound through the grass and led to the top of a ladder propped against the embankment. As Iosuke climbed down the ladder, it creaked under his weight, but was no more dangerous than the potholed roads of the devastated city.

When commuting on the Chuo Line, Iosuke had noticed people living on the far side of the river across from the train tracks. Given the shortage of housing after the war, it was not surprising. It was a depressing sight, he had thought, like people living on top of a junk heap, and he had wondered if it could not have been made a little more attractive. Now he was going there with the old man. As he reached the bottom of the ladder, he realized how different it looked from here, compared to the view from the train.

The area was secluded and quiet. With the river nearby, the grass was lush and there were plenty of trees. He had never imagined there could be a place in the city filled with such magical tranquillity. He was astounded by the contrast between seeing the area close up and looking down on it from the station beyond the river.

Another revelation was the extent of the land there, some 400 square yards. It was on a slope, to be sure, but how many homes in Tokyo could boast such a spacious front yard?

At the upper end, huddled under the bridge and sheltered by the embankment, were signs of human habitation. From one shack a woman emerged wearing a clean white apron and carrying a bucket, like any ordinary housewife. On seeing the old man she beamed and greeted him warmly.

"It's moving day today, I see. You must be happy!"

A middle-aged man came up. "So good to have you back! It's a great day today, now that that woman's gone!"

A girl aged fifteen or sixteen appeared, followed by a small boy and a dog. They even have a watchdog, thought Iosuke.

It was obvious that the old man was respected by the people living there. Perhaps there was some truth to his story of being the first one to build a shack under the bridge.

"Yep, I'll be relying on your kindness again. Now I've got a man for a wife and he'll be living here, too, so please be nice to him. Hey, what's your name?"

It was the first time the old man had asked Iosuke's name.

"Minamimura Iosuke," he replied without hesitation.

He was startled by a burst of laughter, but this was brought on the old man's joke of having "a man for a wife" rather than his name.

"Wow! You're big," said the boy, gazing up at Iosuke.

"I'm Suematsu Sadakichi. I live in the last house on the west," said the middle-aged man in khaki, obviously a former soldier.

"I'm Suzuki, your neighbor," the woman in the white apron said with a slight bow. "My husband works for the Road Bureau, so he's not here."

It was early, and most of the men in the seven households were out.

"So let's get the place cleaned up. That woman's taken everything!"

The old man was peering into the shack he called home, which stood in the middle of the cluster of dwellings. It was about three tatami mats in size and built against the stone supporting wall of the bridge, with the other three sides sturdily, if clumsily, constructed of wooden slats. There was a roof—slightly tilted—and a floor. The old man said he had used thirty-two apple crates for it. The window facing the river had glass in it, and both that window and the front door were professionally made fixtures, no doubt found on early morning scavenges. The window was small and did not open, so its value for light and ventilation was limited. Everything inside the shack was covered in soot, making you wonder if it had been built before the war. The straw matting on the floor had witnessed the passing of many years.

However, after their long stay in the bomb shelter, the two men were content, only too pleased to have a real roof over their heads.

"I'll sweep, and you wipe the floor, okay?"

The old man's wife had at least left some items for cleaning, so Iosuke carried the bucket down to where the old man told him he could get water. It was the communal washing place. Water was gushing from a clay pipe sticking out of the earth. Thinking it might be a sewage pipe, Iosuke hesitated at first, but then he saw that the water was clean and, moreover, had the distinctive smell of city water after the war.

The water was a real find. The old man had picked the spot for his shack because it was sheltered on the north side by the embankment and had a south-facing slope in front. One of the things he had learned from his experience as a vagrant was the importance of water. A natural spring discovered here in the early seventeenth century by the first Tokugawa shogun Ieyasu, had given the area its name—Okanenomizu, or "Spring of Gold." The old man first heard about it at a performance by some *kodan* storytellers, about how it was unused and buried in weeds, so he had taken a look and had found water. He knew, of course, that it was no Spring of Gold but a broken water main. The water's chemical smell confirmed that, but there was no reason to complain that it was not the legendary spring.

The homeless knew of sites with tap water all over the city, but the abundant supply from this one made it better than a natural spring. The old man had installed the clay pipe and placed an abandoned fire-fighting tank as a trough, so the washing place looked new and attractive.

After water, dry soil was the next most important, and the old man found that the earth beneath the bridge, being sheltered from rain, was bone dry. After careful deliberation, he had built his shack under the middle of the bridge. Within six months, he was joined by others who could not afford houses. The Suzukis next door were the first. The old man had showed them how to build a shack, and they had made one next to his. Building onto the side of the old man's shack saved them a lot of trouble. And so it went, with each newcomer building against the previous structure, until there were seven shacks, all linked. Any more would have gone beyond the width of the bridge and been exposed to the elements as well as the gaze of people standing on the station platforms opposite, so it was decided not to allow any more, and the decision strengthened the bonds of the little community.

First, they built a communal toilet and set up a system like a neighborhood association, with the families taking turns to clean the shared open space and around the "spring." This insured better hygiene and also forestalled complaints from the police or ward office. Next, since most of the residents were trash-pickers, they found ways to increase the value of some of what they picked up. Straw and old straw matting were burned and the ash was sold to farmers. Other articles were arranged by type and taken directly to dealers in those goods, in this way avoiding middlemen.

As the community grew and developed, the old man's role diminished, but he continued to be loved and respected. Constantly berated by his vain, domineering wife, he also had everyone's sympathy.

That night there was a party in the old man's shack. By the front door hung a proper name plate with "Hasegawa Kinji" written in black ink.

The old man thanked everyone repeatedly, clearly delighted.

There was a bottle of cheap liquor, strips of dried squid, and some boiled fava beans. To celebrate his return, his neighbors gave the old man and Iosuke six large balls of rice. The five guests who came over for drinks after dinner were all men. The woman called Takasugi did not appear in person but sent a bowl of pickled vegetables.

"Kinji, promise you'll never let your old woman back," urged Ogiya, a single man in his twenties living to the immediate left.

Suzuki, who lived with his family on the right, agreed. "She was awful, always looking down on us." All voiced their dislike of the old man's wife.

Suzuki, the youngest-looking, had a wife and baby, and Kawano, who resembled a bookish student with his long hair, was married as well. The two middle-aged men—Suematsu and Ema—were single. Mrs. Takasugi, living with her daughter on the far right, was a war widow.

The only one with a steady job was Suzuki, who worked for the Road Bureau; the rest were either trash-pickers or day laborers. Listening to them, Iosuke discovered that they were basically gentle-hearted people who had fallen on hard times after the war, not veterans of the streets like old Kinji.

"You must have had an easy life before. I can tell from your hands!" Ema said to Iosuke, the effects of the liquor loosening his tongue.

"I guess so."

"You're lucky to meet the old man and end up in a place like this," said Suematsu. Iosuke learned there was another cluster of shanties beneath the next bridge down and still another farther along the embankment. He was warned not to visit those places and to steer clear of the people living there.

Although Kinji's shack was the largest, with seven bodies huddled inside and all the cigarette smoke, it soon became stifling. The lamp was an old ink bottle filled with kerosene, with a wick stuck through the lid. With no shade, it was like a cigarette lighter burning continuously and was the cause of all the soot. By the time the bottle of liquor was empty, the party had gotten a little raucous.

"While you were away, some fellow built a hut on the other side of the willow tree. It's not our territory, so we didn't say anything, but we should get rid of people like that," Ogiya said to the old man, his voice louder through the drink.

"Don't talk like that. There're seven of us, and we've got a tough-looking ally," said Ema, indicating Iosuke, "so we've nothing to worry about."

Iosuke had made a good first impression in his new home.

The people there were all early risers. By the time a whistle announced the departure of the first train from the station beyond, they had washed at the trough and several were already climbing up the ladder to the main road, their dark shapes shrouded by the mist rising from the river.

Describing a job as one that can be done "before breakfast" suggests it is quick and easy, but for trash-pickers and those headed for the employment office it was important to be there before other people, even if breakfast had to wait.

Smoke rose at an early hour from the hibachi and earthen cookstoves outside the shacks of the Suzukis and the Takasugi women. The trash-pickers would get their breakfast either at the Kanda market or back home at around eight, after finishing their morning rounds.

Beset by fleas in the night, Iosuke had hardly slept a wink. There were fewer mosquitoes than in the bomb shelter, but the dryness of the soil resulted in an astonishing number of fleas. Their jumping about on the floor was like the spray thrown up in a sudden evening downpour, and they pounced on Iosuke's bulk without mercy. These so-called ground fleas were not as common as the ordinary sort, but their bites were just as itchy.

And so it was that Iosuke found himself uncharacteristically up at dawn, venturing out for a walk.

"Good morning!"

Mrs. Takasugi greeted him as she came out of the communal toilet. She was about thirty-seven or thirty-eight years of age, but the old-fashioned *mompe* trousers she wore and the prewar style of doing her hair in a bun made her look older. Her features, however, were not unattractive.

"The fleas here are awful." Iosuke voiced what was uppermost on his mind.

"But you won't find any lice, that's for sure!" She seemed offended and left abruptly.

Entering the toilet, Iosuke saw that someone had rigged up a device with a weight so the door would always swing shut. There was even a Japanese-style porcelain toilet bowl—not purchased, of course, but installed with hygiene in mind. The toilet's location had obviously been carefully calculated so it was far away from the shacks. It resembled a telephone booth without a roof—simple to build and with ample ventilation. Since the residents took turns sweeping, the communal open space and the area around the toilet were clean and tidy.

Iosuke ducked under the iron support of the bridge and continued walking upstream, where the dew-laden grass was thicker. There were many bushes, and a large willow tree stood veiled in morning mist by the muddy river. The graceful bend in the river evoked a bygone age when its beauty inspired poets to call it the "Little Red Cliffs," after the famous "Red Cliffs" of the Yangtze River in the Chinese classic *Romance of the Three Kingdoms*.

Iosuke noticed a white goat in the grass. Strange place to keep a goat, he thought, but then he spotted a lone hut farther along. It was a recent construction and a crude mixture of bamboo, straw mats, and branches, far more primitive than the other shacks.

A man of Iosuke's age came out of the hut wearing a dirty khaki shirt. He glared at Iosuke.

Not one to pass by without a word of greeting, Iosuke addressed him cheerfully. As if he had expected something else, the man looked bewildered. Finally he spoke.

"You're one of the fellas from the bridge, right?"

"Yes."

"So I want to tell you that you don't own this riverbank. You have to let other people come and go freely."

His aggressive tone set him apart from the good-natured people at the old man's shack the previous evening. His hair was cut very short, and his swarthy complexion and squat build were typically Japanese. He gave the impression of being filled with what they call "Japanese fighting spirit."

"I'm afraid I don't know much," Iosuke replied in his usual deliberate way. "I'm new. I just got here yesterday."

"There's no point talking to you then."

Sounding disappointed, the man turned to go back into his hut.

"Is that your goat?" asked Iosuke, looking at the animal busily grazing in the lush grass.

"Anything wrong with keeping a goat?"

"Why should there be? She's cute. Does she give milk?"

"Of course. That's why I keep her."

"You drink the milk?"

"It's my food."

"That's clever. Saves cooking."

Iosuke was genuinely impressed. What could be smarter than having a goat to transform the riverside grass into fresh, nourishing milk. For the inept and indolent Iosuke, producing food without having to light a fire and cook seemed like a wonderful idea. He had tried cooking rice many times but could never get it right, despite being scolded by old Kinji.

"Well, she won't give milk with just grass," said the man, with a wry smile. "You have to feed her something substantial like tofu leas from time to time." A flash of white teeth in the weather-beaten face was unexpectedly appealing in this tough-looking man. His wariness seemed to have relaxed a little.

"How's your hut? Any problem with fleas?" asked Iosuke.

"No way. I've sprayed it with DDT."

"You're very up-to-date. But the toilet must be a problem."

"Not at all. There's a public toilet at Suidobashi Station. It's not far."

"How about water?"

"There's a spring on the embankment. It might even be the old Spring of Gold that Tokugawa Ieyasu found."

By the time they had been standing and talking for ten minutes, Iosuke was on good terms with the man. He was obviously the "intruder" mentioned at the gathering the night before, but Iosuke did not think he was a bad sort.

Iosuke was nearly a full-fledged trash-picker. Everyday he accompanied Kinji on his rounds and whatever they found would be converted into cash. The best items were sold to a buyer who came to the shacks every day, and with the extra income from the straw ash they made, Iosuke earned 150 yen a day, sometimes 200 yen.

Almost all the money was spent on food, but that was inevitable. When he and Kinji cooked, they ate rice every other day, making do with noodles or sweet potatoes the other days. The only person in that community who received a rice ration was Suzuki, because he was regularly employed. Everyone else had to buy rice on the black market. Nevertheless, they had a kind of pride in not relying on the rice ration. They were people brave enough to survive by their own efforts, not depending on the state.

The problem was, however, that there was little money left over.

"Whenever you have some extra cash," instructed the old man, "buy yourself a blanket."

But no such opportunity seemed likely. Iosuke did not possess any bedding. It was so hot he could not imagine needing any, but the old man's words were a warning to prepare for the winter.

Warm bedding was one thing, but what Iosuke desperately needed and was unable to buy was underwear. Exactly as Komako had predicted, with no other clothes to wear, Iosuke worked in the heat in his shirt until it reeked of sweat. He could wash his clothes in the trough, but not having even a loincloth to wear while waiting for them to dry was inconvenient. Taking pity on him, the old man searched a pile of rags and found some streamers used for the Children's Festival in May. From these old strips of cloth he fashioned a couple of loincloths for Iosuke. The old man had been a tailor and was good with a needle, but it was nevertheless unusual to see a man wearing a bright red and blue loincloth.

Another problem was bathing. There were public baths nearby at Yushima and Surugadai, but if the bath attendant deduced from their clothes that they were "from down there," even though it was closing time and there were few other bathers, they would be treated meanly, which left an unpleasant aftertaste.

"We're not beggars!" the easily aroused Ogiya had blustered after being turned away from one bathhouse, but the women could not even say that much. Both men and women only went to public baths with reluctance.

It became Iosuke's habit to wash late at night at the trough, splashing himself with cold water, but this might be hard in winter. Some of the others solved the problem by dressing more smartly and going to a bathhouse some distance away.

The people living by the river all possessed one set of good clothes, and the young men could look quite fashionable decked out in smart suit, tie, hat, and shoes. When they dressed this way to go to the movies or the red-light district, they did not stand out at all. Iosuke finally realized why the old man had advised him to hang on to his suit.

Kinji and Iosuke left very early each day, so that by the afternoon Iosuke had nothing to do.

He had no particular wish to visit the red-light district. Some imagine that people as large as he must have physical urges proportionate to their size, but that is simply not true. Corpulence does not necessarily entail a voracious sexual appetite. On the contrary, obesity can dull the sexual drive. Iosuke's needs had always been modest, which may have been one reason for Komako's dissatisfaction.

Not that he was dysfunctional or anything, but at times when he felt the urge he would stretch out on the grass in the shade of a large tree.

This is where he was that day.

There was a dip in the ground, making it perfect for gazing up at the heavens. The July skies were clear and blue, and, framed by the branches, looked high and distant. The few clouds were white and thin.

I wonder what Komako's up to.

Her sharp gaze and the curve of her nose floated before his eyes. He could see her freckles, especially the three big ones. He projected her face against the sky and studied it for a while, but all he could discern was that it was not unduly troubled. Komako was a woman who could earn a living and was not afraid of ghosts or robbers, so she would not be too inconvenienced by his absence. The face he saw was completely calm as she waited for her husband to come home, humble and contrite. She seemed armed and ready to deliver the requisite scolding and redouble her efforts to control his life.

He could accept that. To be the husband of a domineering wife was not as miserable as it looked. There were ways to escape those pressures. Even the Edo townspeople of a couple of centuries ago managed to lead enjoyable lives despite the feudal restrictions. He was ready to go back if she would just stop being so determined to win every time. He only wanted her to abandon her desire to conquer her husband. In his opinion, the domination of one partner by another ought to be a thing of the past. Besides, he considered himself a postwar husband who had waved the white flag of surrender years ago.

But Komako's face floating in the great blue yonder would not agree so easily.

So let's stay apart a little longer, he thought. That's fine with me. It's not too bad here.

This reaction was not one of sour grapes. Life at the bomb shelter had been miserable, but here Iosuke had adapted like a fish to water. He was free to do as he pleased, and the people were all kindred souls, as gentle and kindhearted as he himself. Moreover, the "society" that had so harassed him stopped at the edge of the embankment, high above. Down here was a group of individuals taking life as it came. No annoyances; no rent for house or land; no water bills; no donations for festivals; and, best of all, no tax!

This sudden realization filled Iosuke with such delight that he sat up, but his excitement was cut short by an urgent call for help.

"Come and help, quick!"

Mrs. Suzuki ran up, looking pale.

"What's happened?"

"Ogiya has gotten into a fight with the goat man. The other men are at work, so there's no one to help him. Come on."

"I'm no good at fights."

Iosuke tried to back away into the shrubs.

"Don't say that." She seized him by the sleeve and began pulling him toward the bridge.

There two men were fighting, dust flying everywhere.

The goat man was small, but he knew some judo. He was desperately attempting a hip throw, but it was ineffective as Ogiya was doubled over, with his rear end sticking out. The goat man's face was growing redder and redder.

"How about stopping there?"

Iosuke approached the two with a broad grin.

"Oh, it's you. See what you've done. I told you to get the word out, but as soon as I try to come through, this fellow tries to stop me."

The goat man glared at Iosuke.

He had indeed asked Iosuke to make the other residents let him pass. He had explained that a little way along the bank there was a path to Suidobashi, but when he wanted to go to Yushima Shrine, there was no other route except the one in front of the shacks.

"Yes, it's my fault. I meant to talk to everybody but I forgot." Iosuke quickly accepted the blame.

"Why should you apologize?" said Ogiya. "Come on, Iosuke, we mustn't let him get into bad habits. I'll give him something to remember!"

Iosuke's arrival had made Ogiya feel stronger, and when his opponent let down his guard, he seized the chance to deliver a solid blow to his head.

"You rat! I'll get you!" retorted the other, and there was no stopping them. They punched, they kicked, they bit—it was back to primeval times, a return to tooth and claw.

"Do something!" Mrs. Suzuki screamed. Women are indeed the more civilized species. Iosuke could not bear to watch, yet hesitated to use violence to end the fight. Finally, after several hesitant attempts, he thrust himself between the two men, probably the first time he had ever deliberately used his strength.

The action, however, had an unforeseen effect. The bodies of the two flew apart and rolled down the slope. They would have fallen straight into the Kanda River had they not been stopped by an iron bridge support.

"Iosuke is incredible!"

"He's so strong! Even ten of us would be no match for him!"

After the incident, the people in the shacks began treating Iosuke like a superhero. Mrs. Suzuki had been the only witness, but no one doubted her word.

The two men had picked themselves up but had lost all desire to fight on. They meekly submitted to Iosuke's suggestion to find a peaceful solution. The matter was settled when it was agreed that the goat man could pass in front of the shacks; in return, he would donate a bottle of liquor to the community.

Iosuke himself had no memory of using force to stop the fight, so he felt he had done nothing courageous. Far from it, when he had moved between them, flinging the men apart, he had felt awkward and had apologized profusely to them. That reaction, though stemming from timidity, was accepted as modesty. When a person who is very strong does not flaunt the fact, it proves he is genuinely strong.

The people under the bridge kept a dog for safety's sake. The world outside was dangerous, and one night a wanted criminal even wanted to stay there. But Iosuke, endowed with the strength of ten men, was much better than a dog. Komako and his colleagues at work had made fun of him, but here people looked up to him.

"How about a cup of tea." Iosuke was constantly being invited in by one neighbor or another. In this way, he learned the stories of all the people in the community.

Except for old Kinji, all of them were either repatriated soldiers or people whose houses had burned down. Before the war they had all led normal lives, so they complained a lot about their plight, but their sympathy for other people had by no means disappeared. The little boy at the Kawanos was not their own child but an orphan they had taken in. He disliked the orphanage he had been placed in and had constantly run away from it, but now he had been living happily here for a year and a half.

When Mrs. Suzuki was about to give birth, Iosuke was told, there was some concern that no midwife would agree to come. Her husband had finally gone to fetch the midwife in the middle of the night, but he had only told her where they were going when they were nearly there. The midwife had been surprised as well as apprehensive, and when they paid her the fee of 300 yen just the same as anyone else, she had been even more surprised.

"There's no difference between us and other people," Mrs. Suzuki said, seeking Iosuke's agreement.

There was nothing strange about their world except its isolation. Still, the postal system treated them fairly, and a letter addressed "Under Okanenomizu Bridge" would be delivered by a postman who climbed down the ladder with his bag on his shoulder like Santa Claus. That was the residents' only direct line of communication with the rest of the city.

Chapter 10
Troubled Times

Winning the respect of those around him made Iosuke complacent, to the extent that his innate laziness resurfaced. Essentially, he only needed to work to eat, and if he did not mind foregoing the luxury of white rice every day, one round of the streets each morning was enough to subsist on. These days he worked only enough to make 100 yen or so a day. There was little point in earning more. His supply of cigarettes came from the butts found on the street. His cold showers sufficed, so he did not need money for the bathhouse. He let his beard grow and spent nothing on newspapers. Cash was only necessary for buying the sweet potatoes or dried noodles that were his staple food.

Despite his diet's simplicity, Iosuke had not grown noticeably thinner, perhaps because he had been so overweight before. Or perhaps it was due to the peaceful state of his mind. He felt calmer and freer than at any time since his employment or his marriage to Komako.

Iosuke seemed to have achieved his objective much sooner than Komako, and he had attained it without a great deal of effort. After obeying his wife's command and leaving, he had let himself be guided by events, by the hand of fate, until he found himself in a place he had thought existed solely in his dreams.

He had never even imagined that he would find his own version of the Garden of Eden so quickly and so close to hand. He wondered if it was a hallucination, but even if it were, it bore a wonderful resemblance to what he had dreamed of. Here on the riverbank the invasiveness of society and the present age was minimal. There was ample space for an individual to breathe. It might not be the genuine article, but in current circumstances it was close enough.

In general, Iosuke was content and grateful, but his natural slothfulness began to assert itself. Paradise and hard work are incompatible. His two-hour stint each morning, with the rest of the day idled away, conformed neatly with the charter of the Garden of Eden. People around him would say, "That Iosuke doesn't seem to want anything," and admired him for it. They assumed he was never bothered about money.

But, in fact, he did want money. Now and then he yearned to be able to buy that fiery "bomb" at the Kanda market, but it seemed easier to suppress his desire than to work for the extra cash. Laziness is not a trait that can be easily corrected, and Iosuke was not the type to reform even if a hydrogen bomb hung over his head.

With so much time to spare, Iosuke eventually grew tired of reading the discarded newspapers and magazines collected by the trash-pickers and became bored with lying beneath the trees gazing at the clouds. At such times, he even missed his arguments with Komako. He needed someone to talk to.

One day it occurred to him to visit the goat owner.

The man had chosen to build his hut in a strange place. There was a path leading from the shacks to an area with dense trees, and the land rose steeply where the branches of the big willow hung down. The goat man had perched his dwelling in an awkward spot up there. Under the bridge was considered the best location, and below Keitendo Hospital the second-best. The choice of this isolated place midway, certainly the worst in terms of situation, must have been deliberate.

Slipping and sliding, Iosuke made his way up to the hut. Standing in front of it, he noticed that the wooden planks were now covered with straw matting, so it was no longer as rudimentary as before. Like all the shacks, it was constantly being improved.

"Hello? Are you home?" Iosuke called out, as though visiting a friend's apartment.

There was no answer. Despite the heat, a coarse mat hung over the doorway. Sounds showed there was someone inside.

After a considerable delay, the mat was lifted and the man glared out. "Who is it?" he asked sharply.

Iosuke had not told him his name, so he simply stood there, grinning.

"Oh, it's you."

It took the man a moment to recognize Iosuke, who was looking like a hermit, not having had a haircut or shaved for some time. He had also recently acquired the demeanor and air of a vagrant, so even Komako would not have recognized him had she passed him on the street.

"I just dropped by," said Iosuke in his usual easygoing way. "May I come in?"

"I don't care, but it's hot in here."

With a clatter the man opened two other doors, which swung outward like trapdoors and were propped up by poles. They let in a pleasant breeze. Crude though it might look from outside, the hut had a floor with canvas and tarred paper spread under the coarse matting, so it was well protected from the damp ground. Inside, apple crates stacked along one wall served as shelves that were neatly filled with dishes. The shack was reminiscent of a camp hut, and was more finished than any of those under the bridge.

"You've got a nice place here," Iosuke said, not out of politeness but from genuine admiration.

"Don't know what's so nice about it," said the man. "I'm used to small places like this. But you'd suffocate here in a day."

It was true that the hut was small, about half the size of Kinji's.

"I don't see you out in the streets in the mornings," said Iosuke, assuming that the man, too, must be in the scavenging trade. "Where are your usual rounds?"

"Well no, actually, I'm . . ." the man started to speak but then changed the subject. "How would you like some fresh goat's milk?"

The milk was in a beer bottle kept in the cold water of the spring on the embankment. It struck Iosuke that this man did things differently from the people under the bridge.

"Umm, tastes good." It had been a long time since Iosuke had drunk milk.

"Go ahead, drink it all," urged the man generously. " I have it every day and I'm tired of it."

He did not appreciate what a luxury milk was, thought Iosuke.

"You're living in style," said Iosuke admiringly. "With your house all neat and tidy, and spraying it with DDT and all."

Iosuke put down the aluminum cup he had been drinking from.

"You seem to be taking it nice and easy, too," said the man.

"I suppose so. If I had a little more money, I'd have no complaints."

"Incidentally, you've been to university, haven't you? You talk like an intellectual."

"I wouldn't call myself an intellectual."

"Do you speak English?" the man suddenly asked in English.

"No. Well, I learned it as well as German, but . . ."

"I knew it. You're right up there with the cream of the crop. What brought you down to a place like this? But you probably don't want to talk about it."

"You sound as if you graduated from university yourself."

134

"Not university. But I did go to a higher school, though it doesn't exist any more." He sniffed sadly and turned aside.

"Never mind. Life's not so bad. I'm usually free in the afternoons so come and visit me. My name's Minamimura Iosuke."

"Oh, sorry not to have introduced myself. I'm from Shikoku. The name's Kajiki Kenpei."

As soon as he had identified himself, the man seemed to regret it.

"I've been going by the name of Nakamura Taro, so I'd prefer you to call me that. Don't tell the people under the bridge my real name," he said.

He seemed quite anxious.

"I won't say anything," Iosuke said. "I don't even speak when I should, and I was always getting into hot water with my wife because of it."

"Thank you. I know I can trust you. Ever since that fight the other day, I've had you figured for a man of character. You're more than what you appear. Whatever did you in," he continued melodramatically, "must have been bitter and crushing—hard for a Japanese to endure."

"Not at all!" said Iosuke lightly. "My wife just told me to get out."

"You're not being straight, but I won't ask any more. Mr. Minamimura," said the man, his tone changing, "what do you think of the state of the country today? How can we let it go on like this? What's going to happen to Japan?"

"What do I think? I suppose it is what it is."

"What do you mean?"

"When a country loses a war, this always happens to it."

Iosuke's words sounded as though they had an enlightened man's detachment, but the truth was that he had given the matter little consideration. Since Japan's defeat, he'd been more concerned about his own circumstances.

Kajiki Kenpei was lost in thought. His face was typical of a man from the country—prominent cheekbones, narrow forehead, and swarthy complexion—marking him as a simple, uncomplicated man. He was thinking so hard that the veins on his temples stood out, and he seemed overcome by some indescribable sorrow.

"Only the gods can know that. Japanese shouldn't have to put up with these miserable conditions!"

Kajiki's declaration escaped him with a high-pitched hiss, like air coming out of a punctured tire.

"Is something the matter?" Iosuke was startled.

"There're different kinds of defeat. There's the defeat of Carthage. There's the defeat of the German Empire. There's the defeat of the Heike

135

clan and the Aizu clan—they all lost. But the way they lost was not the same. If a nation has to lose, it should lose in style. It should be a defeat to be proud of in the eyes of Heaven, the world at large, and the victors. Defeat in an orderly way, without rancor, admitting one's mistakes, acknowledging one's crimes, and cultivating the courage for renewal—that is the true way of defeat."

Kajiki seemed totally absorbed in his impassioned speech.

"But what have we got in Japan today? What is the matter with the people in Tokyo? It's worse than the defeat. It's a defeat messed up by internal chaos. If the people had taken defeat to heart, things would not have come to this. I am ashamed for the millions who died for their country."

Blinking back tears, Kajiki wiped his eyes with a deeply tanned arm.

Declamations of this type had never been Iosuke's strong point. Whenever his colleagues at the news agency got into serious discussions, he had always tried to slip away. Today, though, with Kajiki shedding anguished tears, he could not just look on unconcerned and he did his best to give noncommittal responses.

"Well, people are exhausted and confused."

"Don't use those words! People shouldn't be let off so easy. You're too lenient. How many years have passed since the surrender on the *Missouri*? How long are we going to let this corruption continue? Have you any idea what terrible things are going on in this city? I want you to see them and I'll be happy to show you. Seeing is believing—it will change your ideas. And then I may ask a favor of you. But that's for later. How about going out now?"

Kajiki Kenpei was a strange fellow, and he was determined to show Iosuke what he called "the dark side" of Tokyo. Iosuke, with his ingrained laziness, was not particularly eager to see the dark side, the bright side, or any other side, but he could not bring himself to reject the other's suggestion outright, so he went along.

As they were leaving, however, Kajiki complained about Iosuke's appearance.

"You can't go out with that beard. You look as if you're just back from the jungles of Guadalcanal." He produced a safety razor from one of the apple boxes and told Iosuke to shave.

This took some time, but once rid of his bushy black beard Iosuke's next problem was his clothes.

"A suit is the least noticeable," said Kajiki. "Have you got one?"

After Iosuke had put on his suit, Kajiki was not the only one startled.

Both Mrs. Suzuki and Mrs. Takasugi were moved to comment with knowing chuckles, "Oh, Mr. Minamimura, you look the perfect gent. Where can you be off to?"

Indeed, clean-shaven and dressed in his woolen suit, Iosuke did not fit the surroundings, although the others did not realize how he was suffering in the heat of early August.

"Just don't ask me to wear a tie!"

The shirt he had washed was full of creases, and he undid its top buttons.

They set off with Kajiki in the lead. He had been critical of Iosuke's appearance, but he himself was casually dressed in a short-sleeved polo shirt and khaki trousers. This was probably the most common summer outfit in the city and was thus unobtrusive.

They climbed up the ladder, coming out beside the main road, and were immediately assailed by the smells of the city. They were the odors of gasoline and steel, borne on a southwesterly breeze, but to Iosuke they recalled the society to which he had once belonged. It was never like this when he went out on his early morning rounds, so why should he feel so differently now? He concluded it was because he had put on his suit for the first time in a while.

"Now, where shall we begin?" Kajiki said to himself. After pausing by the road, he headed in the direction of Suidobashi Station.

"Let's go somewhere not too difficult," suggested Iosuke, as they walked down the slope. "For a fellow who lives where you do, you seem to know the city well."

"I know Tokyo's back streets and its dark side better than any journalist," said Kajiki with some pride.

"What work do you do? Not one of the night trades, I suppose?" Iosuke teased.

"Don't be ridiculous," protested Kajiki. "You think I'm a thief or a burglar? I'll soon show you."

At Suidobashi Station they boarded a tram. Kajiki glared in the direction of the baseball and bicycle-racing stadiums at Korakuen Park.

"Just look at those people!" he muttered. "Every one of them has forgotten we lost the war."

When the tram reached the end of the line in the entertainment district, they got off, and Kajiki began looking around him as though in search of something.

"It may be too early to find a good example."

The square in front of the station was full of businessmen rushing to catch their trains and housewives hurrying about their day's shopping. Only the two of them were strolling around in a leisurely way.

Beckoning to Iosuke, Kajiki took the long elevated walkway to the west side of the station. There the view was completely different. Almost all the houses had been built since the war. The shops were ramshackle affairs with garish facades. Their goods spilled out into the street and were protected from the sun by reed canopies. The whole area bustled with life.

"They're good specimens."

Kajiki indicated two young men looking like students who had emerged from a shop with a red sign reading "Mahjong."

"Dammit!" one of the students was saying, "Couldn't win a thing in there." His gaudy tie hung loosely around his white shirt collar, and his student coat was slung over one shoulder with a swaggering defiance.

"But when you tried 'fishing' in there . . ." drawled the other, gesturing as he walked. His aloha shirt was open down the front, and a cigarette dangled from his lips. His chin was spotted with pimples, and they both had long hair, with their caps worn at an angle and threatening to slip off any moment. Their shoes of brown leather looked expensive.

Kajiki began to follow the youths, signaling to Iosuke to do the same.

Iosuke had not been close to students like these for some time. In fact, they did not even look like students, and he wondered if they were only pretending. Any connection with knowledge and learning seemed improbable. When Iosuke was at university, there were plenty of students who should not have been there. Their mental abilities and temperament were better suited to learning landscape gardening or dyeing or another useful craft. But a diploma had been the guarantee of a monthly paycheck, which was why those with no love of book learning went to university. But had times not changed? It was a mystery why anyone would want to wear those outmoded university caps if they did not have to.

The students turned down a side street, which soon grew narrow, twisting and turning this way and that. The area was packed with bars and shops selling secondhand clothing. In one long, narrow store, people were gathered around a horseshoe-shaped counter and a woman was calling something out in a shrill voice. The students joined the crowd.

"What's this?" asked Iosuke.

"It's bingo." The sight obviously made Kajiki livid. "They've been defeated in war, and now this is all they do!"

138

Before Iosuke could work out this new form of gambling, the two students returned to the street. They seemed easily bored. Urging Iosuke on, Kajiki continued following them.

"Did you see that? Even children were there!" said Kajiki with a grimace. Iosuke had noticed a child of twelve or thirteen sitting at the counter like an experienced player.

Having come to a decision at the bingo parlor, the students began to move more quickly to another destination. On the way they bought ice-candy sticks and were licking them as they cut through alleys that were obviously familiar to them until they came to a street of makeshift huts. Cheap wooden structures were everywhere, but these were particularly run-down. It was still early, so few people were about. Every house, however shabby, looked as though it sold food and drink, although there was no smell of cooking. On the contrary, the prevailing odor was of dirty gutters.

As if to cover up some feeling of guilt, the students began humming a popular tune as they ducked into one of the houses.

"I knew they'd come here." Kajiki was congratulating himself on his prescience.

"Where's this? Somewhere like Tamanoi?" asked Iosuke, naming one of the cheaper red-light districts.

"Much worse. For your edification, I'm going to show you what students are up to these days."

Kajiki walked boldly into the house next door.

"Welcome," called a woman, who was wearing only a slip. "You're a bit early." It was three in the afternoon, but she was brushing her teeth.

"We're not here to buy. We want this," said Kajiki, cupping his hands like binoculars in front of his eyes.

"But there aren't any customers yet," she protested.

"Two just went inside."

"Oh, you've been keeping an eye out!" she said.

Kajiki and Iosuke drank a beer while waiting in the small, earth-floored hall. Five minutes later the woman came back and whispered something in Kajiki's ear.

Poking Iosuke in the leg, Kajiki said quietly, "Follow her."

Iosuke did not understand what was going on. He was told to take his shoes off and was led into a dirty two-mat room with a window overlooking the grass in the back garden. Beside the window was a ladder leading to the attic, and the woman signaled that he should climb quietly. In the room above he had to bend to avoid hitting his head. The woman came up after him. She opened a cupboard fixed to the wall at waist height and thrust Iosuke into it like a piece of luggage. In the wall in front of him was a small hole with glass in it. Through it one could see into a room in the neighboring house.

There were two bodies there. The one in the man's position was the student with the tie. But he no longer had his tie on—nor his shirt, nor anything else.

"So what did you think? Shocking, right?" That was the first thing Kajiki asked when they met the next day.

"Maybe, but it's nothing to do with the defeat. Students in Marseilles have been doing that since way back."

The "sights" Kajiki had intended to shock Iosuke with the day before may have been revolting, but they had not upset him. Perhaps he was thick-headed.

"So you don't care if students do such disgusting things?"

"Students were always outrageous, even in my time." Iosuke recalled how around 1932 or 1933, when a taste for the erotic and the grotesque had been all the rage, students had fallen under its spell. One of his classmates had even boasted of sponging off a prostitute for the money to play around. The vices of the students the day before could be considered light in comparison; postwar students were simply following the vices of their predecessors since the Meiji era. Moreover, considering that they had to get their kicks so cheaply that they became the target of peeping toms, they were more to be pitied.

"Nothing seems to upset you, so today I'm going to show you something different." Iosuke's lack of reaction made Kajiki even more determined to find something that would arouse him.

"I'm sorry but I've had enough," Iosuke protested. "For one thing, I don't want you to waste money on this."

He meant it. Kajiki must have spent five or six hundred yen the previous day.

"Don't worry about that. I have something in mind, and for that I need you to be aware of present realities. I'm talking about a cause for the good of the nation, so it's money well spent."

It was unclear what the "cause" was, but Kajiki seemed to have cash, which was curious in itself. The day before he had had a thick wad of notes. He said he was not a thief, but could he be trusted? Iosuke had never given much thought when selecting friends, so he did not bother about the background or character of this unusual man.

"If I do as you ask, will I have to wear my suit?" Iosuke asked.

Iosuke had been uncomfortable the day before. Recently he only felt good in his work clothes. Moreover, if he noticed a good cigarette stub on the street, somehow his hand would not do his bidding when he was wearing a suit. It made him feel constrained, as it was supposed to, and did not allow him the freedom he wanted.

"No one will respect you if you're dressed like a vagrant. Besides, I'm hoping to put you in a morning coat one of these days."

Iosuke had no idea what he was talking about.

That day Kajiki took Iosuke to Asakusa.

First, they went to a strip show at the Rappaza theater. Iosuke had had a foretaste of this in Shinjuku, so he did not find it shocking. Next was a movie about childbirth, but despite all the blood it was no more gruesome than photographs of accidents often seen in newspapers.

"Nothing seems to shock you!" Kajiki complained.

"Everyone knows about all the shady things going on in Tokyo," said Iosuke.

"Yes. And don't you think the fact that people take it for granted is disgusting? Let me try a different tack."

Kajiki began to walk faster. They passed out of the entertainment area and much farther, until Iosuke, who was unfamiliar with Asakusa, had no idea where they were. As they proceeded, the traces of the bombing were still evident, with empty plots here and there. Most of the new structures had signs identifying them as inns. Before the war, this area had been full of cheap lodgings for traveling merchants, and in their place had been built traditional-style "restaurants" bearing signs with three vertical wavy lines in red, the symbol for a hot spring, and boards with large letters proclaiming "X Hundred Yen for Short-time Stay."

"These are cheap hotels with hourly rates. They're all over Tokyo. That hot spring mark is the give-away. It shows the state of our morals since the war. What's happened to this country? It's as if the entire population has suddenly come into heat."

Standing in the middle of a street surrounded by such establishments, Kajiki was fuming. As they walked on, the number of inns diminished and the area became residential. Many of the houses had signs advertising dentists.

"These 'dentists' are where they fix what results from the inns," said Kajiki.

141

"You mean people get cavities from eating too many sweets?" Iosuke asked in all innocence.

"Don't be stupid," scolded Kajiki. "The signs say 'dentist,' but they're for abortions."

It made Iosuke feel very strange, imagining how their techniques might overlap those for extracting teeth.

They went farther, and at one point Kajiki made Iosuke wait outside a coffee shop while he inquired inside. When he emerged he said, "There's something unusual along here."

He turned off into a street with more establishments, though without any hot spring signs, which were avoided as a means of dodging taxes.

Inside one of these, a woman wearing nothing except the top half of a bicycle racer's uniform was pedaling on a stationary bicycle. Iosuke thought it was a ludicrous sight.

"What do you think? Revolting, right?" Kajiki asked confidently. But Iosuke was unmoved.

"Well, it's no more revolting than that childbirth film, is it? Except there's no baby."

The next day Kajiki took him out again.

"It would be better to go at night," said Kajiki, leading the way up the steps at Ueno Station toward the bronze statue of the Meiji leader Saigo Takamori. Iosuke had made it clear that nighttime excursions were out of the question since he had to wake up for work in the morning. In fact, he was beginning to dread the "sights" even in the daytime.

"Listen," said Kajiki sternly. "Keep your eyes peeled and see how depraved people have become. Of course, you can't see all the decadence at one time. I can't show you the wicked doings of politicians, bureaucrats, businessmen, or university professors. But, like a doctor who takes your pulse to diagnose an illness, you can gauge the overall problem by examining the symptoms. A glimpse from the edge of this vile society will demonstrate how bad things are. The past few days I've been showing you society at its worst, and yet you seem unfazed. I'm beginning to lose patience," said Kajiki, revealing his frustration. "Please take what you see to heart."

Iosuke was not just being stubborn or pretending not to be bothered; that he was not shocked by what he saw was due to his placid nature. In fact, the decadence Kajiki had taken such pains to show him had been fully exposed in such weeklies as *Bunmei Shunju* and *Shukan Ashita*. Newspapers and magazines, perhaps from habits formed when reporting on the army's overseas campaigns, were documenting it all with great enthusiasm. In the past two or three years, countless articles had appeared about Ueno Park, sometimes disguised as Nogami Park. One salacious story followed another, and Iosuke had lost interest, so when he learned that Kajiki was taking him there, the prospect depressed him.

"This whole area is out of bounds after dark," said Kajiki, walking while eyeing the grounds around the red Shimizudai buddha hall as if it were a veritable gathering place of criminals. It was midday, so the homeless were napping here and there in the shade. Now that he was one of them, Iosuke did not find them unpleasant or squalid.

"They're doing it over there."

Kajiki lowered his voice and gestured with his eyes toward the shadows behind the buddha hall.

A young street boy of thirteen or fourteen was standing with his shirt-sleeve rolled up and his arm extended while a scruffy, middle-aged man held a syringe.

"That's the stimulant drug called philopon," said Kajiki. The boy's eyes were sparkling with health, and he looked like a teenager getting a typhus shot from the school doctor.

"Now children are becoming addicts," lamented Kajiki. "It's the worst thing that can happen."

But Iosuke did not feel the sight was so heinous. It made him remember the time—how old had he been?—when he had started smoking behind his father's back.

Kajiki pointed out the shelters, some quite imaginative, that the tramps had built among the tombs in the cemetery and behind the billboards beside the train tracks, but they differed little from the shanties he now called home, so there was no surprise there either.

Kajiki's anecdotes about a prostitute being murdered here or morphine being sold there were hardly riveting, especially in the daytime when the park was empty and peaceful. The public toilet said to be frequented by perverts simply stank, Iosuke thought. When told about a police box officer who fell for a prostitute he had arrested and resigned from his job to become a pimp, Iosuke knew he might have done the same in that situation.

"You're a difficult case, Mr. Minamimura. I thought you'd get the point by now. There's only one place left. Want to go to Ikenohata?

Iosuke's apathy was beginning to exhaust even Kajiki.

"I've had enough. Let's go back," said Iosuke, wiping the sweat from the back of his neck with his hand.

"Stopping now would be like a priest giving a hundred days of sermons and ending with a fart—it would make it all meaningless. Let's go to Asakusa one more time. A lot goes on there. What you saw the other day was only a sample."

"But it's so hot."

Kajiki was all sinew and bone and could not imagine how much Iosuke was suffering with his thick layer of flesh.

"You can bear a little warmth, can't you? It's for the good of the nation."

Iosuke had no ready response to this.

"Let's stroll over to Asakusa."

"We're going to walk?"

"It's not a waste of time," said Kajiki. "Tramps and criminals often go back and forth between Ueno and Asakusa, so we'll see lots of signs of them. I'll tell you what to look for."

The indefatigable Kajiki led the way, with Iosuke following reluctantly.

In front of Ueno Station, the street was filled with the "Nogami tribe," a crowd of raffish men and women. Kajiki, aware that most people knew all about them, hurried across without stopping.

Turning into a side street, he continued in silence. When they came to a large concrete building like a ward office, he stopped as if he had had an idea.

"Mr. Minamimura, you look hot. How about a bath?"

It was a tempting suggestion, and a bath was exactly what Iosuke wanted. He was desperate to have a proper soak in a tub. Using the cold water by the river had made his skin dry and scaly. Today, he was in his suit, so he could enter a public bathhouse without causing any complaint.

Kajiki bought a towel and a small bar of soap at a nearby shop.

"In you go," he said, handing them to Iosuke. "Take your time."

"You're not coming?"

"I'll wait here," said Kajiki. "The effect will be bigger if you're alone."

Iosuke did not understand, but he was not bothered.

It was an ordinary back street bathhouse. Far from large, it had been built since the war. Sliding open the frosted-glass door Iosuke saw three other bathers at the taps in the washing area. It was nearly four o'clock, and the lack of bathers at this hour showed that life had grown more stable. The days when bathhouses had been crowded all day had passed. Barbershops and bathhouses, thought Iosuke, were gradually rising above the postwar chaos.

The bath attendant at the entrance gave Iosuke a friendly greeting.

As he was undressing and placing his clothes in a basket in the changing room, Iosuke suddenly remembered his brightly colored underwear, but fortunately no one noticed and he quickly hid it under his trousers.

When he strode naked into the washing area, the other bathers turned to stare at him, not only because of his unusual height and size but because his skin was unblemished and his flesh was as plump and soft as a freshly peeled white peach. He was fairer than Komako, and he recalled how Komako had once given him a playful pinch and said grudgingly, "You've got good curves for a man." That had been a long time ago.

The water in the large tub was still clean, and when Iosuke got in the water level rose noticeably. It was heavenly. Iosuke loved a soak more than anything, and it always distressed him that after the war Komako and he were too poor to afford a proper bath at home. It made him appreciate the luxury of a big bath all the more.

He got out of the tub and began to soap and wash himself vigorously, peeling off weeks of old encrusted skin. It had been six weeks since his last visit to the Surugadai bathhouse, so it was not surprising that so much dried skin came off as he scrubbed. He was feeling clean and fresh, when it occurred to him that Kajiki must have an ulterior motive in bringing him here. There was not even a whiff of the dregs of society Kajiki was always trying to expose him to. Perhaps your clothes would be stolen, and Kajiki had sent him in as a trial. But two of the three bathers had already left, and when he looked over at the basket with his clothes at the far end of the changing room, nothing seemed amiss. The remaining bather was a harmless old man.

Kajiki, you made a mistake, thought Iosuke, and he started to shampoo his hair, working up a lather and scrubbing his head thoroughly. It was when he rinsed off and raised his head that he got the shock of his life.

At first Iosuke thought it was an illusion.

He decided he had entered the women's bath by mistake. He calmed himself and noticed that the old man was still calmly wiping his wizened back, so he couldn't have made a mistake. But four women were making for the washing taps—it must be they who were breaking the rules.

"Get me that basin, will you, dear?"

"Lazybones! Here you are!"

"Thank you, dear. Lovely it's so empty today."

"Yes. When it's crowded I'm too embarrassed to put my makeup on properly."

145

No way they could be the same sex as himself, thought Iosuke. In the enamel basins with red and green patterns they carried were soap, bottles of shampoo powder, and other toiletries, and their hair was done up in both Western and Japanese styles. They had no powder on their faces, but there were traces of it. You did not have to be a genius to conclude that these were women next to him.

How could women charge brazenly into the men's bath without any complaint from the bath attendant? It wasn't a hot spring with mixed bathing. Was it a custom peculiar to this old part of the city?

Perhaps this was what Kajiki is talking about—the breakdown of society. Iosuke tried to think of some explanation. Maybe it was still too early for the women's bath to be open. This would never have happened before the war.

Iosuke was shocked. His upbringing had been good, and he had a gentleman's modesty. He was also a timid man, and the idea of being naked with women other than his wife was not to his taste. It made his heart pound and his head throb.

The women got into the tub and took their time soaking, their heads bobbing above the water. Some of them stared quite openly at Iosuke.

"Renko, how was it last night? Good?"

"No, a disaster! Why is everyone so poor these days?"

"Summer's always dry, but it's a real drought this year. One can hardly earn enough to buy cigarettes."

"If only someone would fall in love with me and be my steady boyfriend."

The woman who said this was flashing coquettish glances in Iosuke's direction.

"Now, now," one of the others answered, "don't be setting your sights too high." All four burst out laughing. Their voices were strangely low and resonant, like the husky female singer Kasagi Shizuko.

From the women's bath on the other side of the wall came the sound of splashing and high-pitched women's voices punctuated by similar outbursts of mirth.

Iosuke became more perplexed since the women's bath was obviously open and being used. And the voices from the other side of the wall were clearly not the same as the women's voices on his side. They were as different as solid metal and cheap plate—miles apart.

There was something odd about the women on this side. Their conversation revealed their work involved serving clients, but flaunting the rules by brazenly invading the men's bath was more than shocking—it was downright incomprehensible.

Iosuke had hoped for one more soak in the bath, but he did not want to get in with the four women. He remained at the taps, washing his face again and again and trying to look inconspicuous.

Eventually the women got out of the tub, one after the other. They seemed to like doing everything together, and they sat in a line in front of the taps, too.

"Give me your towel." The second woman began to wash the back of the first one, while the third began to soap the back of the second one, and so on. They reminded Iosuke of a woodblock print he had once seen of a group of blind men taking a bath.

Noticing that the tub was now empty, Iosuke plunged in and tried to calm himself by looking at the painting of the picturesque islands at Matsushima on the wall. He was still thinking about those women. It was not his eros that was aroused but his curiosity. Surreptitiously he turned his head and saw the women were now scrubbing their own bodies. Their gestures were as graceful and as demure as any well-bred woman's. Discreetly concealing what they should and twisting their bodies this way and that while soaping themselves, like a scene from an ukiyoe print, their voices and the language they used seemed incongruous.

After one of them sat in front of the mirror and covered her chin with foam, a grating sound of shaving was audible. A normal woman would not do that, and as Iosuke looked over he became aware of the woman's Adam's apple. Then he noticed that all the women had Adam's apples. Suspicious, he allowed his gaze to stray to the women's bodies despite his embarrassment.

What he saw—or rather did not see—almost made him exclaim out loud. Their chests were as flat as the back of a hand, without the slightest undulation.

Iosuke felt a shiver run through him. He felt sick, as if he had sniffed poison gas. He wanted to escape from there as fast as he could. He stepped out of the tub and had begun to dry himself when one of the women accosted him.

"My dear, what a beautiful body you have. Let me help you." As the soft hand brushed his back, Iosuke let out a silent scream and ran for the changing room.

In a panic, Iosuke had no idea how he managed to pull on his shirt and trousers. He did not even tie his shoelaces. Only out in the street, with the cool

147

evening breeze on his face, did his world return to normal. But far from the usual freshness associated with a bath, he felt more like a traveler who has barely managed to climb out of a gorge haunted by demons and ogres. What relief to have escaped unscathed!

The feeling of those soft, slug-like fingers across his back lingered. With a shiver he tried to suppress the memory.

I've had my fill of Nogami. All I want to do is get on a train and head back to Okanenomizu. Everything's wholesome and peaceful there, and the people are good.

He turned to go back the way they had come.

"Hey, Mr. Minamimura! I'm over here!" Kajiki called out to him from a little shop selling shaved ice.

"You look pale. What's happened?" Kajiki motioned for Iosuke to sit down. "How about some ice water?"

"Give me something fizzy like cider or soda pop—something cleansing."

Iosuke talked as if he had a hangover.

Kajiki waited for him to finish drinking before asking, "Well, what did you think?"

Iosuke replied in a low voice, "It was a shock."

"So it got to you? You finally saw something that shocked you!"

Kajiki looked at Iosuke, unconvinced.

"These are troubled times, chaotic, as you like to say," Iosuke began. "I was completely taken by surprise. Even now I haven't got over it. But are they male or female?"

Kajiki could not figure out why Iosuke was so frightened by something he did not understand.

"Even without their clothes on, you didn't recognize them?"

"No."

"They're the famous denizens of Nogami. They visit that bathhouse before they go out on the streets at night."

Finally, even the slow Iosuke grasped what Kajiki meant. But it made him feel no better. He wanted to take another bath to wash the memory away.

"Mr. Minamimura, if you're being honest when you say the times are troubled, then as a man who loves his country, you can't keep quiet about it any longer, right?"

Kajiki had turned solemn.

"You mean about these being troubled times? Yes, that's my opinion, but . . ." Iosuke began.

"No buts. You're committed now."

Chapter 11
Man of the Underground

"I'll tell you about myself," Kajiki began. "I was in the navy and I committed a grave, no, an inexcusable error in the service of my country."

Sitting under the willow tree near his hut, Kajiki finally recounted his story to Iosuke. He had begun telling it in the eatery in Ueno, but had stopped for fear of being overheard. Not until they were back at this isolated spot did he feel safe enough to continue.

The sun had set, plunging the riverbank into darkness. Only Kajiki's cheekbones caught the glow from the floodlights of the Occupation forces apartments at the top of the embankment.

Kajiki spoke of Japan's defeat and the responsibility of the professional military for it. Those people could never atone for it, he grieved, even if they were reborn seven times. And he was personally guilty of a serious offense.

"You're a layman, so you may not know how important the Battle of the Solomon Islands was. Before that battle we were winning and our night tactics had brought us a string of victories. We were almost convinced we were unbeatable. After that, our fortunes changed, and we were put on the defensive."

Kajiki was a lieutenant in charge of torpedoes on a destroyer. In the fighting near Savo Island, something strange happened. Although the nights were pitch black, the enemy's shells and torpedoes began to hit with great accuracy. The Japanese navy had trained men to see in the dark like owls, but they were no match for the enemy. At first he suspected a spy was on board, but that was disproved. Finally he became convinced that some god must be on the enemy's ship, and the only way to win was to kill this god or take him prisoner. After a fierce argument with the captain, he instigated a bold attack, attempting to ram their ship into an enemy vessel, but they were sunk before it even hit.

Almost all the men aboard perished. Kajiki himself managed to stay afloat until morning, when he found his way to a small island and was helped by the natives living on it. Later, Japanese soldiers from a transport ship that had sunk reached the same island, and there they remained until the end of the war. To uphold the honor of the navy, he concealed his military affiliation and assumed the name of Nakamura Taro in order to pass himself off as a civilian. During the winter after the end of the war they were picked up by a British vessel and repatriated. When he discovered that he was listed as deceased in the family register, he decided to keep on using his pseudonym.

"As a navy man I felt responsible for the defeat, but after I got back to Japan I learned that the 'god' giving the advantage to the enemy at Savo Island was radar. I will never be able to atone to those who died on my ship or to my country for my error of judgment." Kajiki's voice was trembling with emotion.

He went on to describe how he had lived since then. The account was long on abstractions but short on specifics.

"I could have followed procedures to have myself reinstated as a living person, but my family register says I'm dead and my name's already buried. I am no longer strictly a Japanese—or at least I'm not a person subject to Japanese law. The Penal Code doesn't apply to the dead, nor does the Civil Code. Can a ghost be arrested? So I realized I had attained complete freedom. At the same time I thought that this freedom was not my own possession and I must offer it to my country and my comrade-in-arms in apology for my terrible mistake. And I began to think how I could atone for it."

With excellent health and a dogged nature, he worked in the black market, donating the money he earned to the families of deceased servicemen and helping street orphans. However, soon he began to feel overwhelmed, as though he was trying to extinguish a huge blaze with a water pistol. He realized that in order to help people he had to get large sums of money flowing into the country. He had studied life in the city of Tokyo and concluded that poverty was the cause of all society's ills. What people needed most was not morals or culture but money. They yearned for the jingle of coins, not the clanging of the bells of liberty. So, he resolved, his atonement should take the form of filling the country's coffers.

"I found two comrades who thought the same way," Kajiki went on. "They, too, had been listed as dead, and they are also concerned about the plight of our country. They say there are many 'living dead' like us. We three formed the War Responsibility League, and we have a project. Until recently, we each had a home and went about our work in the open, but now we have to lie low, so we've gone underground. We're dead anyway, and that's where the dead are—underground. We all live in different areas and meet in secret when necessary. I decided to live here. With trains and people passing overhead, I feel literally underground."

As Kajiki finished, his tone changed.

"Mr. Minamimura, you look like one of the living dead. Even if you didn't fight in the war, you obviously want to withdraw from society. And you have presence, which is rare today. You don't need to deny it. I know a giant when I see one. And I want to ask you to join our group and help us."

Iosuke had no idea what to say.

"But I'm nobody."

"The Meiji leader Saigo Takamori never called himself a hero, either."

"I'm only here because my wife told me to get out of the house."

"The old Oishi Kuranosuke story with a new twist! You're clever," Kajiki said, laughing.

He was referring to the hero of the eighteenth-century story of the forty-seven *ronin*. Pretending to abandon his family, Oishi had led a dissolute life to disguise his plan to avenge the death of his lord. Kajiki's knowledge of history was evidently based on the tales of *kodan* storytellers. It was annoying, however, that he insisted on casting Iosuke in a role created by his imagination. His self-confidence was unshakable.

"You're a giant of a man and I'm a little fellow. I babble on, telling you all my secrets, but there's no need for you to do the same. I ask you nothing about yourself. More important, Mr. Minamimura, do you think Japan is in a mess?"

"I suppose so."

The memory of the public bath—with that sluglike hand on his back—was still vivid.

"It's time for you to come out of your retreat," said Kajiki, alluding to the way the great strategist of ancient China had been lured out of his retirement in *Romance of Three Kingdoms*. "I think we have shown you enough courtesy by now."

"I agree the plight of the country is grave, but I'm not ambitious enough to try and do anything about it. I'm hopeless at business, and I'm lazy and useless, as my wife used to remind me all the time."

"That doesn't matter. It's what impresses me about you. There's no need for you to be involved in the actual work. We just need you as a big calm presence in the background. When we want you to do something, we'll tell you. You will be our figurehead, a symbol for us."

If that was all, thought Iosuke, it sounded easy, but he still felt he should find out a little more before agreeing.

"So what business are you in?" he asked, lowering his voice. "Bootleg liquor? Contraband cigarettes?"

"It's better if you don't know for the time being. Eventually you'll hear more than you want to about it. It's best for the nation if our figurehead is not endangered. All you should know is that our aim is to bring foreign capital into Japan. No matter how lucrative black-market alcohol or cigarettes may be, that money only circulates in Japan itself and does not make the nation richer. But that's enough for the moment. All I expect from you is one word—yes."

Kajiki extended his hand in the darkness and gripped Iosuke's. Iosuke gave no answering squeeze, yet Kajiki was ecstatic.

"Thank you so much!"

The following day Kajiki's attitude toward Iosuke had altered completely, and the change was pleasant enough. Not only did he let Iosuke drink as much goat's milk as he wanted, but he gave him real cigarettes—not butts picked up off the streets—as well as a wad of ten 100-yen notes he called "secret funds." Iosuke had no idea why he would need secret funds, but the money freed him from the need to work, and doing nothing was very welcome. The sight of Iosuke idling away his time would have set tongues wagging anywhere else, but here it caused no comment; it was an individualist's paradise. Old Kinji simply assumed that Iosuke had found a wallet full of cash and treated him the same as always.

Iosuke was now free from early morning and could visit Kajiki anytime, but the man was more often out than in. Iosuke had no idea where he went, but it was accepted that Iosuke could come and go as he pleased, and could even take a nap in the hut, treating it as a second home. Iosuke liked animals and would sometimes feed the goat with bran kept in the hut.

Iosuke was tending the goat one day when it began to rain. Unwilling to leave the animal in the wet, he brought it to the hut and tethered it under the eaves. Kajiki let the goat shelter under the jutting roof at night.

Wanting to get out of the rain himself, Iosuke went inside the hut. With their roofs and the bridge overhead, the shacks of Kinji and the others had double protection against the rain, but one result of this was that they did not hear the sound of rain falling on the roofs. As Iosuke listened nostalgically to the drumming of raindrops, he found himself thinking of Komako.

I wonder if she's having an easy time. Or . . .

A startling image of Komako enjoying herself flashed into his mind. Suppose she had taken up with a man? It was fashionable nowadays to have a boyfriend.

It had never occurred to Iosuke that Komako might be unfaithful to him. Komako had always been the jealous one, so it was his first experience with this disagreeable emotion. The new constitution had given wives the freedom to fall in love, so Iosuke was in no position to complain. His jealousy smoldered but failed to ignite, and he let out a groan.

Just then the goat bleated. Goats are intelligent animals, and whenever this one saw Kajiki or Iosuke, it would bleat in friendly recognition. However, this was more like a cry of alarm, as if it had detected a stranger. A moment later, Iosuke heard something hit the ground behind the hut.

Braving the rain, Iosuke went to look. Nothing seemed amiss, but a lead-colored can like a tea canister was on the grass. People often threw trash down the embankment, and he assumed that's what it was, except that the can was new. Iosuke, now accustomed to picking up anything that might be of use, took it into Kajiki's hut.

Stretched out like an ailing serpent, Iosuke's thoughts returned to Komako, causing him to let out occasional moans. He finally dozed off with a wretched expression on his face, like a child who has cried himself to sleep.

He had no idea how long he had slept, but he was woken by Kajiki's voice.

"Sorry to have kept you waiting."

Dressed in dirty working clothes, Kajiki did not look wet, so the rain must have stopped.

"You weren't here, and I fell asleep."

"No problem. It's reassuring to have you here when I'm out."

"By the way, do you have a wife?" asked Iosuke suddenly.

His dream about Komako had provoked the question.

"Couldn't be bothered!" was the immediate response.

"You're divorced then."

"Never had a wife. I was in the navy. In the war, being a soldier was popular and lots of men took advantage of enlistment to rush into marriage before leaving for the front, but not me. It's better to be single when you're living underground. Besides, I don't care for women!"

"You prefer the ones in the bath the other day?"

Iosuke felt on good enough terms with Kajiki to joke.

Kajiki flushed. "What nonsense you come out with!" Then he spotted the metal can in the corner.

"What's this?"

Iosuke told him he had found it on the grass.

"It's a good thing you were here." As if talking to himself, he added, "He ought to have checked I'm home before leaving it. It's careless."

Peeling off the tape that sealed it, Kajiki removed the lid and took out a folded piece of paper. From what Iosuke could see, the penciled message was written in code.

Kajiki looked at his watch and then turned to Iosuke.

"Mr. Minamimura, I need you to put in your first appearance tonight. Do you have anything better than that suit of yours?" Kajiki seemed suddenly impatient.

"No. It's all I have!"

"It'll have to do. Get changed and I'll take you to the barber."

Like a couple of bats darting out at dusk, the two emerged and climbed the embankment and the stone steps leading to Nikolai Cathedral Bridge.

Kajiki was on his guard, as always, checking ahead and behind. When he was satisfied, he flagged a passing White Line taxi with a practiced gesture.

"Okachimachi," he told the driver.

The way he had opened the door and got in revealed he was no stranger to taking taxis. Even before Iosuke left home, he was more likely to spend money on drinks than on a taxi ride.

Kajiki was a curious character. He had not told Iosuke what they were to do, and the latter, accorded the honorable role of "figurehead," felt it improper to ask.

Kajiki had the driver stop in a crowded street near Okachimachi Station. He led the way under the train tracks, then circled around to pass under the tracks again and emerge on the west side. After weaving through a maze of dark alleys, they came to what looked like an ordinary two-story house. It would have been much quicker to come straight here.

The first floor was occupied by a hardware store. In an alley at the side was a door with a wooden signboard reading "Shogi Publishing," *shogi* meaning "clear loyalty."

Kajiki slid open the door and went up the stairs, which creaked under Iosuke's weight as he followed Kajiki. At the top were closed sliding partitions.

Kajiki called out a greeting, and, following a reply from within, he slid a partition to one side and entered. The eight-mat room was furnished with some office tables and chairs. A man with the sleeves of his white shirt rolled up turned toward them.

154

"All's well?"

"All's well," echoed Kajiki before introducing Iosuke to the man.

"This is Hayashi, one of my partners. Think of him as you would me."

Hayashi already knew about Iosuke. "I look forward to your wise guidance," he said, standing at attention and speaking in the clipped military fashion.

"Who brought the message today? Must be Takahashi. It's risky, leaving a message when I'm not there. Luckily the Admiral here picked it up, so it was okay."

Iosuke was apparently "the Admiral."

"Perhaps the Admiral can tell him to be more careful."

This was where Kajiki and his group had their base. The signboard outside indicated a publishing company, but like many such companies these days it did not publish anything.

"By the way," Kajiki asked Hayashi, "do you know a good tailor? We must get a better suit for the Admiral."

To Iosuke's embarrassment, the two men looked him up and down, appraising his sweat-stained appearance. Then they opened a cupboard, pulled out some suitcases, and changed their clothes. Kajiki cut a stylish figure in a fashionable light flannel suit and a burgundy tie. He made Iosuke look all the shabbier.

"I'll arrange some new clothes, but there isn't time tonight. We can fix him up with a new tie, socks, shoes, and so on. He'll look all right."

To Iosuke's astonishment, the cupboard seemed to contain an endless array of clothing and accessories—both costly and cheap—like a theater wardrobe. They ironed his shirt and suit and gave him a new tie, with a matching handkerchief for his breast pocket. Iosuke looked a perfect gentleman, mostly due to his size.

Three bowls of pork cutlet on rice were delivered. Iosuke thought there was something incongruous about three well-dressed men, looking as if they were about to spend an evening at a cabaret, sitting down to this working-class meal. Kajiki and Hayashi wolfed down the food with the gusto of growing adolescents. The way they ate made it clear that this was gourmet fare for them. Iosuke ate ravenously, too, for the tasty meat and white rice were good reason to enjoy it. He was the first to finish, and the sight of him noisily crunching his pickles was almost comical.

"We're going to meet a broker with overseas connections, and we want you to pretend that you possess a certain substance. You won't get into any trouble because we're the ones who actually have it, so you won't need to say anything. In fact, the less you say the better. We simply want you to sit there and nod your head when we give you the signal. You'll be doing your country a great service," explained Kajiki.

Easygoing though he was, Iosuke felt a bit apprehensive.

"But if you are the owners of the substance, why can't you take care of everything yourselves?"

"There's a problem," said Hayashi.

Kajiki explained. "Me, Hayashi, and Takahashi were in the military for years, and we look and behave like junior officers. That always counts against us. This time it's a big sale, and there's no way the client will believe us if we say we're the owners."

"Well, if I don't have to say anything . . ."

Iosuke finally agreed. He did not mind pretending to have some unidentified substance, but, lacking any experience, he wished to avoid having to negotiate.

Soon the long summer's day ended and night fell. The men whiled away the time with anecdotes until after nine-thirty, when Kajiki and Hayashi finally stood up.

"Mr. Minamimura," Kajiki said, "as I told you, we will signal you whether to say yes or no, so just follow that. If you're asked something that's difficult to answer with a yes or no, say nothing specific. We won't signal, but you should say something like, 'We'll let you know later.' All right?"

Kajiki led the way downstairs, all three carrying their shoes and putting them on in the entryway. Iosuke's shoes were brand-new and top-quality.

They came out onto Hirokoji Avenue. The windows of the large department store there were dark and street lights were few. Streetwalkers popped up out of the shadows like mushrooms after rain, but Kajiki walked on rapidly, ignoring them. Now that Iosuke had agreed with him about the state of society, he no longer bothered with them.

Kajiki looked for a taxi. He told the driver to go to Ginza, then said loudly to Takahashi and Iosuke, "Okay! Let's go! The night's still young!"

"I'm good for a couple more spots," Hayashi answered, apparently talking for the benefit of the driver. They wanted to give the impression that they were out to enjoy a few more drinks in Ginza. From their clothes, they could pass for three successful businessmen intending to have a good time.

They left the taxi at a brightly lit intersection and made their way into darker streets, taking a route that confused Iosuke completely. They finally

156

reached a street without a single neon sign.

"This area has the most exclusive clubs and bars," whispered Kajiki.

The men stopped and waited. As if on cue, a man stepped out of the shadows.

"All's well?" the man asked in a low voice, and Kajiki replied with the same phrase.

"This is our partner, Takahashi," Kajiki said to Iosuke. Like his two collaborators, the man was short and unprepossessing.

Takahashi led them to a small building a few doors away. The front shutters were closed, as was a small door at the side. Takahashi knocked on this.

The door opened a few inches. It was on a chain.

"We came with Mr. Mogi the other day," said Takahashi quietly. A middle-aged woman in an apron looked them over through the narrow crack.

After opening the door, she disappeared without a word, assuming that anyone coming here would know where to go.

It was a small building so it had no elevator. Takahashi went ahead up the clean but bare concrete stairs. There was no sign of human presence on any of the floors, although one could not tell what lay behind the closed doors. When they reached the third floor, Takahashi knocked on a door and a man dressed in a tuxedo like a head waiter appeared and scrutinized them suspiciously.

When Takahashi said, "We have an appointment with Mr. Mogi," the man replied curtly, "Floor above," and slammed the door.

That brief glimpse revealed that several secret clubs were operating in the building.

Climbing to the fourth floor, Takahashi seemed to recall a previous visit and quickly approached one of the doors. This time they were confronted by a fat waiter dressed in white and wearing a bow tie.

"Welcome!" he said, as if they were expected, and he ushered them inside.

The room was not large and was furnished as a bar, with a liquor cabinet and counter. There were leather armchairs and a three-seat sofa.

"He'll be here soon. Would you like something?" the waiter asked, coming to their table.

While Kajiki and Takahashi kept exchanging glances, unaccustomed to a place like this, Iosuke understood what the waiter was offering. With the aplomb of someone completely at home, Iosuke said, "Highballs, if you please."

Iosuke's habits from hotel bars and clubs before the war had soon returned. The waiter respectfully withdrew behind the counter to prepare the drinks.

Apart from the waiter and a demure waitress, they were the only people in the room, but through lace curtains drawn across a window in one wall they could see into the brightly lit room next door, where two groups of men were playing cards.

"They're playing poker. The bets are in tens of thousands of yen," whispered Takahashi.

The highballs tasted of genuine Scotch. After sipping their drinks for five minutes, the card game at one table ended. There came the sound of conversation and someone was writing a check. One of the players did not look Japanese.

As they waited, someone from the card game came into the room. He was in shirtsleeves, wearing a light-green tie knotted neatly.

"Sorry to keep you waiting."

The face was unknown to Iosuke and Kajiki, but the reader will recognize him as Mr. Mogi, the man Komako and Henmi had visited for the lunch of sweetfish in the hills of Noborito. Wearing the same cheerful, yet worldly-wise expression, the shortish figure approached, and Kajiki, Hayashi, and Takahashi rose to greet him. They shook hands.

"We've brought the owner as promised."

When Takahashi introduced Iosuke, he smiled but did not rise, merely stretching out his arm to shake hands with Mogi. This was due to his natural slowness, but it could have been mistaken for the self-assurance of a prosperous man.

"I'm Mogi. How do you do?"

"Good to meet you."

Iosuke did not give his name. He remained silent, afraid of saying too much, but to Mogi this indicated a cautious and formidable man. Had Iosuke introduced himself, Mogi would have remembered Komako. He might have mentioned her name and Iosuke would have learned how his wife was doing. Then there would have been no knowing what they might have talked about. However, the opportunity passed.

"So you have the white?" Mogi asked.

Kajiki tapped Iosuke's foot once under the table—the signal for "yes."

"Yes."

"Of the three, what do you have most of?"

Iosuke was stumped, but Takahashi answered for him.

"He has three bottles of Type 2. The rest are P and Type 1."

"All in one-pound bottles?"

One tap on his foot.

"Yes."

"It's the genuine article, right?"

"Of course."

Kajiki had stepped hard this time, so Iosuke had responded firmly.

"Do you have a sample?"

"We'll show you." Takahashi had answered for Iosuke, and he took a purple bottle with a pharmacist's label out of his pocket.

"I'm going to break the seal. Okay?" Mogi removed the flat cork and took a pinch of the white powder inside.

"It came from the navy hospital, right?"

At the signal, Iosuke responded, "Yes."

"Two million yen a bottle, right?"

The price startled Iosuke more than anyone there. Can this stuff, which looks like ordinary boric acid, fetch that sort of a price?

"Well, we'd be happy with one and a half million," broke in Kajiki, "on certain conditions."

"What conditions?"

"First, you don't sell it in Japan."

"I know that. I told you we have a ship leaving soon."

"Second, payment in foreign currency is best. If that's not possible, we'll barter it for some of the goods you're importing to sell in Japan."

"That's difficult. Of course, since I'm selling, it's okay to sell to you, but it's a strange way of doing business. With so much imported stuff about, why would you want that?'

Mogi turned to Iosuke with a smile. It was a question that could not be answered with a simple yes or no, so Kajiki had no way of signaling him.

Iosuke, smiling back, was noncommittal. "We'll let you know later."

Kajiki looked relieved. Iosuke had done exactly as he had been told, without a single mistake, and Kajiki's respect for him increased.

"All right. Then I'd like the stuff delivered here tomorrow, at nine in the evening. You get it together and I'll prepare half the cash. I'll give you a list of goods for the other half. Okay?"

"Okay."

Mogi and Iosuke shook hands.

Drinks were served, with black caviar, olives, and other expensive snacks. They continued drinking highballs.

159

"You look as if you've traveled abroad."

Mogi had obviously overestimated Iosuke.

Iosuke was already in fine spirits from the drink, and he laughed frequently, his large belly shaking.

"How about a game of poker? We're playing in the next room. A couple of friends there would be happy to meet a nice Japanese gentleman like you."

Chapter 12
Thoughts of Home

As autumn winds began to blow in Tokyo's streets, Iosuke's fortunes were blossoming with a springlike vigor.

The War Responsibility League had provided him with two good, fashionable suits, so he looked quite the dandy. And Kajiki had given him more money than he could spend in a month, so he was not short of cash.

"You and your partners don't take any of the profit," Iosuke protested. "It shouldn't be just me that gets money."

At first, Iosuke had refused it point-blank. According to Kajiki, the three of them took some cash for expenses but nothing else. Their aim was to accumulate enough capital to set up a proper trading company once the peace treaty with the Allies was signed. Iosuke felt badly about being the only one benefiting from their activities, but Kajiki would not take the money back.

"No, no, you're more important than us. Thanks to you the deal went through. It was like asking an admiral to fire his ship's guns himself, so let us show our gratitude in this small way."

Iosuke asked the name of the drug they had sold, but Kajiki wouldn't tell him.

"I don't want you getting involved any deeper. It's terrible stuff, and we want it out of Japan. With the military being disbanded, there're lots of goods Japan does not need any more. We must sell those as fast as possible and turn them into cash."

What was bad for the Japanese must be as bad for non-Japanese, too, but Kajiki showed not the slightest qualms. That wartime attitude had not changed a bit.

In fact, Iosuke had no need for funds from Kajiki. On the night of the drug sale, he had returned to the shack under the bridge with his pockets bulging with his poker winnings—more than 50,000 yen.

Iosuke had a talent for card games. Rather than skill, it was his character that was well suited to gambling. His imperturbable nature allowed him to make bold bluffs, and that, plus his intimidating size, made him win big and lose small. He was particularly good at poker, which is essentially a game of nerves. Playing with people for the first time, as in the game with Mogi, his stature and his slow reactions gave him an advantage. That night he won from start to finish. Iosuke had been thrown out by Komako, so the saying "Lucky in cards, unlucky in love" fitted him perfectly.

In short, Iosuke's money problems had vanished, proof of how dramatically a man's fate can change. Now he could invite his neighbors to a party anytime or give money to Kinji without making a dent in the amount he had. Naturally, this had an effect on Iosuke's behavior, and his laziness grew as rapidly as bamboo shoots in May.

For an indolent man, nothing is worse than not having someone like Komako to keep him in line. When he slept till late in the morning or came home drunk at night, not only did his neighbors not reproach him, but they respected him all the more. That he could have so much money without working proved he was no ordinary man, and his popularity increased. Iosuke took advantage of the situation, allowing the orphan boy to polish his shoes and Mrs. Takasugi's daughter to massage his shoulders.

Life became so comfortable that, despite having plenty of money, Iosuke lost all desire to leave. His ship had indeed come in, as the saying goes, and he could not imagine a better life. Able to avoid all things disagreeable, he enjoyed more freedom than other Japanese of the time. If he had any desire at all, it was for Komako to change and become an obedient wife and join him here.

Since leaving home, the fates had been good to Iosuke and he had not suffered the discomforts Komako had imagined. From the outside, his situation might appear wretched, but he was as content as could be. Of late he had resumed his prewar lifestyle—doing exactly what he wanted.

Iosuke spent each day in Ginza. With money in his pocket, the old familiar haunts suited him best. The area had changed a lot with the war, but the drinks and food there were better than at the Kanda Station market or in the back streets of Shinjuku. Ginza may have lost some of its prewar glamour, but it still possessed an aura of sophistication, and Iosuke spent his days dining at the Karinsha and similar restaurants and browsing in jewelers like Ako. As befitted a postwar man of leisure, his clothes were in the latest pastel shades and his shoes were of tan leather. He had also bought himself a hat that you might see on the heads of young men from Hawaii. He looked every inch the energetic nisei from America on a buying trip to Tokyo.

Today, too, he had arrived in Ginza at around four. He was torn between eating at a fancy French restaurant, which would leave him feeling bloated, or having Kansai-style food, which could not be enjoyed properly without company. To help him decide between these two extravagant alternatives, he had a couple of whiskey-and-sodas at a bar.

By evening he was already a little intoxicated. As he sauntered through the crowds from Sukiyabashi toward Ginza 4-chome he heard some commotion behind him, but thought nothing of it until two or three girls, obviously streetwalkers, ran past and disappeared into a side street. The police must be rounding up prostitutes, he thought. It was nothing unusual, and he resumed his stroll.

A hand was suddenly thrust under his arm and gripped his elbow.

"Please keep walking!"

Iosuke could only stare at the creature beside him.

It was a young woman wearing a garish Western outfit. The dress was crimson and edged with white lace, and her arms were bare to the shoulders. She was carrying a white shoulder bag. She was so close to him that he could not see her face. All he saw was a head of cheaply permed hair nestling by his chest.

The girl kept walking without a word, matching Iosuke's stride.

Quite brazen, this one!

Iosuke was often approached by girls like her, but they usually gave up after a few paces, and he had never experienced such persistence. Times were hard, so perhaps they were being driven to extremes.

It was not seemly to walk around the streets of Ginza with such a girl on his arm, but Iosuke was neither courageous nor cold-hearted enough to disengage himself and escape.

As long as I'm not buying, everything will be all right, he decided.

So he kept walking until they reached Ginza 4-chome intersection. There, the girl suddenly guided him into a side street on the left.

Where's she taking me? There're no hotels here.

The area was packed with coffee shops and small restaurants, but the girl kept up her brisk pace, not talking or looking left or right. After walking a full block and just before reaching a main street, she finally gave a furtive look back and let out a deep sigh of relief, loosening her grip on Iosuke's arm.

"Thank you very much. You saved my life!"

She sounded so ingenuous that perhaps she was a newcomer to the business.

"No problem, but you gave me a start, seizing my arm like that!"

"Sorry. If I hadn't, the cops would have caught me. If you're with a man they leave you alone. I'm not that sort of girl, but the cops saw a foreigner talking to me, so I thought I'd better be careful. I've heard that's all it takes for them to haul you off to Yoshiwara Hospital for a syphilis test."

"I'm glad you're okay. So if you'll excuse me . . ."

Iosuke had taken a few steps when the girl came running after him.

"Wait! Forgive me if I'm wrong, but aren't you Mr. Minamimura?"

This startled Iosuke more than having his arm seized.

"Well, yes. But who are you?"

"Don't you remember me? I'm Fujimura Yuriko," said the girl, giggling.

Iosuke studied her face for the first time, and beneath all the heavy makeup he finally recognized the round face of a girl in school uniform he had met about three years before.

"Yuri?" His expression showed his shock. "What on earth are you wearing?"

"You're quite a surprise yourself. You're so fashionable! That hat! And those shoes!" What impudence! She was sizing him up from head to toe like a young prostitute out to hook a fat-cat customer. "You're so stylish. No wonder I didn't recognize you. What're you doing now?"

Iosuke avoided answering.

"You're someone important, I knew it! Mama and Papa are convinced you must be having a terrible time, but I was sure you could look after yourself even when you got thrown out. I know you're a man with plenty of confidence."

"How do you know that?" Iosuke suppressed an urge to scratch his head in embarrassment.

"I know everything. Even things you don't," said the girl suggestively.

Iosuke tried to change the subject. "You've grown up so fast. Do girls turn into women just like that? But you shouldn't be wandering around Ginza. You can get into fixes like that back there."

"It was nothing. I come here every day so I don't know why I haven't run into you before. Do you often get dressed up and come to Ginza for a good time?" Yuri was looking up at Iosuke with a certain respect.

"Well, I just came to eat. I'll stay a little longer, but you ought to go home. I'll find you a cab."

Iosuke wanted to escape from the girl quickly so that his uncle would not find out about him.

However, Yuri stood her ground, shaking her head like a stubborn boy. "No, let's go somewhere to eat. I have a good story to tell you."

Iosuke took Yuri to a branch of a Kansai-style restaurant in Ginza 6-chome.

It might be more accurate to say that the young woman took him there.

"The steamed sea-bream head is good."

It was astonishing that a nineteen-year-old girl should turn out to be an expert on food in a Ginza restaurant.

The building had survived the war, and its brown walls and ceiling boards were old and worn. They were shown into a small room at the back of the second floor, probably because they seemed like a couple on a tryst. After pouring some saké for Iosuke, the waitress disappeared.

"Don't treat me like a child." Yuri glared at Iosuke, pushing aside the glass of soda he had ordered for her. Iosuke had already started drinking and nibbling at the snacks served with the saké.

"Oh, do you drink?"

"A little saké at least." She emptied the soda into the container for rinsing saké cups and held out her glass.

"You're astounding! If you get drunk, don't blame me!"

She was not to be deterred, so he poured her some saké, which she gulped down. Her eyes began to shine and she leaned forward with an alluring smile. What is the world coming to? Iosuke wondered.

"Now let me pour you some saké. Let's drink lots tonight!"

"Yuri, where did you learn all this? Your father's a serious person who doesn't touch alcohol, right? Do your parents know you're wandering around here all the time?"

Yuri seemed so willful that Iosuke, quite out of character, found himself assuming a paternal role.

"There's no need to tell them! If they gave me more pocket money, I wouldn't have to work part-time."

"You mean you come to Ginza to work?"

"I don't have a job this month, but last month I worked at a coffee house where they pay you to talk to customers. It was interesting. You learn all about men's weak spots and you get paid for doing it."

"So your parents don't know. I'm surprised they haven't guessed."

"Parents are hopelessly out of touch. Even if they find out, I'm the one who's working of my own free will, so it's my right."

At this Iosuke fell silent. He noticed that Yuri's glass was empty. How could she drink so fast? She obviously did not know how to enjoy good saké.

"You've had enough. And if you're going to drink saké, use a saké cup, not a glass. By the way, don't you have a fiancé?"

"Yeah. I still see him. He's a dandy who only cares about his hair and his clothes. But I know a story about him, and it has a lot to do with you. So how about pouring me another one?"

This is how Iosuke happened to learn what Komako had been doing. It was his first news of her since he had left home, so he leaned expectantly over the low table, eager to hear the whole story. Chattering with a glibness unusual in someone so young, and wearing a worldly expression, Yuri produced a humorous account of events between Komako and Takabumi.

Surprised at what he had been told, Iosuke sat back with his arms crossed.

As the man in question was Takabumi, Iosuke did not feel in the least jealous. It was Takabumi who was infatuated, and Komako had been playing with fire to pass the time. Anyway, it was a relief to hear that Komako was safe and well.

"Isn't it amusing? Like something out of a recent novel."

"It can't be amusing for you." Iosuke sympathized with Yuri, who had been betrayed by her fiancé. He felt he should apologize on Komako's behalf.

"Why not? I even asked her to become Takabumi's lover!"

"You did what?"

"I'm sick of *boys*. What I'm after is a *man*." She used the English words. "Only a real *man*—in the physical, mental, and financial sense—is capable of affecting a woman deeply. After all, I'm a grown-up woman, too!"

Understanding Yuri was beyond Iosuke. He had not yet read *Lady Chatterley's Lover*, so he had no idea what affecting a woman "deeply" might involve. He could not admit that, however, so he simply said it would be safer not to be affected too much. He had more questions.

"How is Komako doing? Did she agree to your request about Takabumi? As far as I know, she's not the sort to do what anyone asks."

"You're right! And Takabumi got into a state and came to me begging for help. I don't know what to do with him. But I don't blame him. A rival appeared."

"You mean another *boy*?"

"No, this time it was a *man*. An ideal *man*, financially at least. You know him. He's in the Goshokai—the son of Mr. Henmi, the hospital director who died."

"Oh, him."

"Well, he was totally smitten with Komako. He has a wife, but she has weak lungs so she's likely to be in a sanitarium for some time. Their mar-

166

riage wasn't good to begin with, and things were like that when your wife came on the scene. Mr. Henmi's no sissy like Takabumi. He's sophisticated and intelligent, and on top of that you weren't around." Yuri's tale ended abruptly.

"Don't stop there!" Iosuke's attitude had changed.

"See? I know everything. I deserve to be taken to dinner."

She sounded cocky and self-assured, but everything she was telling Iosuke she had learned from Takabumi. Driven by his youthful jealousy and his rather womanish personality, Takabumi had spied on Komako's every move.

"So your wife decided to go for a drive to Tama River with Mr. Henmi. It was a very long drive, from before noon until seven in the evening, so they must have had plenty of time for a 'rest.'"

Iosuke was reminded of the streets he and Kajiki had passed through in Asakusa, with those ubiquitous hot spring signs. He felt a hot spring of jealousy bubbling up inside him, which prevented his hand from reaching for his saké cup.

"And what happened?"

"Well, something must have gone wrong, because after that drive your wife suddenly decided to *waste* Mr. Henmi."

"She did what? Please use proper Japanese."

"You know in Japanese baseball they talk about a *waste ball*, when the pitcher intentionally walks the batter. And this really was a *waste*. Mr. Henmi would be a great catch, but your wife didn't seem interested."

"She must have had something else on her mind."

Iosuke breathed a sigh of relief.

"I hear Mr. Henmi's heartbroken and has stopped going to the Goshokai. Komako must have hurt him terribly."

"That sounds like her. Komako likes stringing a man up by the neck. So now that she's driven Takabumi and Henmi away, is all quiet on the Komako front?" Iosuke gave a hopeful laugh.

"No. An even greater threat appeared. A real he-man."

"You're exaggerating. Komako went for one of those nouveau riche types?"

"No, he's a local. A repatriated soldier, in charge of the ration office where you live. Takabumi also met him. He's not as big as you, but Takabumi says he's super-strong. It happened when Komako was attacked by a robber. He comes along and tosses the wretch ten yards into a field. He's the physical, muscleman type."

"But Komako wouldn't fall for someone just because he's strong."

"You're behind the times. Strength alone counts for nothing, but if there's spirit and passion, it has a powerful sex appeal that touches a woman deeply to her core. No aristocrat or intellectual, however wealthy he is, can attract a woman like one you might find in the forest."

Iosuke found it increasingly difficult to follow Yuri. The psychology of postwar women was more difficult than advanced mathematics, and he could not fathom what made Yuri talk like this. Since the end of the war, men had been "reborn" and were saying such things as they "understood" and "respected" women, but Iosuke was uncertain how honest they were being.

"This ration officer must be good-looking," he ventured, revealing not only his conventional attitude but also his poor grasp of the situation.

"I was told he has the face of a smoked herring."

"You've lost me completely."

Iosuke turned to his food and began to eat the autumn delicacies of fragrant *matsutake* mushrooms and simmered eel, but he failed to enjoy them.

"You see, Komako belongs to a different generation from me and Takabumi. She's a postwar woman in theory only. As soon as she begins to regret what she's done, it's over. In the end, she threw that guy a *waste ball*, too."

"And that's not the end?"

"There's much more. This guy—he's no gentleman like Mr. Henmi— doesn't go quietly after being dumped. He gets aggressive and starts pursuing Komako. He's kind of like Tarzan—once his passions are aroused, he's unstoppable. So now Komako's afraid. She's scared to be alone in the house at night and even asked the landlady to let her stay with her."

"Is this true?"

"If you don't believe me, ask Takabumi. Both Takabumi and Mr. Henmi are really worried about the situation, and they've even got together to discuss how to protect her."

"That sounds odd."

"Why? Takabumi can't fight worth a damn, so it's natural for him to ask Mr. Henmi's help."

"I suppose so. But Komako . . ."

Iosuke started to speak but did not know what to say. The idea of your wife pursuing another man is not pleasant, but he had no wish to prevent it. However, the news that the man was threatening her came as a shock. But he was not ready to rush to her defense. If it came to a fight, he would have no choice, but it was not an option he had much confidence in. He had settled the dispute by the bridge, but that was purely by accident. If he were to rush off blindly to save the damsel in distress, the damsel might give him a sound tongue-lashing. There was nothing to show her anger had abated. So what was he to do? Just thinking about it put him in a bad mood.

Iosuke suddenly stood up.

"Yuri. The saké here's no good. Let's go somewhere else."

Outside the restaurant Yuri hooked her arm into Iosuke's, the same as earlier, but now darkness had fallen and the streets were alive with neon lights.

"What about going dancing?" Yuki asked.

Young as she was, she was using her sexiest tone of voice.

"I dislike dancing!" Iosuke's reply was uncharacteristically curt.

"Well then, let's go and relax somewhere. I have something else to tell you."

"About Komako?" he asked, more gently.

"No. About me."

"In that case," said Iosuke, "not tonight. I've got to get back, and you're going to miss your last train if you're not careful."

"That's not fair! Didn't you say we should go somewhere else for a drink?"

Iosuke was feeling miserable. He wanted to drink seriously, but not with Yuri. He wanted to get rid of her, but she was so persistent he could find no way.

As they walked down the tree-lined avenue and passed the Spanish-style bar Madrid, Iosuke could barely resist the temptation to escape inside. There was no way saké could taste good with a young girl at his side. He was a man of ordinary tastes, and he had as little interest in seducing a young girl as in being indulged by an older woman.

With no other alternative, he said firmly, "Tonight, I'm going home."

"Then I'll go home, too. I'll take the tram from Shimbashi," said Yuri, unexpectedly compliant. "How will you go?"

"I'll take the train."

"Where do you live? Please tell me."

Iosuke was in a fix. He could not say he was living under Okanenomizu Bridge.

"Near Kanda," he lied. "In an apartment."

He lengthened his stride in the hope of avoiding more questions. There were few street lights, and the two walked in silence.

"Well, a dark street is probably better for asking," said Yuri, her voice softening. "How would you like to marry me?"

"What did you say?" Iosuke almost fell off the pavement in astonishment.

"I want to get married as soon as I can. I'm sick of being treated like a child. I want to sail into the big wide world of adulthood."

"But you've got Takabumi."

"He's no good. He can't even earn a living. Besides, I'm dead against arranged marriages. I want someone like you, a mature man who's big and strong and knows how to make money."

"But I'm married to Komako."

This sudden declaration even surprised Iosuke himself.

"That doesn't bother me. You can carry on loving Komako for who she is. Just set up house with me."

The next morning Iosuke woke up later than usual, and it was after ten when he went to wash his face.

It had been difficult to sleep at first. The autumn fleas were vicious, and the story of Komako's situation had thrown his mind into confusion. Memories of home that he had pushed away came flooding back. He could picture the man he had never met sitting on their veranda threatening Komako.

Maybe I should go back and take a look.

The train running in the Tachikawa direction was right there on the other side of the river. Nothing held him back except Komako—she was no ordinary woman, and more independent than most. There was every possibility she would confront him with the words, "Who asked you to come and save me? I haven't given you permission to return." Even if she were in trouble, she might say something like that. If she was desperate to have him back, she would place a missing-persons ad in the newspaper. She was certainly bold enough to do that.

It occurred to Iosuke that he should try to forget Komako once and for all, but it was not easy to suppress the yearning for home that Yuri's story had aroused in him. All men possess an instinct that drives them out on the hunt, a trait no doubt dating to primeval times, but they also have a homing instinct that inevitably brings them back. Iosuke was no exception.

I shouldn't have parted with Yuri like that, he thought with some regret.

Yuri knew every detail of Komako's life, and from now on he wished to keep track of what was going on. Only Yuri could keep him informed, but when she had suddenly asked him to marry her in the middle of the street, he had been panic-stricken and had bolted into Shimbashi Station.

Maybe it had been a joke. The idea of asking him to make her his official wife and keep Komako as a friend was topsy-turvy; if she had been serious, she would have suggested the opposite.

The psychology of young women in the postwar era was too much for Iosuke, and he had no interest in it. Even if it had been a joke, he had taken it seriously and had fled with such haste that he had failed to find out how and where he might meet Yuri again. Now he was ruing this.

Iosuke was rarely this edgy and out of sorts. He had no appetite for breakfast and paced up and down the riverbank. He wanted to think things out, but was soon spotted by Kajiki.

"I've been waiting for you to get up. It's excellent news. We made big money from the deal the other day, so we bought a ship. We're loading it with stationery, tools, and electrical equipment, and it'll be sailing soon with Takahashi as captain."

The way Iosuke was feeling, he couldn't care less about foreign currency or the glory of the nation. All he wanted was for Kajiki to go away and leave him to his thoughts.

"Have you got a fever? You don't look good." Kajiki seemed worried. "Take care," he said, before returning to his shack.

Relieved to be alone, Iosuke went and sat under the willow tree, but then old Kinji came up, almost on tiptoe.

"Iosuke, I couldn't talk in the house, the walls being so thin and all," he began. And the story he recounted was completely unexpected.

Kinji's wife had taken a live-in job in Hongo, working for a manufacturer of medical equipment, but soon realized how restrictive regular society could be. She wanted to come back to the shack—in other words, to come back as Kinji's wife and live with him. Since Iosuke had put up half the money, she would return 500 yen if he would let her move back.

"But we'd never think of kicking you out. We're happy for you to live with us, if you don't mind. There's also a suggestion that you could become an owner yourself. It's worth considering. It'd be best all around."

Kinji's suggestion was also completely unexpected.

"You know Mrs. Takasugi, who lives on the east side? Well, her daughter has found a live-in position, leaving her mother all by herself. She may look a bit haggard, but she's only thirty-six, one year older than you. Instead of living alone, how about marrying her? She's an older woman and will take good care of you. Besides her house is the newest and doesn't have so many fleas."

"Kinji, please stop! It's out of the question."

Iosuke's irritation boiled over, making him raise his voice. The old man had come at a bad time. Usually Iosuke would have listened good-naturedly.

"I'm sorry! Don't be angry."

With that, Kinji withdrew, looking crestfallen.

Iosuke felt disgusted with himself. This place no longer seemed a haven of peace and quiet. He was still wearing his work clothes, but he wanted to go into town for a drink.

He climbed up the ladder and was about to step into the street when a bright red skirt caught his eye.

"You're living here, aren't you? I followed you last night. What an exciting life you lead!"

Yuri seemed fascinated.

Chapter 13
The Wild One

Komako found herself in an impossible situation, and it was all her own fault.

She had never dreamed that she would provoke such a catastrophe. Her interest in Heiji, the ration officer, had not been idle curiosity, like an aristocrat accustomed to eating sea bream attempting to try common saury. Nor did it stem, as Yuri had surmised, from some primeval attraction to a hairy-legged, Pan-like creature of the forest.

It was as a pilgrim along the road to womanhood that Komako had stumbled upon this unusual specimen of manhood. While her idea of the road differed somewhat from the paragons of fidelity and obedience envisioned by Confucian scholars of old, if Heiji had been the first man to appear after Iosuke's departure, she might not have noticed him. After all, a housewife dabbling in English literature and a taciturn bachelor living in a ration office are hardly likely to be compatible.

However, Komako was well along on her pilgrimage. It had started with her marriage to Iosuke and moved to Takabumi, who was audacious but as pliant as a jellyfish. Her journey had then brought her to Henmi— conservative, cultivated, and, like a banana, possessing a pleasing aroma but lacking a substance one could sink one's teeth into. Both suitors had their strong and weak points, but neither came close to attracting her, in either mind or body.

In fact, Komako felt rather exasperated by her experiences so far. The terrain had been anything but inspiring, with not one viable prospect on the horizon. She had begun to despair about the dearth of specimens of genuine manhood following the nation's defeat when the ration officer loomed into her life.

She saw a side to Heiji that did not exist in Iosuke, or Takabumi, or Henmi. Or so Komako had thought. She was tempestuous by nature, and this being a time when the pillars of her mental stability were shaky, inevitably her impression of Heiji was somewhat distorted at first.

Her interest had been kindled when she went to the ration office to thank Heiji for saving her from the robber. He had ignored the carton of cigarettes she had given him; indeed, he had complained about Iosuke's rice ration. Normally Komako would not have submitted so easily in an argument, and it was odd that she conceded defeat.

"Sorry about that," she had heard herself say, and it had actually felt good. She thought that she had glimpsed the strength of Heiji's character.

After returning home and hearing the landlady's gossip about Heiji's personality and his unfortunate past, her interest in him grew. She began to think of him as a man rather than as the ration officer. One might assume that this was the influence of postwar democracy, but it was more the effect of her earlier mental flirtations with Takabumi and Henmi.

Komako had not exactly fallen in love with Heiji. A modern housewife over the age of thirty does not fall in love so easily, but attraction to and affection for a man can blossom more often than an innocent girl might imagine. When the bud of an affair begins to emerge, though, the woman usually nips it off or lets it shrivel and die.

In the normal course of events their relationship might have developed no further, despite Komako being impressed by Heiji's peculiar character and superhuman strength. But one day Heiji found it necessary to visit her house.

"Mrs. Minamimura, I was mistaken the other day. Since you are not receiving chits for eating out, your husband's ration can be issued here. That's what my boss says."

Heiji had brought along a small bag of imported rice. Since her visit to the ration office, Komako had not been receiving Iosuke's share.

"It doesn't matter. After all, there's just me, and I can't eat it all."

She was telling the truth, but Heiji had insisted, so in the end she had accepted the rice. She paid for it, served him tea, and gave him some cakes she had at hand to take home.

"You're living in the ration office, I understand. It must be rather uncomfortable."

That remark—made as Heiji was sitting on the edge of the veranda— had been the start of a conversation that told her a lot about him.

Heiji was not much of a talker. His answers were a brief "yes" or "no," but there was a pleasing dignity to that, and Komako gradually warmed to him. It might have been impolite, but she found herself offering sympathetic comments on his wife's betrayal.

"How could she do that? After you had put your life on the line and managed to get home."

"Ma'am, all I can say is that women are bandits."

Heiji had spoken quietly, but there was pain in his face. This tough-looking man seemed shrouded in a mist of melancholy, and Komako thought she had guessed its source.

"Don't say that. I'll keep an eye open for a woman who'd make you a good wife."

"There's no need for you to trouble yourself."

All was well as long as they were merely exchanging pleasantries, but Komako noticed that the seam at the back of his army jacket had come un-stitched, and she felt sorry for him.

"Take your jacket off and I'll sew it up on the machine."

Her order was kindly meant, but it revealed Heiji's basic shyness. He was not wearing an undershirt, so he was reluctant to remove his jacket. When he finally did so and was naked from the waist up, Komako could not help admiring his rippling muscles and his skin, which, unlike his face, was not tanned.

When Komako, having deftly sewed the seam, handed back the jacket, Heiji overcame his usual reserve to say with great sincerity, "Thank you, Mrs. Minamimura. You're very kind."

After that, Komako had shown him one or two more small kindnesses, once taking him some food she had left over.

Heiji's attitude toward Komako slowly changed, although it was not always consistent; at times he would be extremely shy and at others almost brusque. Never once did he look Komako in the face, and though well over thirty he still shied away from her like a child.

He's a simple-hearted fellow, she concluded.

Komako found this quality rather endearing. She was aware, of course, of the feelings she had stirred in him. Women of all ages, young or old, have excellent radars for detecting emotional frequencies, which, if used to excess, can result in overconfidence.

Komako did not find Heiji's attention unwelcome. A woman who makes a man said to curse women in general fall in love with her deserves to be pleased with herself. Since Iosuke had left, not one but two men had sought her affections, and Komako found that curious. Now a third had taken a fancy to her, making her a little confused. She wondered if she possessed some irresistible appeal of which she was unaware. Otherwise three men would not have become infatuated with her in the space of a few months.

Heiji's way of showing his feelings was not disagreeable. He was not flamboyant and fawning like Takabumi, nor nervous and indecisive like Henmi. Despite looking lovesick, he said nothing. The flame of his passion may have lain so deep that it burned more intensely than that of the other two.

One thing that troubled Komako was that Heiji did not speak the language of her class and was not familiar with the customs of that world. Depending on how you looked at it, of course, this factor may have fanned her interest. After all, differences in class or education were no longer supposed to matter.

What's more important is his worth as a human being! she told herself.

Komako did not want to be stuck in the mold of prewar women, who measured everything by appearances and conventions. In her emotions and actions, she wanted to experience greater flights in the realm of freedom.

Just as modern women keep their kimonos stored in chests instead of wearing them, Komako might be said to covet freedom for its possibilities, but on the practical level she was inclined to be satisfied with only the prospect of freedom. This was what protected a middle-aged woman from danger. No matter how strong her interest in Heiji, it never occurred to her to be the first to make overtures to him.

Heiji was a patient man, and because he was satisfied with going through the motions, Komako accumulated one more kimono in her chest. One stormy night, however, the situation changed dramatically.

The weather report had forecast a typhoon that night, so Komako had closed the storm doors around her house and was reading when she heard Heiji call out, "Good evening."

Even Komako felt frightened.

The typhoon might not arrive as predicted, but alone in the house at night, with a strong wind moaning in the trees, she did not welcome a visit from Heiji.

"Goodness, what brings you here tonight?"

She tried to sound friendly, but she opened one of the wooden panels only a little.

"I have something to tell you," Heiji said.

Peering into the darkness, Komako could see that it was raining lightly. A rather dejected Heiji was holding a traditional oil-papered umbrella. At times like these it was most inconvenient not to have a proper entry hall. Since the veranda was wet, he could not sit in his customary place.

"Come in. But only for ten minutes. I have a job to finish tonight."

Hoping that this would have the desired effect, she let him into the house. She intentionally did not close the panel.

"Sorry to come so late."

Heiji was unusually nervous and bowed to Komako. Instead of his army clothes he was wearing a kimono in an attempt at dressing formally, but the gray material and striped pattern were cheap and provincial, making him look seedy.

"Is it about the rations?"

Komako did not offer tea or cakes. Her voice, too, was uncharacteristically stiff. Affected by the tension, Heiji seemed to shrink visibly as he sat there.

"No, it's nothing like that." His voice trailed off and he fidgeted, gazing fixedly at the tatami.

It was the first time Komako had seen Heiji looking cowed. Her initial fears abated. If he was going to be a toothless tiger, she had no cause to worry. Yet she also felt somewhat disappointed, too, for half of his usual appeal was missing.

Komako waited for Heiji to say something, then grew impatient and spoke first.

"I don't know what business brings you here tonight, but please tell me."

"Well," he began tentatively, but fell silent again for two or three minutes before resuming in a faint voice.

"I don't want you to do what you mentioned the other day."

"What was that?"

"You said that you'd look for a wife for me."

"Oh, that!"

Komako came close to laughing. She had just been making conversation and had forgotten about it.

"I can't see any other woman as a wife," he murmured with a sigh.

"Was your first wife such a fine person?" Komako was curious.

"You can guess the kind of woman she was, who'd take up with another man while her husband was off in the army." Heiji glared into space and his expression turned vengeful. "If I ever get hold of her, I'll make her pay!"

His tone intimated that he would strangle her if he met her. The beast has not been defanged, Komako realized, and her fear returned.

"You should find a nice young woman and get even," said Komako, attempting to calm him. It would be dangerous, she thought, if he got more excited.

But the embers smoldering within Heiji seemed to have come alive, and he vehemently rejected her suggestion.

177

"Never! I'll never take a young woman. What use would that be!"

"How strange! But who would you marry if not a young woman?"

Komako said this jokingly, to defuse Heiji's wrath.

Heiji stared ahead. Then he turned to Komako and looked her full in the face for the first time. It was hard to tell whether it was a look of great yearning or deep resentment, but it had a ferocious intensity.

"Who would I marry? I'd help myself to somebody else's wife." He spoke quietly but with confidence.

Komako shuddered. Her interest in Heiji vanished. She was ten times more afraid than when she had been attacked by the ruffian. She was in no state to answer him and was wondering how to defend herself.

Heiji kept staring at Komako. Gone was his former reticence. That had not been a pretense, but it revealed a character that swung sharply from one extreme to another. Komako felt even more frightened.

The wind was still strong outside. The lights flickered, fading one instant and growing brighter the next.

Heiji continued. "You understand, don't you? Someone took my wife, so I can take someone else's wife."

Komako was too scared to listen further. Rising, she edged closer to the shutters.

"Excuse me, but I just remembered something I have to tell the landlady," she said in a voice that was almost a scream. She darted through the opening, leaping barefoot into the garden and running for the safety of the landlord's house.

Komako asked the landlady to put her up for the night. Thinking that if she mentioned Heiji's name it might cause trouble later, she told the landlady she had been frightened by strange noises, and that had sufficed.

The next morning, however, when she returned home, the place was a mess.

Heiji was nowhere to be seen, of course, but the house looked as though it had been hit by an earthquake—pictures flung off the walls, the bookcase thrown over, and the sewing machine overturned, one cast-iron leg snapped off.

It was horrifying. When Komako looked at the garden, she found that it, too, had been ravaged—a parasol tree lay on the ground, ripped out by its roots; the stone washbasin and its pedestal had been toppled; and the azalea and nandina bushes beside it had been flattened, the white centers of their broken branches exposed.

He did it! He certainly did it! This man of superhuman strength had lost all control. Enraged, Heiji had let his brute force run riot.

Komako's initial reaction was resentment—after all, she was not the adulterous wife—but there was a comical aspect, too. His rampage did not look like the work of a human being but of a machine—it was as if a bulldozer had been let loose in the house.

Komako's opinion of Heiji plummeted from forest Pan to bulldozer. Little had she dreamed that it would come to this. He might have been a passing fancy, but the fact that his true nature had been revealed in this way was deflating.

Can Heiji not distinguish between his faithless wife and me? Or did he just go on a rampage because I escaped?

She pondered this at length but did not arrive at an answer. Probably both were correct.

In any case, Heiji had come the previous night harboring the violence that had been wreaked on the garden. Whether it was the force of passion or of revenge mattered little, for it went against all her instincts and caused her a lot of trouble. He might be innocent and in no way evil, but he was still as frightening as those pure young ex-kamikaze pilots who had turned to crime. No, even an ordinary robber would be less dangerous because he would not harm you unnecessarily.

Yes, I am afraid of him because he's like a bulldozer!

The devastation was a reminder of Heiji's strength. There was nothing comical about it. When she recalled how she had shared her food with him and sewed his clothes, she understood she had been putting her head in the tiger's mouth, and the memory sent a shiver down her spine.

She set about clearing up the mess, thinking she had learned a good lesson.

I won't be able to do any more dressmaking work until I get the sewing machine fixed, she realized.

That afternoon, at the most inconvenient time, Takabumi appeared.

"What happened? Looks like the typhoon scored a direct hit." Seeing the state of the garden, anyone would have thought the same.

"Never mind. Here, help me!"

Disgruntled and sweaty, Komako had been trying to raise the stone pedestal of the washbasin, but it was too heavy.

"Of course."

Takabumi removed his jacket, and on the count of three he and Komako heaved, but the young man's strength was negligible.

"What's the matter with you!" scolded Komako. "You're a man, aren't you? Try harder!"

Although he dug his heels in and heaved with all his might, the only result was that his fashionable hairdo was spoiled. He gave up, exhausted. Young men of his generation had not been drafted to work in munitions factories during the war, and the shortage of good food when they were growing up had made them physically weak. They held great promise for a country pledged to peace, but when it came to cleaning the house or moving, they were less than useless.

"Look at you! Even I'm stronger than you." Komako continued working by herself. The image of Iosuke passed through her mind.

He'd be a tremendous help at a time like this, she thought.

That went without saying. Of course, she would have to hustle him to get him going, but once he started he would have been more than a match for Heiji.

For the first time since Iosuke had left Komako admitted that she needed her husband, even in this insignificant way.

"This is not a natural disaster, is it?" Takabumi asked. "I can see big footprints all over the place."

The earth was soft because of the rain, and Takabumi had found traces of Heiji's wooden clogs. He could be quite observant.

"I know! It must be that man. Tell me what happened! I'll help protect you."

Takabumi was aware of Heiji's strength because of the incident with the robber, and he was more than a little jealous of Komako's interest in the ration officer.

"I don't know what you're talking about! Takabumi, how can you say that when you're so useless!" Komako was fuming. "And what are you doing here, anyway, asking all these questions? You know that ever since that self-righteous mother of yours came and insulted me, my house is off-limits to you!"

Today, she was filled with anger at the uselessness of men.

It was the time of year when evening starts to arrive much earlier. Komako had vented her frustration on the objects around her and on Takabumi, but when night fell her mood changed and loneliness set in. So desolate was she that she almost regretted sending Takabumi away.

As the house sank into darkness, chill waves of fear swept over her again.

The typhoon had moved on, so it was a starry night with a bright moon, and the wind had died down. However, Komako's nerves were so much on edge that even the slightest whisper of a breeze sounded like footsteps creeping outside. There was no assurance that Heiji would not come back again.

Another problem was that she did not want to have to go to the ration office again. The thought of coming face to face with Heiji even in the daytime was terrifying. She supposed she could subsist on bread for a while, but she could not imagine doing without her rice ration for long.

I don't want to live here any longer. I must move.

There was a clatter in the kitchen. Komako jumped to her feet and began to pace around the room, wondering where she could flee. If she ran outside he might catch her, but if she stayed in the house, he might break in.

There were no more sounds, so it must have been a mouse.

Komako thought she would go mad if she remained there, tormented by every noise. She took her night clothes and a bed sheet from the cupboard, wrapped them in a cloth, and, like a girl setting off to work as a live-in maid, she ran over to the landlord's house.

"Good evening. I'm sorry to bother you, but would you mind putting me up tonight as well?" she begged the landlady, who was sewing on the raised floor near the entryway.

"That's easy enough," the landlady answered, but a look of slight annoyance passed over her face.

The landlord was seated by the sunken hearth smoking a pipe. He looked questioningly at Komako.

"If you don't get that husband of yours to come back soon, you'll get nowhere," he said pointedly. Komako had told them that Iosuke was away on business, but the more time passed the closer her neighbors came to guessing the truth.

That night, as Komako tried to sleep, covered by a none-too-clean quilt and gazing at the soot-covered rafters of the old farmhouse, tears of frustration and self-pity ran down her cheeks.

If only he would come home, all these problems would be solved. Regarding the things between them, however, she would no doubt have to compromise.

With autumn drawing near she could hear people practicing music for the harvest festival. It reminded her suddenly of Iosuke's uncle in Oiso.

I should go and talk to him again, she decided.

Chapter 14
Out of Tune

"What on earth can Iosuke be doing?"

Haneda Ginko brought the subject to her husband's attention as she was clearing the table after lunch, putting the bowls and plates onto a tray.

While Haneda Tsutomu drank his tea, it was his habit to maintain the formal position with legs folded under him, with his back straight and his shoulders squared beneath his faded serge kimono. Known for his talkativeness in company, at home he tended to be silent, absorbed in his own thoughts. Even when eating, he eschewed the more relaxed posture of sitting cross-legged on the tatami. He was not being pretentious; like many other eccentrics he was basically a serious fellow.

"These false teeth." He was moving his jaw from side to side in obvious discomfort. "What they say about Americans getting a new set made every three years must be true."

Accustomed to her husband's habit of ignoring her questions, Ginko knew how to keep him from changing the subject.

"Your false teeth may need attention, but I'm concerned about Iosuke," she said.

"Yes, that fellow's a problem. He should be home any day now." Haneda sounded nonchalant, but his wife of nearly four decades knew that was not the case. While he feigned indifference to his own relations, he was comparatively attentive to her side of the family. Thus, she knew better than to accept her husband's coolness toward his relatives at face value—particularly as far as his only nephew, Iosuke, was concerned.

"Knowing how slow Iosuke is, he's unlikely to wander as far as Hokkaido or Kyushu," said Ginko. "He must still be in Tokyo. Is there any way we can find him?"

"Even if we find him, that won't solve the problem. He's not a child and may not want to come back, so it would be rather pointless."

"Maybe, but think of poor Komako, waiting and waiting for him."

"Komako must be doing all right. She is capable of managing on her own, both in her daily life and in society at large. I wouldn't worry too much about her."

"But she's a woman, after all. No matter how many times a woman may change her clothes, she's still the same person underneath. Even that Fujimura Yuri, who's behaving so outrageously just now—she'll settle down in time and make someone a fine wife, even if perhaps a little too spirited. So don't expect Komako to alter that much."

"How can you be so sure? Women are changing these days. After suffering a defeat like ours, people can't help but change. It's a revolutionary time for men and women. The only ones who won't change are people like you and me."

Haneda lit an Ikoi cigarette and gazed out at the sunny garden. Clumps of late-blooming portulaca on the sandy soil lent a splash of color to the simple scene of five or six pine trees bathed in the early afternoon light.

"Well," laughed Ginko, "I don't know about men, but women won't be that different just because the country was defeated. They have more grit than that! When it comes to women, you don't have it right at all. It's strange how little men understand women, while women see other women as clear as day. It's difficult to believe men can't understand women's true nature."

Not having a maid, it was just the two of them, so they could chat at their leisure after a meal instead of having to clear the dishes away immediately.

"You may say that, but women don't know the true nature of men, either," her husband countered.

"Oh, but they do," said Ginko. "A woman studies her husband very carefully. Knowing her husband is part of her profession."

"So I'll have to watch out. I always thought no woman could understand me."

"You! You're one of the easiest to understand. But Iosuke's more of a puzzle."

"Iosuke? He's not so hard for me. But to be quite honest I don't know about Komako. She's certainly intelligent, but is she faithful or is she having an affair with one of those fellows?"

"Neither, I'd say. Only a man would think in such simple terms."

"So you think men tend to generalize while women are better at specifics?"

"I don't know about that, but Komako is a woman. She's probably the most feminine of women. But because of her education she's developed some ambition."

"That's not the purpose of education."

"Not for men maybe, but education makes women want to imitate men. That's what they hanker after."

183

"That sounds like some new theory."

"But once a woman reveals her ambition, she loses out. When women imitate men, they stand to gain nothing. That's because they don't understand men."

"So there's no advantage to imitating men."

"Well, I'd say that if a woman wants to win the battle, she should use her own talents rather than copy men. In any event, women have to win somehow!"

"Oh, so you're out to conquer me!" chortled Haneda.

"Let's see now," said Ginko with a laugh. "Oh, look at the time. It's already one o'clock. But please think about Iosuke, all right?"

After his wife disappeared into the kitchen, Haneda took a cushion onto the veranda. The sun had already moved well to the south, but he sat with his back against a post, ignoring the glare.

Men and women—what a dilemma!

He and Ginko had had a normal arranged marriage, and now they had lived together for thirty-six years without any discord. Not that he had no experience of the pleasures of the geisha houses, but his affections had never shifted to another woman, so there had never been trouble at home. He had not actively courted Ginko, yet she soon became someone without whom he could not live even for a day, and he had come to think, perhaps rather naively, that this was the nature of all marriages.

Observing the world today, however—and the problem between Iosuke and Komako was a case in point—relationships between men and women were becoming frightfully complicated.

Young people nowadays are to be pitied, he thought. Where will all this lead?

As a scholar of law, Haneda was critical of certain clauses in the new constitution, but he approved of its general direction. All the same, he did not think it would necessarily result in happiness for the men and women of Japan. He knew full well the limits of freedom guaranteed by the law. He also knew from long experience that there was no direct connection between freedom and happiness. On the contrary, he felt sorry for the younger generation, who had had freedom deposited so abruptly on their doorstep.

The problem between Iosuke and Komako was especially difficult for him because he was equally fond of both of them. Since he had no children of his own, he felt a strong attachment to his nephew, but no less for Komako. He felt as much affection for her as for Iosuke, even though she

184

was only related by marriage. If he had been able to favor one over the other, the situation would have been much easier, but he was determined to find a solution that would make both happy. If he could not, he was convinced that the problem would not be solved.

Finding a solution would be hard, he realized, for siding with one meant siding against the other.

He did not need his wife's urging to want to mediate between the two, but for the time being there was nowhere to begin, which left him little option but to fold his arms and wait. Still, he did not want the situation to drag on indefinitely. As his wife had said, the first thing they had to do was to locate Iosuke. For this he was thinking of asking a former student of his who was now an inspector in the Tokyo police to see if he could get any information.

I should consult Komako as well, but I wonder what she's doing? She hasn't come for a long time.

As he was thinking this he heard the gate open. There were two sets of footsteps and male voices, so it could not be Komako.

"Well, well, come in, come in!"

Having gone to the entryway himself, Haneda immediately broke into a smile, for standing there were his Goshokai friends, Hishikari Otomaru and Fujimura Koichi, the two most welcome guests he could imagine.

"We've come to ask you about the ensemble," said Fujimura, with his usual grave expression.

"I've been feeling a little dismal today, so your timing is excellent. Please come in."

When one reaches the age of the Hanedas, it is not easy to make new friends, which was why Haneda was so delighted to see Hishikari and Fujimura. Indeed, he was as happy as a child as he showed his guests inside. As might be expected, all thoughts of Iosuke and Komako vanished from his mind.

Hishikari and Fujimura, Yuri's father, were both men of the traditional mold, and their greetings, even to an old friend, were habitually courteous and formal. They bowed as they broached the subject of their musical gatherings.

"Indeed," Haneda began, "the matter has been on my mind of late, and I have been thinking of visiting both of you to discuss it. I'm sorry that you have had to make the long journey out here. But do come in and let's talk about the group and tell stories and so on. These days, should I have an inclination for a talk, I have few opportunities to go into the city, and I miss

185

the pleasure of good conversation. With only the old woman to listen to me, even if a witty phrase should arrive on the tip of my tongue, it has nowhere to go but back inside! Ha-ha-ha!"

With guests present, Haneda was soon bubbling with cheerful chatter, a completely different person from when he was with his wife.

Haneda Ginko appeared with tea. Far from thinking guests a bother, upon seeing the two visitors she was already planning what kind of evening meal she could serve the old men. Indeed, both the Hanedas were sociable and outgoing—birds of a feather, one might say.

"Times have gone sadly amiss, I feel," said Hishikari. "I suppose I should not complain, but things were much better in the old days. The Goshokai meetings before the war were so amicable." The erstwhile aristocrat mopped his broad forehead as he voiced his mild protest. He was wearing not his customary kimono but an old-fashioned, double-breasted suit with four buttons.

"They were," Haneda added with a deep sigh. "Dr. Henmi was with us in those days, and Hori, too. Indeed, the zither's five strings were all in place."

None of them was satisfied with the present state of the Goshokai.

"How about here in Oiso? Is there no one suitable with time on his hands?" Hishikari asked Haneda.

"There's no dearth of people with an abundance of free time, but most around here aspire to aristocratic tastes, even though they are not aristocrats. Unlike a bona fide blue blood like yourself, who has a preference for more plebeian arts, they are more inclined to noh chanting and suchlike."

"So our idle jangling is not to their taste," said Fujimura with a wry smile.

"Still, we need to do something to rally our fellows," said Haneda. "We waited patiently for the war to end and were at last rewarded with the chance to restart this year, but after two or three meetings we've reached this pitiable state of affairs. If it's going to be like this, we shouldn't have bothered to start again." Haneda revealed an old man's petulance.

"So why did Henmi junior stop coming?" asked Hishikari.

"That's not at all clear," Haneda responded indignantly. "If you ask me, the fellow's motive for joining was inappropriate to begin with. He lacked respect and affection for festival music and probably sees it as a sort of unusual hobby—like wearing a flashy tie. Given his youth, that's to be expected, but in that case he is not qualified to join the group. We have dedicated ourselves to it and are determined to devote the energies of our remaining

186

years to this purpose."

"Exactly," said Hishikari. "And when we think how admirably it has helped us to forget the slings and arrows of outrageous society . . . ."

"And, in an unobtrusive way, to sustain independence and freedom of the spirit."

The two elderly gentlemen, Hishikari and Haneda, were in complete accord. Their words confirmed their shared camaraderie—reminding one of the *Sprechchor* choral speeches in leftist plays.

"Indeed, the ten years since the failed coup d'état of February 26, 1936—that unhappy period for Japan—were perhaps the most pleasant for the Goshokai, although it's awkward to admit."

"As we're talking about the pleasures of men of virtue, we need not let that worry us. We enjoyed ourselves, but with great reluctance."

"But once we got going, we were reluctant no longer."

"Now, now, men of virtue should not reproach themselves excessively. Besides, given the present state of the country, we will probably have to distract ourselves again this way."

"That's right. At a time when the Goshokai may become truly significant, the lack of a gong and a flute player will be a serious impediment."

The discussion had returned to its starting point.

"Dr. Haneda's interpretation may adequately explain young Henmi's absence, but I'm somewhat puzzled why Mrs. Hori's flute was so unpolished. I thought she had been taught by her late husband, so one expected her to show a little more enthusiasm," said Hishikari, quietly revealing his dissatisfaction.

"Henmi sent a note to say he would be absent, so that is excusable, but that woman has been absent twice without letting us know, which is unacceptable. Is there some unspoken message in this? Has she just tired of the instrument, though I must say her flute playing was too elementary for her to have tired of it already." Haneda had ceased to mince words.

"'Elementary' is also an apt description for Henmi's gong. His father was no more skilled, but his sense of rhythm was better."

"It's a matter of spirit, you know. After all, old Dr. Henmi was our generation. The blood of people whose lives have spanned the five decades from the Meiji Constitution to the present one is such that myriad emotions can be expressed in the music they play. I cannot say the same for our postwar members."

"And yet we seldom played in harmony," put in Hishikari with a laugh.

"Maybe so. But it's what's called 'harmony without blind agreement.' It reflects the code of the man of virtue and a gentleman's respect for the individual. It is also the secret of ensemble playing," said Haneda. "But our postwar contingent does not understand the true meaning of harmony and just follows along. They cannot distinguish between the freedom you should seek and the one you shouldn't. They probably assume that being absent without notice is some kind of human right. Postwar ethics are quite vexing."

Haneda was venting his irritation, but if Yuri and Takabumi had heard that he considered Mrs. Hori and Henmi their "postwar contingent," they would doubtless have burst out laughing.

As the reader will have gathered, the Goshokai meetings had been canceled for two months due to the absence of two members. Unlike other groups, even if one member was missing the ensemble could not perform. The lack of a gong player was not serious, but without the flute the drums became ineffective. The absent players might think it was just "fool's music" and of no importance, but it seriously spoiled one of life's pleasures for the three old men. This was the reason for their criticism of the unreliability of the new members and of the necessity to consider the group's future.

"Perhaps we should dismiss those two and replace them with professionals to keep us going for the time being," said Haneda.

At this, Hishikari shook his head.

"Dismissing them seems a little extreme, and having professionals goes against our very purpose."

"What should we do then?"

Fujimura, who had remained silent throughout the discussion, finally spoke up.

"I've been hesitant to say anything since I'm not supposed to talk about it, but I recently saw Mrs. Hori and heard her side of the story."

"And what was that?"

Fujimura had won the full attention of Haneda and Hishikari.

The engagement of Yuri and Takabumi had been arranged some time before and the two families were close, so there was nothing unusual about Fujimura meeting Horan. Something in his tone, however, had alerted the other two.

"That woman, as you know, can be very stubborn." Fujimura lingered over the preliminaries, since what he had to say was difficult.

"She's not just stubborn," declared Haneda, without any hesitation at all. "She's downright obstinate."

"Well, while she appears to know the ways of the world, when it comes to her own son she loses all sense of proportion."

"In other words, she's uneducated," said Haneda, still furious at her unpredictable absences. "No matter how much one may study noh chanting or ink painting, if a human being is cut from inferior cloth, there's little to be done. All she can hope for is to become an instructor at some back-street art school."

"Be that as it may," said Hishikari, trying to pull the conversation back on track, "is there any connection between her absence and her son?"

"Yes, there is. Her son is the reason. Takabumi has become involved, shall we say, with someone related to one of our members." Fujimura avoided looking at Haneda. "This is extremely hard for me to say."

"You don't have to hold anything back. Is that woman saying it's awkward to see one of us because of her son?" asked Haneda suspiciously.

"It's not just a matter of awkwardness. She feels resentful, or perhaps I should simply say she's angry."

"Really? And who is the object of her anger?"

"Well, it is you, sir."

"She's angry at me? How unexpected! I haven't the slightest recollection of doing anything to make her angry."

Haneda looked as amazed as he would have if all his students had decided to go on strike.

"I understand your bewilderment perfectly. I told her repeatedly that you could not possibly know anything about the matter, but her maternal instincts have got the better of her and she's lost her powers of reasoning."

Fujimura went on to tell the story of Takabumi and Komako. Since he had heard it from Horan, it was inevitably biased in favor of Takabumi. It sounded as if Komako, unhappy at the absence of her husband, had seduced the young man.

"Shameful," fumed Haneda, "if that is what really happened."

Haneda's plan of enjoying the rest of the day in cultivated conversation with his old friends was completely ruined.

"If that really took place," said Haneda, his voice rising, "I must first of all apologize to you, Mr. Fujimura, since it casts a shadow over the future of the liaison between your daughter and Takabumi."

Haneda may have considered himself a liberal, but when it came to morals involving himself or those around him, he was a firm traditionalist.

"I'm sure you all know that daughter of mine—more of a boy, I'd say.

But she is not in the least bit bothered by it."

Fujimura revealed that he, too, had a soft spot for his offspring.

"You cannot be sure about that," said Hishikari. "A girl is not likely to say what she feels. She would probably be too shy." His thinking was also out of date.

"No matter what your Yuri thinks, Komako should not be allowed to get away with this. Still, something makes me doubt that she would do such a thing." After his initial outburst, Haneda had begun to feel doubtful.

"Mrs. Minamimura impressed me as a respectable person, but then I heard rumors of another liaison with Henmi junior." Fujimura had not intended to mention this other piece of gossip from Horan.

"What do you mean? Has Komako been up to something with Henmi, too?"

Haneda's agitation returned.

"Well, it's not very clear, but it seems there was something between them, and that Henmi's absence from our group is related to it."

"Is that true?" Haneda's expression grew darker.

"It is probably a mistake. One cannot readily believe it," said Hishikari, always an advocate of the moderate path.

"Possibly. But the fact is that the two went for a drive somewhere."

Fujimura, as Yuri's father, seemed to have lost any good feelings he might have had toward Komako.

"That's even worse. Not only has she made trouble with Takabumi, but now you say she's making eyes at Henmi, a married man," said Haneda. "Whatever they may say about the decline in morals since the war, this is surely unforgivable. And if this is the reason the Goshokai has lost its flute and gong players, then Komako is responsible for our woes. It's outrageous! I will question her and get to the bottom of it."

Haneda was already upset by the difficulties with the ensemble, and he now revealed his abhorrence of immorality.

"*Oi! Oi!*" Haneda shouted, clapping his hands at the same time. This traditional way of summoning one's spouse was no longer acceptable in postwar households.

"What is it?" Ginko soon appeared, wiping her hands on her white apron.

"A terrible thing has happened," sputtered Haneda. "Komako has seduced Hori Takabumi and is suspected of making a pass at young Henmi, too. She's shown her true colors. If we don't do anything, who knows how many men may fall into her poisonous clutches." In his excitement, Haneda's language had grown colorful.

190

Raising a plump hand to her lips, Ginko tittered delicately, much amused.

"It's no laughing matter!"

"Is this why you called me? It's all a lot of nonsense. Now, let me tell you that I've managed to get hold of some very fresh yellowtail and sea pike. I'll serve it right away." She was about to return to the kitchen when her husband stopped her.

"Wait. The sashimi sounds good, but we need you to help us with this Komako problem."

"Do you really believe that story?" Ginko looked at her husband as though she was disappointed with him.

"Even if I don't believe all of it, as long as rumors like this are circulating I can't sit and do nothing, can I?"

"Well, what did I tell you earlier? The first thing is to find Iosuke as soon as possible."

"Nobody's saying that Iosuke's done anything wrong. And if he has, he hasn't caused any problems. The person who has is Komako."

"No, it's Iosuke. If Iosuke were at home where he belongs, none of these rumors would have started."

"You may be right."

Haneda yielded surprisingly quickly to his wife's reasoning.

"If husband and wife are together, then problems do not arise. Don't you think so, gentlemen?" Ginko looked at the two guests.

"I couldn't agree with you more," affirmed Hishikari, while Fujimura, showing his background, gave a typical engineer's straightforward, "In principle, yes."

"The fact is that we cannot ignore Komako's alleged behavior. It affects the Goshokai. To get our gong and flute back, I'm thinking of going to see her tomorrow," said Haneda, glancing at his wife.

"Oh, don't do that. Poor girl, she wouldn't do anything stupid. If you don't trust her, I'll go and see her myself. This kind of discussion ought to be between women."

"Yes, it would be best if you went. If that's settled, I'm greatly relieved. And yes, we'd be very grateful for that sashimi."

The sashimi and saké were served before the sun went down and dispelled the gloom that had hung over the gathering.

Haneda was holding his saké cup to his lips but doing more talking than drinking,

"I'm beginning to think it's too much of a strain to get along with post-war people, so I don't see any likelihood of visiting Tokyo much. But I want to keep the ensemble going. I can't imagine retirement without it."

"Besides, it's not just for our amusement. It will help to preserve the tradition of Kanda festival music. No one else seems interested in it," said Fujimura. "The imperial court will stick to its *gagaku* music, and the middle class will support noh, but there's only this small band for festival music, so we have a responsibility to continue." He had completely forgotten about the unpleasant topic of the previous hour and was enjoying himself, his cheeks pink after a few cups of saké.

The former viscount helped himself to a slice of yellowtail and offered his own perspective.

"Indeed. Of course, we're not very good, but we can take pride in the fact that we learned the basics from our late teacher, Hasegawa Kintaro. Although we're amateurs, it's because we're carrying on the correct tradition that we can talk to professionals. It's another sign of the decline of tradition." With that, he directed his chopsticks toward the sashimi.

"Exactly. How nostalgic to think of the days when we studied under Kintaro! You were very talented, Mr. Hishikari, so you made quick progress, but I couldn't master the small drum and kept getting scolded by him," said Haneda.

"No, it was Dr. Henmi on the gong who was the worst. He never became very accomplished."

"Old Hori's flute always lagged behind the most. Whenever we were supposed to speed up, the flute would always trail behind the drums."

"But those two were so enthusiastic. And they were such good men."

"Nothing is sadder than losing them. Henmi junior and Mrs. Hori are, truth be told, substitutes at best."

"Yes, I agree. As it was the son of one member and the widow of the other, we thought the harmony of our group would be maintained and I let them join, but the old atmosphere has gone."

"Perhaps we should continue with just the three of us. I'll play the flute and you, Professor Haneda, can handle the small drum, and Mr. Fujimura can play the large drum," suggested Hishikari.

"With no gong? It would be forlorn without the gong."

"It's just a suggestion. If we can't find anyone suitable, that's what we'll have to do. It's better than not playing at all," concluded Haneda.

"Yes, we can't stop meeting. That would be the worst." His two guests responded almost in unison.

192

Haneda heard the front door open and someone call out "Good evening."

Neither of his guests seemed to notice, but to Haneda it sounded like Komako.

Continuing the conversation, he said, "The ideal would be to find two or three members our age. There must be people such as Mr. K, the former count we met at your house. He seemed a man of taste."

"No, he wouldn't be right. He's got his heart set on politics and is just waiting for the purges to cease, so he's only free temporarily," said Hishikari.

"That's a pity. So it'll have to be someone whose hobby is either the tea ceremony or golf."

"Right. K is involved in the tea ceremony. Anyone interested in our sort of music would have to have graduated from the tea ceremony and noh chanting stage."

"Moreover, people like yourself, Mr. Hishikari, have graduated from the universities of Shimbashi and Akasaka as well."

Haneda made a joke by granting academic status to Tokyo's major red-light districts, but he was distracted by his awareness that the new arrival must be Komako. His mind was more on what he would say to rebuke her, and his banter was flagging.

"In our day," said the respectable Fujimura, "we enjoyed the company of geisha, but where do young people go for amusement nowadays?"

"Oh, dance halls and cabarets," began Hishikari. Then he recalled something and turned to Haneda.

"It may seem a strange question, but have you heard from your nephew Iosuke since we last met?"

"No, he's as elusive as the wind," answered Haneda, making a wry face.

"I may have been mistaken, but I saw someone in Ginza a week ago who looked like him."

Haneda moved closer and asked, "Did you talk to him?"

"No. If I had, I could have been sure, but I only saw his back."

"How did he look?"

"Well, he was wearing an expensive suit and he had a fashionable woman on his arm."

"It must have been someone else. He doesn't have that kind of money."

"Not many people are his size. The woman was quite young, and from the way she dressed she was either a dancer or a high-class call girl."

193

"If only you had confronted him."

"The two of them disappeared into a restaurant in a back street."

Ginko came into the room with more saké. Moving to her husband's side, she asked him to excuse himself for a moment.

"We're talking about something important."

"But it's Komako, and she's asking us to put her up for the night."

Chapter 15
Women Together

That night Komako stayed with the Hanedas. She had done that only once before, shortly after she and Iosuke had been married. Since then, no matter how late it was, they had always caught the train home. Komako could never feel entirely relaxed there in the same way as in her parents' home.

As a result, Haneda was curious as to why Komako had asked to spend the night.

"Something must have happened," he told his wife.

"You're probably right. But act as if you don't know anything. Whatever it is, I'll try and coax it out of her tomorrow."

This exchange took place at night, before the old man and his wife went to sleep.

It is true that Komako had come to Oiso to consult about Iosuke, but the main reason for asking to be put up was her fear of Heiji. She could not keep troubling the landlady, but it might be dangerous to stay in her own house. She wanted to be able to enjoy one good night's sleep somewhere safe. Although she was reluctant to impose on the Hanedas, it was better than staying with the landlady.

The next morning Komako woke up at the same time as Ginko and immediately set about helping with the chores. Haneda was also an early riser, and it was his habit to take a daily walk along the shore at daybreak. After he had left, swinging his walking stick as usual, Ginko spoke to Komako while adjusting the fire under the pots on the cookstove.

"Komako, you don't come often, so please don't feel you have to work so hard. We can clear up after last night when we've had breakfast, so leave it for now. Tell me, have you had any news of Iosuke since we last saw you?"

"No, and I don't know what to do."

Komako's voice trailed off as she stood at the sink washing the plates and bowls of the previous night. From her tone Ginko could detect that Komako was truly at a loss.

"One of the guests last night said that he saw someone who looked like Iosuke in Ginza recently. He said Iosuke was wearing a nice suit and he saw him go into a famous restaurant." Ginko thought it best not to mention the young woman on Iosuke's arm.

"It must be someone else. Iosuke couldn't possibly afford that." Her rejection of the idea was tinged with disappointment.

"Where do you suppose he's been hiding? It's high time he came home, isn't it?"

"Yes. I thought he'd be back in two or three days, so I went ahead and . . ."

"Went ahead and what?"

"Told him to get out, just like that."

Komako's tone seemed unusually subdued, and Ginko sensed it was the perfect chance to discover what was going on in the younger woman's mind. Unfortunately, at that very moment Haneda returned.

While the three of them ate breakfast together, Komako was bothered by her uncle's apparent ill humor. After the guests had left the night before, she had gone to pay her respects to him, but he had treated her to none of his usual witticisms. She had never seen him in such a bad mood.

She wondered if yet another critical magazine article about him had appeared. During the war, Haneda had been under surveillance by the secret police. After the defeat, too, he had been a frequent target of ridicule by more progressive professors. So, things had not always been easy for him.

Unaware that she herself was the reason for her uncle's irritability, she tried to make conversation.

"Uncle, I noticed you didn't play any music last night. Is that because you can't play unless there are five of you?"

It was not the most diplomatic question.

"If someone is causing trouble, we can't play no matter how many members are present," said Haneda sourly. Seeing that he had finished his rice, Komako held the tray out for his rice bowl so that she could fill it, but he ignored her and handed the bowl to his wife instead. Ginko silently passed it to Komako.

Even that, however, failed to alert Komako that it was she who was the cause of Haneda's displeasure, so she asked an even more insensitive question.

"Uncle, these days I've been doing a lot of thinking about the meaning of freedom for a woman, and . . ."

"A woman's freedom? If you're referring to the freedom that has come about because adultery is no longer a crime, I don't want to talk about it!" he snapped with such vehemence that Komako felt she had been physically struck. Something was wrong. Ordinarily, if she had ventured a naive comment like that, he would have entertained her with a jolly thirty-minute lecture spiced with his brand of wry humor.

After breakfast, Haneda withdrew to his study without a word.

"Is Uncle not well? I came because I want to discuss something with him." She appealed to her aunt for support.

"Well, perhaps not today, Komako," Ginko said, with a warm smile. "Why don't you stay two or three days and bring the matter up when it seems a good time?"

"It'll be trouble for you, but perhaps you're right, though I don't know if I should be away from home for so long."

"But don't you always ask the landlady to keep an eye on the house?"

"Yes. There's nothing of value in it anyway."

"So what's bothering you?"

"It may sound strange, but what if he were to come home while I'm gone?"

A little before noon, Ginko went into her husband's study.

"I'd like to ask you to have lunch by yourself today," she said.

"Why?" Haneda asked, taking off his glasses and placing them on the large sandalwood desk.

"I'm going to take Komako to lunch at the Shokintei restaurant."

"That's quite an extravagance," he remarked.

"There's a lot to discuss and she'll find it difficult to talk freely here. If it's just the two of us, I can find out what's going on."

"Do you think she'll tell you?"

"Oh yes! She's already told me she's worried that Iosuke might come back while she's here."

"Don't be fooled by what she says!"

"Just leave it to me. All I ask is that you don't say anything and have lunch by yourself. I'll set everything out on the table."

"Fine with me. Have you got enough money? Not that my wallet would be much help."

"Don't worry. I can manage lunch at the Shokintei when necessary."

"Oh? The nest egg has hatched, eh?"

Haneda made his first joke of the day.

Ginko went back to speak to Komako.

"Komako, we're going out for lunch—my treat. So get ready and we can leave."

197

"I don't want to put you to such trouble."

"Nonsense. Sometimes we women need a break."

"Uncle's not coming then?"

"How can we relax with a man around! Besides, it's good for him to mind the house and eat lunch on his own now and then."

Ginko went to get changed. She put on an Oshima lined kimono but decided to forego the *tabi* socks. Komako was wearing the dress she had come in, so she only needed to freshen her makeup.

As they left the house, Ginko turned toward the study and announced loudly, "We're off now!"

It was answered by a roar.

"Listen to that! Sounds like a tiger in its cage!" joked Ginko to make Komako relax.

They walked past villas enclosed by hedges and bamboo fences, climbed the hill by the train tracks, and entered the open area in front of the station. With the beach-going crowds of summer gone, it was deserted.

"Is this your first visit to the Shokintei? It's at the top of this slope," said Ginko. They passed through an imposing old gate and walked up the tree-lined path.

The Shokintei was just one of many villas in Oiso that had been converted into inns after the war. Standing atop a pine-covered hill, it consisted of a Western-style building dating to the Meiji era, surrounded by several smaller structures serving as private dining rooms.

Ginko entered the empty vestibule and called out, but it was some time before anyone came to greet them.

"I telephoned earlier. Is one of the cottages available for lunch?"

"Yes, this way, please."

The maid showed them into an eight-mat room that resembled a teahouse set among the trees.

"What a beautiful view! From here it hardly looks like the sea at Oiso."

Standing on the veranda, Komako was looking toward the ocean, which was visible between the trunks of the pine trees. It was a fine autumn day, and the Miura Peninsula and the small island of Enoshima were outlined against the deep blue of the sea. The waves lapping unheard against the shore looked like frills of white lace.

"Komako, you're my guest today," said Ginko, directing Komako to the seat of honor in front of the tokonoma.

"When I came to Oiso as a child, this villa was so splendid, so magnificent. We never dreamed it would become an inn," Komako said, thinking that its decline mirrored her own life.

"You may be mistaking this for the Villa Iwai nearby. That has been turned into a somewhat unusual orphanage."

"Oiso has certainly changed, hasn't it?"

"And not just Oiso!"

The maid came in with tea.

"What would you like to have for lunch?" asked the maid.

"Komako, let's treat ourselves to something special, all right?"

"Oh, not on my account, please."

"Why not? Please bring us two orders of the Sumiyoshi restaurant's famous broiled eel as well as the lunch."

"Certainly, ma'am."

"And a bottle of warm saké."

"Goodness, we're going to drink?"

"What's wrong with women having a drink? It's not against the law. If we women don't enjoy ourselves now and again, how can we survive?" Ginko laughed.

She's acting a little out of character today. What's going on? wondered Komako.

Komako was perceptive enough to know that Ginko would not normally do this. The Hanedas were not well off, so it was odd that her aunt would take her to an expensive restaurant and treat her like an honored guest.

"Sorry to keep you waiting," announced the maid, bringing the saké and appetizers.

"This restaurant is a favorite with lovers, and I suppose they drink saké like this. So let's pretend we're one of those couples. As two women, we can really let our hair down."

After one or two cups of saké, Ginko's eyelids were flushed, but she kept pouring for Komako. It was fine to talk about drinking, but she could not take much. Komako, on the other hand, was still steady after several cups. Her fainting fit with Henmi had been the result of the unfortunate combination of alcohol and cigarettes.

"In that case, you can be the man and I'll be the girl who's being seduced," said Komako, playing along.

"That's right. Think of me as a balding executive. But I hear girls these days don't care how old a man is provided he's rich. Is that true?"

"That seems to be the trend. But unlike the professional geisha of the old days, they're not just after money. They're looking for men who're on their way up socially and professionally. They trust a man who has the ability to earn a living and get ahead, and that is lacking in young men these days."

"Why?"

"Times are hard for men in their thirties. They're exhausted from the war and they can't think straight, so loving a woman or being someone a woman can rely on seems to be furthest from their minds."

"That's too bad. And what about younger men?"

"You mean boys who grew up during the war? They are the real postwar generation—completely self-absorbed and unable to think of anything except their own limited desires. They don't know how to love a woman in the true sense, and they don't even want to. When their passions are aroused they're like children. They behave erratically and they're selfish. That's why girls are so disgruntled with boys their own age and look for people who are older and more dependable."

"Really? That makes men in their twenties and thirties seem hopeless. Isn't that bad news for women? When I was young, there were plenty of attractive men around. I felt like a kid in a candy store."

"I heard that Uncle was rather dashing and brilliant in his day. He'd graduated with honors from Tokyo Imperial University and looked like the kabuki actor Onoe Eisaburo!"

"Come now, you mustn't tease an old lady. But I'm puzzled how young women nowadays feel. Unlike my generation, young women today are progressive and strong-willed. And of course the world is different, too. Women have been liberated and men and women have equal rights. Everything is changing. Which means that neither helpless young men nor conventional older men are really satisfying for women today, are they?"

"That's true. But ultimately a woman wants to love someone, and if she can't find that person, she at least wants someone she can trust." Without realizing it, Komako had found herself confiding in Ginko. To conceal a surge of emotion, she picked up her chopsticks to sample the *amadai* fish cooked teriyaki style that had been served.

"So they're not very different from women in the past. But this doesn't apply to you, does it, Komako?" Ginko was enjoying the dish of simmered chestnuts while listening alertly to what Komako was saying.

"Lately I'm surprised by my own lack of confidence. My age group is in the worst possible position. We're not exactly postwar, but we're not traditional women either."

"You're living in the best age—the richest in every respect but also the most confusing."

"Yes, nothing's clear at all. I get disgusted with myself. I don't know what to think about Iosuke or what I should do. I'm at my wit's end."

"I can understand that and I don't blame you. Your husband left and hasn't come back for nearly six months."

"But it was me who drove him out."

"All the same, it's strange for a husband to walk out like that without saying anything. Even if he did leave, you'd think he'd wait for the right time and come back."

"I don't think he can figure out how to do that. But where do you suppose he's gone? I'm worried about him these days."

"But isn't it easier not having him around? It gives you a chance to live the way you want for a change."

"I've done that."

"And how was it?"

"Disappointing." Komako answered honestly, looking up with her large, round eyes.

"That's too bad," commiserated Ginko. "And what was disappointing?"

"There wasn't a single decent man anywhere."

Komako had spoken calmly, but Ginko was visibly shocked.

Good gracious, has this girl done something awful? she wondered.

"Forgive me for being frank," continued Komako, "but since you were married, was there never a time when you were interested in someone apart from your husband?"

Komako was staring at Ginko. Perhaps the alcohol was having an effect.

"Well, I'd be lying if I said there wasn't."

"And were there times when you couldn't stand Uncle any more?"

"Plenty!"

"Even you?"

"Naturally! Have you ever met a more cantankerous, critical, and egotistical man than my husband? You can't imagine how many times I've thought of leaving him. Then, about the time I turned forty, my thinking began to change. I realized that even if I left Haneda for another man, I might not end up with anyone better."

"So you put up with it, right? People of your generation were able to do that."

"Hold on a minute. Even a traditional woman couldn't put up with the impossible, you know. You bear what you can, and if you can't, that's too bad. In any case, I stopped complaining about Haneda when I finally saw the true nature of men. I had always had a high opinion of men, but something unexpected made me understand them."

"What happened?"

"It was when we were living in Aoyama. Your uncle had just been made dean of the law faculty at the university, and naturally this carried a lot of prestige. And as far as I can see, when a man attains some status in society and people start to fawn over him, that's when things are worst for his wife. He tries to lord it over her, too."

"I'm afraid I've never had that experience."

"You're very lucky not to have. In those days, Haneda was quite obnoxious. And because one's husband is so highly regarded, one gets taken in by it, too. Against my better judgment, I'd try to please him in every way, but then it all got out of hand. He became thoroughly spoiled, throwing his weight around all the time. Finally, we had a big quarrel one morning."

"The fact that you can quarrel sounds fortunate to me. With Iosuke, it's just me getting mad all by myself."

"Let me finish. I was so angry that I thought I'd kill him and commit suicide myself. It was that bad. And then your uncle comes into the room with his old cutthroat razor and starts shaving."

"Sounds dangerous."

"No, it was his habit to shave there. Usually I would lather his face, but that day I just sat there and let him get on with it. I was watching him, and he starts shaving, trying to look dignified. He's tipping his face up, then down, tugging his nose this way and that, pulling his skin back, making funny faces, pursing his lips like a clown—you know the faces a man makes while he's shaving! It was quite a show. Finally I thought I'd burst out laughing. But it wasn't because his face was so funny. It was because I suddenly saw how comical men are. They're such fools—silly, muddle-headed, impatient, arrogant, vain, and, on top of that, stingy, cowardly, and obsessed with you-know-what. It was like a revelation that showed men's faults all at once."

"What an amusing way to see men."

"Anyway, all the faults I'd observed in men and kept bottled up inside flashed through my mind. And from that time on I could not get angry with your uncle whatever he said or did. On the contrary, I found it sort of endearing. I suspect young women today have too high an opinion of men. They're not satisfied unless they believe their husband is important, right?"

"I'm a bit different."

"No, I think you may be like them. Aren't you unhappy with Iosuke simply because you believe a man ought to be someone wonderful whom you can have complete trust in?"

"But isn't it possible that somewhere there's a manly man—someone a woman can wholly devote herself to without any regrets?"

"If there were, he'd be a monster."

"How can you be so sure?"

"Komako, be patient and let the years pass. For a woman, does an 'ideal bride' or a 'paragon of beauty' really exist? Of course not! But men are out there in droves hoping to find just that. They never will. And you're trying to do the same thing."

"What you're saying is quite depressing."

"It may be depressing, but it can't be helped. Look at the proof. Didn't you yourself say that you haven't found a single decent man?

"Yes."

"Right. And while we're at it, tell me frankly if you went all the way with one or two of them."

"No. Before anything like that could happen, they turned out to be such disappointments."

"I'm relieved to hear it. If you'd become seriously involved, you could get out of it, but it would be more complicated. If 'the affair' is only in your mind, it doesn't cause any trouble, so you're safe. Have another drink."

"You know, freedom for a woman is very limited, isn't it?"

"Isn't it the same for men? After all, God plays fair. Isn't Iosuke out there somewhere, experiencing who-knows-what difficulties and wanting desperately to come home?"

"Even if he does come home, I'm worried that the same thing might happen again. Which is why I came to ask your advice."

"I see. If you're considering a divorce, we won't stop you, but let me tell you one more thing. Earlier you asked if any other man had attracted me besides your uncle."

"Yes. I wanted to ask who it was."

"No reason to hide it now! It was Iosuke!"

"What?"

"Don't be so surprised. You can search high and low throughout the country, but you'll never find another man who'd give his wife as much freedom as Iosuke. But you already know that, don't you?"

Chapter 16
Storm beneath the Bridge

"May I impose?"

Iosuke was in bed, his head covered by a blanket, when he heard this call, spoken in a style more likely heard among middle-class madames than the people living under the bridge.

Oh dear, here she is again!

He knew who it was, but he was dozing, and the dreamy feeling of being half asleep was so comfortable that all he did was turn over.

It was ten o'clock. Old Kinji had long since left on his rounds, and the other residents were out at their jobs. Only Iosuke was there.

"Are you still asleep?" Her voice did have a certain refinement.

Iosuke was forced to wake up, but he still made no answer.

Autumn was now well advanced, and the morning sun slanting over the rooftops of Surugadai to the south and spilling through the window of the hut brought a comfortable warmth. It was too bright to sleep in for long, but though Iosuke opened his eyes, he did not get up.

"Oh, you are awake," said the widow Takasugi with a laugh. Her face with its prominent cheekbones was peering through the small window. Iosuke had no choice but to get up.

"Good morning. Nice day, isn't it?" He lumbered to his feet and pushed open the door.

Brisk and cheerful in a freshly washed white apron, Mrs. Takasugi was carrying a tray with a pot of tea and a teacup. Her hair was done as usual in a bun at the nape of her neck, but the morning light showed she had applied a touch of powder to her rather dark-complexioned face.

"I have brought you some tea. Why don't you go and wash your face," she urged, using the same middle-class style of speech.

Without saying anything, Iosuke took his towel and toothbrush and walked to the spring. The water was colder now, and washing his face had become enjoyably exhilarating, but that was not the reason he took his time.

Mrs. Takasugi's kindness was becoming bothersome.

After Kinji suggested that Iosuke live with her, the widow's attitude toward Iosuke had changed noticeably. Her morning and evening greetings carried a flirtatious undertone, and she adopted an affected way of speaking that was incongruous in that community. She also insisted on doing Iosuke's laundry and often gave him pickles she had made. Lately she had taken to bringing him tea in the morning, for her house was the only one with a fire going all day. But Iosuke was not too pleased with these developments. Slow-witted as he might seem, the widow's motive was clear.

"Mr. Minamimura, I've swept the room," she called out as Iosuke returned to the shack. She poured the tea into a cup free of cracks or chips, saying, "I'm sorry, but it may not be hot any longer." No one else living there had the luxury of a cup of tea in the morning, and after muttered thanks Iosuke knelt formally on the floor to drink it, like a guest at a tea ceremony.

The pajamas he wore in place of his work clothes were tight around his bulky thighs, making it uncomfortable to kneel. His posture and his expression showed clearly that he wanted her to leave as soon as possible.

Unfazed, she set out to charm him. "Would you like *miso* soup today or would you rather have toast?"

Using the time-tested strategy that the way to a man's heart is through his stomach, the widow would renew her assault each morning. Since Iosuke and Kinji had stopped cooking rice together some time ago, Iosuke had accepted her offer once or twice, but recently he had begun refusing.

"Thank you, but I'm not hungry today."

"There you go again. It's not good to go without eating in the morning. Have something light—some toast—all right? My late husband liked toast for breakfast, and I'm good at making it," she said. By adding the polite inflections to her speech, she sought to show him that she had once lived a regular, middle-class life.

"But . . ."

"There's no need to be shy."

Far from being shy, Iosuke was just distancing himself from his self-appointed housekeeper, but, faced with such persistence, he did not have the heart to refuse outright. In the eyes of the doting older woman, this made him all the more attractive.

She took bread and some butter from what Iosuke had on his shelf.

"I'll be right back," she said, and with that returned to her own shack.

This gave Iosuke the opportunity he had been looking for, and he immediately began preparations to leave. He had no idea where he would go, but if he could be out before Mrs. Takasugi returned with her constant prattle, his purpose would be served.

However, despite hurrying, clumsy Iosuke could not move fast enough.

Just as he was knotting his tie, he heard footsteps outside. So she had beaten him to it, he thought. He sat down with his back to the door, his head sunk into his shoulders.

"*Hey, Daddy!* Isn't it a beautiful day!" a voice called out brightly. It was Yuri, come to his rescue.

"So you're here again," he said, happy not so much at seeing her as having received a timely defense against Mrs. Takasugi's offensive.

"Are you going out?"

Yuri had noticed Iosuke's shirt and tie and, untroubled by the shabbiness of the shack, had sat down on the matting, ignoring the fact that it was as hard as a plank.

"Well, I don't have anything special to do, but . . ."

"Great!" she sang out. "So you can spend the day with me, can't you?"

She took some makeup from her handbag, a gift Iosuke had bought her shortly before, and began touching up her face.

Yuri had taken to visiting Iosuke once or twice a week and was well known to the people there, who gave her the nickname "Miss Panpan." She had acquired it when Kajiki had asked Iosuke in all seriousness, "Who's that? Is she a panpan girl?" There were lots of such girls in Tokyo, as Kajiki knew, and indeed most of the people in the shacks considered Yuri a bona fide prostitute. How horror-stricken the Fujimuras would have been had they known!

"Let's go then," said Iosuke.

He was about to put on his shoes when Mrs. Takasugi reappeared with a tray.

"Sorry to be so long, but the fire went out."

As well as toast, she had brought a soft-boiled egg, but the moment she saw Yuri in her stylish light green suit and Iosuke dressed to go out, her manner changed abruptly. She was livid.

Yuri continued nonchalantly powdering her nose, but the gentle-hearted Iosuke could not help apologizing. "Thank you very much. I'm just going out, but I'll gladly eat it before I go." He reached for the tray.

"You don't have to force yourself, Mr. Minamimura!"

"I'm not," he said. "I'm beginning to feel hungry."

"Don't lie! I know you don't like what I've made!" With that she threw the tray to the ground. Dishes shattered, the toast went flying, the egg splattered, and she ran back to her shack with an anguished cry.

"What a mess! Should I go and apologize?" asked Iosuke, picking up the broken dishes.

"No need to bother. We've got to fight against feudal hysterics like those if anything's going to change." Yuri sounded like one of those progressive columnists in the newspapers.

"That's easy for you to say, but I don't like this kind of thing."

It had been some time since he had suffered the destructive force of "Typhoon Komako," and the threat of a storm there in the quiet idyll under the bridge had shaken Iosuke to the core.

Why are women so emotional? he wondered. Why can't they be more peaceful and reasonable, and get along with men? Why do women, whether educated or not, always resort to violent acts or violent language? He had heard of one woman who had even thrown nitric acid into a man's face. And there was a certain other woman who had told her husband to "Get out!" What Mrs. Takasugi had done was less extreme, but it still amounted to violence. It was ironic, indeed, that the goddess of peace was a woman! All women are hysterical, he thought, and no form of militarism could compare with the irrationality and egoism of a woman on the warpath. The world might one day be rid of war, but it would need a million years to eliminate women's hysteria.

Absorbed in such pessimistic thoughts, Iosuke found it difficult to move.

"Let's go," Yuri pressed him.

Iosuke finally stood up, but he felt depressed.

"Yuri, you're a woman, too, right?"

"What are you talking about? You're acting very strangely today. Are you okay?" She peered at him curiously. Iosuke's gloomy thoughts continued.

This young woman hasn't got into the habit of getting hysterical yet, he thought, but one or two years into her marriage and she'll be an expert at it. She may belong to the postwar generation, but there are not likely to be any exceptions.

Slowly he came out of the shack, but they had to pass Mrs. Takasugi's shack to go into town, and Iosuke sneaked by as quietly as if it were a tiger's den. Perhaps she was still crying, for her door remained closed and she was not to be seen.

It was no longer as easy to live there as it had been. Old Kinji was dropping hints that he wanted Iosuke to leave, and now the widow was in tears, so life was not all that different from the world above. What had happened to the wonderfully free atmosphere of earlier days?

The two finally reached the path leading to the bottom of the escarpment. The green grass was turning an autumnal hue.

At that moment the sound of running footsteps behind them made Iosuke stop apprehensively, thinking that Mrs. Takasugi was after him again.

"Mr. Minamimura, where are you off to?" It was Kajiki.

"Oh, hello. You haven't been around for a while."

Happy to see Kajiki, Iosuke walked toward him. Kajiki had not been in his hut for the past four or five days, and Iosuke had been feeding his goat.

"I got back this morning. I went to your place but you were asleep. I went back later, but you'd just left, so I came after you."

"What did you want to tell me?"

Kajiki noticed Yuri's flamboyant clothes, and with a glance over at Okanenomizu Station said, "She attracts too much attention, you know. Look, they're all staring this way. You'd better not do anything to get yourself noticed."

Kajiki hunkered down among the tall grass so the people up there could not see him, and Iosuke did the same. Yuri went ahead up the ladder to wait for Iosuke at the main road.

"Oh, it hadn't occurred to me," said Iosuke.

"Nothing wrong with playing around, but it's dangerous to bring her here. There're plenty of places to meet, like Shinjuku Station or the corner of the Hattori PX."

Despite looking like a farmer, Kajiki knew his way around Tokyo.

"I don't need to say it, but don't tell her anything about our project and our hideout," he cautioned.

"I won't."

"Women are dangerous. They have magic powers to make you talk."

"Why are you so worried all of a sudden?"

"The situation's not good. There're problems about the second shipment. It's ready to go anytime. We closed the Shitaya hideout two days ago and moved somewhere else. It's best if you don't know where. I'll be moving out of here soon, too."

"You're leaving?"

"It's not safe here any more. I'm in charge of the next ship so I'll be on board. I have a lot on my hands right now, and this evening may be the only chance I have to meet you, so please come back early."

"I will."

"If anyone asks you any questions, just swear you don't know a thing. In fact, you don't know anything and had nothing to do with it. Now go and

208

have a good time."

Emotion infused Kajiki's voice as he gripped Iosuke's hand.

Walking beside Yuri along the riverside street toward Okanenomizu Station, Iosuke was completely lost in thought.

So Kajiki's leaving!

He was not so much worried about the danger Kajiki warned him of as saddened to lose a man who had become a good friend.

Of all the people living under the bridge, Kajiki had been the one he had talked to the most and grown closest to. And Iosuke liked Kajiki. He might be stubborn, but his straightforwardness and his passionate beliefs, as well as his sense of duty, appealed to Iosuke. In that regard Kajiki was far superior to anyone at the Tokyo News Agency. For some reason Kajiki had respected Iosuke. In front of his comrades he called him "Admiral" and had always treated him deferentially. This may have been due partly to his military training, but Iosuke, accustomed to being the butt of ridicule, was gratified. His leaving reminded Iosuke of how he had felt as a boy when a student lodger he liked left the Minamimura household. He had been filled with a sense of loss.

"How about a day trip to Hakone," Yuri proposed.

Iosuke mumbled a vague reply. As they turned toward Okanenomizu Bridge, he heard a friendly greeting.

"Hey, Iosuke! Going out?"

Iosuke turned and saw old Kinji about to cross the road from the Keitendo Hospital side. He was carrying bags of shopping and was followed by a heavy-set woman of about fifty.

"I guessed you wouldn't be in today, so I invited the missus over for a drink. She's got the day off."

Grinning, Kinji gestured with his chin toward the woman. She was wearing a striped cotton kimono tied a little lower than usual, with a small *obi* sash that was in danger of coming undone. She approached Iosuke and launched into a speech.

"This is the first time I've met you, sir, isn't it? You know, I get homesick for the place under the bridge, so I've been visiting now and then when you're out. A gentleman like yourself doesn't have to live in a dirty shack like that. Wouldn't you rather live somewhere different? Even at our age, him and me still want to live together. Be a sport, eh?" she said with a lusty laugh that revealed her gums.

The two couples—the hulking Iosuke with the loudly dressed girl, and the shabby old man and his wife—were quite a sight as they stood talking. Passersby stared at them, making even Yuri blush.

"Let's go," she urged.

So now Iosuke was free to go anywhere. No one would call him back. His despondency deepened.

Yuri was bubbling with excitement as they reached Okanenomizu Station. "If we're going to Hakone, shall we go from Tokyo Station or take the Odakyu Line from Shinjuku?"

Iosuke wanted to reject the idea and said, "It's late now, so we'd have to stay over."

But Yuri was not discouraged. "So let's stay over. What's wrong with that?"

"You should have a bit more self-respect! Your body is worth looking after," he growled gently.

"Are you saying my body's a 'national treasure'? Don't worry! It's not going to burn up and disappear. If you don't want to stay over, we can rest in a hotel for a while and come back. If we just go to Yumoto, we can easily make the last train back in time."

"We can't go. I haven't got the money." Iosuke's refusal was firm.

"How much do you have?"

It was not a question a girl who was not on the game should have asked.

"About 1,200 yen. I checked last night."

Iosuke was being honest. In the three months since that poker game he had spent most of his winnings, and since Yuri had begun asking him to take her out, his expenses had increased noticeably. However, as long as he had any money left, he was determined not to ask Kajiki for more; neither had he accepted any of the cash Kajiki had offered, so his wallet was exceedingly thin.

Yet Iosuke was unconcerned. Compared to the 300 yen Komako had doled out to him, 1,200 yen was a small fortune. Besides, ever since he had left home money seemed to fall into his lap, so much so that if he was ever short, he felt that it would just somehow appear. In fact, he was convinced that if he returned to Kajiki's secret club, he could win as much as he wanted at poker.

"Why don't we give Hakone a miss and have lunch around here. It's too early to go to Ginza."

With that, Iosuke started down Surugadai Avenue.

"That's no fun!" Yuri snorted.

210

What was no fun, however, was not giving up Hakone but finding out that Iosuke's seemingly inexhaustible funds had shrunk to 1,200 yen.

"Is that really all you have?"

"For the moment."

"But you can go to the bank, right? You have lots stashed away there, don't you?"

"That would *never happen*."

Through spending so much time with Yuri, Iosuke seemed to have adopted some of her new vocabulary.

The two ate a simple lunch in a coffee shop catering to students in the Kanda area.

"This ham salad's rather shoddy."

Yuri might complain about the food, but it was far more palatable to Iosuke than Mrs. Takasugi's lovingly prepared breakfast, and he ate with appetite.

"You know what?" Yuri said, putting down her fork, "you look rather shoddy, too."

"On a par with the salad, I suppose."

"You're a man who has to have lots of cash or you're nobody. You're such a big man, you need big funds to match."

"I think so, too."

"Only having 1,200 yen is dismal. It makes me feel August 15th has come around again."

Yuri sounded truly saddened. She might talk like a streetwalker, but her sentiments were those of any young woman whose dreams, materialistic or romantic, have just been shattered.

The two sat in silence, drinking the saccharin-sweetened coffee.

It was still early and the coffee shop was not crowded, but two or three groups of students were lingering over their drinks. They looked enviously at Iosuke and darted furtive glances at Yuri. Unlike the people under the bridge, they knew that Yuri was no prostitute. The fact that she was with an older man with plenty of money did not strike them as outrageous or contemptible. On the contrary, they seemed to be lamenting their own impotence. They kept stealing looks at Yuri until she glared at them so fiercely that they looked away, cowed. It was a scene unimaginable in prewar days.

Yuri crossed her legs, lit a cigarette, and was lost in thought.

Iosuke was similarly occupied as he replayed in his mind the encounter with Kinji and his wife. Kinji's wife reminded him of a brothel madam, not a type he cared much for. Yet he sympathized with their desire to nurture their affection in their old home during their remaining years. For Iosuke, life under the bridge had lost its former friendliness, so he had no objection to leaving the shack. But in order to rent a room or get lodgings over a store, he needed money. With the small amount he had in his pocket he could do nothing.

Yuri suddenly emerged from her thoughts and stood up.

"I'm going to make a telephone call," she declared and disappeared downstairs.

She returned after a while, looking animated.

"Let's go to Hama Rikyu. I called Takabumi and he's going to meet us there."

Beyond Shimbashi was a bridge called Horaibashi, and over this and a little beyond on the right was the Hama Rikyu garden. Iosuke had never heard of it, but Yuri seemed to know it well. Along with the Shinjuku Gyoen Park, it was one of two former imperial gardens open to the public in Tokyo. Like London's Hyde Park, it had become a popular trysting place since the war.

They paid the 20-yen entrance fee and walked down a gravel path, passing a damaged gateway and overgrown lawns, testament to the neglect the park had suffered since the nation's defeat. The man-made pond, elegant bridges, artificial hillocks, and old pine trees, however, were clearly the legacy of a lordly estate and more refined than Hibiya Park, which had been designed by Western-trained engineers during the drive for modernization in the Meiji era.

They crossed the pond and walked among the trees beside the bay. It was still early, so nearby couples were busy taking souvenir photographs and generally behaving themselves.

Yuri called to Takabumi, who was waiting under an oak tree, one hand in his pocket and a cigarette dangling from his lips in imitation of an American movie hero. The two had located each other easily so they must have met there many times before.

"Mr. Minamimura! How nice to see you. It's been a long time." Takabumi greeted Iosuke warmly, doffing his hat to reveal his fashionable Ginza haircut. For a young man to greet someone whose wife he had been courting and with whom his fiancée had been cavorting without a trace of resentment or hostility would have been unthinkable before the war.

"My, you've grown up." Iosuke treated the young man like a playful puppy, and nothing indicated that they were involved in a sort of love triangle.

They sat down companionably on the grass looking out over the water, although the view there was rather shoddy, too, with the old Odaiba battery and Landfill Number 4 on the other side of the bay.

"Sad news, Takabumi. Iosuke is in a *pinch* for money," said Yuri, using the English word.

"That's too bad. But you have a knack for making big money, right?"

"It's not that I don't, but that doesn't concern you two. Frankly, Yuri's getting on my nerves these days. Do you two really intend to get married?"

"It's not that we don't," said Takabumi, mimicking Iosuke, "but if we just get married as our parents wish, we'd look as if we had no independence, wouldn't we?"

"That's right," said Yuri supportively.

"Perhaps, but what about a little respect for my independence?" Iosuke then broached another important topic. "Young man, is it true you're in love with my wife?"

"We young people don't believe love is absolute. With that limitation, I can say yes, I do love her."

"That's right," Yuri chimed in again.

"But I heard Komako did not fall in love with you."

"True. But that doesn't matter. Without wishing to, I chose her as my teacher in matters of love."

"And did you learn anything?"

"Yes, about technique. But it was frustrating because she was so afraid of being happy and so suspicious. She wouldn't take any chances."

"That does tend to be the way adults behave. So what's Komako doing these days? Did Mr. Henmi fare any better than you?"

"Oh no. That episode came to an end some time ago, and Mr. Henmi's at present courting a blue-blooded novelist. After him came Superman, which has also ended, and now she's disappeared altogether. She's not living at home any more."

"You mean Komako's left the house? That doesn't make sense."

"She's been gone over a month," said Takabumi. "Not that she needs to fear Superman any more. He quit the ration office and joined the police reserves."

"So where's Komako? Do you have any idea? Her family lives way out in the country, where they were evacuated during the war."

"Are you so worried?" asked Yuri. "In that case, I think I know where

213

she's gone."

"Tell me and I'll treat you both to dinner at the Karinsha."

"How can you? You don't have any money!"

"Oh, I forgot about that," said Iosuke, deflated. "So I can't ask."

"Poor man. I feel sorry for you. I heard Papa say that she's in Oiso."

"Are you sure, Yuri?" asked Takabumi, suddenly looking concerned. "If that's true, there may be trouble down there."

"Why?"

"Because today Mama said she was going to Oiso to discuss something with Professor Haneda."

"That should be interesting! Your mother, Mrs. Minamimura, and the professor all together? How exciting!" exclaimed Yuri.

"But there's more. I told Mama that Iosuke was living under Okanenomizu Bridge and everything."

"How could you be so stupid! How many times did I tell you not to say anything? So your mother's decided to tell the professor and make him get the two of them back together again. That way she thinks she can get us married. I bet that's her plan. Adults never give up!"

"What a mess! It's going to be a tragedy!"

Listening to the two chattering excitedly and often incomprehensibly, Iosuke stretched out on the grass.

"Whatever happens, happens. You kids would be safer if you stuck to your own games. Why don't you go and have a good time in Ginza?"

"Not a bad idea," said Yuri brightly. "You didn't have any money, so I asked Takabumi to come."

"But don't you need to comfort Iosuke a little more, Yuri?" asked Takabumi.

"Don't worry about me," said Iosuke. "You go and enjoy yourselves. Here's my contribution."

Iosuke took a 1,000-yen note from his wallet.

"Don't leave yourself so short," said Yuri. "You only have 200 yen left!"

"Never mind, there's something promising on tonight." He spoke with such confidence that the two happily accepted.

"I've changed my mind about you!" Takabumi said.

"No compliments, please."

"I really admire you," said Yuri. "Anyway, we're off. Bye! And come to Ginza later, okay?"

At moments like this, the postwar generation could be quite endearing. They set off like a couple of kids on a picnic. Left alone, Iosuke was finally able to relax.

Why did Komako decide to go to Oiso?

It seemed strange, even amusing, that a woman so strong-willed and sensitive about what others might think should have stayed for a whole month at his uncle's home. Something terrible must have happened for her to abandon the house in Musashi-Hazama.

Iosuke thought all these developments might break down her obstinacy. In that case, she might act less oppressively toward him. Perhaps it was a good time to go home. And going to her while she was in Oiso might be better. With his aunt and uncle present, she might be more reluctant to lambaste him with endless reproaches.

Maybe I'll go to Oiso tomorrow.

It seemed a good idea until he remembered the state of his finances. What to do about money? Not that he needed to go back to Komako pretending he had become rich, but to give the impression he was returning because he was broke could cause more trouble later. Quarrels over money had been frequent throughout their married life, and remembering those days made him hesitate to return to the same situation. He needed to go to Komako with at least enough money to buy her a new suit as a present.

I will need fifty or sixty thousand yen.

So he decided to go ahead with a plan he had been contemplating all day.

It was still early however. There were more couples in the park now, but the clouds reflected in the bay were not yet tinged with an evening glow. Gazing across at the cream-colored TQND building and the freighters moored in the bay, he passed the time daydreaming. A motorboat was pulling a string of rowing boats, the throb of its engines echoing across the water, and as Iosuke listened to that rhythmic pulse he fell asleep.

When he awoke, the scene was shrouded in a bluish twilight, the breeze was cold, and the waves of high tide were lapping noisily against the stone parapet.

Iosuke had slept well. He stretched languidly and stood up. His brooding thoughts had disappeared, and the conviction that he would win a lot that night flooded through him.

Money! Everything depended on money. Whether he was going to rent a room somewhere or go back to Komako, he needed cash. Without it, no kind of freedom was attainable in this day and age. Until now Iosuke had not been aware of the tremendous power of money, so being away from

215

home had taught him a valuable lesson. It had never occurred to him that money was difficult to obtain. He dismissed the hit-and-miss approach of buying lottery tickets and suchlike, because you only had to use your will-power to call it forth—"Let there be money!"—and money would appear. Several times since he left home he had had proof that money did indeed favor him.

Tonight, for the first time in a long time, he would summon that power, so his stride was confident and his step light. No matter what the young couples were up to under the pine trees and by the artificial hillocks, Iosuke paid no heed. He thought no more of them than of the cats and dogs following nature's imperatives in the streets of the city.

Iosuke hurried out of the garden, crossed the bridge, and plunged into the crowds at the Shimbashi intersection. The neon signs of bars and restaurants were coming on, drawing flocks of customers. He felt hungry, but as he could not afford to eat, he decided to indulge in three 40-yen glasses of liquor at a market stall.

He lingered over the drinks, and by the time he stepped into the street again it was completely dark.

Still a little early perhaps, but I'll go and see.

The liquor dampened his hunger and filled him with a cheerful optimism. Crossing Dobashi Bridge, he walked down the broad avenue in the direction of Sukiyabashi. Eventually he reached the corner where the taxi had dropped Kajiki and his partners the other evening.

Retracing their steps that night, Iosuke managed to locate the building. The entrance was shuttered, but unlike that occasion the side door was open. As he entered, the woman standing by the door stared at him but said nothing. Once inside, memory of his previous visit returned and he soon found the right door and knocked.

The bartender was the same, and he remembered Iosuke and welcomed him. Iosuke learned that Mogi, whom he had come to meet, had not been to the club for several days.

"He may be on a trip somewhere. If you want more information, you can wait. Someone will know. Sit at the bar if you like. Do you want a highball?"

That night, shortly after ten o'clock, Iosuke was thrown out of the club.

"Don't ever dare to come back!"

With that, the hitherto affable bartender tossed Iosuke into the corridor. The man was of average size and slightly overweight, so he had no hidden reserves of strength like Heiji, the ration officer. Despite this, he picked Iosuke up as easily as a kitten and thrust him out of the door because Iosuke was as unresisting and as pliant as a jellyfish. It was the same when Komako had pulled him up by the collar.

The events that had led to this began after Iosuke had been drinking at the bar for a while. One of Mogi's friends and a poker player of the other night came into the club, and Iosuke had asked him about Mogi.

"Oh, he's gone to cool his heels in Hawaii. How about another game? I want a chance to win back what I lost."

It was what Iosuke had been waiting for. Mogi had been the excuse for a game of poker and the chance to make fifty or sixty thousand yen. He wanted to gamble, but it did not have to be with Mogi.

After making up a foursome with two others, they entered the side room and opened a new deck of cards. The other three were heavy drinkers and downed whiskey after whiskey. The stakes were high. Iosuke was winning at first, but then his luck ran out. On the previous occasion, Iosuke's misfortune with women had brought him luck, but this time he was a man enjoying the attentions of both Mrs. Takasugi and Yuri, so his luck did not hold. He ended by losing continuously and heavily.

When it came time to settle up, Iosuke turned pale and his head drooped. He had no excuse, for he knew it was a shameful breach of etiquette for a gentleman (if that is what he was) to come to a place like that without any money.

The attitude of the players changed completely. They stood up, stubbing out their cigarettes. Iosuke was not to be let off so easily.

The bartender appeared and apologized to them, saying, "It was my mistake for letting him in." Calling Iosuke over, he took the opportunity to exhibit how hard he could punch.

Iosuke boarded the train near Yurakucho and got off at Okanenomizu. His gait was like that of an ailing elephant, and his mood was as black as a rag soaked in India ink.

The day after he had left home, when his wallet and watch were stolen at Meiji Shrine, he had been disheartened, but that was nothing compared to his present misery. The earlier incident had shown him what it meant to be penniless, but he had not felt humiliated. This time he had received a hard blow psychologically. Slow as he was, he had been well brought up, so the shame was harder to bear.

If only you were here, Mother, he thought.

If she had been alive, she would have been outraged and shed bitter tears of mortification. She would have told him that what he had done was unforgivable. The very thought filled him with anguish. He had not felt as wretched as this when he picked up his first cigarette butt. Indeed, at that time he was like a young man setting out on life's stormy seas for the first time. Dispirited, he stopped by the railing on Okanenomizu Bridge. The overcast sky made the water below appear even darker. Raindrops began to fall, striking his large nose, but his face was already wet with tears. It had been many years since Iosuke had wept.

Mother, I'm miserable!

The man had reverted to childhood. The liquor he had drunk earlier and the whiskeys at the club had weakened his self-control, and childish thoughts and feelings odd in a man his age and size flooded into him. In company or in front of women, a man acts tough and confident, but when things get difficult, he may abandon all pretense and become again a tearful, weak-hearted boy. Most people in this situation appeal to God for help, but the person Iosuke invoked was his mother.

I won't do it again, Mother. I've learned my lesson. Please forgive me!

He felt exactly the same as when he had been shut in a dark storeroom as punishment for some boyish infraction, though he could not remember what that was.

Yet no matter how often he called, his dead mother did not appear. Strangely, it was Komako's face that floated up from the darkness under the bridge.

Komako, I want to come back, but I don't have a penny. Will you let me in anyway?

His inner voice pleaded with her, but Komako, gazing out of the black night, seemed to shake her head.

In the depths of despair, Iosuke let go of the handrail. It had begun to rain heavily. On the other side of the bridge he was assaulted by a strong westerly wind that had been lying in wait. He had a lot to think about, but in this weather he had no choice but to go back to the shack. As he felt his way down the ladder, he remembered promising to visit Kajiki that evening. He would keep his word, regardless of how he felt. He was trudging through the wet grass when a dark figure blocked his way.

"Where are you going?" came an authoritative voice.

By the light from Okanenomizu Station beyond the river Iosuke could make out the shape of a man, but he had no idea who it was. He took a step back, and as he did so anger welled up in him. His misery turned to rage.

"I'm going back to my home. Don't try to stop me or there'll be trouble."

These were strong words for a man of Iosuke's disposition.

"You live under the bridge?"

"Yes. Who are you?"

"Please wait here a while. I'm from the police."

Iosuke peered at the man's face, but all he could see was what looked like a hunting cap on his head.

"You're lying! No policeman would stop a man going to his home. You're the one who's suspicious. If you stick around, the people here will set their dog on you."

Iosuke started to walk forward but was seized by the sleeve.

"You can't go there. Don't move!"

"But it's raining. I don't want to stay here."

There was a scuffle, with Iosuke trying to break free and the man in the hunting cap holding him down.

"So you're not going to obey?"

Realizing that Iosuke was strong, the man jumped back a couple of paces, showing some martial arts training, before he lunged for Iosuke again.

Just then two pistol shots rang out from the darkness under the bridge, followed by a series of shots a little farther away. The sounds ricocheted around as though a hunt was in progress in the mountains.

Forgetting the man holding him, Iosuke looked toward the bridge and could just make out a figure scampering up the steel beams as quickly as a monkey. Only someone in a circus or used to climbing ship's rigging could be so agile.

As if sucked into the darkness, the man disappeared behind a steel girder, which Iosuke knew stretched right across the river.

A number of figures were milling about under the bridge, and police whistles were being blown.

The figure behind the girder came into sight again, sliding down a bridge support on the far side of the river so fast he seemed to be falling. For an instant he was lit up by the station lights, and the whistles sounded again.

Was it Kajiki?

Iosuke's immediate reaction was to run, but he felt a sharp pain in his right wrist. He had not noticed he had been handcuffed. Enraged, he tried to throw off the dark figure that held him.

219

Chapter 17
In Prison and Out

"What a surprise! I had no idea she was that sort of woman," Haneda Tsutomu said to his wife and Komako as he emptied the last drops of his evening saké from a dark red unglazed container into his cup. His anger toward Komako had dissipated at last.

"She could certainly talk. I never knew she had so much to say," Ginko offered as she filled her husband's rice bowl.

"Oh, I've known that for a while. What I didn't expect was the woman's cunning, or her one-sidedness and her vulgarity. She was so Manno-like."

"What does that mean?" asked Komako.

"You know that character in the kabuki play. A woman named Manno appears on the stage and calls out the name of a prostitute."

"Oh, I thought it might be someone in French literature."

"In the play, she's a spiteful waitress in a brothel, a manifestation of women at their worst. But I didn't expect our guest to have all those qualities. How could Hori have married a woman like that, even if it was his second marriage?"

"But haven't I heard you praising her and her geisha-like accomplishments?" said Ginko, taking advantage of the opportunity to show her displeasure at his earlier compliments.

"Well, she did have some good qualities, but she showed her true colors yesterday. I knew she was mean and catty, but I didn't visualize her as such a cat monster."

They were talking about Horan.

The previous afternoon Horan had come to the Oiso cottage and taken it by storm. First, she had delivered a scathing attack on Haneda for failing to supervise his nephew's wife properly, demanding that he return Iosuke to his love-starved wife as soon as possible so that Komako would stop her seduction of Takabumi.

That was the first cause of Haneda's anger, but what had really made his blood boil was what she said next.

"What's wrong with all you venerable gents and that plebeian music of yours? I put up with it because I have my relationship with the Fujimuras to think about. And I thought I might need a professor and some of the others to help my son get on in life. That is why I tolerated piping away on the flute with a bunch of old men. It is all for the sake of my dear boy. For him I would gladly starve, that's how important he is to me! I can't sleep at night until I see him married to a good woman so I can look forward to some security in my old age. I've no time for that *ten-ten'ya* nonsense of yours. I'm not joking. I'm different from all of you—society doesn't need you any longer, so you waste your time clanging your gongs and banging your drums."

Her indictment of the Goshokai ensemble and her insults of its members threw Haneda into a blind rage.

Horan had come to Oiso willing to give up not only her membership in the Goshokai but her friendship with the Hanedas, which she had continued after her husband's death. Her maternal instincts had been the spark that caused the huge explosion.

If Haneda had been more understanding, the commotion would have been less serious, but being childless and obstinate as well as a legal scholar, her clamorous, self-centered diatribe outraged him. Then Komako, who thought the problem concerned herself, entered the fray and began to tell her side of the story. This precipitated an ugly and protracted slanging match between the two women that echoed through the neighborhood, the like of which had not been heard since the house was built. If Ginko had not intervened, it could easily have escalated into screams and fisticuffs.

After Horan left, still fuming, the aftershocks of her visit continued to be felt for the rest of that day and into the next. It was all they could talk about.

"I am determined to expel that woman from the Goshokai. Komako, you put up a good fight. You were not speechless with fury like me. I admired the way you argued calmly, pointing out the faults in her logic. I see now that Iosuke did not stand a chance." He decided not to finish the thought.

"Speaking of Iosuke, do you think what Mrs. Hori said is true?" asked Ginko, her head cocked to one side. "I can't imagine him living under Okanenomizu Bridge."

"How can you believe anything that woman says! Iosuke may be meek and indecisive, but he's an epicure. He couldn't live that kind of life, don't you agree, Komako?" said Haneda as he moved to the veranda after his meal.

Komako did not agree. When Horan had said that, Komako had instinctively known it to be true.

221

That must be where he is!

It would explain why she had found no trace of him. It was the ideal hideout for someone with no skills or abilities, and it must have suited Iosuke well. She had noticed the shacks under Okanenomizu Bridge from the train, and she had a good idea what life there must be like. If he was living there, what she could not account for was the rumor that he was looking well off. Perhaps that was simply a mistake. In any case, she decided that he was most likely there, and she was considering going to have a look that very day. But she hesitated, knowing it would be difficult to win the Hanedas over to the idea.

I'll go and look tomorrow without telling them.

Her mind made up, Komako went outside to collect the evening paper from the postbox at the gate before doing the dishes.

It was still bright out, and golden clouds were floating toward the Izu Mountains. In her usual way Komako paused at the gate to scan the news before taking it to her uncle. Bold headlines announced the attempted arrest of a smuggling gang consisting of members of the former Imperial Navy. Komako was less interested in this than in the latest developments in the lawsuit to ban publication of a translation of a famous novel. Then she noticed a column headlined "Chase under Okanenomizu Bridge," and the name "Minamimura Iosuke (35)" caught her eye near the end of the article. She ran through the garden, leaving one of her clogs stuck in the mud as she leaped onto the veranda and held the newspaper out to Haneda.

"Look! Look at this!"

"What's the rush? Has someone bombed Kyushu?"

Haneda was sitting on the veranda, leaning against a pillar with one knee drawn up. He took the paper from her but he needed his reading glasses so his reaction was delayed.

"Oh, those smugglers again," he said calmly, but as he finished reading he looked up stunned, his lips twitching, too shocked to speak.

To regain his composure, he stroked his mustache and took off his glasses, but his voice sounded far from normal.

"What a fool!"

"What shall I do?" pleaded Komako.

"What shall you do? Well . . ."

"Please help him!"

Komako's voice sounded shrill. She was ten times more upset than her uncle. She felt as if she had jumped off a high cliff without knowing it.

"Iosuke's in the papers?" Ginko had come out of the kitchen.

"It doesn't give any details, but it seems that only Iosuke was arrested and all the others got away. He was always so slow. It's hard to believe that someone like him could be involved in smuggling."

"Exactly. If only Iosuke was smarter," Ginko said, but no one noticed her tactless remark.

"Where is he now?" pressed Komako.

"According to this article, probably at the headquarters of the Metropolitan Police."

"Then I'm going there right away to find out more."

"Good idea, but you don't know who to ask."

Haneda lapsed into thought and remembered his former student, now in the police, whom he had intended to contact to help look for Iosuke.

"I'll go with you. Ginko, check the timetable and find out the next train to Tokyo."

When Haneda and Komako boarded the Shonan Line train at 5:23 p.m., they sat facing each other, but both were absorbed in their own thoughts, and they exchanged few words.

Was there any man who caused so much trouble? Did any husband create so many worries?

The shock and dismay she had felt a little earlier turned to irritation. Not once in their nine years of marriage had she been able to lay her head on her husband's shoulder and rely on him in times of difficulty. It was she who always had to support him. Recalling the words of Iosuke's mother, who long ago had asked Komako to care for him and treat him as an eldest child, she realized that she had been doing that all along. Indeed, her problems with Iosuke had not been those of a wife but of a mother. And what a handful the child had been! And now the final straw—his name in the papers announcing his arrest!

She was furious, yet underneath her anger she felt strangely relieved. At least I know where he is! In fact, it was that knowledge that allowed her the freedom to be angry with Iosuke. Mothers whose sons had been imprisoned in Siberia and were repatriated to Maizuru years after the war had felt much the same. Many of the men had formed communist groups, but their mothers sighed with relief just to know that they had returned alive.

Komako began to see her troublesome husband—and herself—with fresh eyes. Despite all her difficulties, in nine years she had not once wanted to escape from the marriage.

Am I not to spend the rest of my life with him, just as I have up to now?

223

she asked herself.

She was thinking of it not as destiny but in terms of her own character and personality. She recalled the three men who had entered her life in her husband's absence, and not one of them even came close to her ideals.

Does this mean he's the one I can tolerate the easiest?

How could that be? He had already exceeded the limits of her patience. She had not told him to "Get out!" simply on the spur of the moment.

So why am I rushing to police headquarters? Komako had no answers. Her thoughts were scattered and her mind was in a whirl.

You horrid and useless man!

If Iosuke had been there, she would have seized him by the hair, scratched his face, and kicked him.

By the time she came out of her reverie, the train had passed Yokohama. The man sitting next to her had opened his evening newspaper and half of one section was hanging down. She could see the story about the smuggling ring, reported in greater detail than in the *Tokyo Evening News* she had read in Oiso. Even Haneda swallowed his pride and leaned forward to glance at the article.

At Shimbashi Station the two took a taxi to the police headquarters in Sakuradamon. The government office buildings in the district had all been rebuilt and their lights were shining out through the evening mist. Climbing the crescent-shaped steps of the main entrance, Haneda asked the policeman on duty, "Where can I find Inspector Fujita?"

"Deputy Inspector Fujita's office is upstairs to the right. He is chief of the General Affairs Department of the Criminal Affairs Division."

"So he's been promoted. Is he still here?"

"I'm not sure, sir."

Urging Komako on, Haneda led the way into the huge impersonal building. After locating the right office, he entered alone.

Komako had never been in a place like this, and despite her self-confidence she found the atmosphere oppressive. In the concrete corridor where she was waiting, a group of grim-faced people passed by, with policemen leading five or six men in handcuffs. Remembering her husband, she shuddered at the thought that he might be among them.

Haneda appeared at the door of the office he had entered and beckoned to her. Late though it was, Department Chief Fujita was still there.

The high-ceilinged room was impressive. A secretary or assistant neatly dressed in a suit led Komako through it and opened the door to Fujita's private office.

"This is my nephew's wife, Komako," said Haneda, introducing her to a clean-shaven man of about forty who was wearing a gray suit and a carefully knotted dark blue tie. His hair glistened with pomade, and he made a polite bow.

"I'm Fujita. In my student days I benefited tremendously from Professor Haneda's guidance."

He looked no different from any company employee. Komako had imagined she would have to deal with a gravel-voiced man in a uniform with metal buttons, so she was relieved.

"I am sorry to have caused you so much trouble." She felt she had to make this formal apology. Phrases typically voiced by a criminal's wife flowed out naturally.

Haneda and Komako sat side by side on a large sofa, while Fujita brought a chair around in front of them for himself.

"It's quite a surprise to learn that this man's your nephew, Professor. Why was he living in a place like that?" he asked, offering Haneda a cigarette.

"Well, there were various circumstances," said Haneda, glancing briefly at Komako before continuing. "We read the newspaper report, but I cannot grasp the whole story. Could you tell me my nephew's connection with the case and the reason he was arrested? We don't even know that, which is why we have come."

Haneda brought the cigarette to his lips, unaware that it had gone out.

Fujita summoned the officer in charge of the case, who explained everything to Haneda and Komako. The charge against Iosuke was unexpected: obstructing an officer in the performance of his duties. Iosuke had not been among the men sought by the police.

"What did he do?" asked Haneda.

"He beat up the plainclothes detective on duty there. Even though the detective told him he was from the police, the suspect assaulted him, causing injuries that will take a week to heal. The suspect is a big man and was under the influence of alcohol, so it was difficult to control him."

The officer squared his shoulders and spoke without hesitation. He was not aware of the relationship between Haneda and Iosuke.

"I see. That is indeed obstructing an officer in the performance of his duties. Did he engage in the aforementioned behavior with the intent of aiding the criminals to escape or did it have that result?" asked Haneda, using formal police language.

"From what we have found out in our interrogations, there is no proof that his actions had any direct effect on the criminals' escape. The incident with the detective took place more than a hundred yards from where the police exchanged fire with the smugglers."

"Thank you, officer. I understand."

Haneda began to look more relaxed. Due to the darkness of the night and the alcohol he had consumed, Iosuke might not have believed the man was a policeman, and there was no indication he was trying to help the culprits. That meant that Iosuke would probably not face any serious charges.

"Although we tried to arrest the smugglers at two other places as well, they all got wind of the raids and fled. We heard that Minamimura Iosuke was associating with Kajiki, the gang leader, so we have been questioning him, but he hasn't told us anything."

"That's the way he is," Komako commented. "He doesn't talk much, and, besides, he's easily intimidated. A place like this would make him nervous."

"However much he dislikes talking, he has to give us whatever information he has."

"There'd be no problem if it were only regular smuggling, but we suspect narcotics are involved, so it's more complicated," continued Fujita quietly.

According to him, the three who escaped were all former Imperial Navy officers, and the smuggling was carried out not for their own gain but to obtain funds to set up a nationalist group. That was the principal concern of the police. They had not caught Kajiki and any of his accomplices, and even if Iosuke was not part of the ring, as long as he was suspected of having a connection with the three, he was considered an accessory and could end up in the prosecutor's office.

"After all, he's guilty of obstructing an officer," added Fujita.

"He's in a bad fix," Haneda muttered to Komako as they left Fujita's office.

As he saw them out, Fujita tried to offer some encouragement.

"Professor, it's not definite he'll be charged, so don't be too concerned."

"Could you tell me where the holding cells are?" asked Komako.

"I'm afraid you can't go there, but from this window you can see down into the exercise yard where prisoners are allowed to walk and smoke once a day.

"They're allowed to smoke? Can we also send them food?"

"Yes, but it will be inspected."

From the window Komako looked down at the exercise yard; it was enclosed by wire netting and resembled a pigeon cage. She pictured Iosuke in an underground room not far away, surrounded by concrete walls and iron bars, and a sharp pain clutched at her heart.

After leaving Fujita, they went outside.

"What should we do?" Haneda asked Komako. "I'm still worried, so I don't think I'll go back to Oiso tonight. I'll ask the Fujimuras to put me up so I can think what to do."

"I'll stay in Tokyo, too. I'll go back to our house. I haven't been there for some time."

Komako was apprehensive about returning. She did not know that Heiji had already left the ration office, but Iosuke's predicament took precedence. She would stay in Tokyo for the next two days and learn what would happen to Iosuke.

"I'll go to the Fujimuras' house tomorrow morning to talk it over with you," she said.

They parted at Sakuradamon, but Komako did not go home right away. She took a bus to Ginza, where she bought cigarettes, sweet buns, chocolate, and other snacks before returning to police headquarters.

Fujita had already left, so she had some difficulty getting to see the officer in charge of the detention cells.

"Wait there," said the officer, pointing to a bench by the wall. Nearby were some cans for kerosene, but the smell indicated they contained DDT, probably to disinfect the prisoners. To Komako it represented an alien world. She watched as a prisoner led by an officer disappeared down the corridor. There was a fierce command—"Enter!"—followed by silence. No other voices were heard. The corridor must lead to some sort of dark hell.

"Oh, Iosuke." She had to use all her willpower to refrain from shouting his name out loud.

By that time Iosuke was already in bed, two blankets pulled up to his chin.

The inmates of the detention cells went to bed early and got up early, a regime more suited to old people and hard for Iosuke and his cell mates to get used to. Moreover, the lights were kept on all night, making the room as bright as the lobby of a first-class hotel, so it was hard to sleep. Rather than saving electricity, the priority at police headquarters was ensuring that the guards could see into the cells at all times.

The floor of the cell was wooden, but the bedding, consisting of a new thick rush mat and a soft futon, made it relatively comfortable. There was a strong smell of DDT, but Iosuke was grateful there were no fleas, unlike in the shacks.

227

No wind penetrated the cells since the walls were of thick concrete. In the shack he shared with Kinji, they had had six square yards between them for sleeping, whereas here each inmate was allotted just over two square yards. There were eight men in cell No. 17, their futons lined up like sandwiches neatly packed in a lunch box. On Iosuke's right was a petty thief and on his left a dealer in stimulants; by his head was a bicycle thief. The others were a pickpocket who had assaulted his victim, a racketeer, a man who had kidnapped a girl, and a factory worker who had attacked his personnel manager during a strike.

Nearly twenty-four hours had passed since Iosuke had been placed in the cell. The night before, in an office resembling a small courtroom next to the detention center entrance, he had undergone a physical examination and then many of his personal effects, including his tie and leather belt, had been taken from him. Each one was labeled and stored away, not under his name but his number. On entering the center, each inmate was handed a small black card with a number written on it in white, like the cards issued in hospitals to show your place in the queue. With that, the procedures for entering the cells were complete.

Only when the order was given would the guard at the door let you in, so it was not easy to gain entry. The moment Iosuke passed through, his name ceased to exist, to be replaced by a number.

"Cell 17, Number 36!"

From now on he would be addressed as that. Numbers were convenient and easy to remember. The system had the same aim as the recent limit to the number of Chinese characters in use and the new rules for the *kana* syllabaries. The convenience, however, meant little to the inmates.

As a number, Iosuke had been summoned twice that morning to the interrogation rooms of both the financial security section and the narcotics section. When he was first asked whether his name was Minamimura Iosuke, he felt he was meeting himself for the first time in quite a while.

"It was dark," he had answered. "I couldn't tell he was a policeman." He also said that he had been drinking and felt he was being physically threatened. He kept his answers brief to demonstrate he had no criminal intent, as he had been advised by the pickpocket in his cell.

But the officer was more interested in his relationship to Kajiki and his gang.

"Well, he was living in the same place, and he would give me goat's milk, so we became friendly."

The officer, dissatisfied with the answers and annoyed, tried to bully

Iosuke, but that was about as effective as trying to wrestle with a curtain. The officer was convinced that suspects who adopted this attitude were seasoned criminals, and he glared fixedly at Iosuke, but the only response was a blandness of expression, look, and voice. The suspect seemed to lack anything conclusive.

Concerned for Iosuke's safety, Kajiki had deliberately not told him details of their plans, so Iosuke had no information to give in response to the officer's persistent questions. Iosuke's eyes strayed to the view of Miyakezaka that was visible through the barred window, and he was filled with sadness. How wonderful to be free to walk out there!

Now, lying in bed with eyes wide open and unable to fall asleep because of the light, the same sadness washed over him.

Nevertheless, he was not completely dissatisfied with conditions in the detention center. Life was not so bad there. Police cells had been reformed after the war, and the fried rice and tofu soup served that night had been good. The rice ration of 130 grams per person was the same as for people outside. In the afternoon they could bathe, and the bath was clean and large—probably better than that in the police director-general's own home. But what Iosuke was most grateful for was the flush toilet. There had been one in the house in Akasaka, but in Musashi-Hazama as well as under the bridge the toilet had been the non-flush type Iosuke had always disliked. All in all, he was quite comfortable.

Not being allowed to smoke was irksome, but for fifteen minutes every day they could walk in the exercise yard and smoke the cigarettes that were kept for them. Some inmates would even smoke two at once, and old-timers managed to smuggle cigarettes into their cells to smoke in secret.

His other minor complaint was that since he had no belt, his trousers were always in danger of falling down, but Iosuke's large stomach made this less of a problem for him than for the other inmates.

With such amenities, living standards were comparable to the average man's outside. One night's lodging with three meals a day of the same quality cost four or five hundred yen. If movies and television had been provided, no government branch would have merited more praise than the democratized police.

The social life in the cell was also to Iosuke's liking. From the first, the occupants treated him with respect, partly because of his size and unusual appearance but more because he was connected with a big smuggling ring with ideological leanings. Ideals were respected even in a place like this. The pickpocket, who appeared to be the cell leader, had also treated Iosuke with consideration.

"Here's a good-luck charm for you," he had said, handing Iosuke a tiny *waraji* travel sandal he had made with twists of toilet paper. To while away the time, the inmates would fashion these little sandals or small dogs as charms. They also made dice from bread and would use these for various gambling games. Repeat offenders were especially skilled, producing charms that could have won prizes. Both in the cells and the world at large, these creations were prized as talismans by those who made their living in the nightlife and gambling trades.

In other ways, too, Iosuke's cellmates treated him well. He was given cigarettes in the exercise yard, and sometimes extra rice at meals. He was just as well esteemed as he had been under the bridge, so he felt he was in green pastures once again. Only one factor made him not want to prolong his stay—the iron bars.

Police cells usually have walls on three sides, sometimes with a window, and bars on the other side, making it almost like an ordinary room. In this building, however, the twelve cells were in a large underground chamber, and all four walls consisted of iron bars. The result was a series of cages just like in a zoo, and the bars ran vertically as well as horizontally, with iron mesh in between. Iosuke disliked this arrangement intensely.

At times the desire to use his strength to pry the bars open and escape was almost overpowering. But it would have been futile, for the chamber was enclosed by thick concrete walls, with only one small exit that was always guarded. Even if he had managed to make it through the door, there would be other guards and policemen. And even supposing it was possible to knock them all unconscious, the emergency bell would go off, summoning another three thousand policemen armed with pistols and tear gas.

Escape was a fantasy he should abandon, but a life without fantasies is the saddest of all. Iosuke was aware of the stark reality of where he was and what had befallen him. He recalled what he had confessed to his wife the day he had left: "I wanted freedom."

And look where I've ended up! he thought.

A teardrop fell on his blanket. No wonder he could not sleep.

The next morning, after roll call and breakfast, the inmates were seated cross-legged with their backs against the bars, saying their farewells like departing travelers.

"They're sure to send me on, so I'll probably get called this morning.

230

May not see you again, so hope it goes well with you. Make lots of money!"

"Me, too. I'll have been here forty-eight hours by two this afternoon, so I won't be spending the night here. If I get out again, I'll send you something. Take it easy."

Prisoners did not remain long in the detention cells, and within two days they were sent to the prosecutor's office, where it was decided whether they were to be charged or not. If further interrogation were needed, they would be detained for up to ten more days. The happiest fate was to be questioned at police headquarters and released.

"You'll probably be let out today. After all, they have no proof," one man told Iosuke.

"But it was a big job, so who knows," said another.

"Even if they send you to prison, a politico like you will have it easy there."

Deaf to these consoling words, Iosuke sat with his arms folded, not saying anything. By the evening, he, too, would have been there forty-eight hours, so his fate would be sealed that day. He thought he had done nothing worse than scuffle with a policeman, so he would be freed, but he had no knowledge of police investigations. If he was sent to the prosecutor's office, he knew the situation would be more serious. Although he had not confessed, he had been a member of the smuggling gang and was present when the narcotics were sold, even though he had played no active part. Furthermore, he knew the gang's hideout, so there was no telling what might happen.

He had not been there two full days, yet he had had enough of life behind bars to want to escape by any means. He was about to invoke his mother's name again in the hope of being rescued when the guard called his number.

"Cell 17, Number 36!"

"Yes!"

The bearer of his fate had arrived at last.

"A parcel for you. Come and get it."

His hopes were dashed, but he was glad to be able to go outside the bars even for a minute.

Near the door leading to the exercise yard was a wooden table and a bench, where he was handed a package of sweet buns and chocolate. "It's from your wife. There are cigarettes, too, but we'll keep those until exercise time."

Iosuke was astonished. He had not expected Komako to know of his situation, and her sending a parcel was even more unexpected. He was so moved he could hardly reach for the food.

Another guard appeared and said, "When you've had that, you'll be taken to the prosecutor's office."

It was nine-thirty in the morning.

Iosuke was put on a bus with fifteen others and driven to the Tokyo Regional Prosecutor's Office. The vehicle was clean and looked like any sightseeing bus except for the double bars on the windows. Nevertheless, with all the passengers in handcuffs and two guards with pistols on their hips, it had a slightly sinister air.

The prisoners were taken to a large room with a sign reading, "No. 1 Holding Room." After a simple physical examination, they were told to sit on a hard bench and wait. Talking was strictly forbidden, and the tension in the room was high. When Iosuke moved his arms slightly because the handcuffs were hurting him, he was sharply reprimanded by a guard sitting on a raised platform.

Iosuke waited and waited to be called. Even after eating the boxed lunch they gave him and watching the sunlight start streaming in through the windows on the western side of the room, his name had still not been called. The prosecutors had a full schedule. Within twenty-four hours, each had to pronounce judgment on seven or eight suspects, and a single prosecutor could only deal with one case at a time. It was a time-consuming process.

The guard finally called his name at a little past four o'clock. Iosuke was taken to the second floor, still in handcuffs. The gloomy corridor was flanked by interrogation rooms, and sitting on benches were what looked like ordinary citizens. Iosuke kept his head bowed in embarrassment. In the distance he thought he caught a glimpse of someone resembling Komako.

"What a miserable state you're in! Aren't you ashamed?" He seemed to hear her voice lash at him like a whip on his back. He could say nothing in reply. Fortunately he was distracted by the guard opening a door in front of them.

"Enter!" he ordered, pushing Iosuke in.

The room—No. X Interrogation Room of the Crime Division—was long and narrow, and the prosecutor's desk was under the window. A clean-shaven man was sitting there in his shirtsleeves. Nearby was a stenographer's table, and a guard was standing at attention by the wall, on which hung a small glass vase holding an artificial rose that was covered with dust.

Iosuke was told to sit on a chair across from the prosecutor.

"You have been sent here under suspicion of the aforesaid offense. Is that correct?"

The prosecutor was about the same age as Iosuke and had a scholarly air as he peered through his glasses at the documents in front of him. His speech revealed the slight trace of a Tohoku accent.

"Yes."

"I have questions for you. Answer as accurately as possible. However, you do not have to answer any questions if you do not wish to. That is your right." The fresh breeze of the new constitution was wafting through the room.

The interrogation lasted about an hour. Iosuke was not asked much about what he had done to the plainclothes detective. Most of the questions concerned his relationship with Kajiki and his gang, and the interrogation was milder than at police headquarters. On the crucial points, however, Iosuke was conscious of the prosecutor's piercing gaze. Trembling, he did his best to respond "as accurately as possible," as requested.

Both the prosecutor's words and his own were recorded by the stenographer on ruled paper. The document was certain to be attached to his indictment. Iosuke was resigned to his fate.

"I think I understand."

The prosecutor looked Iosuke over again, his face as expressionless and cold as a whetstone.

This is when I receive my sentence, Iosuke thought, looking down.

"By the way, what is your relationship to Professor Haneda?" The question came as a complete surprise.

"He's my uncle. My mother's brother."

"And Minamimura Komako, aged thirty-one?"

"She's my wife," replied Iosuke weakly.

"From now on, will you follow your uncle's advice and live in the same house as your wife? In other words, do you intend to cease living under Okanenomizu Bridge and return to normal life? Of course, what you decide is not within the prosecutor's jurisdiction, and this is not an order. I ask merely for reference."

"Yes, I intend to do that."

Iosuke responded without thinking. He had never in his whole life expressed his determination so clearly. The moment Komako's parcel had been handed to him his feelings toward her had changed drastically. It was an instinctive, impulsive response, a wish to reach out for the strand of hope let down from heaven to save him. Behind the prosecutor's words, he could

233

hear voices calling to him from beyond the prison bars.

"Please bring the two people who came earlier," the prosecutor instructed the stenographer.

Soon the door opened and Haneda and Komako entered the room. With his back to them, Iosuke did not know that Komako was pressing a handkerchief to her eyes as she gazed at her husband's head.

"Professor, please sit down." The prosecutor had a chair brought for Haneda.

Haneda, looking exceedingly formal—so different from when he was with his Goshokai friends—bowed.

Iosuke realized his uncle was present and then saw Komako. Immediately, his head sank into his massive shoulders and his thick arms seemed to shrink and wither. The change was faster than a punctured balloon deflating.

"The investigation is about complete. Professor Haneda and Mrs. Minamimura, I want to consult you," said the prosecutor, looking at them.

The prosecutor told them that Iosuke's offense of obstructing an officer in the performance of his duties had not been deliberate, and he would not be charged. However, regarding his connection to the members of the narcotics gang, it might be difficult to prove he had committed a crime, but on certain points his record was not entirely clean. The details would not become clear until Kajiki was captured. At that time the suspect's testimony would be valuable, but for the time being there was no reason to detain him. However, if the suspect continued to live as a tramp and did not take up regular employment, he might suppress evidence or even abscond, so some measures were necessary. Fortunately, the suspect's uncle was a scholar and a respected member of society, and his wife had a fixed address and was leading a normal life. If these two people would vouch for the suspect, the prosecutor would order his immediate release.

"That is basically what we would like to do," said the prosecutor less formally, after pronouncing his verdict, gazing at Haneda and Komako. "However, as you know, accepting responsibility for the suspect is not legally binding. It is a formality, but some documentation is needed. If you will file a signed document accepting custody of the suspect, he can be turned over to you."

"I accept."

Haneda replied with great seriousness.

"I will also," said Komako, raising her head.

Komako was about to go in search of the appropriate form, but the prosecutor said that a formal document was not necessary and a letter in plain language would do. He asked for paper to be brought to her so she could write the letter herself.

"With regard to the suspect Minamimura Iosuke, after his release we accept custody on our own responsibility and promise to have him report when summoned."

Komako wondered why it was necessary to write the letter in the *katakana* syllabary, but she did so using a brush, as the stenographer instructed, and brought it to Haneda. He signed it with an impressive flourish and affixed his seal. Komako had no seal, so she was allowed to put her thumbprint on it instead.

The prosecutor read the letter, nodded, and placed it in a tray on his desk. He then turned to Iosuke.

"Now you are free to go. When you pick up your belongings at headquarters, it would be proper to apologize for causing them trouble. From now on, avoid associating with shady characters. You should be aware that a mild person like yourself can be taken advantage of by criminals. You have no idea what serious charges might result. I hope you and your wife will become reconciled and live a normal, healthy life."

Although the prosecutor was giving him valuable advice, Iosuke was only half listening. His heart was soaring into the open sky and the wide world beyond the prison walls.

The sun had set. At the main entrance of Tokyo Station, they bought tickets for their respective destinations: Haneda for Oiso, and Iosuke and Komako for Musashi-Hazama.

"Iosuke, I hope that now you will settle down."

Only then did Haneda speak. On the way to police headquarters and from there to Tokyo Station he had not said a word.

"Yes, I intend to." Iosuke stumbled over his words and bowed as awkwardly as a middle school student.

"A good marriage is hard to find," said Haneda, looking at the faces of the two. "It's similar to the relationship between an individual and society at large. No one is satisfied with his or her lot, but there are ways of mitigating the dissatisfaction. I suggest you investigate those."

Leaving them with these words, he walked briskly toward the ticket gate. By the stairs leading up to the Chuo Line tracks, Iosuke and Komako tried to bid him a formal farewell, but he merely touched his hat and disappeared into the crowd.

It was rush hour and the platform was full of people. When the train arrived, there was a brief struggle to board the train typical of train travel after the war. People's chests, shoulders, and arms battered Iosuke's large body, but he was happy. Jammed against him were soft human bodies, not iron bars and concrete walls.

His experiences over the last two days had scarred him mentally and physically. He was determined never to enter that world again. When they had emerged from the Prosecutor's Office building, he had automatically stretched out both arms above his head, reaching toward the evening sky.

Even the packed train seemed like paradise. And next to him was his wife. She was not tall, so he was looking down on her. She wore no hat, and her wavy black hair with its brownish tint held the fragrance of her hair oil that he had not smelled for six months.

Komako must have some regrets, he thought. She may have changed, too.

He noticed she was grasping the sleeve of his jacket tightly. She had never touched him in public before, so what could it mean? And what did the parcel at the detention center signify? What else could it be except that she had changed?

Just then Iosuke realized the train was pulling out of Okanenomizu Station. Peering between the passengers' heads, he strained to catch a glimpse of where he had lived. He missed the shack, the shared outhouse, and the open space there. Now that he had left, old Kinji and his wife must be living together.

He felt a tug on his sleeve.

"Don't even look over there!"

Komako's voice was low but imperious.

Those were the first words Komako had spoken directly to him. When Haneda was with them, she had addressed him a few times, and her tone had been quiet and bereft of emotion. But these words were different, uttered with even more severity than the former Komako would have used. The two were surrounded by other people, so he had not expected them to be her first words to him. If she were penitent in any way, wouldn't she have been less harsh?

As the train passed Yotsuya and Shinanomachi, night was already falling. The Outer Garden of Meiji Shrine reminded him of the day he had left home, and the stop at Shinjuku Station recalled the strip show he had seen the same day.

After Nakano the carriage became less crowded, and Iosuke leaned against the doors on the side of the train that did not open. Komako stood next to him, still keeping tight hold of his sleeve. To others it probably indicated a happy couple, but Iosuke felt threatened.

She's acting like the police guard in that bus.

The train finally reached Musashi-Hazama. As Komako bought bread, ham, sausages, and so on for their evening meal, Iosuke enjoyed seeing the familiar streets again. Wanting some cigarettes, Iosuke set off for a store he knew, but Komako followed him.

"And where do you think you're going?" she asked.

Even on the way home Komako maintained a constant vigilance, staying close the whole time. He felt as though handcuffed to her. On the dark road she began to talk to him.

"I've made up my mind, you know."

"About what?"

"I won't leave you. And I won't let you leave me."

It was like a blow to Iosuke's chest. The words were more than blunt: they revealed absolute, passionate determination. She had never talked like that before.

Iosuke did not understand her. She was different, and if she had changed in his absence, was the change favorable to him or not?

Despite the darkness, they had no trouble finding their way. The fields on both sides of the road were pitch black, with only an occasional light glimmering in the distance. Over them stretched the vast sky with moon and stars, and in front loomed a dark stand of cedars.

Komako said nothing further, and Iosuke was not eager to ask questions. The only sound was of their footsteps on the road.

When they arrived at the house, Komako opened the door with her key and took a step back, just as the guard in the detention center had done.

"You, go in first."

It was late, so they sat down to eat without changing their clothes. Suddenly ravenous, Iosuke hastily buttered some bread and ate it with the cold meat.

Making tea in the kitchen, Komako called, "There's one bottle of beer left."

Iosuke glanced around the house he had not seen for months. The rain doors and sliding partitions were closed, but it seemed exactly the same. The 40-watt bulb was casting a dim light, the same as when he came home late from work. There was no sign that anything had changed.

I escaped wanting to find freedom, Iosuke thought.

Komako brought the bottle of beer and two glasses. She was going to drink, too.

"In any case, congratulations."

Without a hint of a smile, she raised her glass.

"Sorry for all the worry I caused." He sought the right words, but a long silence followed. The bottle of beer was soon empty. Komako seemed a little drunk.

"As it has turned out, you can't go anywhere, can you? The prosecutor put you into my custody, right?"

She relaxed her posture, and a cunning smile spread across her lips.

Astonished, Iosuke looked at Komako's face. This did not sound like her. Was she drunk, or had she begun to show a woman's crueler side?

"If Uncle and I had not backed you, you'd have ended up in prison. Now you're under an obligation to me and have to obey me."

She was laughing, but her eyes were cold. Iosuke felt a chill run through him as he imagined the life stretching before him. The room partitions suddenly turned into iron bars.

He stood up.

"Where are you going?"

"Thanks for your trouble, but I don't think I belong here. A place like Okanenomizu Bridge is probably right for me."

"How can you say that? I was given custody of you on condition you would not go back to living like that."

"But the prosecutor said neither you nor Uncle has any legally binding responsibility. You don't have to worry about me."

Iosuke took his hat from the nail by the door as he had six months earlier. Seeing this, Komako rushed over to him and stared into his face. She raised her right hand and slapped him hard, the sound reverberating through the room.

"What did you do that for?"

"I'm sorry—I give up. Please don't go away!" she pleaded. "Please don't go away again!"

Sobbing, Komako collapsed at Iosuke's feet. With her arms around his legs, she was wailing like a small child.

Chapter 18
All's Well

The year was drawing to a close, and in less than ten days it would be New Year's. In the parlor of the Haneda house Hishikari and Fujimura were perspiring as they struggled to tighten the red cords of the drums with their host. It was a quiet, warm winter's day in Oiso.

Looking across the garden at the neighbor's hedge, Hishikari gave an exclamation of surprise. On the gnarled branch of a wild plum tree there, two or three blossoms were showing white in the sun.

"They're four or five days early this year," observed Haneda, who was accustomed to plum trees blooming comparatively early in this area.

"I'm not sure whether this winter is cold or warm. Yesterday morning it was so cold in Tokyo there was ice everywhere," remarked Fujimura, sitting down to rest.

It was the Goshokai's first meeting for some months and the last of the year. So much had been happening that the group had not managed to get together. Henmi and Horan would not be present this time, and no suitable new members had been found, but the remaining three had staunchly decided to continue even without a gong player. Hishikari would play the flute, Fujimura the large drum, and Haneda the two small drums, so they had an ensemble after all. They would have preferred a gong, too, but it was better to do without than to endure a member who did not fit in. Their experience with Henmi and Horan made the three old men realize how unreliable new members could be, and they resolved to limit the group to the original three, even if this involved changing the name to the Sanshokai, the "Three Laughs Group."

"Now we're all here, shall we begin?" Haneda suggested brightly, taking his place in front of the drums, well aware that an ensemble of three inevitably felt somewhat forlorn.

Before they could start, Ginko appeared with tea and some cakes.

"Thank you so much. Sorry to always be so much trouble," said Fujimura politely.

"Not at all. May I offer our warmest congratulations? We are very happy for you. I'm sure your wife is relieved it's all settled," said Ginko, uttering the customary polite phrases.

Takabumi and Yuri had been married about ten days earlier. The wedding had been sudden, due partly to Horan's efforts and partly to the Fujimuras' concern, on learning of Yuri's alarming adventures, that she might do something outrageous unless she was married quickly. Strangely, although the young couple had denounced the feudalistic custom of arranged marriages, they had yielded to their parents' wishes. A family much like any other was now in the making.

"It happened so quickly," said Fujimura with an embarrassed smile.

"Did you know that young Henmi is back with his wife?" offered Hishikari, sipping his tea and smiling benignly.

"No. It's the first I've heard of it."

Their curiosity was immediately aroused.

After Komako, Henmi had become friendly with a rising blue-blooded novelist, but a New Year's issue of a magazine had featured a short story by the woman modeled on her relationship with Henmi. This infuriated him, and he severed all ties with her and even recalled his wife from the Fujimi Highland sanitarium. Hishikari had met him since then and encouraged him to return to the Goshokai gatherings, but he said he had decided to avoid all unhealthy indoor amusements to concentrate on his golf.

"For a fellow like that, golf is about all you can expect. He's still a strapling—far too young to join this illustrious company," said Haneda pompously.

"By the way, what happened to Iosuke?" asked Fujimura, recalling the events of two months before.

"Sorry about all the worry he caused, but he seems to have settled down. The other day he and his wife came down to thank us."

"They've set up an interesting arrangement," Ginko added. "Komako goes out to work while Iosuke looks after the house."

"That's an unusual turn of events. Not exactly American-style, is it?" asked Hishikari.

"It's no particular style. Komako's the one who knows how to work. She's got a job in a trading company, doing something that requires her skills, with a starting salary of 20,000 yen a month. Iosuke is useless, and I don't know what he was thinking about while he was away but he's lost all desire for a regular job—at least until the Peace Treaty is signed and the Occupation is over, he says! Instead, the lazybones is working away at household chores like a man reborn."

"With only cooking and cleaning, he has time to spare, so he says he might learn to use the sewing machine," said Ginko with a giggle, causing everyone to burst in laughter.

"Can you imagine Iosuke working a sewing machine. He'd break as many as he put his foot to!" said Hishikari.

"In other words, they've exchanged roles. Well, that's one solution. How are they making out?" asked Fujimura.

"They seem to be doing well. Komako says she's happier. How long it will last, I can't say, but while one tries various experiments, time passes. Gradually, one stops complaining, as we all know from experience," mused Haneda.

"Yes," said Hishikari, continuing the sentiment, "and then we find diversion in the flute and drum."

"Yes, indeed! We're forgetting our business," said Haneda with renewed vigor. He began unwrapping his drumsticks. Looking pleased, Hishikari picked up his flute and Fujimura his drumsticks.

"All right, here we go!"

Ten-tenya, ten-tenya. Ten-tenya, ten-tenya. Even without the gong, there was no mistaking the cheerful festival music of old.

Afterword

School of Freedom (Jiyū gakkō) was a best-selling novel in the 1950s, and Shishi Bunroku was among Japan's most widely read authors of the Shōwa era (1926-89). The novel was selected for the Japanese Literature Publishing and Promotion program because it stands out as a work of refined humor in the era of modern Japanese fiction. Published first in daily installments of roughly 1,200 characters in the Tokyo morning edition of *Asahi shinbun*, the leading national newspaper, from May to December 1950, it came out in book form in 1951 (Asahi Shinbunsha) and was reprinted several times thereafter. Like many of the author's other short and long works of fiction, *Jiyū gakkō* was adapted for film (twice, by Shōchiku and Daiei; both films opened May 5, 1951) and television (Fuji Television in 1965). The novel was divided into chapters from the outset, but the subsections of each chapter seem to have been created when it was published as a book. This translation is based on the edition published in *Shishi Bunroku zenshū* (16 volumes, 1 supplement, Asahi Shinbunsha, 1968).

Shishi Bunroku is the penname adopted by Iwata Toyoo (1893-1969) when he turned to professional writing to support his family after his second marriage in 1934. Echoing the names taken by *rakugo* comic storytellers, it has the ring of a writer of humor. The author left no clear explanation of the derivation of the name, the parts of which are *shishi* (lion), *bun* (letters), and *roku* (six), but Kobayashi Hideo (1902-83) recalled his close friend's love of puns and wry logic: since *bunshi* is a writer (*shi* means both "samurai" and "four") and *bungō* is a great man of letters (*gō* means "great man" and *go* is "five"), surely to be called *bunroku* would place him a cut above them all.[1] Subtly, then, the name also expresses his pride as a serious writer of literature. Iwata used Shishi Bunroku for his fiction and essays, reverting to his family name for his plays and for the few stories he wrote during World War II.

CHILDHOOD IN YOKOHAMA AND KEIŌ GIJUKU EDUCATION

Born in 1893, Shishi Bunroku's life spanned the eventful era during which Japan emerged as a modern industrial power, its cultural and intellectual life was internationalized, its political and military power was tested—with devastating results—on the world stage, and it rebuilt and reformed itself out of ashes. His life and work, to which there is surprisingly little access in any Western language, offer a chronicle of this dramatic time. Contemporaries such as Tanizaki Jun'ichiro, Kawabata Yasunari, Sakaguchi Ango, and Dazai Osamu have dominated the literary limelight and appealed to the tastes of the leading translators of modern Japanese literature, leaving the rich store of Shishi Bunroku's fiction and essays almost untapped for English readers.[2]

His father was Iwata Shigeo, a former samurai of the Nakatsu domain of Ōita Prefecture, who was inspired by Fukuzawa Yukichi, a prominent educator, founder of Keiō Gijuku University, and thinker from the same domain, to move to Yokohama to start a silk-goods business in the foreign concession there. The connection with Fukuzawa, though indirect, later made it possible for Shigeo's son Toyoo to receive a private school education at Keiō, where his peers were members of the intellectual and social elite. The business, which catered to foreign residents of Yokohama, prospered, providing an urbane and cosmopolitan environment in which the young Toyoo spent his childhood. This background appears to have nurtured the open-minded, progressive, and culturally sophisticated personality that is manifested in his prolific work.

The Iwata business and family faced a crisis with the death of Shigeo in 1902, when Toyoo was nine, and a gradual decline in the family fortunes began. His mother tried to support the family (which also included Yoneko, Toyoo's sister three years his senior, and Hikojiro, his brother two years his junior) on a steadily shrinking volume of business. Despite the difficult financial circumstances, Toyoo continued at Keiō Gijuku through higher school and entered the university division (Keiō University) in 1911, where his fellow students included many who would play leading roles in Japanese culture, politics, and business during the twentieth century. The friendships and contacts he formed there were to support his activities and achievements throughout his career.

Interested in theater, including the traditional kabuki and *shingeki* (one strand of the new Western-style, realistic theater movement), from the age of 16, Toyoo steeped himself in literature and tested his writing skills in the pages of a circulating magazine founded with high school friends. Although he remained on the Keiō Gijuku rolls, he spent most of his time with writing and publishing projects, or absorbing himself in the works of Tolstoy and Dostoyevsky. He finally dropped out of the university in 1913 when he was 20. He earned small amounts of money by publishing short stories in *Yorozu chōhō*, a popular newspaper of the time. The period between 1915 and his mother's death in 1921 following a stroke appears to have been the crucible of reading and experience that set him on the path to become a writer.

THE PARIS YEARS AND INVOLVEMENT IN THEATER

The name Iwata Toyoo, not Shishi Bunroku, is associated with the introduction of French theater to Japan and with important contributions to the New Theater movement that started up in the 1930s. Better known leaders of the movement, like Kishida Kunio (1890-1954) and Kikuchi Kan (1888-1948), were a few years his senior, both in age and in their engagement with the theater.[3]

Like many other young Japanese writers, artists, and intellectuals in the 1920s, Iwata wanted nothing more than to immerse himself in the culture and arts of Europe, and so in 1922, with the remainder of his inheritance, he left for France. His sojourn there coincided with a renaissance in French theater, which was thriving from the stimulation of numerous new companies emerging in Paris and of visiting companies from Moscow. Iwata quickly discovered an affinity for the genre. He attended the theater all over Paris as well as in other European cities, he met performers and directors in the Russian as well as French theater, and he took assiduous notes about the plays, stage settings, and performances that he observed. During his three-year stay in France, he developed a deep appreciation of and discernment about theater.

In Paris in 1923, when he was 30, Iwata met and fell in love with a woman named Marie Chaumy. She was the daughter of a school principal from a small town in central France. She had gone to London to study English and with that skill had found a job with an American company in Paris, where she and Iwata became acquainted. They married and returned together to Japan in June of that year. A daughter, Tomoe, was born in August 1925. At the outset of their life in Tokyo, Marie helped support the household by tutoring French, as Iwata had no income to speak of until he began receiving some payments and royalties for translations of plays and other writings. In 1926 he published *Gendai no butai sōchi* [Modern Stage Settings] (Chūō Bijutsu Sha), translated Jules Romain's *Knock*, and became involved in the New Theater movement. He joined the Shingeki Kyōkai (New Theater Society) and then helped to found the Shingeki Kenkyūjo (New Theater Research Institute) as well as the short-lived Kigekiza (Comedy Theater). Iwata's writing generated little income at this time, and so life was difficult. According to his

244

autobiographical accounts, however, his family of three was happy.

In 1930, around the time their daughter turned six, Marie became ill with a combination of a chronic heart condition and depression. Realizing the cost of her effort to accustom herself to the Japanese lifestyle, Iwata moved her to a hotel run by a French woman friend, but when after some time her condition did not improve, he decided to take her back to France for a rest.[4]

Leaving their daughter in the care of his sister, who was then living in Pyongyang (Korea at the time was under Japanese colonial control), the couple went back to France. While Marie convalesced with her family, Iwata spent time in Paris, where he again frequented the theater and, at the request of Ōtake Takejirō (founder of the Shōchiku Theater Company), studied the popular *théâtre de boulevard*. After six months his funds were running low and Marie was still ailing, so he decided to go back to Japan for a while, leaving her with her parents. He traveled across Siberia to Korea and picked up Tomoe in Pyongyang. He then returned to Tokyo, where he set up housekeeping in the Tokyo suburb of Higashi Nakano.

Iwata then plunged into the activities that would make him one of the driving forces in the development of Japan's modern theater movement of the 1930s and 1940s. He worked as director and in the development of stage settings, and he translated a number of European plays for performance in Japanese. His first play, *Higashi wa higashi* [East Is East] did not receive much critical interest, but his second, *Asahiya kinumonoten* [The Asahiya Silk Goods Shop], published in 1934, was more successful. It was staged by the Shingeki Kyōkai that year. Although he is not remembered as an original playwright, his translations were highly praised, and theater became his passion. At age 70 he wrote, "I would have made my career in the theater, but you cannot support a family that way. So I began to write fiction, but even while I wrote, half of me remained in the world of the theater."[5]

In 1937, together with Kishida Kunio and Kubota Mantarō, leaders of the "artistic" branch (*geijutsuha*) of the New Drama movement, he founded the Bungakuza theater group. Created to provide an alternative to the ideologically motivated movements that dominated many aspects of Japanese theater at the time, the Bungakuza aimed at artistically refined theater, attuned to and mirroring real life in modern Japan. It was run by a council system led by Kishida Kunio, Kubota Mantarō, and Iwata. Iwata played a particularly important role in maintaining harmony among the strong personalities involved. Iwata continued to work with the Bungakuza after the Pacific War ended, and he was active in experimental studio performances and as advisor to the new theaters that branched off from the Bungakuza.[6] Writing became his principal occupation during and after the war, but he continued to pursue his interest in theater as well as film acting.

REMARRIAGE AND SHISHI BUNROKU

Marie Chaumy passed away in France in 1932, and Iwata faced raising their young daughter alone. He wrote about that time later in his well-known autobiographical work *Musume to watashi* [My Daughter and I], which was published in serial form over three years from 1953 to 1956 in the *Asahi shinbun* and was later serialized for television (NHK, 1961). In 1934 he married Tominaga Shizuko, a native of Ehime Prefecture (Shikoku) and a sewing teacher at Kyōritsu Women's School. A serious and hard-working woman, Shizuko reared Tomoe and ran the household that sustained Shishi as a professional writer. While continuing his engagement with the theater, he launched his professional career as author with short stories published in such magazines as *Shin seinen* and *Kaizō*.

With *Konjiki seishunfu* [The Gold Youth, 1934], he first published under the pen name Shishi Bunroku. His reputation as a popular writer became established with long newspaper fiction, starting with *Etchan* in *Hōchi shinbun* (1936-37), *Koshō musuko* [Peppy Boy, 1938] and *Nobuko* in *Shufu no tomo* (1938-40), and many others, all of which were quickly published in book form. Several of his stories were also made into films, among them *Rakuten kōshi* (Prince Optimistic; Nikkatsu, 1938), *Koshō musuko* (Tōei, 1938), and *Sara Otome* (Tōei, 1939).

The attack on Pearl Harbor in 1941 and the outbreak of the war, wrote Iwata, "was to be the most important event in my life . . . the aftereffects would reverberate until I drew my last breath."[7] He wrote a number of works about the Japanese and the war, including *Obaasan* [Granny] and *Kaigun* [The Navy], the latter setting down the personal history of one of the nine submarine pilots who participated in suicide missions as part of the Pearl Harbor attack. These he published under his given name, Iwata Toyoo. He was awarded the Asahi Shinbun Prize for *Kaigun* in 1943.

Iwata saw himself as a "homefront writer" (*jūgo bunshi*), and though his portrayals of individual characters and their responses to experiences in the war were hardly meant to serve the purposes of warmongering, inevitably *Kaigun* was used as propaganda to whip up popular militaristic fervor.[8] Popular images of the novel were affected by the propaganda film based on the story, which was widely publicized on the 1943 anniversary of the Pearl

Harbor attack.

Regarding his writing during the war, Shishi later reflected:

> I did think I would do what I could if it would help my country
> win the war, but writing was something I wanted to be allowed to
> do my own way. If I could not, then I would find no meaning in
> writing. In the early years of the war, it seemed that my own way
> of writing was more or less successful. As the war situation grew
> more difficult, however, the censors' policies became increasingly
> strict, even a bit mad. If you weren't keeping the exact same beat
> of the war drums as everyone else, you were quickly branded as
> "anti-war." So everyone's writing became filled with meaningless,
> coarse war sympathizing.[9]

Hampered by increasingly rigid censorship and controls, Shishi's writing
slowed. In 1944, primarily for the health of his wife and daughter, he moved
his family to a house near Yugawara on the coast of Kanagawa Prefecture,
where they remained until the end of the war.

After Japan's surrender in August 1945, food shortages even in the
countryside became acute, a situation the Iwata family felt more keenly than
they had during the war. When their landlord requested they vacate the
house they had been living in, Iwata decided to move to Shikoku, to the
hometown of his wife, Shizuko. Another factor in his decision to move to
that distant place was his awareness that his writing, particularly *Kaigun*,
would likely be seen as having played a role in inciting war fever among
his countrymen. He terminated a novel being serialized in *Shufu no tomo*
magazine and turned down further writing assignments. He wrote a will
and waited for the sentence of death he felt sure was coming.

POSTWAR WRITING

The Occupation and the "purge" proved somewhat different from what
rumor had depicted, and Iwata returned to Tokyo in October 1947. Housing
was still in short supply in the city, but he and his family were given an
apartment in the employee dormitory of Shufu no Tomo, whose monthly
women's magazine had published many of his stories and essays since early
in his writing career (1937). The property in Kanda Surugadai where the
dormitory was located was spacious, and about half of Ochanomizu (called
"Okanenomizu" in the novel) bridge was visible from a wooded area on
a rise toward its north side. Depressed at the devastation of Tokyo, Iwata
spent many days secluded at home or walking in the dormitory garden:

... then, while gazing at the cliff on the other side of the bridge, I spotted several crudely built dwellings, obviously built by amateurs, halfway up the steep slope. At first I thought they must be some sort of tool sheds, but then I noticed that sometimes there was laundry hanging up to dry and smoke or steam rising . . .

As the days went by, I began to observe the life of those houses from between the trees of the garden whenever I went for a walk on the grounds. I ended up feeling very envious of the people there. It seemed to me that their lives must be the freest of any people in Tokyo. If one lived simply like those people, I thought, it might be possible to put up with the unpleasantness of Tokyo as it was. I later included my imaginings about that settlement in *Jiyū gakkō*.[10]

In March 1948, just as he was trying to recover his momentum in writing, he received notice that he had been provisionally designated as one of the writers subject to the Occupation purge, mainly on the basis of the reputation of *Kaigun*. He submitted a legal protest, carefully following the procedures established by the authorities to challenge the designation. Backed by his editors at the *Asahi* and *Mainichi* newspapers, where he was a precious asset, he argued that his writing as it stood should not be confused with its interpretation by readers and propagandists. His name was removed from the list, and he then resumed writing, again under the Shishi Bunroku pen name. Soon thereafter, the monthly *Shufu no tomo* began to serialize his first long postwar work, *Ojiisan* [Grandfather]; it ran until May 1949.

In late 1948, the first installment of *Ten'ya wan'ya* [This Chaotic World] appeared in *Mainichi shinbun*, and the rest followed over the next five months. *Ten'ya wan'ya*, along with *Jiyū gakkō* [School of Freedom, 1950] and *Yassa mossa* [This Way and That Way, 1952] were what Shishi called his "defeat trilogy," or record of the history of Japan's defeat and occupation as he saw it imprinted in people's lives. The hallmark of these works is their vivid portrayal of the confusion, distortions, and scars that the war and defeat wrought in the lives of people in various walks of life. Shishi was convinced that the awful experience Japanese shared would, perhaps not in obvious ways, one day be useful to them. There is no self-pity, sentimentality, or pessimism in these novels; they are narrated with wit and humor and the kind of poignancy, affection, and empathy found only in a keen observer of human foibles and social phenomena. Adding to the seasoning acquired in overcoming the personal difficulties of his younger years, the individual and national experience of the war brought further maturity to his writing, which he learned to burnish with a fine quality of humor rarely found in popular literature. Having absorbed the spirit of the cultural renaissance of Paris of the 1920s and having been fascinated by the humor and satire in French literature and theater, Shishi made a significant contribution to Japan's literature by articulating and nourishing its untapped comic dimension, which, as he himself wrote, had been left virtually uncultivated in post-Meiji Japan.[11]

Ten'ya wan'ya chronicles the adventures of an employee in a company whose owner faces charges of war complicity as determined by the Occupation purge of persons in "official" positions, and the opportunism he witnesses in both the city and the countryside as people absorb the impact of Occupation-imposed reforms. *Yassa mossa* is set in the Elizabeth Sanders Home for mixed blood children born to American GIs and Japanese during the Occupation. The home is located in Ōiso, not far from the place where Iwata lived during 1951-58 and spent his summers for many years thereafter.

ŌISO AND THE REGULAR LIFE

After two years in the midst of the *ten'ya wan'ya* (chaotic; a word coined by Shishi) of Tokyo under the Occupation, Shishi's health faltered, but what initially appeared to be cancer turned out to be an ulcer. Resolved to live out his life quietly, Shishi had begun to make arrangements to move to Ōiso, a coastal resort area south of Tokyo. He and Shizuko had found a house they both liked, when suddenly in February 1950 Shizuko died from a stroke. Shishi was overwhelmed by the sudden loss of his partner of sixteen years, but he moved to Ōiso as planned with his daughter, and he devoted himself to writing *Jiyū gakkō*. Its serialization began in the *Asahi shinbun* in May and continued until the middle of December. In *Musume to watashi*, he wrote:

> In the midst of writing [a serial work], I avoided going to Tokyo as much as possible and lived a life of rubber-stamp regularity. It seemed to me the best way to recover more quickly from the shock of Shizuko's death.
>
> My quite ordinary, rather somber life seemed to demand that the newspaper novel I was writing be a bit boisterous, dramatic, and colorful. This became *Jiyū gakkō*, in which I sought to portray characters far removed from my own life, placing them in the tumultuous world that was unfolding under the fiction of "freedom" in those days.[12]

The following year Shishi underwent stomach surgery, which resolved some health problems. In May he remarried. His third wife was Matsukata Yukiko (née Kikkawa, then 39), daughter of a former daimyo family who was raised among the social elite. Since being widowed at 35, she had been living in Ōiso. The following month Iwata Tomoe married diplomat Date Muneoki.

And thus a new phase of the writer's life began. In her memoir, Iwata Yukiko aptly captures the contrasts her new husband must have found in his three spouses:

> At the time we married, Iwata was living [in Ōiso] with his daughter Tomoe and two maids.
> His first wife was French, and since to the French eating and conversation are inseparable, he told me he had been scolded for not talking during meals. His second wife, true to her name (Shizuko ["quiet woman"]), was a quiet person, and Tomoe, whom she had reared, was also very reserved despite her youth. The trivial chatter I brought into this household seemed to amuse Iwata at first, but it was not something I kept up for long.[13]

By this time, Shishi Bunroku was the consummate professional writer, his days shaped by a steady, deliberately paced routine of completing daily installments for a work being serialized in either a newspaper or magazine, as well as shorter stories and essays. Yukiko's memoir describes his early-to-bed/early-to-rise routine, the fiat of quiet that reigned in the household during his writing hours, the numerous visitors, his custom of taking regular walks, his enjoyment of theater, and his pursuit of good food and drink. The couple continued to reside in Ōiso, and in 1953 their son Atsuo was born, to the sixty-year-old author's great delight. In 1958, as Atsuo reached school age, the family moved to Akasaka, in central Tokyo.

According to Shishi's other major biographical work, *Chichi no chichi* [My Father's Milk], he began to suffer from depression starting around 1963 when he turned 70, and he was hospitalized for stomach pain. Many of his closest friends had passed away, and economic growth was bringing dramatic change to the country. The following year the first Shinkansen super-express train went into service, and the Tokyo Olympics gave Japan a whole new identity. Nevertheless, he appears to have been at pains to remain outwardly cheerful. *Shishi Bunroku-sensei no ōsetsushitsu*,[14] the memoir of an aspiring writer who came to work as a maid around that time, evokes a lively household created by the self-centered and hard-to-please, yet inherently considerate and sometimes even jolly, writer and the irrepressible, hard-working Yukiko.

During a visit to the Ōiso house in April 1968, the author recorded his inner thoughts in a touching ode of gratitude to the bush peony (*botan*), a flower for which he had a special fondness and thought he might be seeing for the last time. The essay "Botan," written in April 1968 and found in Shishi's desk after his death, reveals suicidal thoughts that he restrained in his final years.

In November 1969, Shishi received Japan's highest honor, the Order of Cultural Merit. Called to present himself at the imperial palace to receive the award, he stood before the emperor in a morning suit that he had had custom-tailored in Paris forty-six years earlier. His account of why he decided not to have new attire made for that august occasion, and instead don the formal wear that had followed him throughout his life, is rich with humor and recollections.[15] It was written only days before he passed away on December 12 in the midst of his daily routine.

The special character of Shishi Bunroku's humor—which represents the supreme challenge for any translator of his literature—derives from his uncommon insight into human nature and his affection for human idiosyncrasies and foibles. Shishi captured the hearts of readers starved for light or humorous topics with writing that touches the comic lode in the serious stuff of history and the realities of ordinary people's lives.

Shishi Bunroku's literary achievements extend over three genres. One area consists of his contributions to the development of the *shingeki* theater. The second is fiction, a genre in which he produced roughly four different types of work. The first is autobiographical, namely, *Musume to watashi* and *Chichi no chichi*. Both serious in tone, they are moving stories about an author and the path he took through tumultuous times. The second type consists of works of a biographical nature that grew out of Shishi's strong interest in certain individuals. Examples are *Tajima Tarōji den* [The Story of Tajima Tarōji; based on the life of Satsuma Jirohachi, 1901-76, scion of a nouveau riche family who made a reputation for himself in European society], *Kaigun* [The Navy; the personal history of a Pearl Harbor submarine attack pilot], and *Anderu-san no ki* [The Story of Mrs. Anderson; a woman of mixed parentage who worked at the Elizabeth Sanders Home]. All are fascinating life stories. The third type focuses on dimensions of society in a certain period, and it includes *Ōban* [Large Size], which depicts a stockbroker's world before and after World War II, his "defeat trilogy," and *Hakoneyama*, a fictionalized documentary account of the struggle between two railway companies for control of the Hakone resort transportation system. The fourth type is light humorous fiction and adult comedy; it includes *Etchan, Koshō musuko*, and *Seishun kaidan* [Youth's Mysterious Tales].

The third genre of Shishi's writing is essays, for which his style is

251

uniformly light, readable, and deeply informed. His essays explore the minutiae of personal memories, society, daily life, human character, and so forth, but among the most popular are those on dining and good food. Some admirers consider them to be unsurpassed examples of gourmet writing. In things related to the theater or to human nature Shishi had a rare instinct for knowing what was genuine, and that served him well in the realm of good eating as well.

THE WORLDS OF *JIYŪ GAKKŌ*

Tokyo in 1950 was a city only five years removed from the months of firebombing that left the city a scorched plain and drove tens of thousands to evacuate to the countryside. Those who remained teetered at the brink of homelessness. The war and the destruction of the cities, even before the Occupation instituted its reforms and ordered a new Constitution, had toppled the prewar social structure, reducing the circumstances of people of all classes. The evacuees had returned and rebuilt homes and businesses, and the most difficult, hungry, and demoralized period finally lifted, although the American-led Occupation, begun August 1945, was still in place. Most people had a place to live, some kind of work, and hope for the future. By 1947 the new Constitution had been promulgated and the Occupation reform program was in full swing, energetically, if naively, attempting to change a traditional, patriarchal society into a democratic nation of "freedom" and "individualism."

The Constitution guaranteed "freedom" and "equality" to everyone, and everyone had a different take on it, as Komako observes in the story. Iosuke experiences freedom in many forms, all of which turn out to be transient; he tastes freedom from Komako after he leaves home, freedom from the burdens of ownership and work, freedom from the constraints of society in his carefree life under the bridge, and freedom from concerns about money while serving as the "symbol" for Kajiki's secret project. It is only when he lets freedom from scruples go too far that he finds himself in deep trouble.

The freedom that Komako explores in the absence of Iosuke is in the pursuit of a "real man." That search takes her through a succession of associations with other men—Takabumi, Henmi, and then Heita (Hei-san), and as she tests the expression of her own drives and values, finally her own naïveté brings trouble down upon her as well. Women in Japan, subordinated to their fathers, then their husbands, and finally their sons under the Meiji Constitution (promulgated in 1889), were changed by the deprivations

252

and heavy responsibilities forced on them during the war, and now they were legally equal to men under the new Constitution. The Occupation forces had one idea about what freedom should be for Japan, leftists had their ideas, national patriots had theirs, and men and women had theirs—but for everyone, "freedom" had some lessons to teach.

Occupied Japan was a time and place when the outlines of freedom were being tested at every level of society: by the long-suppressed socialists and communists through the labor movement, by brokers and black-marketeers in the economy, in literature by the translation of D.H. Lawrence's controversial novel *Lady Chatterley's Lover,* and in language by the influx of English brought by the Occupation personnel and American culture. The protagonists' stories take us on a lively tour of this postwar interlude, making the history of those years come to life.

The special appeal of a Japanese novel on this endlessly interesting subject, however, lies in the social and cultural backdrop, especially when it is depicted by an author with a veteran's eye for stage setting. Shishi's Tokyo in 1950 is a city where rural farmhouses with thatched roofs are part of the suburban landscape, where the public transportation system, though decrepit, runs on time, where good restaurants and fashion shows entertain a growing middle class even while a living could be made from selling trash and cigarette butts on the recycle market. It is a city where those left behind by the recovery effort still live in makeshift shacks.

In the narrator's asides we glimpse vignettes of early postwar metropolitan life. In Iosuke and Komako's abode we see the reduced circumstances of former members of the upper middle class; we see the markets and strip shows of Shinjuku, the secret poker pubs in the backstreets of Ginza, the under-the-tracks markets of Kanda, the cradles of *kasutori* culture in Ueno Park and the backstreets of Asakusa,[16] the fashionable front streets of Ginza (front cover illustration), and the open-spaced, somnolent Hama Rikyū Park (back cover illustration[17]), not to mention the community under "Okanenomizu" bridge. With Komako's visits to the Ōiso cottage and the broker Mogi's vacation home in Noborito, the story also chronicles the transformations taking place in Japan's social fabric as the prewar upper-middle class gave way to the mass middle class of the postwar era.

The passing of the heyday of *yamanote* ["high city"] culture in Tokyo is another sub-theme of *School of Freedom*. Reminders of that passing keep recurring—in the older couple, Ginko and Haneda, in Komako's memories of her girlhood, and in Iosuke's family background. An essay written just before Shishi started work on *School of Freedom*, "Yamanote no ko" [The

People of Yamanote], is a farewell to the Yamanote-ite qualities that vanished in the destruction of the war—a sense of honor, gentility, modesty—and a disposition that "abhorred the mean, cowardly, or dishonest as well as the obstinate or unreasonable."[18] In the original Japanese narrative, terms of address (e.g., "Obasama"/"Ojisama"), unspoken understandings between men and women, and the family culture that forms the backdrop of the main characters of the novel are echoes of the *yamanote* culture to which Shishi is witness as it passes into history.

The settings of the novel are real, but it was written while Occupation censorship was still in force, and thus some names are thinly disguised fictions. Komako and Iosuke live in "Musashi-Hazama," which is likely a reference to the then-remote Musashi-Sakai suburb west of Tokyo. The area where Iosuke spends most of his absence from home is described with a mixture of real and fictitious names of local landmarks then and now: the real Shinjuku, Shinanomachi, Suidōbashi, the Nikolai Cathedral, Surugadai, Hongō, Kanda, along with "Okanenomizu" (Ochanomizu) Bridge and "Keitendō Hospital" (Juntendō Hospital). The landscape of Ōiso, the popular Meiji-era resort where swimming in the ocean for recreation began in Japan, and where Meiji and later leaders built luxury seaside villas, is vividly portrayed. There is mention of the pines along the shore, "Sōrōkaku," Itō Hirobumi's seaside residence (now part of a hotel wedding facility), and the Shōkintei restaurant next door to the "unusual orphanage" (the Elizabeth Sanders Home near the station that cared for orphans of mixed blood born of the Occupation). The story mentions several landmark establishments in the Ginza district of the time, altering the names of some—Akō jewelry shop (Wakō)—but not others—like the Daikoku hat shop and the Senbikiya fruit parlor. Corporation names are transparently fictionalized: Iosuke's father's company, the Manchurian Transport Company, evokes the South Manchuria Railway Company; the Tōkyō News Agency is reminiscent of the Kyōdō News Service; and Mr. Fujimura's company, Mitsuboshi Heavy Industries, is written with a different character from that for the well-known Mitsubishi company.

While the documentary aspects of *School of Freedom* are the product of the author's careful research, his insights into human character and views on gender are entirely his own, testimony, too, to a particular era in the history of modern nations. All cannot be consigned entirely to history, however, as many aspects of this story of nearly six decades ago resonate with unexpected immediacy to events and experiences of our world today.

ACKNOWLEDGMENTS

This translation is much more than the work of one individual. In accordance with the process adopted by the JLPP project, the draft was checked by an experienced translation editor, in this case Takechi Manabu, of the Center for Intercultural Communication and my long-time collaborator in translation. After an extended process focused on faithfulness to the quality, tone, and meaning of the original, the translation was edited by Jules Young, who was requested by JLPP to assure the accessibility of the story to as wide a readership as possible. I am fortunate for the opportunity to translate Shishi's first major work to appear in English, and grateful that it should appear as the collective product of a high level of professional expertise. For support in compiling the afterword, I would like to express special thanks to Minamitani Akimasa, professor, Gunma University.

ABOUT THE COVER ILLUSTRATIONS

The front and back cover illustrations were selected from the more than two hundred illustrations created by Miyata Shigeo for the *Asahi shinbun* serialized version published May-December 1950. Printed with permission from the Miyata estate, the reproductions were provided courtesy of the Kanagawa Museum of Modern Literature (Yokohama), where the entire collection is kept. Miyata Shigeo was a close friend of Shishi Bunroku, known as a member of his amateur golf group, and the two seem to have consulted closely about the images, which provide a precious and skillfully captured visual record of Tokyo in 1950.

NOTES

1. Kobayashi Hideo, "Botan" [Peony]. In another remembrance, Akutagawa Hiroshi speculates that the author may have had the *shi-shi jū-roku* ("four-times-four is sixteen") line from the multiplication table in his head, but when asked about it, Shishi remarked dryly: "They talk about *bungō*, you know—I just added one more." See "Meimei no meijin"; both essays in *Botan no hana: Shishi Bunroku tsuitōroku* [Peony Flowers: In Memory of Shishi Bunroku] (Shishi Bunroku Tsuitōroku Kankōkai, 1971).

    2. The Japan Foundation "Japanese Literature in Translation Search" database lists three works published in English. "Memories of a Meiji Boyhood" (*This is Japan*, 14), "Shoes in the Tokonoma" (*This is Japan*, 16), both in 1967, and "The Young Know Best" (*Seishun kaidan*) translation by Hiroo Mukai, in *The Yomiuri*, March 2–July 15,

1959. *Etchan* has been published in French (L'École des Loisirs, Paris, 1991), translation by Jean Christian Bouvier, and a German translation of *Musume to watashi (Meine Tochter und Ich)* was published in 1967 (Japanisch-Deutsche Gessellschaft, Tokyo).

3. A partial English account of Iwata's involvement in the New Theater movement may be found in *Toward a Modern Japanese Theatre: Kishida Kunio*, by J. Thomas Rimer (Princeton: Princeton University Press, 1974). In Japanese, see "Shingeki to watashi," in *Iwata Toyoo engeki hyōronshū* (Shinchōsha, 1963).

4. *Musume to watashi*, Shishi Bunroku zenshū 6, p. 224.

5. Iwata Toyoo, *Iwata Toyoo: Sōsaku hon'yaku gikyoku shū* [Original and Translated Plays by Iwata Toyoo] (Shinchōsha, 1963), p. 483 ("Atogaki"). This volume includes the two above-mentioned plays, *Higashi wa higashi* and *Asahiya kinumonoten* as well as Japanese versions of eleven French and other European plays.

6. Comment by Fujiki Hiroyuki in *Botsugo jūgonen Shishi Bunroku ten* (Kanagawa Kindai Bungakukan, 1984), unpaginated.

7. *Musume to watashi*, Shishi Bunroku zenshū 6, p. 379.

8. "Gunshin" [War Heroes], essay in Shishi Bunroku zenshū 14, pp. 530–31.

9. *Musume to watashi*, Shishi Bunroku zenshū 6, p. 399.

10. *Musume to watashi*, Shishi Bunroku zenshū 6, p. 461.

11. "Yūmoa to fūshi" [Humor and Satire], Shishi Bunroku zenshū 13, pp. 362–65; "Yūmoa bungaku kanken," Shishi Bunroku zenshū 13, pp. 442–44; "Yumoa shōsetsu to tantei shōsetsu," Shishi Bunroku zenshū 13, pp. 444–45.

12. *Musume to watashi*, Shishi Bunroku zenshū 6, p. 515.

13. Iwata Yukiko, *Fuefuki tennyo* [Flute-playing Angel] (Kōdansha,1986), p. 129.

14. Translated as Shishi Bunroku-sensei's Parlor (Kage Shobō, 2003).

15. "Mōningu monogatari," *Zuihitsu II*, Shishi Bunroku zenshū, bekkan, pp. 243–52.

16. The scenes of the strip club that Iosuke visits in Shinjuku and the ones that Kajiki later shows him in Ueno and Asakusa, which represent the "dark side" of Tokyo life, will be more meaningful after reading John W. Dower, *Embracing Defeat: Japan in the Wake of World War II* (New York: W.W. Norton, 1999), chapter 4, "Cultures of Defeat," pp. 121–67.

17. Hama Rikyū was a luxurious villa for shoguns and emperors and a guest house of foreign dignitaries like U.S. President Ulysses S. Grant in the early twentieth century. During the Pacific War it became the site of anti-aircraft emplacements and a target of the bombing by American forces. Air attacks in November 1944 left the grounds a vast empty space. See Edward Seidensticker, *Tokyo Rising: The City since the Great Earthquake* (New York: Alfred A. Knopf, 1990), p. 139. It is in this setting, requisitioned by the Occupation and made open to the public as a park when not in use for training (Seidensticker, p. 160), that in chapter 16 we find Iosuke, Takabumi, and Yuri amicably conversing on the lawn.

18. "Yamanote no ko," in *Yamanote no ko*, Shishi Bunroku zenshū 14, pp. 71–82. See also Minamitani Akimasa, "A Reading of Shishi Bunroku's School of Freedom: Gender in Japan through Defeat and Occupation," *(Gunma University) Journal of Social and Information Studies* 13 (March 31, 2006): 209–29.